Mendocino

Also by Judith Greber

❦

Easy Answers
The Silent Partner

Mendocino

A NOVEL BY

Judith Greber

Crown Publishers, Inc.
New York

Author's Note: Nicolai and his descendants are fictional, but the events during which they live and struggle are as true to historical fact as conflicting written records and a human researcher could make them. For their unstinting help I would like to thank the generous, knowledgable and enthusiastic staffs of the San Francisco Public Library, the University of California's Bancroft Library, the California Historical Society, the Marin County California Room, and the Mendocino Historical Society.

And special thanks to my editor, Betty A. Prashker, for putting all of the above in perspective.

Published by Crown Publishers, Inc.,
225 Park Avenue South
New York, New York 10003 and
represented in Canada by
the Canadian MANDA Group

CROWN is a trademark of Crown Publishers, Inc.

Manufactured in the United States of America

Library of Congress Catalog Card Number: 88-47649

ISBN 0-517-56761-X

10 9 8 7 6 5 4 3 2 1
First Edition

for
my father
and
the memory of my mother

"The past is not a bad witness."
—*Russian proverb*

FORT ROSS, CALIFORNIA
1842

At the moment just before dark, Nicolai Beriankov stood on a long plateau between the crimson Pacific and primeval forests. He squinted to see a distant ship, little more than a cinder against the sunfire-stained horizon.

Near him were the marks and leavings of civilization: half-shadowed barns, a windmill, barracks, tanneries, mills, a church, a fort, fenced fields, orchards, and a rose garden.

But the buildings were empty, the fields half-turned, the plows abandoned, and the oxen wandering aimlessly.

That morning, church bells and cannon had summoned everyone who'd put an imprint on this place, and all of them, save Nicolai, had answered the call and boarded the waiting ship.

Now the departing ship blurred into the dying sun, carrying Nicolai's comrades, language, God, and childhood. For a moment he thought he heard familiar Russian voices, but it was only a seabird's final cry of the day.

He was not an impetuous child or an adventurer. His blond beard was streaked with gray. For thirty years, since 1812, he had served the Russian-American Company and his country well. Now, at fifty, he should have been home by a fire, whittling cups and baby toys, drinking vodka, and telling stories of his foreign adventures.

1

Instead, he faced old age and death among strangers on a continent lacking even a priest to say his last rites.

He had chosen to remain, but still, he momentarily wondered at his decision to be the last of his kind. His wife, waiting in her nearby village, knew the songs and stories of the Kashaya Pomos, not of Russia. Even their children, blends of peoples and continents, were unlike him. They were as new and mysterious as this country was.

The colors faded until the ship was an indistinguishable smudge in the gradations of night and Nicolai had no choice but to raise his hand in a last salute, a final wave.

Hail and farewell.

PART I
1 8 4 4

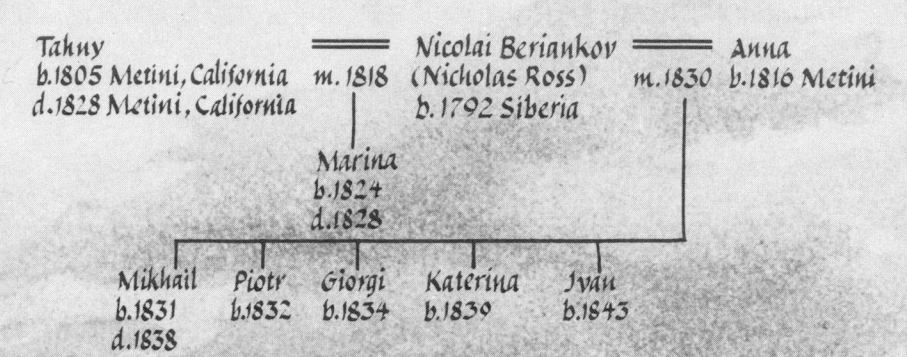

Tahny
b.1805 Metini, California   m. 1818
d.1828 Metini, California

Nicolai Beriankov
(Nicholas Ross)
b.1792 Siberia

m.1830   Anna
          b.1816 Metini

Marina
b.1824
d.1828

Mikhail   Piotr   Giorgi   Katerina   Ivan
b.1831   b.1832   b.1834   b.1839   b.1843
d.1838

1

"You're like a panther ready to pounce," Anna said. "What's wrong?"

How could Nicolai explain? There was nothing amiss, nothing as it shouldn't be. Today was indistinguishable from yesterday, from, indeed, the two years of yesterdays since he had chosen to remain in this country.

Beneath an innocent sky, his wife squatted in front of the tipi, preparing acorn mush. Elsewhere, his children gathered berries and village men played gambling games in the long grass. An ordinary, harmless, inoffensive day.

Except he couldn't bear it any longer. Life had become a quiet sitting pool reflecting only what he already knew. Nothing nameable was wrong, but nothing felt particularly right, either.

Nicolai's restlessness had been building since the ship had left. He had no work to engage and free his mind or take the cramped waiting out of his muscles. What was the meaning or use of a master builder in an Indian village?

He was no longer certain who or what he was. No one would mistake him for the naked Kashaya, but neither would he be recognized as a Russian. His feet were bare, his boots left in the tipi for bad weather. His last *kosovorotka* was long-since threads and scraps. In

place of the high-collared belted shirt he wore a deerskin vest and another deerskin tied around his hips. His beard and hair were wilder than ever.

It was becoming difficult to remember and believe what he had once been. Suddenly and intensely he needed the grainy touch of a different world, craved it as much as, other times, he craved Anna's gold flesh, gentle hands, and low, throaty laugh.

"I need to walk," he finally answered his wife.

She scowled. "You're going there?" Her voice became razor-edged whenever she spoke of the fort. She resented his past because he cherished it, and she couldn't comprehend the attraction of square buildings, windowpanes, tapestries, pianos, and leather-bound books, let alone international trade and rivalry and imperial ambitions. Nicolai didn't blame her—after two years as a bearded Kashaya, he himself half-believed that such things were not memories, but feverish hallucinations.

Still, more and more, he missed the old Nicolai buried under buckskin. The new Nicolai, the blond Kashaya, carved toys for the village children, surprising them with intricate Matryoshka dolls—Russian peasants one inside the other—or, in his new version, braves and shamans and tiny babies in baskets. But even while he worked, while he took pleasure in his clever artistry, a mocking inner voice asked how toy making compared with hewing trees into ships, staircases, or a perfectly made chapel.

By day, he lived Kashaya. But at night, in either the congested tipi or the sweathouse filled with sleeping men's silhouettes dark in the firelight, perspiration and tobacco peppering the air, he escaped to Russia, or at least to Ross. In his dreams, he wore cotton and linen, nankeen and worsted, and heard songs, the balalaika, the swish of Princess Helena's gowns, her music floating from the drawing room onto the beach, the prayers of the priest at vespers.

And in the dark corners of his mouth he tasted rum, kasha, piroshki, dark, heavy bread, his mother's delicious *pryaniki*, gingerbread cakes in fantastic shapes.

Never did he hear the strange music of the foot-drum and birdbone whistles. Never did he taste maggots or army worms or even the ever-present acorn mush.

Surrounded by good and gentle people, he nonetheless felt terribly, irrevocably alone. He didn't know which way was better—Anna's or his. Her people lived so lightly on the land they left almost no traces. Like the other species in these woods and streams, they took what

was needed, gave thanks for it, and left the rest. There was no value in or idea of storing and hoarding. If there was an abundance of food, messengers were sent to announce a feast and the largesse was shared with another village.

And when Anna's people died, they were burned along with all their possessions, so no one fought for what a man once owned. Only songs, secret charms, and powers could be inherited.

It was a good way, but still, Nicolai couldn't let go of the idea that man, made in God's image, should prevail—should flex the muscles, talent, and imagination God had given him, create new things, change the landscape.

He loved the dark forest and the open, flower-sprinkled meadows, but even so, he missed human imprints and the kind of men who left those marks. Their bark tipi would never be as beautiful as well-shaped rooms and beams whose notches locked like lovers.

Long legs taking oversized strides, Nicolai rushed away from the village toward his past, a hillside or so away. There, until fog and winter storms would grind them to dust, timber skeletons stood surrounded by wild, weedy gardens, silent proof that something quite different had once been on this piece of America. Something Russian. Ross.

"We'll make the Pacific our lake," the officers had bragged. The words echoed, even after dreams of conquest had died and Ross was no more than denuded, hollow buildings. The dreamers, the art and icons, the carpets, the beautiful Princess Helena's piano had gone on that last ship. The ambitious Swiss Sutter had bought the rest—the livestock, the lumber and window glass, the tools, the last crops, and whatever else he could lift, herd, or cart away. Even the cannons that Napoleon had left in Russia, the cannons that had been shipped to the New World to guard Fort Ross—even they were in the Delta, protecting yet another national dream, defending Johann Sutter's New Helvetia. Everything, in fact, was gone except the few objects Nicolai had hidden in the well. What, after all, did a man from Switzerland need with a samovar and where would Nicolai be in a new world without a few tools?

The word *Sutter*, the idea, left a foul taste in Nicolai's mouth. He'd never met the man, but he'd had enough of his emissaries, particularly one whose red face looked like boiled pudding. He and his fellows had herded the sheep with the wool nobody knew how to spin and the cattle, underfed and exhausted from their rocky hillside grazing. If the stupid livestock had had minds enough to suspect the long and

dangerous trek ahead of them, they'd have given up on the spot.

Sutter didn't get the pigs. Years earlier, the pigs outsmarted their fate by eating shellfish and beach refuse and becoming unpalatable so that they were set free. And now, wild and triumphant, their children owned the hills and their own destinies.

Sutter's red-faced man had gestured toward Metini, the Kashaya village. "Diggers!" he said abruptly, and he spat. "They're everywhere. Animals!" He used a mix of Spanish, English, hands, shoulders, and his own guttural language.

Nicolai understood. "Americans," he said gently. "Americans are good."

"Good for nothing!" The man's face darkened. "Scum of the earth. Trash. Eatin' worms and—"

"Stop," Nicolai said quietly. The man was in a sudden, full rage of loathing, as if it were important, necessary for him to despise those quiet people. Why? The Spanish missionaries had been just as bad, arrogant and sneering as they enslaved and "saved" the Indians until they died of starvation or heartbreak.

"What's wrong with you?" Red-Face demanded. "You must be a goddamn *squaw* man!" He spat again. "Married to one of them— them *things!* Jesus!"

For a second, Nicolai froze, paralyzed by the man's violent disgust. What was it? What did he mean? Why shouldn't he have married an American? No less than Alexander Andreivich Baranov, governor of all Russian America, had married a chief's daughter. What was wrong with this foreigner? What had any Kashaya ever done to him?

"Diggers ain't worth *shit!*" The man coiled rope and prepared his pack. "Not hardly people. How could you—"

Nicolai stopped caring about the how's and the why's and the sense of it. "Stop!" he growled.

"Everybody knows diggers—" The man's face went slack as the giant Russian loomed over him.

"I'll kill you." Nicolai was strong, muscles hardened by felling redwoods and hoisting beams, and he felt his strength increase a hundredfold. A torrent of Russian exploded out of him as he cursed the man and all the generations that had bred him.

"I didn't—I only—" The man stammered, barely breathed, stood in place, trapped, arm still in midair as if Nicolai's power had tied him up.

Nicolai didn't move, didn't say a word as he watched, prolonging

Pudding-Face's fear before he crushed the life and the lies and the insults out of his foul throat.

The man knew it. He grew still and pale, like an upright corpse.

Nicolai lifted his hands—and heard a gasp from the nearby trees. When he looked, there was Anna, wide-eyed, her hand clasped over her mouth.

This wouldn't be the end of it, her eyes said. The whites would avenge this death. More newcomers would return and kill the Indians, always easy prey. He wanted rid of them, of all of them, forever.

He dropped his hands and stepped back a pace, releasing the man. "Go!" he shouted. "Out!"

When the man, tripping and falling, had run out of sight, Nicolai again looked toward the trees. Anna had disappeared.

That had been two years ago. The red-faced hate spewer was the last white man Nicolai had seen. The last, he thought ironically, of "his kind."

Now, as he had on earlier visits, Nicolai went into the stockade, climbed the bastion, and looked over the bluff onto the glistening horizon. He felt like a tsar surveying his realms as he listened to the fierce but comforting cracks of waves against rock. Some things were forever.

This place had been the centerpost of his life, had forged him, taken him from the snow, mud, and poverty of Siberia to a new life, a new world. *Bolshaya zemlya.* Great land.

Behind him, inside the stockade walls, the silence mounted, pushing through empty window sockets and smothering the barracks and chapel, rising until it surrounded and suffocated Nicolai.

He was no tsar. He was a live ghost haunting a dead dream. There was an ache in his middle, a soft sore, like the empty place where a tooth had been. He didn't belong here, either.

He walked away heavily, suddenly much older, his mind muddled with memories. He crossed the little valley where he and Anna and their children had lived along with other Russian-Kashaya and Aleut families, halfway between the worlds they were mixing.

All that remained were chimneys and compromises. Nicolai's children spoke two languages and were called by two different sets of names, but the balance scale had tipped and they were firmly in the one remaining world.

As if underlining the confusion and unsteadiness of the morning,

Nicolai's legs buckled. He tilted, gasped, and toppled, a confusion of flailing arms and shouts.

He sat on the ground, catching his breath, gingerly touching his ankle and shin. Nothing broken—except the earth. A gopher hole had trapped his foot and caused the fall.

Damned creatures! He snorted with disgust, stood up, and kicked a clod of earth into the hole, then kicked at the edge of the hole itself. Rotten underground rats! They were the villains, the culprits. Ruined the last hope of staying here.

The first hope, of course, had been the oceans with their treasure-house of the most valuable fur in the world. But after the otters had been harvested to extinction, there was still the land, lush and green and mild. Ross had a second chance at existence if it could feed the Russian outposts in Alaska.

But the men were trappers and builders and soldiers, not farmers, and their crops withered, spotted, wilted, and shrank. What little was left was munched from below by ravenous gophers, co-conspirators with the fog to damn forever Russia's imperial ambitions.

Nicolai brushed his legs and headed back to the village, drained and exhausted. His head hurt and he was tired even though the day had barely begun.

Men still gambled in the meadow.

Nicolai walked by them. He needed to be alone.

"Digger!" The man spat onto something furry and dead, paws up, belly split, and entrails dragging. "Digger! Digger!" His face expanded, pressing into and smothering Nicolai, hot spittle drowning him, while the words, like a war cry, thundered. "Digger! DIGGER!"

"Papa! Come look!"

The voice edged through the shouts in Nicolai's head.

"Wake up, Papa. There's a dead whale!" Katerina shook his shoulder.

Nicolai sat up, nauseated and disoriented. His bleary eyes still saw the enormous face of Sutter's man. And the otter, paws out, head to the side, like, God forgive him, Christ on the cross, blood pouring from its open wound.

Another otter dream.

"Papa, you're wet." Katerina touched the perspiration on his face.

The dreams had started when the otters disappeared. But they'd become more severe the last few years, ever since the encounter with Sutter's man. Nicolai didn't understand why.

10

"It's stuffy in here," he said by way of explanation. The tipi was dark even at midday, and musty, with leftover human smells mingling with smokey basketfuls of meal, roots, and dried fish.

"There's a dead whale on the beach. Come see!" She danced from foot to foot.

He wiped his face and shook himself back into the day. He hadn't meant to sleep. When he'd returned from Ross, he'd simply meant to be alone, to think awhile. What a lazy creature he'd become, his head filled with nightmares because there was nothing more important to occupy it. "Mustn't go near," he said. "Bears will be after it. And wild pigs."

The fences would fall, the orchards go to seed, the buildings collapse, and memory fail. How strange if wild pigs became the only Russian legacy.

"But Giorgi's already at the beach. And Piotr. Why can't I?"

Nicolai roused completely. "Come, then." He blinked in the dazzling sunshine outside. His sons were not so stupid as to interrupt a feasting grizzly, but Piotr was training for the hunt and might decide to practice. He'd better check.

He walked behind his animated daughter, half his mind still in his dream as he climbed down the steep rocks to the beach.

"Oooh!" Katerina said, wrinkling her tiny nose and waving her hand at the air.

No one in the village had bothered the sacred whale. But predators had no such taboos and they obviously had discovered the carcass before the boys had. Now, the odor was enough to discourage anyone but adolescent boys and their tagalong sister.

Piotr, tall and healthy, was dwarfed by the rib cage looming behind him.

Suddenly, Nicolai was consumed by a hunger that had nothing to do with his stomach. "A man could build a fine bidarka with those bones," he said, trying to contain his excitement. Yes, he shouted inside. Yes, yes. The Aleut's kayak could take him away, and he knew how to build one. He felt fully awake for the first time in days.

Anna's people had no boats. For thousands of years they'd lived near rivers and the ocean and the most they built were rickety rafts for one day's river fishing. Nicolai could scarcely believe it.

But then, they never wanted to get anywhere, to escape or explore. They didn't understand or desire the sort of freedom a strong boat promised.

Nicolai walked closer to the dead animal, fanning away flies and pestilential odor. There were still sinews he could use to fasten the bones together, and fat enough for oil to seal the chunks and seams. He'd strip it today, before the entire animal kingdom heard about the windfall on the beach.

Of course, he'd need skins. Sea lions or seals. He could cure them. He'd watched the process often enough, had sometimes helped, knew how to stretch them over the bones, stitch them with gut.

How *could* a people have no boats? How could they watch Russians and Aleuts go to sea and never once imitate the process?

Instead, once a year or so, a handful of strong young men prayed for peace from the sharks, swam a mile and a half to the rocks, killed a seal apiece, and swam back, dragging it. And when Nicolai offered to build a wooden boat so they could carry a larger haul with greater ease, they'd said, simply, "Why?"

"If the gut's not ruined," he told his sons, "I'll show you how to make kamleikas for the rain. Sew it up with gut thread, and not a drop gets in. And boots, too, from the esophagus."

"You've hunted whales?" Giorgi asked.

Nicolai shook his head. "How different can they be from seals and sea lions, except bigger? A gut's a gut." He stepped back and viewed the dead animal. "Then," he announced, saving the best for last, "we'll build a boat."

"Why?" Piotr asked.

Why? *Why?* What kind of question was that? It was sometimes hard to believe they were his sons. "Because!" he bellowed. "For travel, and—just because!"

Katerina's eyes were enormous in her small face. "Wouldn't it be harder than walking, Papa?" she asked. "And what's its good in the hills?"

He snorted with exasperation. They couldn't envision going anywhere except the same route their people had followed for thousands of years. To the rivers for the fish in season. To the coast for abalone and seaweed. Inland when the fog and chill became too bad.

A very small circle, and he was surprised at the irritation, boredom, and sense of constriction it produced in him. He hadn't let himself admit how much it frustrated him until this moment. Even this morning he had looked for other causes for his restlessness. But this feeling wasn't new at all. It was as if he had been casually tossing scraps of lumber and resentment into a remote storeroom. And then, when he turned around, he found that he'd built an enormous con-

12

struction, with towers and subcellars and room after room of mixed emotions, and he was trapped inside it.

"Where would you travel?" Giorgi asked tentatively, with a mix of respect, fear of his father's temper, and real curiosity. Where, after all, was there except where they always went, and the ocean, from the bottom of which they were sure their father came?

"Bodega." Nicolai surprised himself with the answer. There it was, as if it had been waiting a long time for the question. "To Bodega. To see Dmitri, the other one who stayed on."

To hear Russian again. To smoke a pipe or—he didn't even want to think about it—God be praised—drink rum or vodka with someone who understood. Who didn't ask "Why?" whenever adventure was suggested.

So yes, to Bodega, which he still wanted to call Port Roumianzoff. The Khlebnikof Ranch.

His sons were tired of the whale and its stench. He followed them, as did Katerina.

"Are you going away, then?" Piotr asked quietly when they were halfway up the bluff.

Nicolai nodded. "As soon as I build my boat."

"Why do you need one to go there? Nobody else does," Katerina said. Her brothers looked at her, then warily at Nicolai, checking whether she had gone too far out of line. Katerina never worried about such things and never seemed to annoy her father either.

"You're right," Nicolai said, surprised. Why did he need a bidarka? He wasn't going to sea, merely down the coast. The Kashaya had traveled to Bodega for millennia for the special shells used as money. They made the trip overland, crossing on sandbars or swimming the river. He didn't need the whale or the imagined bidarka, except as prods toward change and escape.

In which case he could leave right away.

A too-long missed excitement welled up. Russian sounds, Russian tempos, Russian laughter beckoned a few days away. He smiled, his strong teeth gleaming above the gold and silver beard. It was the dry season. The streams wouldn't be flooded and traveling would be its easiest. He could even use one of the horses Sutter had missed.

His children looked at him, solemn-eyed. They showed no visible curiosity about his trip's motives or expected rewards. It was simply another sign of their father's oddness, part of what set him apart from other fathers.

13

"We'll all go," he said. "Time to see the world!" Bodega wasn't much, but it was a beginning.

"And Mama? And the baby?" Katerina sounded nervous.

"Both. All of us. The whole family."

"But I—"

"What? What is it, Piotr?"

His son looked at him uncomfortably for a moment, then looked down. "Nothing."

"And Grandma? Grandpa?" Katerina continued her inventory as they neared the top of the hill.

Nicolai sighed. "Maybe not. They're old." They could keep their narrow ways. They didn't need to be disturbed.

Besides, they wouldn't approve of going into another tribe's territory on what they'd consider a wild impulse. Nicolai would have to reassure them and the toyon that he wouldn't collect money, assume anyone else's special profession, or secretly trade with the Olamenko. And that he and Anna would gather kelp and abalone again when they returned, that nothing terrible would be lost by a few days' or weeks' absence.

But Nicolai's family would go. He felt straighter, taller, younger, and stronger than he had in years. They reached the top of the hill. "You'll have fun," he said. "It's an adventure, a holiday."

Before they could respond, the world around the four of them plunged into darkness. The grass encircling their feet faded to shadowed gray. Silently, they looked up.

A condor hovered above, its enormous sweep of wings blocking the sky.

The vulture inspected each one of them in turn. "What you want is on the beach," Nicolai told it softly. "You know you don't want us." His heartbeat pounded in his throat. Of course the bird wouldn't trouble them. It cared only for the already dead. But still, its glinty-eyed curiosity filled him with dread. "Go," he whispered. "Leave us in peace."

But the bird wasn't yet satisfied. It ignored him, judging, floating, suspended above their heads. None of the earthbound creatures said another word. They stood immobile, waiting, holding their breaths until finally, its private questions answered, the condor moved toward the beach with a great whoosh of air.

Even when they were again in sunshine, Nicolai felt chilled.

"Yes," he said, more loudly than intended. "We'll have a holiday. It will be wonderful."

"Wonderful," he answered himself when nobody else did.

14

2

"Look there! See? What's that bird?"

Giorgi and Katerina skipped and danced and explored their way toward Bodega, excited about each new discovery.

Nicolai walked beside the pack horse and watched his family with great pleasure. He'd make adventurers of them yet. The trip to Bodega had been a fine idea. They traveled at a leisurely, late-spring tempo, honoring Katerina's short legs. Bright days full of flower-spattered meadows, long gold grass, and laughter merged with one another. Even baby Ivan seemed pleased by the passing scenery, despite his position on his mother's back, which made him see everything as it retreated.

"It's a woodpecker," Anna answered. "There's a story about him."

Even she seemed happier, lighter, and younger, laughing along with her children. Sometimes, in the long sameness of their days in the village, he forgot what an animated sprite the child-woman Anna had been. It was her gentle humor, her wide clean smile and enveloping warmth that had pulled him out of his mourning for his first wife and child, both lost to measles.

He could see young Anna reborn in Katerina, but too often he forgot the source.

"Once, when a brave woodpecker saved his babies from a fire, he burned his face and choked in the ashes," Anna said. "And that is why, to this day, Woodpecker's face is red and his neck and chest are gray with the ashes that clung to him."

This was the Anna of long ago, before her first-born, Mikhail, had died, before Ross had ended and Nicolai had become neither Kashaya nor Russian.

Nicolai's smile faded. This would be perfect, the family intact and together, if Piotr had come.

Anna had sided with her son. "He's trained for so long," she'd said. "My brother taught him as if he were his own." She'd put red-hot stones into a water-filled basket and kept mush boiling while Nicolai, the foreigner who couldn't teach his own sons the songs and charms that enticed deer, absorbed her polite rebuke.

"There will always be another deer hunt," Nicolai insisted.

"Not a first hunt. Not this one." She looked up and her eyes were like the burning stones in the basket. "It's more important to hunt deer than memories!"

And so it was decided. Still, Nicolai missed Piotr and not for the first time wished his oldest son had shared this trip. Did Piotr, born into this place, recognize its breath-catching beauty? He would have liked to talk to him about it.

Paradise. The Mendocino coast surely was nothing less. Nicolai should know. Sixteen Siberian winters followed by Sitka, Alaska, where murderous storms ripped trees out by the roots—and what they didn't kill, the Kolosh tribesmen did.

But here, a man could take root. Here, nature was generous, the woods alive with game, and the streams so full of fish you could pull them out with your hands.

He loved its wild contrasts—dark, mysterious forests against achingly clear light, soft fog and stony cliffs, gentle people and dangerous sea. Everything stretched toward eternity—the sky shattering trees, the endless sheet of ocean, the blue bowl of heaven, and the burnished people who blended into their lives with astounding rightness.

It was the garden with no serpent. Except for the loneliness. The confusing nightmares.

But what of them? He shook away worries and replaced them with a song.

He wondered if his family found his Russian melodies as uncomfortable to their ears as he found Kashaya songs, but if so, he didn't want to know. He missed music almost more than anything else. It

16

made work easier, pain milder, and pleasure more intense. He could play his balalaika, yes, but without a chorus of male voices as accompaniment, it wasn't the same at all.

That night, as the children lay sleeping by the river, Anna embraced him. "Love me," she whispered, her lips close to his neck, making each word a kiss. "Let me give you so much pleasure, you won't fall into the sun-girls' hands." She patted leaves and soft grass into a nest for the two of them.

"Who?"

"You know. The beautiful sun-girls who live near water. They seduce men. Especially a man like you, with your beard full of sunshine. A man who came from the bottom of the sea."

It did no good to explain, once again, about ships and horizons. Besides, this wasn't the time. Anna pressed against him, nuzzling his neck, kissing the hair on his chest. Her bare breasts touched and teased like two extra hands. "You must be one of them yourself," he said softly. "I feel very seduced."

"Oh, no." She laughed, that low, dark sound heard only when they were alone and close. That laugh that bubbled up from a deep and welcoming warmth inside her and made the blood pound in his ears. That laugh that pulled him into it, into her, that knew it and rejoiced in it. She ran her hands across his chest, around his sides, under the buckskin vest. "I'm saving you from the sun-girls, because they kill men when they make love. They have rattlesnakes in their vaginas. But I don't. No, I truly don't. . . . Come here, let me save you. Let me make you too satisfied to ever notice anyone else, even them." She kissed him, all the while undoing his buckskin and hers, until they lay naked on the leaves.

The next morning, he walked behind his youngest son, making faces until the baby broke into a toothless grin and a deep, breathy laugh. "My Ivan. Like Ivan Tsarevich, who overcame the evil Kaschei and gained his heart's delight. And so will you." They would both tell their stories, fill their children's heads with the whole world's heroes and legends.

"Tell us more," Katerina said, and he complied, making her forget the miles they walked with stories of the Snow Maiden, who melts the spring sun, and of evil Kaschei the Immortal, whose power is a needle hidden in an egg.

"More, more!" Katerina said.

"Always more. Don't you know about the fisherman's greedy wife who burst from asking for too much?"

17

"No, tell me. Tell me *more!*"

Nicolai laughed. "No more stories. I can't remember another one. Instead, I'll tell you about where we're going and how once a grand party was held there for Princess Helena."

He heard Anna's soft snort. "His *princess*," she muttered. "His *princess* again."

He ignored her. What was to be made of women, jealous even of a man's impossible dreams. Anna would never understand what Princess Helena de Rotchev, the commandant's beautiful wife, niece of the Tsar, had meant. A royal touch of Mother Russia, a world Anna's imagination could never encompass, a world Nicolai himself found as remote, exotic, and enchanting as the fairy tales his grandmother had told him.

But to be jealous of her? Of even her memory? "His *other* princess," he said with a smile in his voice. "For you, Anna, are my American princess."

It was Anna he wanted and loved, but she was afraid of his past, of what she didn't know and he remembered fondly. When she was in a dark mood, he couldn't convince her that he was glad no Russian women had been available to wed.

"What decent woman would come here without a husband?" Commandant Kuskov had said early in their first tour of duty. What a strange figure he'd been, half leader, half pirate with his peg leg. "Marry a good American girl," he'd advised, and wisely.

"Princess," Anna muttered. "Silliness."

Anna. Anna. Without her, he turned to gray slush, but all the same, she could be difficult.

"What about Princess Helena's party?" Katerina demanded.

"Ah, yes. For two days people came and danced, celebrating her birthday. The officers from Ross, officials from the presidio, mission people."

"Were you there?" Giorgi asked.

Nicolai shook his head. "I wasn't an officer." They couldn't understand why only certain people would be invited to a festival. They had no comprehension of rank or caste, or what it meant to be born a step or two up from peasant. Son of a *mestchannin*, the lowest grade of small trader, ineligible for even the town guild of merchants. And in his case, son of a drunk to boot.

As they approached Bodega, Nicolai's excitement grew. He tried to hide it so that his wife and children would never suspect how much he yearned for and needed something they could not provide.

18

But as they neared, his anticipation was replaced by apprehension.

The houses and threshing platforms had been stripped away. The distant hills had been changed. From afar, they looked patched, the green treetops missing in great long scars. And above them hung a strange, heavy mist and the burry whine of a million bees.

There was no sign of Dmitri or anyone, no sign of anything remembered or Russian. Indeed, except for the nonstop buzz, there was no sign of life. He called and called, but no one responded.

Finally, he left Anna and the children near the water and walked toward the noise. No matter what it turned out to be, he knew it for the sound of a key locking away the last piece of his past.

He suspected, correctly, that the noise and mist were a sawmill, steaming the air, eating the hill, patch by patch. It was impressive—three hissing boilers above a roaring fire steam-powering not only a sawmill, but a new gristmill as well, but it had nothing to do with his life or needs or dreams.

He walked slowly back to the beach.

Anna nursed Ivan. "No Russians are left," she said.

"How do you know?"

"People came while you were up there. They told me that Sutter's man—Bidwell?—he was here awhile, but he's gone. Somebody named Smith, now. Look what he did to the hills."

The horizon was as empty as it had been throughout his walk. "Who talked to you? Where are they? Why didn't they come when I called out?"

"They're afraid of you. Your own people taught us that white men with wagons wanted to trade and were safe, but white men with horses meant danger."

"Not me—not a man with his family!"

"They thought we were your prisoners."

"Prisoners? Of what war? There aren't even missions now. What nonsense!"

"They said that now the ranchers take people. Make them work the fields."

"That's ridiculous." He was very annoyed. Anna must have misunderstood, or they were tricking her, frightening her off. If he could talk with them, he'd make some sense of it.

The distant whine blended into the sound of the sea. The baby was sated and asleep, and Anna stood up. "Let's leave, too," she said firmly. "It's no good here."

"Don't be scared by their talk."

She shook her head. "Something's wrong. I feel it. I was here before, when it was happy. Normal. When nobody was afraid. When the air didn't sound like insects and the hills were full of trees. Now it's no good." She shuddered, stood straight, and went to get Katerina and Giorgi.

He had hoped to spend a long time, to visit and explore, reminisce and sing, to picnic in the meadows and bathe in the sea, but the landscape's disintegration to rubble and steam upset and dislocated him as much as it did Anna. He didn't mind turning his back on it—if only he could understand what it meant and what was next.

It meant nothing, he decided as they left Bodega. Someone named Smith was cutting trees. It didn't mean anything else had to change. It didn't have anything to do with Nicolai's life.

Days later, when they were close to the village, Anna admitted fatigue, and decided to ride the horse. Until then, she had chosen to use her feet—the way people were meant to travel, she insisted. Now, as Nicolai helped her up, she smiled easily, completely, for the first time since Bodega. "Those people on the beach were so frightened." She closed her eyes as if to block the memory. "Well, we're away from it, and I'm glad." She urged the horse on with greater speed. "There it is. There's the village. I've missed it. And most of all, Piotr." A smile of expectation, of good and familiar delights lit her face. "We've never been apart this way before. I hope he caught a fine, large deer. I hope—"

Her sudden silence was absolute, as if she were choking.

Nicolai looked up. Anna's mouth still shaped whatever words she had meant to say. But her body, her neck, her eyes strained to see into the distance. "What's the matter?" he asked.

Even Katerina, glancing up, was alarmed. "Mama? Why are you so . . . Mama, what—"

"Shhhhh!" Anna said. "Listen! What do you hear?"

"Nothing," Giorgi answered, his voice worried.

Anna shook her head. "Nor do I. Nothing. I hear nothing. What's wrong there?"

"Oh, Anna," Nicolai began, "the stories upset you, you're imagining things."

"Shhhhh!" She put her hand up. "Where's the smoke? The fires? The noise?" Her voice was low and wary, as if pressing, hiding, against the ground. "People make noise. A village has fires. What's wrong? What's happened?"

Nicolai saw tipis across the meadow, but Anna was right. There

were no curls of smoke, no sounds of laughter or play or conversation. He shuddered.

And then a single sharp keening cry, a mourner's wail, cut the malevolent silence.

Anna gasped and slid off her horse. The children were already running across the meadow. "Wait!" Nicolai shouted, "Don't go in there!" Something unknown and terrifying could suck them all up the way it had the smoke and sound.

But the only thing ahead was Anna's mother, tiny and wailing, staring blindly at a gray ring of ashes.

"Where is everybody?" Anna cried. "What happened?"

Her mother looked at her with dull incredulity. "They didn't take me. I'm too old. The rest are gone. Except your father, who is dead." Her voice was sluggish. She looked at the ashes again. Funeral remains. "They raped three women, then took them, too. Took everybody they could. The rest ran."

Piotr.

"Took where?" Anna's voice was barely audible. It sounded full of cracks and fissures.

Piotr.

Her mother shook her head.

Piotr! The tragedy was enormous, incalculable, but Nicolai heard only the name of his son, Piotr the deer hunter. "Took who? Who took who?" he said. He was suddenly unsure of the Pomo language although he'd spoken it for years. Surely he'd misunderstood the old woman.

Her silence and the black sorrow in her eyes did not need translation.

Anna doubled over as if hit. Then, head still bowed, she covered her eyes and wailed with her mother.

Katerina pressed against her, afraid, and Anna dropped her hands and looked to the skies. Her voice became low, coming from her belly, a growl, a curse, a spell being cast. "My father climbs to the happy land in the heavens, but the evil men who did this will fall off the ladder, become rattlesnakes burning their bellies on the hot earth forever. Or grizzly bears who—"

Piotr! "Somebody *took* everybody?" Nicolai ripped at his hair, his beard. "Took people? Stole"—and he dared to say it, even though Anna's eyes looked hollow and still more terrified—"my son?" Pressure built in his chest, in his lungs, in his fists, and behind his eyes until he knew he would burst.

His mother-in-law stared up at him through the web of wrinkles holding her skin together.

"Who?" he roared. *"Who dares to do this?"*

"Strangers," the old woman said softly. "Men of Sonoma."

The Spanish, kin to the ranchers who had frightened the Indians at Bodega. Mexicans they called themselves now that they'd broken with Spain. His people's old antagonists, the ones who hadn't let them breathe, the ones who claimed all the lands they used as well as the land they didn't touch at all. They extended the missions, built San Rafael and Sonoma only to contain the Russians, only to keep Ross from rightfully expanding. And now the Russians and the missions were both gone and still the enmity persisted.

The village was a graveyard, except instead of crosses and redwood slabs, there were tipis to mark the dead and missing.

If only he hadn't gone to Bodega. He could have been here. The Russians had always protected the Indians, had been welcomed for it from the day the treaty was signed. He could have saved Piotr. He could be here with his son, with the people who were, for better or worse, his people now.

And then he admitted that was no more than the wishful boast of an old man. He would have been killed. There were many of them, one of him. He couldn't have protected them. He had failed to protect Piotr, victim of the white man's poison just as much as Tahny and the baby had been with the measles, just as much as Mikhail had been with the smallpox. But this was the worst disease, this greed that led to enslavement.

He looked at his three remaining children, grateful that his foolish expedition had saved them, although Piotr's name screamed through his heart with each beat.

Katerina and Giorgi stood stricken and confused.

"My brothers." Anna's voice broke. "My sisters. My son. Why?"

And Nicolai heard the words of Alexander Baranov, ruling for years in the wasteland of Alaska. "The heavens are high and the Tsar is far away." There was no one to rule here, not God nor man.

There was only Nicolai.

Anna watched him pace, look at the sky, up to his God for answers. He was like a trapped wild thing. "I'll find them," he said abruptly.

"How," she said. "Where." These weren't questions. "And how could you get them back." It made the pain worse, if that were possi-

ble, to see him thunder and rail for nothing. He was like them with his violence, his insistence that he could do anything. She hated thinking about how much he was like them.

"There are laws! These are people!" he bellowed.

"The men of Sonoma will kill you, too," her mother said in her flattened-out voice. "They killed my husband and possibly others. They raped women. They stole so many. And how would you get to them without being killed yourself?"

"They have my *son!*"

"The stolen ones will try to escape," the old woman said. "And so must we. Take your things from the house, and then we'll burn it as a dead thing, and hide like those who weren't taken did."

"I'll find them and bring them back," he said again, more calmly.

"All of them?" Anna's eyes stung and her throat hurt for the missing, for her son, for the man across from her. He was a child sometimes. Anna felt a thousand years old. Older. But he made plans, world-shaking plans that required whole armies. He was so restless, so Russian. "How?"

"I don't know! I'll just do it!"

"Where would you look?"

"Anywhere—everywhere! Wherever we have to go, wherever they took them! That's where we'll look."

"Look first at me, Nicolai," she said harshly.

He looked her way, unseeing. His mind still spun around his plans.

"Look at me!"

His eyes cleared. "What do you want?"

"Look at me—look at Katerina or Giorgi or the baby."

"Yes, yes?"

"*Look at us!*" She held up her right arm.

Slowly, his eyes focused on her purple tattoos, moved to her hair, to Giorgi's bottomwillow earring with its quail plumes and beads, to Ivan in his carrying basket.

"We're what they want," she said softly. "We can't travel with you." Why did she have to remind him? In some ways he was so clever and in some ways so exasperating.

He was old and refused to admit it. He had to believe that he and his kind could change whatever bothered them, do whatever they thought of—and look where such thinking got men! He thought she wasn't smart, didn't want enough. But all she had ever wanted was the life everyone had lived since time began, the kind nobody thought about. Why wasn't that enough? Wouldn't it be enough still

to have Piotr? Still to have the whole village and world?

He blustered and stormed, "I can't stand by and let them take my—"

"Would you leave us unprotected, then?" she asked, keeping her voice low so as not to frighten the children, although that was ridiculous. They stood like gray shadows, afraid to move or consider the future.

Only Nicolai charged into action, directionless but in motion. "I'll do it," he said loudly. "I'll find them. But first, I'll find you a safe place."

Safe. She tried to make herself tight inside so that her heart would stop leaking. Safe, he'd said, thinking that if he said it loudly enough, he'd make it so. Safe. Safe was when his kind was here, when the Russians kept the Spanish away; safe was when she lay with him, became one joined new creature that defied death itself. Safe was in legends, in traditions and ancient knowledge. Safe was a village, many people, many hearts. Safe was a memory and nothing more.

Only a fool still believed in "safe." His own kind had changed the language, erased the word.

He walked away from his family and looked out over the ocean as the day began to fade.

The sky seemed colder and further away than ever before, or else he was lower, diminished and dwindling as if under a curse. Three of his children gone and all their losses on his head.

He had nothing important to do on this earth except protect his family, and he hadn't done even that.

He was fifty-two, an old man, but he hadn't felt his years until this moment. Once his rage cooled and he thought sanely again, once he gave up the idea of finding a hundred people and bringing each one home—and keeping them safe from future attacks—he felt a dead weight, heavy and cold, clamp onto his back and bend him low.

He remembered his dream the day of the whale and the condor, the day he decided to leave for Bodega. The man who'd snarled "Diggers!" and the otters both had been in it, and only now was the connection clear.

Years ago, he'd coordinated a dozen bidarkas, the whole work crew, on a hunt.

The water churned that day, the wind was fierce, but the Aleut hunter said that was good. Sometimes, he said, they'd catch an otter

while the timid animal buried his head in a kelp bed, hiding from the noise of a storm. Nicolai had tried not to think of the terrified animal, blocking out the world and dying for it.

"Another good time to get them," the hunter said, swigging his vodka, "is when the mother dives for food—the only time she leaves her pup its first year. Then you spear the pup. It cries like a real baby, and when the parents try to save it, we spear them."

"They care so much, then?" Nicolai felt a chill that had nothing to do with the darkening sky.

The Aleut nodded. "They have only one at a time. If it dies, they starve themselves with grief. Odd creatures. You'll see. I myself have seen them hugging." He stared at the horizon nonchalantly as the first splats of rain hit his wooden hat.

"Does that ever make you feel—well, as if the killing might be . . ." Nicolai didn't want to offend the man or sound unmanly. "I mean . . ."

The Aleut shrugged. "They're animals!"

It was then that the dreams started, when images of otters impaled on spears became confused with gilded icons and pictures of Christ and the saints that had decorated the corners of his house, his church, his chapel, and his mind since infancy.

He ignored his qualms because the otters kept the company going and the company kept Nicolai in California. Besides, he couldn't combat the insatiable lust of Chinese mandarins for otter-skin robes, or of their ladies for pearl-trimmed otter sashes or lush otter capes.

But now, when otters cried only in Nicolai's worst dreams, he wished somebody, perhaps he himself, had really listened sooner.

Anna's people, so gentle and unwarlike, were like otters to Sutter's men, who spit and called them names and thought them less than human. And to the Mexicans, who had once starved and permanently imprisoned them at the missions and now stole and enslaved them on ranches. How many creatures disappeared that way, with a final unheeded cry, then silence?

He walked the darkening fields, over the hill, down through the valley where they'd once lived, into the stockade walls, and then, into the chapel, the "cross-house," as Anna called it.

He touched its silvered wood. He had built it, and it still filled him with pride for its simple grace, its weathertight planks topped by cupolas, little wonders of engineering, holding crosses.

He went inside and sat silently, waiting for illumination or relief. He fingered the cross he wore around his neck, then held it tight.

The chapel was quiet and empty. The icons were gone, remembered through smoky outlines etched by ancient, guttered candles. The worshipers were gone. Comfort was gone. For all he knew, God, too, was gone.

He stood up, creaking like dry wood. "Good-bye," he whispered, abandoning it to be swallowed by time and salt air.

It was all memory now. Deserted fort, destroyed village, dismantled houses in between. He stopped at the site of their old house. The logs were long gone to Sutter, but the fireplace still stood. He bent and scraped some ashy dirt into a small leather pouch.

"For the *domovoy*," he said, as if already explaining this eccentricity to Anna. Until now, he hadn't moved the house spirit. He'd left behind the old dwarf who lives under the threshold. Or perhaps he had simply known his ancestor's spirit wouldn't thrive in a Kashaya tipi that lacked even a windowsill on which to leave it pancakes and treats.

He hadn't understood, two years ago, that they would need every bit of luck and spirit they could scrape off any corner of the earth. God forgive him.

He walked carefully through dark meadows. The night sky was blind and black, stars and moon hidden.

Anna sat, keening with her mother. "We'll leave tomorrow," he announced. "We'll go away from Sonoma, from everything and everyone. We'll go north, where there is no one."

He had hands and the land had trees. He would build them a new fort. Anna would have to get used to his ways now, because it was no longer safe to live like a Kashaya.

From now on, all of them, even the *domovoy*, would live in a house with square rooms, wooden floors, and doors that swung smoothly and had bolts to lock against dark things coming through the forests.

3

"It's harder to poison white men," he heard through the open door. "But you might as well try."

Nicolai stopped and held his breath so as to remain unnoticed. A skinned rabbit dangled from his hand.

Anna had the children in a semicircle. She held a roughly crafted figure, a small forked stick with a crudely carved oak ball head on its end.

"Get the person's hair. Or better, his urine or feces, and rub it on the stick. And have your poison ready, your snake venom, your spider poison, and I've told you the curses, and you give the poison to this"—she held up the awkward little doll—"and say his true name. It's easy with white men because they tell everyone their true names. And when this is dead, you burn it."

The rabbit trembled in his shaking hand. Nicolai had thought they would be happy here, that time would make a difference. But here she was in a safe and good house, more than a year after they'd left Metini, teaching her children how to poison white men.

They had trudged north until they agreed on a remote and sunny clearing at the edge of a forest. It was a silent, timeless spot against an infinitude of brooding, ancient firs, oaks, and redwood trees. High above the craggy coast, it overlooked approaches by land and sea,

just as Ross had. The trees would provide acorns aplenty and the ocean was not an impossible trek, so there'd be kelp and the salt that collected on rocks. There was a river nearby, though not so close that it was likely to flood them during the winter rains.

Nicolai built his house. He found a fallen redwood, large enough to provide wood for a village, and he formed rough planking. He built, as always, "by the eye," notching and joining beams expertly without need of nails or metal parts.

He began with a spacious single room, hoping that except for its heavy, bolted door, it would make Anna feel somewhat at home. But "home" was a complex and populated word to his wife, and while she grudgingly lived in the wooden box, she didn't adopt it in her heart.

She adopted nothing but pain, he thought. She had clamped down over it and grown a shell to make it untouchable.

Her world was gone and she blamed him for being part of the process of change and ruination.

She was lost, he knew, but she wouldn't let him lead her to a new place. She had been born to be the same woman her mother was, as her great grandmother and the first Kashaya woman had been, back to when the earth was formed. The new, the altered, and the unknown held no attraction.

Of course, she had married him, but then, by that time, the Russians were part of her world and seemed permanent. It was only when the rest of the fort left that Anna started treating him as something foreign, uncomfortable, and suspect.

Anna's world view was like one of her brilliantly intricate baskets —so tightly woven that not even water escaped. The way to live had been woven when the earth awoke, and design variations were unsafe and suspect.

She refused to join hands with him in finding a new way to live and be strong together. In turn, he stopped trying to please her and made his house less an adapted tipi, cutting window openings although he had neither glass nor sea lion intestines to stretch across them. Instead, he covered them with thick shutters to close out the night and foul weather. He built an enormous fireplace, patterned after the one in the commandant's house at Ross. While the winter rains raged, he lay beautifully fitted planks on the floor. The room by firelight was solid and comfortable, if austere. Anna's storage baskets lined one wall and furs served as sleeping mats. Eating implements and toys Nicolai had carved lay about, but otherwise, the room was bare. He carved an icon, wishing he had bright paints and gilding for

it, and created a "beautiful corner" that reminded him of his home in Siberia, his *izba*.

He cut a wide plank out of the fallen tree and put legs under it, then he built sturdy stools and a bench and convinced Anna that they should eat at a table, not on the floor by the fire.

She didn't fight with him over that or much else, and it disturbed him. She seemed broken and limp, wobbling her head in agreement at any suggestion. She was still actively mourning, with white clay balls in hair cut short across her forehead and temples, and singed at the tips. She mentioned, too often, that she should have spent the year "feeding the dead" back at the village. Instead, she had brought the dead along with her and she herself moved like a phantom. Her rebellion was hidden, like an undertow, but it was always there. Nicolai saw it in the glances she and her mother exchanged. He heard it in the stories she told the children.

". . . then Marumda said to Kuksu, the people that we made are behaving wrongly. They are intermarrying, they are turning into idiots, and their children grow puny. Therefore, I will wash them away!"

The children of the intermarriage, neither puny nor idiots, listened with wide eyes.

And when spring arrived, bursting with sunshine and color after the rains, it only increased her rigid pain. Nicolai understood. The rhododendron and the meadow blooming yellow, white, and lavender, and each glint of sunshine off the hard and endless ocean brought back memories of another summer, another meadow where they had idled near the sea while their son and the others had been stolen or killed.

Now she was teaching their children how to poison the unseen enemy. She was not getting better, softer, or happier.

He strode into the house. "I've decided to go," he announced with vigor. "I'm leaving."

Anna looked terrified.

"I'll find him," he said, more softly. "I can do it." It revolted him that his safety lay in being the same breed as murderers and kidnappers. He hoped Anna wouldn't bother to think it through and come to the same realization. He hoped she hadn't meant the poison doll for him. She had once told him that the strongest destruction for a man is worked when you can use his own semen. He refused to think about it, pretended he didn't notice Anna hide the stick doll behind her. "I'll be safe," he said. "I'll pretend that I owned Piotr."

Anna looked appalled, stared at him as if he were truly her enemy. "I don't know how else to do it," he said weakly.

He was away the entire dry season. He searched Sonoma's fertile farms and then went up to the Delta. He found men draining swamps and building Sutter's empire. He saw Sutter's Indian slaves forced to eat like pigs, from troughs. But he didn't find Piotr among them, or any of the lost Kashayas. When he returned to the house in the woods, he brought window glass and a still heavier heart in place of his son.

There was no ease, day or night. Cold rain beat on the new windows through the short winter days and inside, despite the roaring fire, all was equally chill and remote.

He turned to her in the night. Her shoulder was outlined with light from the fireplace. He ached for warmth, for a forgiveness beyond words, and he remembered how she had consoled him when he had been a mourner. When all he could think of was death and loss, Anna had brought him herself, slender and young and very much alive. She had not only touched him, reminded him of his own living flesh, but she had taken his hands, put them on her naked body, and led them over her. His palms could still feel the impress of her gentle swells, the curve of her breasts and hips and buttocks as she led him around her, reminding him through his fingertips and heartbeat that there was still a world, still life, still pleasure.

"Anna," he whispered, although the children and her mother were sound asleep. He ran his hand over her silky shoulder. It felt so right, so natural—until she tensed.

Where was his wife, the woman he had known and loved, the laughing creature on the trip to Bodega, wrapping herself around him to prove there was no rattlesnake in her like in the sun-girls? She had seemed half mythical herself in the moonlight.

Now she seemed like a breathing corpse.

Surely, he could make her feel something again. He ignored her passivity, touching her the ways she had always enjoyed, arching her toward him, pressing into her, moving in the rhythms that she had always joined and loved.

Only the cracks of the burning logs broke the dark silence. Anna accommodated him, but it was as if in defeat, as if her body and spirit were unrelated and she was elsewhere, avoiding his touch. She was always this way now, no matter what he said or did, so that even in

the moment of most intense pleasure and release, he felt an equally acute bitter sorrow.

When he was spent, he lay on his back, staring at the ceiling. "There are other places to look," he said. "I'll go again after the rains. I'll find them all."

She said nothing.

Winter was a long cage. Nicolai tried to be content sitting by the fire, telling stories to his children, and carving spoons and bowls. He sipped tea brewed in the samovar he had hidden in the well at Ross and waited for a sense of rest, but the nights were too long, the dark days too short.

Anna, with unreadable black eyes, announced in a flat voice that she was again with child.

"Tell him," her mother said to her. "It is forbidden for a man to hunt or fish until his wife's child is born."

She held tight to the old ways, never speaking directly to her son-in-law. And on his part, he used only the formal, placating language reserved for mothers-in-law and sharks. But how to tell a shark that the rules had changed, that this was a new village and he was its toyon? This chief had to feed his family, even in the rainy season, even during pregnancy, and there were no other grown men to take his place. He spoke softly, gently, and felt like a man walking a dangerous parapet. Anna tightened her lips and said nothing.

Still, Nicolai's muscles ached with underuse. Finally inspired, he went back to the fallen giant and hewed more planks and beams. "You want to come outside with me?" he asked Anna.

"Go," her mother said. "It's safe."

Anna, unlike her unruly husband, listened to the old woman and obeyed the pregnancy taboos. She never viewed the sun or moon lest she delay birth. She ventured outdoors only with someone else, but when she did, as now, she was sullen.

"What do we need with another room?" Anna asked when his purpose was clear. "There aren't enough of us to fill the one we have." She was irritable and withdrawn.

"This is where we'll sleep."

"Why? The room we have is enormous. Why do you always want to pull people apart?"

"Because," he said as he neatly fit the notched boards together. "Because." Because only peasants, serfs, and soldiers slept in crowds. Because he had the talent to turn that fallen redwood into a castle.

Because Indians and tipis were not safe anymore, and he had to find a way to save his remaining children.

She accompanied him day after day, looking dubious, her arms resting on top of her swollen stomach, insisting she did not need a second room.

It would do him no good to suggest that the new baby could sleep elsewhere. This baby would sleep exactly as its brothers and sisters had, swaddled in its basket until it was strong and big enough to turn it over and crawl out. The idea of a spacious and separate nursery would horrify Anna. He was suddenly inspired. "This will be the birthing room. The menstrual hut. You don't want to have our child in the big room with everyone there, do you?"

She said nothing, merely shook her head. And when he came to her and held her, his arms around her in the unfinished skeleton of a room under a gray and foggy winter sky, she still said nothing, but he could hear her soft weeping.

The pain hovered for a second, deciding, and then it grabbed her abdomen and squeezed, a hard fist inside, pulling the impossible.

Anna inhaled sharply. It was coming, then. Finally. Child of misery. Child with no true family, no true home. The no-child.

Her mother and husband looked up at the same time. Her mother's face was dark, like a leaf just before winter. She waited.

Anna nodded.

Nicolai seemed excited, actually glad. But then, he'd been that way all along, building a birthing room.

Anna carried a much heavier weight than the child accounted for, Nicolai didn't understand anything. As far as she was concerned, this baby could be born in a great knothole or funeral pyre. Her husband, smiling, nodding with encouragement and expectation, didn't know how much she dreaded the idea of another life, of new lips suckling at her breast.

To what purpose? To spend its life hiding?

She had become nothing and they were nothing and she had no idea of how they could have escaped the endlessly sorry way they lived, but she knew she was not bringing another soul into this misery.

She stood up and walked slowly toward the second room. Her mother came to her side, helping her. Nicolai also rose.

"Tell him no," her mother said.

"You can't come in," she told her husband. "This is for women."

She heard him outside the birthing room door, listening, waiting. She was quiet, letting the pain roll and recede in waves. The child was impatient and strong, getting itself born more quickly than any of the others.

Why, she wondered. Why the rush?

And then, after a final squeeze of the fist inside, head and shoulders and legs passed through her into the day and the light and wailed at the shock of its life.

She looked at it. At him. And then at her mother, who cut the cord with a sharp mussel shell, just as she had done for all the others. "Should I make the wish?" her mother whispered.

She had never asked before. She had cut and wished for health and food, for skill at the hunt, then buried the placenta and cord in a secret place. But this time she knew. It—he—wasn't wanted, couldn't be wanted.

Anna shook her head. The baby made soft, needy sounds. "Give him to me," she said, but her voice was hard and unloving.

"He's handsome. Large and strong. My daughter—"

"*Give him to me!*"

Her mother stepped back, holding the newborn. "You'll have to take him yourself."

Anna leaned forward and grabbed the child so harshly his cries turned sharp.

"It's wrong," her mother hissed. "Wrong! Too many were lost already."

"Don't you understand?" Anna cried. "There's no place for him on this earth. No place for any of us." She put her hands on his tiny neck. Better that she destroyed him quickly than that white hands took their cruel time with the job. She closed her eyes and squeezed.

And the world went orange and hot and roared in her ear where an open hand struck her, so hard that she burned. The baby was out of her arms, gone. The door still banged from the force of Nicolai's entry. He passed the baby to her mother and pinned Anna's hands behind her.

"What were you doing?" His voice cracked, his eyes were crazed, he gripped her wrists with unbearable pressure.

"Get out!" she screamed. Shameful, hot tears of frustration and pain blurred the sight of her mother bending over the child.

"What were you doing to my son!" He dropped her wrists as if they

33

were poison and took back the newborn from his mother-in-law, holding the wailing baby close, patting him, reaching for a rabbit skin to wrap him in. "What were you doing?"

Anna's mother began a long wish for life, for enough food, for a good hunt. And then she left to bury the cord.

"Anna?" he demanded. "How could you want to kill him?"

"It's too hard," she whispered. "Too hard for him. Too hard for me, losing them. Losing everybody. I remember Piotr—I remember carrying him. I remember the day he was born and—"

"I'll find him." His voice was gentler. "I remember, too." He looked at the red-faced squalling infant. "He's beautiful."

"You always say that," she said weakly.

"They always are. I name him Alexander." All their children had two names, one for each parent's family, as was the custom. Nicolai called them by their Russian names, Anna by their Kashaya names or by a nickname. "What is your name for him, Anna?"

"Boy."

"Boy?" Nicolai said. "But what's his name?"

"That's enough. That's what he is, all he can hope to be."

"No, Anna. His name."

"It's a secret."

"From me? From his father?"

Anna took the baby, gave him her breast, then wrapped him in swaddling and put him into his basket, acknowledging that he would live. "Yes," she said. "It's all right now. You see?"

"But his name! You think I'm a poisoner and I can't know my own son's true name?" Nicolai's voice was too strained to be a shout, but it was a terrifying sound. "That I would use his name against him? My child?"

She held her hands up to stop him. He noticed how lined her face had become. "Please," she said. "Let it be."

"What is it? That only you can keep him safe? That I've . . . that I . . ." He stepped back a pace.

She looked down at her hands and said no more.

He watched Alexander carefully for months, relieved to see the child thrive. To Nicolai, he was a promise and a hope, and the most beautiful of all his children, long-limbed and quick-eyed, watching intently from his cradle, gasping with delight at the duck heads and abalone dangles hanging on wampum strings to amuse him. His hair

came in a deep red-brown and his eyes turned the slatey blue of stormy skies.

But sometimes the tiny features became pensive and withdrawn in a most uninfantlike way, and Nicolai wondered if Alexander somehow knew how troubled his arrival had been.

Ivan, sturdy and extroverted, spent hours making faces at the baby and forcing deep, moist laughter out of him. Katerina played little mother when the baby's actual mother sank into despair or lethargy. And Giorgi, now a young man himself, was able to hunt deer and fish for the salmon that ran in the river nearby. A few times they walked down to the beach at the end of the river where a tribe of Pomos still lived. But they weren't Kashayas and even Anna had trouble with their language and didn't consider them family.

By summer, Nicolai felt he could leave again, and this time he stopped at Ross. Some of the tribe, those who had fled and hidden, had returned, but not his son or his wife's brothers, and no one knew where they might be. There were rumors that they might be to the south, in Marin. Nicolai continued toward Bodega, remembering the frightened eyes of the Indians there. He rode into San Rafael, down as far as Sausalito, and found no sign.

He brought home a second horse and a bolt of fabric traded for carpentry skills, but not Piotr.

That winter and the next he built additional rooms on the ground floor, then a staircase and a second story, much to Anna's incredulity. At the top of the stairs he built still more sleeping rooms, imitating the grand houses of landowners back in Siberia, houses so splendid that no family members shared a room, let alone a bed. And then, his crowning achievement was a tower above the great room below, multisided like the cupola atop the chapel at Ross, except that one side of this tower opened to the sleeping chambers.

He sat in his treetop room for hours, content to watch the ocean shimmer from pearl-gray mornings into scarlet, purple, and orange sunsets, to study the shifting contours of the forests in the wind, the changing greens as clouds bumped into branches that scraped the sky, to watch condors and hawks hang motionless in space. Sometimes he brought all the children upstairs with him, and even the baby sat still while they told stories and watched the world.

Anna never joined them. He tried to ignore the unpleasant meaning of this and to use this time to tell his children about his life at Ross, without Anna's snorts of derision.

"The commandant's house was rich," he said. "The rooms had thick soft rugs, tapestries, a piano, and—"

"What's a rug? What's tapestry? What's all that?" Katerina asked.

"Rugs are like . . . like leaves or fur or feathers on the floor. Only of sheep's wool dyed bright colors. And tapestries are wall rugs, pictures. With designs, like mama's baskets." The piano was even more difficult to define. "A music box," he finally said. "Like my balalaika, but much, much larger. Larger than you are with your arms stretched out. And it sits on legs."

"Legs?" Giorgi said. "Like you told us about Baba Yaga's house? With the rooster legs?"

"No." Nicolai laughed. "Legs like sticks, like on the table downstairs."

"What does it do, Papa?" Katerina asked. She was always in motion, that one, dancing like a butterfly, and even when she was still, her mind fluttered over everything, inspecting and questioning. She was his bright, shining jewel.

"You push on little pieces of bone," he said, "and they push pegs that hit on strings inside, and that makes music. Princess Helena played it, and beautifully."

Katerina, Giorgi, and Ivan exchanged a glance, unsure whether this was another of their father's fairy tales. Even Alexander's eyes grew wide, but he was like that, sucking in stories like a child still at the breast. "More," he said, sounding like his sister.

So he told his children about the bleak time on the Farallon Islands, right across from San Francisco Bay. The islands had fur seals but nothing else. No water except what collected and stagnated on rocks. No way to leave after being dropped there. No materials on the stony surface with which to build a boat.

"We lived in earth dugouts, collected rainwater, and cooked by burning sea lion bones soaked in oil. People got the scurvy. They bled under the skin, and sometimes were so weak they fell into the sea and were washed away." And then he hugged and kissed each child. "It's very good to sit here dry and safe and strong in a tower above a green world," he said.

Anna wasn't interested. Instead, she went about her business, leaching, drying, and grinding acorns, with grim dedication. Her mother was barely there at all, a small, silent brown woman. She wasn't much of a shark anymore. She dried up like the leaves in autumn and just as quietly, and midway through one winter, with little fuss, she became too brittle to live.

36

Nicolai helped prepare the cremation, and he honored his wife's mourning as she again cut and singed her hair and put the clay balls into it. But the intensity of her expression frightened him. "You will not burn down this house," he said emphatically. "This is not a tipi to be destroyed after a funeral."

Anna's eyes slit, making her face with its hacked hair even more strange and foreign. "I know this isn't a tipi," she said in a low, angry voice. "I know what it isn't."

However, she didn't burn it or declare the ground it stood on condemned.

Even so, they were at war.

A few weeks later, he found her bent over a mussel shell, mashing wild violets and soot into a purple paste. A sharp deer bone lay on the floor. Katerina sat across from her mother, carefully observing.

He watched silently for a moment, admiring the skilled and practiced way Anna's strong arms ground the bright-colored mixture.

And then he connected those arms and their purple tattoos with his daughter and the mussel shell. "No!" He grabbed the sharp bone. "Absolutely not."

Anna's chin went up. Her eyes were dark and furious. She lifted her arm with its lightening strikes and cross-hatches and deliberately reached for the deer bone. Nicolai clutched it tighter and raised his hand into the air, crouching near them, glowering.

Anna's eyes grew wide. "Will you kill us, then?" There was fear and contempt in her voice.

Nicolai realized his hand was poised as if his family were his prey. He relaxed his grip. The bone clattered to the floor.

"Would you have her be plain? Ugly? Every Pomo woman—"

She is not only Pomo!" How would he make this woman understand the world? He stood up and loomed over her. "She is Katerina Nicolaiovna Beriankov. My daughter."

"She's mine, too!" Anna scrambled to her feet. "I'll make her beautiful!"

"You'll mark her for destruction!"

They stood there, a small, dark woman with large brown-black eyes, a fine-bridged nose, striking high cheekbones, and purple tattoos on her chin, and a tall blue-eyed man with a wild silvery beard and long gray-blond hair. They froze into their positions, hands clenched on either side of a block of air that might as well have been made of iron.

"Anna," Nicolai finally whispered.

37

"My daughter—"

"Our daughter. She is—they are all—not like you or me. They're something new and they have to find new ways. When they're grown and they go into the world—"

She shook her head. "There's no world left—"

"—it will be a new place they enter. Both our worlds are gone. Please, Anna, put away the dyes and needles and let's be friends again. No tattoos. No earrings for the boys. No—"

"No family. Nothing, nothing left!"

"We're a family."

"No! We're a piece of something—a severed finger without its hand. People die, families don't."

"We're a family," he repeated. "A new kind."

She pressed her hands against her heart and bowed her head. Then she lifted one hand and covered her tattooed chin as if suddenly ashamed. A moment later, she threw away the mussel shell and deer bone.

So there seemed a truce, although Nicolai knew there would be battle after battle as he, blindfolded and confused himself, nonetheless guided his children toward a new definition. Anna, bewildered, resentful, angry, still refused to tell him Alexander's true name.

Weeks later, the view from the tower room changed again, adding more color on the land by midday, more fog over the morning and evening ocean. It was again time to leave.

Whenever he gathered his children together, he saw his ghosts as well—Mikhail before smallpox disfigured him, Piotr, tall and strong, and, still more ephemeral and desolate, his first wife, Tahny, and first child, Marina. All gave mute testimony to the dangers wrought by his kind, to his powerlessness to protect even those he loved best from the sicknesses of his own people.

Piotr was his only hope of redemption, and so once again he set out to find his son, not allowing himself to wonder if he would even recognize him. He had lost a slender boy. Would he recognize the young man years of dislocation and suffering had produced?

And would the boy recognize him? After each search, despite the deeply lined tan of his skin, Nicolai returned a paler shade. Not only his hair, but also his heart lost color. Something vital drained away as each circular exploration shaped itself into another zero.

This time Nicolai went back to Sonoma, but it wasn't the same place. The streets were ominously silent, the fields so empty that Nicolai shivered. There was a spell on the land.

Finally, he found an elderly Mexican outside a store in Petaluma. "It's the gold," the man said. Nicolai understood the simple words, but not why they had been said. The old man coughed for a long time, then repeated himself. "Gold. You deaf? Where you been? There's gold near Sacramento. Sutter's Creek."

"Sutter? The Swiss captain?"

The man shrugged. "How'd I know? All's I know is that there's gold and people went to get it."

"But they can't leave crops, or livestock, or—"

The man's laugh triggered another coughing spell. When he recovered, he looked up at Nicolai. "For gold they leave everything. And not just here. Cargoes rotting in San Francisco harbor because the crew's at the gold fields. Hundreds of thousands up there already. Whole world's coming to California. Me, I'm too old and sick, or I'd be there, too. A man can get rich overnight. Where you been, you hadn't heard?" He shook his head in wonder, then coughed.

"And the captain?" Nicolai asked. "He lets everyone come onto his land to take the gold?"

The man shrugged. "Ain't a matter of letting. I hear Sutter's place is ruined, that he's mad as hell. But who cares? There's *gold* there."

"He wanted farms, a community," Nicolai began. Then he, too, shrugged. The cannons hadn't protected Sutter's dreams any better than they had those of Napoleon or the Russian-American Company.

However, Nicolai felt a flicker of hope. "Where are the Indians? The field workers." Perhaps they were unguarded, ready to flee.

The man spat. "Took 'em up as servants. Some in chains, some more easy. They pan for the owners."

It didn't matter what happened—good luck or bad for the whites, they made a hell on earth for everybody else. Nicolai's fists clenched, and then his shoulders sagged. Who was he going to punch?

"Now you know about it, you gonna make a claim?" the old man asked.

"What's a claim?"

The man looked at him with wonderment. "When you say part of the ground is yours. Like you would for your ranch. Where you from?"

A claim. Nicolai mulled this over. Should he be claiming his house? "Where do people claim?" he asked.

"In the gold fields? They—"

"No—for a house."

The man coughed. "You don't make sense, you know that?"

"For house—where?"

He shrugged. "Sonoma courthouse. Dunno for sure."

"I thank you." Nicolai remounted his horse.

Behind him, the man coughed.

The hunting was over, then, without conclusion, without redemption.

There seemed no point continuing. For years he had combed the area from San Francisco to Sacramento without a shred of luck or a single worthwhile clue, and now the whole world was upside down and at the gold fields. He had no way of winnowing his lost son out of hundreds of thousands of newcomers. He turned his horse homeward from his last summer search.

He couldn't resist another look at Ross. He wanted to see the fort and then the village. The remaining Pomos were always interested in the results of his searches, and now he'd have to tell them of this new upheaval, although he himself didn't know what to make of it.

Each time he returned to the fort, he marked the progress of decay. This time the ocean glared through gaps in the wharf's planks. Nearby, great portions of the fences that had once divided wilderness from gardens had been burned away by nature or man.

It will soon be gone, he thought, chaff in the wind, and no one will remember that we were here. Except for stumps where there once had been trees, the land will be as it always was.

He remembered the iron markers saying "lands of the Russian realm" buried on this coast. And Mount St. Helena, named for the Tsarina, also had markers saying "Russian, Russian" in two languages. How optimistic they had been with their markers. Perhaps the copper plates would be found, but the dreams behind their placement were lost forever.

He remounted his horse and rode the short distance to Metini.

The village had never been much, certainly nothing like Nicolai's idea of a true village with streets and tidy homes. But whatever it had been, it was less of it now.

He felt lightheaded, dizzy, afraid to look closely and find evidence of another tragedy, because otherwise, he would have seen tipis, children, the normal summertime work of gathering and drying abalone and kelp.

A man galloped toward him, calling greetings. He seemed friendly enough, although he spoke rapidly and incomprehensibly. His language had the hard cadences Nicolai remembered from a Yankee ship

40

captain who had traded with the Russians in Alaska. He even looked a little like him with a big square jaw and pale brown hair. But that didn't help Nicolai comprehend his words.

"Please," Nicolai said in Russian.

The man squinted, shook his head.

Nicolai pointed at the empty expanse in front of him. He raised his shoulders and held up his hands, palms up, to show confusion. "Kashayas?" He tented his hands, trying to describe a tipi.

"Oh!" the man said, smiling. "Sure." He rattled off another confusing string of sounds, pointing, however, to the hills in the distance. "Working," he finally said clearly and by itself. He pointed in several directions. He made signs of digging, or pulling plants. Farming? As they'd reluctantly done for the Russians?

"Working?" Nicolai repeated.

"For *me!*" The man nodded vigorously.

"Why *you?*" Nicolai said. "Why they work for *you?*"

The man's voice became louder, he spoke rapidly, gesticulating. Then he slowed himself down, took a deep breath, and again pointed to everything around them.

"Pri-vate-prop-er-ty now."

He said it once, twice, very, very slowly, intently. Nicolai knew he could hold on to the sounds and someday, therefore, find out what they meant. "Privatepropertynow?" he asked, to doublecheck. What an enormous, complicated word.

The man nodded, looking relieved. Then he lifted his hat in a farewell salute and rode off.

"Privatepropertynow," Nicolai repeated, to fix the sounds in his head. Perhaps that was the new name of the place. He shook his head and sighed and was just about to leave for the north and home when he heard a rustle, a shifting in the air. He felt it, although even after he wheeled his horse around, he saw nothing. Prickles of hair rose on the back of his neck.

It was the past watching him. It visited often, pressing against him more and more, sometimes more alive than the present. He heard childhood songs, remembered Russian voices, the sounds of the deep Siberian woods, the awesome silence of new snow, his village priest's voice.

And this village, this life. The thirty years he'd known it; the two wives it had given him; his children, dead, missing, and alive; the men's sweathouse; the dark tipi; the gambling; and mostly, the peo-

ple, the group that had been decimated and then had disappeared—they all returned, whispering so urgently that he was sure they were there, behind a tree or down below on the beach.

And then one ghost called out loud.

Nicolai's hand was on his knife as he spun his horse around again.

"Nicolai! Remember me?"

This ghost spoke Kashaya Pomo, but he must be a hallucination, another figment of Nicolai's unhappy memory, because he was dressed strangely in buckskin and leather, with high soft boots tied around his legs and a wide-brimmed hat that hid his hair.

"I'm Renny," the apparition said. "That's what you called me. We fished together." He pulled off his hat.

And then, with a glad whoop of recognition, Nicolai dismounted and embraced him.

"You're dressed so strangely!" Nicolai said with a laugh. The man would have been more quickly recognized in his customary nakedness. "You don't look Kashaya anymore."

"I hoped it was you," Renny said, "but I've hidden so long from the white man, I waited until I was sure. Until I thought, Who else but that crazy Russian would stand and sigh and stare so long at this place."

"Where were you?" Nicolai asked. "I've been looking for Piotr, for all of you for five years, looked everywhere. Where did they take you?"

"Missouri."

"Where in California is Missouri?"

Renny shook his head. "Not California, Nicolai. Very far away. Across many mountains. The men of Sonoma sold me. I was a slave with black men until I escaped."

Missouri. A word he'd never heard before, a word that meant all his searching had been futile, doomed from the beginning. Missouri. A world beyond his grasp, beyond endurance, beyond salvation. Missouri. The tribe was gone. Scattered. No old Russian could ride across mountain after mountain and bring them back from Missouri. His hopes had been based on nothing and he had been a fool.

"Heaven is high and the Tsar is far away." He hadn't thought of that line for years, but it seemed this world's motto. There was no order or system in this raw land and things beyond man's imagination could and did happen in the most casual way.

Missouri. The word tasted like ash.

"I hoped others would have also escaped," Renny said. "I hoped

that the whole time I walked home." He shook his head. "There's nothing left, is there?"

"It's all different. Some are back. They were here last year, but now—they work the fields of a white man on a horse."

"I saw him."

"He doesn't call it Metini anymore. He calls it 'privateproper-tynow.'"

Renny smiled, then grew serious. "It means he owns the land now. It's his, not ours. It's all ruined, destroyed. And it'll be worse. Many, many of them are on the way. I saw them myself, coming on horseback and in tented wagons."

"For the gold," Nicolai said. He felt too tired to move. Too heavy to crawl back on his horse and ride home. "They come for the gold."

"And for us," Renny said. "For us."

4

Nicolai wished Renny had accepted his offer of a home with them in Mendocino. But Renny went off to the gold fields despite Nicolai's warnings.

Perhaps it was just as well. Renny would only be more upset by what had happened to laughing, sunny Anna.

His house was bolted, the shutters closed over the window glass, although the day was fair and sunny. And when he touched the latch, Anna screamed.

"It's me!" he shouted. "Anna, it's Nicolai."

Nothing. He could feel her breathing, sense her heartbeat through the bolted door. "Anna," he said more quietly. "Please."

Nothing.

He said her secret, her true name.

She wailed in despair.

He pounded on the door. "Open up! This is my house! Children, are you in there? It's Papa."

Without a word, the door slowly opened. Giorgi looked ashamed. "Mama's afraid," he said simply.

"She saw a man," Katerina said.

"*I* saw the man," Ivan said. "We went to the beach for kelp and he was on the bluff."

"Who?" For one elated moment, Nicolai was sure Ivan had seen Piotr, searching for them all these years.

"A white man." Ivan shrugged. "Pretty old. His hair was funny, almost pink."

The fantasy of Piotr fermented and turned sour. "Where is he?" Now Nicolai understood the terror in Anna's eyes. They were here, too, then. They were everywhere, those hundreds of thousands coming by foot and by wagon. Nicolai grabbed his son with both hands. "Did he see you?"

Ivan shook his head.

"Are you certain?"

Ivan nodded. "We waited until he walked away. Then we left."

Nicolai released his grip. His head still swam, but at least they were safe for a while longer. "It will be all right, Anna," he said, hoping he could convince her, if not himself. She sat like stone, barely acknowledging his presence. He noticed a stick protruding from behind her and shifted himself for a better view of it, and then he saw the little wooden head, the crude features.

A poison doll for the white man on the bluff. Or for Nicolai and the evil that had accompanied life since his kind had arrived.

Nicolai's head was exploding.

"We need food for winter," Giorgi said in a low voice. "Mama's afraid to let us fish, but—"

Nicolai nodded. "Mama's right." Anna momentarily glanced at him without her customary veil of separation. Still, she looked paralyzed by her fears. "I'll fish," he said. "You and Ivan hunt away from the water. And Katerina, help gather acorns. The baby, too." Alexander could pick enough acorns off the forest floor to keep them alive. "And none of you go near the river or the ocean until we know what is happening."

"But the abalone—" Giorgi said.

"Until we know," Nicolai repeated. "And we'll plant a garden. Make things grow as we want them, right here." He didn't look at Anna as he forced more and more of his ways onto her.

That night, Nicolai sat in a rocking chair he had completed before his trip. He had hoped it would be a chair of contentment, a place for an old man to warm himself by a fire, to dream. The scene around him was pleasant enough. Anna was calm, if withdrawn, playing music with her children, gentle with them as always. Whatever her private sorrows and terrors and as much as she had not wanted Alexander to exist, once he was there, she loved and respected him as

much as she did all the others. "Raise them ugly, they turn out ugly," Anna had once said, explaining to a surprised Nicolai why he never saw Kashaya children beaten, never heard the sounds of painful crying. If only his father had had such a philosophy.

He wondered how they would be, Anna particularly, if he had insisted that they return to Russia with the others. Had he picked the most rigid Kashaya bride? Most of the others sailed off with their husbands, willing to learn about snow and ice, petticoats and staircases. The only ones who stayed behind, aside from Anna, were those whose departing husbands suddenly remembered that they already had wives back in Siberia.

Anna had never been tested. Nicolai hadn't wanted to leave, but perhaps he'd been a fool. Life was going on for those who left. They might be cold and poor, but they weren't hiding. Their children weren't stolen, treated worse than stray dogs.

Anna and the children blew hollow-bone bird whistles and rattled insect cocoons filled with pebbles. They made their music and then Anna told stories, trying to single-handedly replace all that had been lost with her tribe.

"Tonight, I will tell you about the woman who married a rattlesnake," she said. Nicolai's uneasiness increased and took up permanent residence. Her voice droned on, calmly, until she approached the part of the story where the woman's rattlesnake children asked why she looked different from them.

Then she paused, her head tilted as she considered her children. Nicolai could almost read her mind, see through her dark eyes as the firelight intensified the alien red of her children's hair, as she looked into eyes that weren't black like hers, but brown, gold, and blue-gray, as she saw bodies that weren't naked, weren't tattooed, weren't draped in buckskin, and heads that weren't decorated with bright woodpecker feathers.

Her voice thickened. "'I am not a rattlesnake,' the woman answered. 'I am a human being, different from you and your father. You cannot become a human being and I am not really a human being any longer, so . . .'" She shook her head and refused to complete the story.

Nicolai, the rattlesnake, backed further into the corner, the beautiful, icon-decorated corner of his splendid house.

The next day, Nicolai set out to find the man. Perhaps, he thought, as he rode in wider and wider circles away from his house, perhaps he was nothing. An aberration. A solitary mountain man

heading away from the crowds in the gold fields. A hallucination.

Nicolai climbed up to the first plateau above the beach at the mouth of the Booldam River where Ivan had seen the white man. The wind swept across fields of wildflowers and, he suddenly realized, across a small shack. Crude as it was, it in no way resembled a tipi. No one was in or near it, but Nicolai's heartbeat accelerated as if thousands of people had appeared, screaming.

He prowled the area and found, near a small ravine, a post with letters carved on it. He touched the post, trying to make sense of it through his fingertips.

"Hello!" The man stood back warily. He seemed as surprised to see a white man as Nicolai would have been had he not been warned.

Nicolai nodded, then pointed at the carved post.

The other man nodded back, pointed at himself. "I own."

"Ah," Nicolai said. "Is—claim?"

"Ya."

They fumbled back and forth with languages, using Spanish, a few English words, and much gesticulation, until Nicolai understood that, as the Mexican had suggested, such things were handled in Sonoma, at the courthouse.

When he left, his mind was a jumble of new fears. He wasn't alone in the woods anymore. He sat by the river, sorting his thoughts while he fished. He built a dam with a hole in it to trap the trout, and he had time to consider, waiting for another fish to slip through the hole and be caught in his net. Sometimes he used another method learned from Anna—stupefying the fish with the root of the soap plant. Either way, he wound up with racks of fish drying close to the house and Alexander standing sentry to keep away the flies.

Alexander reminded him of Mikhail. He was growing tall like a redwood tree and had chestnut hair, just as Mikhail had.

Every time the dead boy's name came into his mind, Nicolai re-played his futile attempts to save him, as if now, this time, he could change the progression of events and eradicate the smallpox.

He'd tried to save his son and the rest, too, racing through the settlement, begging the Indians to let him inoculate them. But they were understandably suspicious and only a few were willing to let Nicolai run a string full of Mikhail's diseased pus through a cut on their arms.

He couldn't blame them for their revulsion, but all the same, they died. He had saved Anna and her family, and tried to save more in other villages. But there was only so much string, only so much

energy and urging, and the disease traveled faster than he could so that hundreds, perhaps thousands, died.

The river ran in clear contrast to his murky thoughts. He thought of what he had not saved, and realized, firmly, that he must save his land. Protect it from whatever danger came next. He would go as soon as the storms ended.

That winter, while he waited to leave again, while the wind howled and the river roiled and spilled over its banks, Nicolai, tired of adding rooms, embellished those he had. He began with the fireplace, carving a story onto a large, solid mantelpiece.

"Look here," he told Alexander, who watched him with unflagging curiosity. Nicolai pointed to the left side of the frieze that emerged, bit by bit, from the wood. "This is my first village—in Siberia. See the fancy little house? My father was a merchant, but he was also a master carver, like me." He saw no need to tell Alexander what had happened to his grandfather's skills when he began to drink vodka day and night. "And then here is the Pacific Ocean, and the ship. And then—"

"Our house," Alexander said.

"No, no. It's a chapel with a cupola like we have, but it was in my second village—Ross." It made him weary to talk about what had been. It was so much more pleasant describing it through his fingers and knife. "And your mother's village was here. Those were the houses." He had carved the rough-sided bark tipis and people, and had gotten great satisfaction in the sense that he was, at least partially, restoring what had been stolen at "privatepropertynow."

"And this is my third village," Nicolai continued. "After the trees in between."

"This house!" Alexander said again, and this time his father nodded. "And that's us." Anna peeked out of the windows, Nicolai sat by the river, Giorgi and Ivan carried a deer, Katerina's lanky body was bent over a basket, and Alexander, chubby and small at the right edge, used a digging stick to uncover delectable root vegetables.

Anna grunted at the final product. "So that's it, then." She pointed at the tableau on the far right. "This is the end of the story. Right here."

He put his arms around her. She was so desperately unhappy, and she didn't deserve to be. She had never done a consciously cruel thing in her life. But all the same, she was racked with a melancholy that wouldn't leave and that tainted every hour of every day. "It isn't such a bad life, Anna," he said.

"Oh, Nicolai," she said with more sorrow than he could comprehend, "it isn't a life at all."

Still, it was the best life available, so he made the trip to Sonoma, finding the courthouse and a surprisingly patient clerk, who worked with Nicolai's small store of Spanish to explain the preemption laws which allowed the first settler to claim and improve the land.

"And do you promise to become a citizen of the United States?" the clerk asked in a matter-of-fact way.

It took a while before Nicolai could understand. "Is possible?" he asked.

The clerk nodded.

"I promise." He felt a warm, expectant rush. On his way back to his house, now officially and forever *his*, he kept asking after the Indians, but more and more, his answer was a shrug. And then slowly, through a patchwork of conversations with Mexicans, he found out that while he had been fishing and gazing out on wild perfection from the watchtower, the world beyond his horizon had grown darker and more harsh. Nothing had improved when California became part of the United States instead of Mexico or Spain.

The law—the white man's law—squeezed like a fist around the Indians whose land it demanded.

There were more kidnappings than ever. A new law, pretending to protect Indians, now allowed their indenture. Any Indian to any white man, so that Indian children were stolen, declared prisoners of war as young as two years of age, and sold for twenty-year "terms of service." Enslaved.

The law also said that any white could declare any Indian a vagrant to be bound over to a white landowner to work for subsistence. To be a slave.

Nicolai had trouble believing this—that men who had stampeded here for gold could turn their frustrated fury on the peaceable people who had never asked them for anything. Each time he heard a new story, he challenged it, questioned the teller again and again, but it was all horribly true.

A new law said that no Indian could testify against a white man, no matter what. It was a different kind of enslavement and an invitation to destruction.

It had been a short trip, the accumulated new knowledge searing and pushing him back toward his house in Mendocino like a hot, angry dragon's breath. Now he sat fishing, heavy with the knowledge

49

that he could never move his family back toward people, back to places where his skills would be useful. Where he could sit and smoke a pipe or drink a glass with another man who knew how to make things with his hands.

And the truth was, he was bored and felt almost as out of his element as Anna did. He carved the newel post of the staircase, filling it with blossoms until it became a wooden garden.

But this wasn't enough.

Perhaps he should go to the gold fields. He couldn't think what gold could buy his family, what freedoms it could reclaim or what they needed and didn't already have.

His garden produced fine potatoes and cabbage. They had fish, venison, now and then bear, and once a ferocious but delicious wild boar that had grown fat on acorns, not seafood. They had abalone and kelp and crabs, baked eggs and pine nuts. They had acorns and manzanita cider, pinole from wild oats, mushrooms and clover and pepperwood balls, huckleberries, and quail. Sometimes, when Anna truly believed the dangers were absent, she went after grasshoppers, trapping her delicacy in a circle of fire. Or, during very foggy summer days, she plucked the red-striped caterpillars that she thought a special gift of the thunder god. Nicolai tried to appreciate these treats.

They had deerskin, shredded redwood bark, and rabbit-skin blankets and rugs on their grass sleeping mats. They were warm through the winter. If Anna and Katerina didn't wear all the beaded jewelry they might have in the village, that was no tragedy.

They had a house that was, he honestly believed, splendid. A wealthy man's house.

Gold could buy him nothing except adventure. But now that seemed enough.

He had thought about it for days, filling his lazy riverside times considering all aspects of the trip.

On this day, he nodded to himself and decided, once and for all, that he must have some excitement or dry up and die as his mother-in-law had done. His sons were old enough to guard the house and provide everyone with food. Nicolai would go to the gold fields.

Suddenly the surface of the water broke and with it his daydreams. He scrambled to his feet. Downstream two men splashed across the river at one of its highest points. The fools didn't test a thing—simply plunged ahead.

"Aiii!" one of them screamed.

A mule, in similar distress, paddled frantically toward the far shore.

The water churned until Nicolai could barely see the head of the man. Without thinking, he raced down the slope by the river and stuck his fishing net on its long pole out over the water. "Grab it!" he shouted.

For a moment, the man was so stunned by the sudden appearance of Nicolai that he nearly finished his business of drowning. Then he collected himself as much as possible, grabbed hold of the net, and was hauled in.

By then, his companion had bobbled close enough to shore to crawl back up.

Both men thanked him in Spanish, then, with some despair, they watched the donkey reach the far side of the river and disappear. They stood, dripping wet and pathetic.

Spanish, Nicolai thought. Slave-catchers. Beware. But they looked singularly inept. All the same, what were they doing in his woods? "There is...easy crossing...there," he said, pointing. "Sandbar."

The men looked sheepish and embarrassed. "This Big River?" one asked.

Nicolai nodded. "Very big in winter," he said. "Not so big now."

"No, no—Big River. That its name?"

"Booldam," Nicolai said.

"What the hell's Booldam?"

Nicolai became wary. Was this a trap? A way of proving he knew Indians and what they named rivers? He changed the subject. "Where do you come from?" he asked.

"Gold fields," the shorter of the two said. He spat on the ground. "Can't you tell?"

They most certainly did not look rich.

"Bad place," the man continued. "Too many people. Costs more than the gold you find to stay there."

"Don't keep the gold anyway," his companion muttered. "Lynchings. Murders. If they don't like you, you're dead."

The first one laughed harshly. "And they don't like nobody 'cept themselves. No Chinese, no Indians, no Mexicans—*foreigners*, they're calling us—and they make us pay taxes they don't pay, they try to make us slaves, they—"

"I'm Californio!" the second one said. "My family lived here one

hundred years. One hundred years! This is *my* country—they're the foreigners! But they say 'only Americans'! They come from a thousand miles away—from somewhere else—from *nowhere*—into *my* country—and they say that to me!" He spat on the ground.

"What," Nicolai finally asked when they paused, "what brings you here?"

"That," the short man said, pointing up the hill, directly toward Nicolai's house.

Nicolai's heart froze. He faced the kidnapper, the slave-stealer. He thought frantically of ways to kill both men before they took another step in his direction, before...

"The woods," the man continued. "The big trees."

It took too long for Nicolai's muscles to relax and his mind refocus. He, along with the men, looked toward the dark forest. What of them?

"Those trees are the next gold," the man said admiringly. "San Francisco company's building a mill up here. Didn't you hear?"

Nicolai shrugged. He heard nothing in his fortress except the birds, the wind, a mountain lion sometimes, and his own family.

"Came looking for cargo from a shipwreck and found the trees instead. Whole world's coming to San Francisco and they need houses and hotels. The good trees further south are gone and the damned city keeps burning itself down. They're shipping wood from halfway around the world now. That's why this here's good as gold."

"They're coming now?" Nicolai asked.

The men nodded. "On their way. Be here any day now." And then, with renewed thanks and hopes they could still catch the mule, the two men went toward the sandbar to cross the river.

Nicolai stood rooted in place. His mind whirled. A mill! Work, adventure. Men who knew wood, who knew trees and forests. Better than the gold fields.

But frightening. It would be those lawmakers, those kidnappers who came north for work.

What about his family?

He shook his head. They'd stay in the house in the woods, the way they had when the first man crossed the river. There were millions of trees and he wouldn't let them touch the ones near his house.

It would work out. It had to.

He felt a keen and complex thrill of mixed emotions working in opposite directions—fear for the safety of the center of his life, his wife and children, and, all the same, a nervous, welcoming anticipa-

tion of a future suddenly charged with excitement and adventure.

Oh, he shouldn't want them to come at all, but he did.

He stood by the riverside, alert, on guard, and, in his confused and secret heart, welcoming.

They were coming. They were coming.

5

Anna's scream lanced the nightmare landscape.

For months, she and the children had stayed close to home, invisible to the loggers and ox teams filling the forest. They had felt the impact of giants hitting the earth, but had seen nothing. Even on the roaring, crashing day that sounded like the end of the earth—the day of the river drive—Anna remained at home.

Nicolai had gone to watch, driven by his white side, as he thought of it, the side that took pride in the way men chose their monuments, changing the landscape at will. Even so, he'd been unsure of what he felt as the dams opened. River men stood nearby with long poles and spikes in their boots, ready to stop logjams. The water rose as they watched until it lifted the thousands of logs stacked forty feet high, uncountable tons of logs rising until they floated and, with a deafening roar, gained speed and strength. The river of logs headed for the sea, capped by a cloud of steam from their own furious friction.

Nicolai still wasn't sure of what to make of the chaos, the sight of the giants forging the river, but at least he was prepared for the ravaged riverside. And because he'd also spent time building the mill, a ravenous insatiable animal with a taste for wood, he knew how much fodder the men in the woods would have to prepare.

"Why are you *helping* them?" Anna had often asked.

"They'll do their work no matter what I do," he answered. "But if I'm with them, I know what's planned." He meant it, but he also knew that he wasn't simply helping them, he was helping himself. He could feel his blood and hands and imagination spring back to life.

So he helped them and knew their ways with the woods, but his family waited until the loggers were gone. Then Anna asked to see what the noise and tumult had meant.

Now she knew, and she screamed with horror. When she could speak again, her voice was a hiss. "They kill everything. Men, women, children, trees. Their greed is an abomination." She walked to the edge of the nightmare, to what had been from time eternal a silent, shadowed forest of giant trees and lush ferns, to a place where in earlier springs they'd admired the deep pink rhododendron and the clean slants of sunshine breaking through the leafy roof above them. To Nicolai, it had been holy, a great green cathedral, an ancient sanctuary.

Now the towering trees, the rhododendron, the feathery ferns, and the underbrush were gone and in their place stumps and charred, spiky splinters.

Anna stood next to what had been a redwood, stroking the high stump. "Poor hurt thing." She turned to Nicolai. "White men hack the world until it is sore and aching all over."

The trees had been chopped off high above ground level, avoiding the thick base altogether for the straight, symmetrical, more easily milled expanse above. Then, to clear the ground and make it easier to haul the trunks to the river, the loggers had set fire to the brush.

Nearby, the river ran sluggishly with silt and wood bits and logs pushing aside the fish.

"Everything," Anna said. "They murder it all."

She looked numbed, stunned. She came from a people who shook acorns and fruit off trees and left what they couldn't use. The rare times Nicolai remembered their taking a tree, their methods hurt nothing else.

Nicolai was flooded with shame for having been involved in the death of the forest. For not being completely unhappy with the arrival of loggers, mills, and machines. For what his people called civilization. For his kind of people.

"We must leave again," Anna said. "Run away again."

His guilt increased. He was a thief about to steal her last ounce of

innocence. "There's nowhere left," he said softly. "This is the edge."

He had wanted to keep it a secret from her. The whites were everywhere, and the situation for Indians worse than ever. When he worked on the mill, he eavesdropped, and many nights he stopped at a saloon for a comforting drink or two and someone would be reading out loud from a newspaper that was only a week or a month old. But it wasn't so wonderful understanding how things were. He remembered how the commandant and officers had pretended not to understand the Spanish when they arrived with unpleasant messages, and sometimes Nicolai pretended to himself that he couldn't comprehend the English news. Certainly, it made no sense.

In any case, he kept it to himself. The death of the forest was enough for Anna. She didn't have to know that the governor of California had, a year ago, predicted the extinction of his state's Indians as sad but inevitable.

A man at the saloon, a man from Maine, took a long time to explain the word *inevitable*. Nicolai had been sure his English was lacking because how could the head of a state say something that terrible in such a matter-of-fact way? How could something you make happen be "inevitable"?

And Anna didn't know that the Superintendent of Indian Affairs —she didn't even know there was such a person—estimated that fifteen thousand California Indians had died of starvation the previous year.

She didn't know that the Senate of the United States had rejected all the treaties that had been negotiated with California Indians.

And even with all that not knowing, she stood so still, barely breathing, a petrified, eternal, and mournful part of the desecrated forest. Finally she spoke. "This is the end of us, too, Nicolai. The trees near our house are just as beautiful and strong as these were." She walked away from the charred ruins. "Yes," she continued, "they'll find our trees and they'll find us and we'll all be gone, one way or another."

"Anna, you forget. This is our land. I have the paper!"

Anna sneered. "Nothing stops them," she said. "Unless your paper is bewitched. Does it have a spell on it, Nicolai? How else could it possibly make a difference?" Then, her back to the river and the black, burned earth, she walked slowly, like a mourner, toward her house.

Of course, Nicolai told himself, she didn't understand that white men had their own kind of rules.

The next morning, sleepless and feeling every day of his long life, Nicolai took his precious piece of paper out of a carved redwood box and prayed that it had the power to stop saws.

He showed its unintelligible signs, seals, and signatures to the foreman of the mill, who took it and Nicolai to the office of the mill owner. He raised an eyebrow in surprise, but he never once challenged the power of the paper and the law as he knew it. "Are you right on the river?" he asked.

"Partly." Nicolai's house was well away from it. An inconvenience when it came to getting water, but it was better storing rainwater in barrels and digging a well and living in sunshine, out of the dark trees and ferny forest floors.

"Would you consider selling that portion?" the man asked. "We don't need the wood further in. Too hard to get and move it. Easier to go somewhere else. God knows there's enough trees. How about it? You'd still have access to the river, for water. We'll mark the limits and be no further trouble."

The paper was magic indeed.

For the next three months, Nicolai stood guard at his house, the only visible, available member of the family, should a logger stray beyond the marked limits.

Meanwhile, he changed the wall of the big room where they cooked and lived most of the time. He pushed a portion of it out, and now that window glass was available nearby in town—and now that the mill owner had paid him enough gold to buy a hundred windows—he built a three-sided bay facing the sea and the untouched part of the woods. Beneath the window, he built a storage chest with a hinged top. He put his little chamois bag of gold pieces inside the chest along with his carved box and the powerful piece of paper.

Now his family could sit in the bay and view a landscape that looked untouched. If they stood and peered carefully, or if they went upstairs to Nicolai's tower, they could see the mill's raw sprawl and the framework of a few houses, but here in the window seat only forest, ocean, and sky were visible.

He carved a wooden plate with the house in relief and put it on the new windowsill for the *domovoy.*

The loggers and Nicolai finished their various redecorations at about the same time. The decimated woods near the river were painful to view, but despite that, Nicolai felt a survivor's surge of pride.

The loggers had come and gone without seeing or questioning

or being able to remember or endanger his family.

Civilization had roared right by. Nicolai breathed more easily.

Suddenly, between one swing of his hammer and the next, Nicolai was filled with amazement. His hand stopped midair, and he stood still atop his ladder, viewing the newly minted world around him.

It had happened so gradually, so resolutely that he hadn't fully grasped the enormous changes. One day the first saws cut into the unmarked wilderness and the next there was a thriving mill town. People flocked north where they could find work and not find malaria or Spanish land grants that challenged their settlement. Everything had changed. How had he not truly noticed? He looked down on the town that had already outlasted a name or two. Big River had become "Meiggsville," after "Honest" Harry Meiggs, who had built the mill—until Honest Harry sailed to Chile in the middle of the night, leaving scandal, debt, and near destruction behind.

But the town shook itself straight and survived, turning into Mendocino City.

He stood and surveyed, rooftop high. Main Street stretched through a row of saloons, hotels, and stores to a solid sprinkle of streets and houses.

Even the ocean was different. Beside it, a steam mill sliced enormous logs into planks to be shipped around the world. And stretching over it, into it, a chute reached out like a thin hand donating lumber to ships that had no proper harbor. They bobbled at sea, planks and railroad ties sliding down onto their decks.

Nicolai felt a considerable surge of pride. He'd helped build the mill that had begun the town and then he'd helped build the town itself.

It hadn't been difficult becoming part of the work force. Everyone was a new arrival, and there wasn't time for or interest in credentials.

The town and woods were a Babel of languages and much was done through slow and tedious pantomime. Nicolai was as quick a learner as the next man, and long before he could say so in English, he indicated and then demonstrated his skill in building the first mill.

The first millwright's designs were all wrong and there were false starts and setbacks. Before Nicolai had completed his portion of the roof, the winter storms began. A nightmare. Even by spring, when a mill stood on the point, men who arrived with high hopes became angry with the delays and problems and left just as abruptly as they'd come, so there were not enough workers, further delays, increased frustrations and leave-takings.

And then the winter after the trees near his house had been re-moved, after the forest had been so cruelly ravished, all the accumu-lated logs washed out to sea. A year's work and a forest of thousand-year-old trees, all lost.

"Good," Anna said when he told her. "Now they'll understand that what they're doing is wrong, and they'll leave."

She lived in a house curtained by dark forests. She never observed the new owners of the land, their determination and sense of destiny. Nicolai didn't have the heart to challenge her assumptions. He merely rode his horse back to the bluff and, as he expected, began work on another mill, this one further inland, sheltered from the winter seas. The point remained the ship-loading area and storage yard and a railroad with ox-drawn cars was built between the two spots. There was suddenly an axis and a reason for a town.

After a short term of employment in the mill, Nicolai realized that he much preferred crafting planks to creating them. He built a small cabin for a mill worker, and then another, and then a rooming house for loggers and barracks for unmarried mill men. And then one of the wealthy men asked him if he could build a house for his wife and family. From then on, as the town grew on the clear plateau at the ocean's edge, Nicolai had all the work he could desire.

He stopped surveying the village and returned to the work at hand —another bride's pretty bungalow. Her house would have a peaked roof and trim that resembled lace, a speciality of Nicolai's.

The brides came sailing around Cape Horn, or on the Atlantic and Pacific with a trek across the Isthmus of Panama in between. They expressed a mixture of joy at being reunited with their husbands and sorrow for what they had left behind. Nicolai understood exactly.

He didn't understand the terms they used when they tried to re-create their New England villages here in Mendocino, but their love of curls and scrolls and fancywork was not so different from the lacey ornamentation of the houses in his childhood village. Besides, he could build anything "by the eye." Russians were the best wood-workers in the world and he was one of the best Russians.

The State of Maine brides always tried first with fancy words: "cor-bels," "pediments," "cornices," "gables."

"A picture, missus, please?" he would say politely. "You draw for me what you want."

And then, their pale faces intent, apologizing for not being fine artists, they sketched their fantasies and Nicolai turned their memo-ries and hopes into redwood truths.

The delighted brides thanked their husbands and Nicolai for making them feel "right at home."

"Right . . . at . . . home," he repeated, adding this to his growing storehouse of English. He would have to remember it and teach it to his children. "Right. At. Home."

"Where are you from?" they'd ask, somewhere between a pediment and a balustrade. It was a standard question. The entire globe sent representatives to the woods. Nicolai worked alongside Finns, Chinese, Portuguese, Italians, Chileans, Germans, and he wasn't sure what else.

"Mad-sui-nui," he had answered the first bride.

She'd looked bewildered, and then he realized he had, by force of habit, used Anna's name for the fort's site. "Near the Slavianka? South of here?"

"Ah, well." She gave up.

Later he found out that what he'd called the Slavianka had also been renamed and was now called the Russian River. Wonderful, he thought. Now these new United States people would remember who had lived there.

"Where are you from, Nicholas?" Their long gowns and petticoats reminded him of Princess Helena. He had forgotten that rustle and fine silky swish.

He didn't correct the "Nicholas." Names were in flux all around him, and nothing remained what it had once been called. Whatever made them feel comfortable was fine with him. He stayed the same person nonetheless. "From Rossiisko Amerikanskaia Kompaniia—" And most often, before he could explain about Ross and the company, they'd clap their hands and say "Of course! My husband told me about you—how silly I've been. From Ross—you're Nicholas Ross."

"Nicholas the Russian, yes," he'd agree.

"Nicholas Ross, the best builder in all Mendocino!"

They thought that was his name. He considered it. Nicholas the Ross, the Russian, didn't sound bad at all. It was more the way Anna's people addressed each other—"he who is clever," "the man who knows charms," "the one from the flat rock." He was the one from Russia. More than indicating his father's name, it seemed right and proud to name his country, to have his skills identified with the motherland. Nicholas the Ross it became, and then, simply, Nicholas Ross.

House after house slowly lined the new dirt roads. And as Nicolai

walked down a street he'd helped create, the brides, now turned busy mothers, waved and greeted him as they swept their porches. They always swept, only to have more mill dust replace whatever they had removed.

He never quarreled with any of them when they called him "the best builder in town." He was. Indeed, he was midwife to the town. He walked its streets with pride, and then he went home to the woods.

Nobody questioned his personal life. It was assumed that he was single like most of the other men. He didn't choose to live in the rooming houses, saying he had a shack in the hills, and his companions accepted his idiosyncracy and need for privacy, writing it off to his crazy Russian temperament.

Anna couldn't believe it. She hadn't thought about such things for years, certainly not since Alexander was weaned, and now he was a long-limbed seven-year-old.

Nonetheless, her body was thickening, spreading even more quickly than aging could account for. Her breasts, soft and lower these last few years, were enlarging, the nipples darkening, her lower abdomen felt hard and heavy, although nothing yet showed beyond its now-normal soft bulge.

She sat in the window seat, a half-completed basket on her lap, and looked out at the trees and her children. Katerina was bossing her younger brothers around, haughtily informing them of the best method of cleaning and preparing a fish for drying. Ivan said something Anna couldn't hear and all three children laughed until Katerina dropped her supercilious pose.

She was lovely, full-bodied and ripe at fourteen. The age Anna herself had been when Nicolai, a lost and bereaved blond giant, had become her husband. Anna shook her head. Where would they find Katerina a husband and a safe place to live?

Which thought immediately moved her mind to Giorgi, who had, with his father's reluctant blessing, made his way back to Metini and, despite all the changes there—despite Nicolai's warnings that it had been swallowed by the white men—Giorgi stayed. Now he worked for wages at what had been his people's summer village since time began. He had a wife and a tiny son of his own. They had visited just a while ago and promised to do so again. It had been an uneventful trip, Giorgi said, and Anna quietly, without a word to Nicolai, began to plan her own eventual trip back to Metini. She ached to see

someone familiar, even if Giorgi said those she most loved were lost forever in an unnamed abyss. Nicolai would object, would fume and rant and hint at terrible possibilities, but she was determined to leave.

But now, with a baby, another baby. . .

I'm a grandmother! she thought. How is it possible to also become a mother again?

Her hair was graying at the temples, her face was lined. She pressed her palms against her middle. "What are you in there?" she whispered. "How are you possible?"

Alexander and Ivan were ignoring their work and Katerina scolded them, hands on her hips, while they tossed a ball Nicolai had carved from a redwood burl.

Ah, well, Anna thought, no one was meant to work every hour of every day. She felt a fierce rush of tenderness for them both, for Ivan, who reminded her of her brothers with his sturdy, muscular build and quick, easy laugh. And for Alexander, so different with his long limbs, tawny skin, and gray-blue eyes. At seven he was already taller than Ivan, and he seemed to stretch day by day.

He didn't laugh the way Ivan did, and Anna always worried over it and felt responsible. As if he had known, inside her womb, that she planned to murder him. As if he had been built of the misery she contained day and night, of her mourning for everything she held dear.

She looked at her hands, innocent and talented holding the delicate basket in her lap, and she felt a mild incredulity. How she had hated that unborn child, believing him part of her unendurable and despised exile. Believing him an intruder—an arrogant creature insisting that he was the equal of, could take the place of her lost Piotr.

How her hands had ached—she could remember it in her tendons even now—to unmake his existence and deny him a moment of life.

And look, look at what he had turned out to be.

She sighed and knew she would let this baby, the surprise baby, live as well. She had none of that burning hatred left anyway. She was cinder and ashes inside and had thought herself completely dead, but here, miraculously or perversely, was a refutation, was life itself.

Nicolai held the squalling infant at arm's length. "She's beautiful," he said, his pale eyes misty. "Beautiful."

"You don't think she's too scrawny?" Anna asked. The child was tiny, as fragile as a hummingbird. Perhaps Anna had been too old to

dare to hold life again, perhaps she had failed the job.

"Scrawny?" He kissed his newborn daughter's forehead. "What do you want? A thick-boned peasant? She's fine, like an aristocrat. Like you, Anna. You've worked a miracle."

Anna looked at the child that barely filled its father's two hands. "Nicolai," she whispered. Her breasts and her heart became full, and she felt as if she had just surfaced after years underwater, as if she were seeing clearly and without distortion for the first time. She remembered him when he'd seemed forged of gold sand and clear autumn sky, a foreign god. When the very sight of him had turned her as liquid and turbulent as the sea from which he'd emerged. She had known from that first moment that he was a man as passionate as the waves that had carried him to her, and she'd been right. Even now, she flushed to think of how it had been between them.

What had he ever done to change that? What had he ever done but love her and share the life and burdens they were given?

But she had closed her eyes and heart to him so long ago—as if she didn't know that he, too, was a stranger in this land. Why had she made him a stranger to her as well? He, too, bled for the lost and the dead, but she had made him mourn alone.

His hands that knew so well how to love and create were gnarled with time and hard work, the veins large and prominent, but he held his newborn daughter so gently, so securely, that the sleeping baby seemed to smile.

"Nicolai," Anna whispered again, her mouth full of his name.

He put the baby down on the pallet beside her and took her hand, and she felt their clasp span and bridge the enormous open wound of the past nine years.

"Perhaps she is a princess," Anna finally whispered.

"A princess?" He looked wary. She knew he tried to never mention such things for her sake.

"We can name her Helena." Anna grinned. "And you'll have your Princess Helena, all yours. Satisfied?"

He said nothing, waiting, looking worried.

Anna continued to smile and nod. "It's all right," she whispered. "It's all right."

Nicolai relaxed and looked at his daughter. "Helena," he said, and nodded, then he burst into laughter, and Anna, surprising herself, felt a laugh bubble up in her, as urgently in need of birthing as her baby had been.

The baby, the princess, slept through the racket.

"May laughter be the most familiar sound in her life," Nicolai finally said.

And all the while they held hands.

Nicolai ordered rum. The saloon didn't stock vodka, had never heard of it in fact. But rum was fine.

He wished he could treat the room, tell everyone about his glorious princess child, stop pretending to be a lonely hermit in the hills. How jealous they would be, how happy for him. They'd clap their hands on his back, congratulate him, buy him a drink themselves.

Sometimes it was hard remembering, after a rum or two, why it was so important to keep secrets from his friends at the bar.

Still, silently, he raised his glass himself, nodded his gratitude, and thanked God for the way his life had once again become blessed. Giorgi married, Katerina grown and lovely, Ivan and Alexander different as could be, but both healthy, handsome good sons. And now, the princess and a gift he had never thought to receive again, Anna smiling.

And his house, his castle and citadel and chapel, safe and secret in the woods.

He drank the rum and signaled for more. This one and then he'd go home. Which reminded him it was time to think about loosening the strings on the chamois bag and buying a new horse, maybe two.

Why not? He had the money. He wasn't like so many of the others in the saloon. Getting the money was easy. But to most of them, keeping it was another matter. The logging camps paid in twenty-dollar gold pieces, "Big River Bits," they were called. The men hid them in their shoes, and then got so drunk they'd pass out in a back room. Next morning, their boots were next to their cot but the gold was gone. Half the time, they'd start to drink again and stagger out, oblivious, only to wonder over their disappearing funds when Nicolai next sat next to them at the bar.

Nicolai saved his earnings. Besides, he had none of the other men's expenses. No room to rent, no boarding charges, nothing to do with his money except for a bit here and there on some of the new luxuries shipped to town—calicoes and linens for clothing, window glass to replace panes broken by his sons and their wooden balls. Coffee, now that it was available, for him.

At first, Anna had boiled the coffee beans the way she had boiled the acorns, and when they had refused to soften, she threw them away, saying they were bad.

64

Now that she left his coffee alone, he truly had everything a man could want. He grinned, nearly laughed out loud. He was a rich man, a king with a castle, and now, a princess. There was a good and just God. He heard the dim echoes of Baranov, "Heaven is high and the Tsar is far away," but this time he dismissed it. This wasn't that hell on earth, Alaska, this was California. The United States. A paradise. The bad times were over.

"*Vsyo proidot,*" his old grandfather used to say. "Everything will pass." Impatient, moody Nicolai hadn't wanted to listen, but his grandfather had been right.

"*Vsyo proidot,*" Nicolai said out loud, surprising his neighbor, a Swede.

"Shhh, Nick," a Portuguese said, "Bill's got the paper."

Bill came from somewhere on the other side of the country. A Yankee, he called himself. He'd had three years of school, could read, and was respected for it.

Nicolai listened politely, his mind only half on the rather monotonous recitation. Bill read every printed word: advertisements, notices, shipping news in San Francisco, fistfights in the gold country. Everything. You never knew who wanted to know what.

There'd been another fire in San Francisco. "More work for all of you, more money," he said to the mill workers and loggers. They agreed, nodding happily.

Bill read the description of a homesteader's tangle with a grizzly.

Nicolai thought of his own family in the woods and needed them suddenly and acutely. Why was he listening to Bill's flat voice when he could be . . .

"'. . . Reports that certain Sonora Mexicans are buying and selling Indians of various Coast Range mountain tribes at fifty to two hundred fifty dollars each.'"

"Selling Indians?" Nicolai asked loudly. "Who says so? Who reported?"

Bill looked up, confused. "Who'd I say?" he asked with a shrug. He could never remember what he had read.

"Go on, go on," the Swede said.

"No—who reported such a thing as selling people here?" Nicolai asked.

"Indians," someone said, and he suddenly realized the man was correcting him. Not people. Indians.

"California Superintendent of Indian Affairs Edward Fitzgerald Beale," Bill read slowly. "There. Does that answer you?"

Nicolai's throat had gone dry. He needed another drink. Bill waited. "Thank you," he said.

"Why d'you care about Indians so much?" Bill asked with more animation than he showed while reading.

The rest of the faces around the bar waited for his answer. His friends. His drinking companions. He had almost told them about Helena and Anna and his other children. He had almost thought they would share his joy.

Instead, they'd corrected him. Indians, they believed. Not people.

His heart raced and he knew it was not going to stop. He shrugged. "No reason," he said. "I . . . was daydreaming—is that how you say it?—and didn't hear, that's all." He ordered another drink and listened to every word Bill read to the room.

And when Bill's flat voice stumbled into a story from San Francisco, Nicolai strained to sit as nonchalantly and impassively as anyone else in the room.

"'Two Indians,'" Bill said, "'were found murdered in our streets the past week, by persons unknown, and dumped into the common receptacle made and provided for such cases.'"

How had he believed in safety, in miracles, in anything?

His ears rang and his pulse beat so loudly he expected the Swede to shush him again, but Yankee Bill calmly went on to the tide tables.

6

He would leave and search once again, this time to the north.

For six years, Nicolai had gone to the saloon regularly. Anna thought it was for the rum, but it was Yankee Bill's monotone reading of the news he craved.

Nicolai had grown up in a village so remote from the outside world that nobody knew for years if the Tsar died. A "deaf village," they called it, making fun of its complete ignorance. But now Nicolai thought there might be a virtue and certainly a pleasure in not being informed of the true state of affairs.

Yankee Bill's stories pressed against him, forcing him deeper and deeper inside himself. He was at ease and comfortable only when he was alone on a ladder or quietly sanding a floorboard or carving his special wooden lace trims, when he was Nicholas Ross, master builder and carver, and nothing else. Otherwise, he was swollen with secrets and disguised by a mask.

He had never been courageous or cruel enough to tell Anna the stories he heard almost every week at the saloon. Let her live as happily as she could in her own tiny deaf village.

He had never been drunk or stupid enough to tell the men at the saloon that he was what they called, with disgust, a squaw man.

I'm protecting my family, he'd remind himself when the isolation and loneliness of his situation strangled him.

Now, he told Anna, he had to leave. "I never went to the reservation."

She shook her head. The reservation had existed a few miles north of Mendocino City for years. Since 1856, it housed a hodgepodge of tribes but few, if any, Kashayas. "You told me people from Metini weren't there, Nicolai."

"But yesterday I heard about an 'Indian Pete.' They said he was large for an Indian, too."

"Who's Pete? What's Pete?"

Sometimes he forgot how little of American ways Anna knew. "'Pete' is short for 'Peter,'" he said carefully. "American for 'Piotr.' Maybe it's—"

"Why would he go there?" She shook her head. "If my son escaped, he'd go back to Metini, or he'd try to find his family."

Nicolai noticed, with a twinge of pain, how Anna always acted as if she alone had created their children whenever she spoke of their honor. My son, my child. In her heart, she must have doubted whether a white man had any of that trait to transmit.

Well, her son might have gone back to Metini, but her son might not have wanted to work for its new white owners. Or her son might have been forced north against his will, rounded up, lassoed as if he were a steer, and forced to "choose" the reservation, like so many others.

Nicolai heard the stories with every glass of rum. Indians pushed off their land, forbidden access to acorns, their main food, now given over to the white man's pigs. Desperate Indians eating dead cattle, then being exterminated as cattle killers. He heard about "pranks"— strychnine put in sugar or flour that a starving Indian would be likely to take.

One man at the saloon laughed out loud at that. "Good trick," he said. "Serves 'em right for stealin'."

Worse. He heard worse. In Siskiyou County, Indians invited to make a treaty with the whites were feasted with bread and meat— both poisoned.

He heard, with incredulity, a statement by the Superintendent of Indian Affairs. "Neither the government nor California recognizes the right of the Indians of that state to one foot of land within her borders." He waited for someone to comment, to hoot or protest the way they did with news of scandals or outrages against property. But

the men simply ordered more drinks, ate more sandwiches, and listened for the next story.

The very day before, in the saloon, Yankee Bill, his voice older and creakier and no more lively, droned his way through a chilling story that still echoed in Nicholai's brain. An Indian man and his wife were gathering clover on land now owned by a white settler. Three vicious dogs were let loose on them. They tore the woman's breasts off and mangled her until she was dead.

"'Of course,'" Bill read on, "'it was the dogs' fault, although their character was well known. . . .'" Nicolai's brain roared, deep at his center. "'But he only set them on for fun," Bill read, "and they were only Diggers.'"

Nicolai's heart pounded as he remembered Sutter's man, the spitter, the Digger-hater, the nauseating demon of his nightmares. "I can't believe it," he said out loud, downing his rum. "Isn't this America? Can people murder people for *fun* and not be punished?"

"'There was a report of a grand pageant held at—'" Yankee Bill stopped himself and looked over, surprised. "Something wrong?" he asked.

"That story's wrong! Where's the justice?"

A few men nodded, but less in agreement than in impatience. They were eager to hear the next story, whatever it might be about.

"Maybe you're a blue-eyed Indian," Yankee Bill said, one eyebrow raised.

"Must be," the man next to him said. "Nick gets real upset whenever you read one of them stories."

Nicolai felt unmasked, cornered, and half-ready for a killer dog to lunge for his throat. "I'm Russian! United States citizen now," he stammered, protecting his secrets but also betraying the people he loved.

"Jesus, can't you take a joke?" Bill said. "Didn't mean to insult you, Nick."

"What happened to the news?" somebody complained. "Ain't you reading no more?"

It was over and forgotten, except by Nicolai, who resolved, not for the first time, to show no emotions ever, no matter how bad the story.

But Anna shared none of his ugly knowledge and had only the sketchiest idea of what was going on in the world outside.

"You searched all those years," Anna said, much readier than he now to give up her ghosts. "Piotr's gone. Maybe across the moun-

tains, like Renny was. Don't go to the reservation. Stay home, Nicolai."

"How can I not look for my son? My son, Anna. My honor, too."

And so he went, a tall, slightly stooped man with a frosty mane, a white beard, and eyes as pale as river water. He took his favorite horse, salmon jerky, a bottle of rum, and gold coins in the chamois bag, and headed north, to the great experiment, the reservation, where poor displaced Indians would finally be given some measure of dignity through blankets, shoes, food, clothing, and land.

When Nicolai was still an hour or more from the Mendocino Reservation, he stopped for water at a small farm. The young Indian worker backed off at the sight of him, instantly wary.

"Please," Nicolai said, "don't be afraid. I come in peace." He spoke Kashaya, hoping the boy understood the dialect even though the chances were slim.

The Indian frowned, stared blankly. That was not his language.

"I'm going to the Mendocino Reservation," Nicolai said in English. "Do you know it?"

The Indian nodded.

"Any Kashaya there?"

The young man shook his head. Nicolai wasn't sure if it was a considered answer, or just a way of getting him to move on. "I'm looking for my—for a Kashaya named Peter. Or Pete. He'd be about your age."

The Indian did not seem interested or impressed.

"Talk to me, please," Nicolai said. "You speak English, don't you? A little! You seem to understand what I'm saying. My name is Nicolas Ross. I'm not your enemy. I am Russian, from the fort."

The Indian's posture became more rigid.

"No, not Fort Bragg. I have nothing to do with the reservation. Fort Ross. Not that kind of fort at all. We weren't guarding Indians, we were their friends. Near Metini. Long ago, I lived at Metini with the Eruskis." He chose the nickname that had been given to those Russianized Kashaya. "Many were stolen. I'm looking for them. Will you help?"

The man considered for a long time. "No Kashaya Pete at Mendocino," he finally said. "Which is lucky for him. It's hell there."

"But I heard—the money, the shoes and food, and—"

"They steal it."

"Why steal it? It's being given to them."

"The *whites* steal it. The Superintendent—Henley. His friends. All

70

of it. And more. They lie about how many Indians are there so they get double rations and money and keep it for themselves."

"Oh, no, you must be—the newspaper said—"

"You'll see. They built a farm near the reservation. Used government funds and materials. Had us work it—had us plant crops and build their barns instead of taking care of the land the government gave us. They sold it for a profit and kept the whole thing.

"They've got a sawmill and a general store built out of the money's supposed to go to us. They gave our provisions to the white men building it. Let us work on it, too, for fifty cents a day, except they didn't ever pay us. I left because I was starving to death. Dying on the white man's gifts. So I ran off, fell asleep in this man's fields, was accused of trespassing, of vagrancy, and now I'm 'indentured,' they say. I'm his slave is what I say, for ten years." He gave a hard, mirthless laugh.

Nicolai nearly wept, seeing not only this man's endless misery but his son's as well. Somewhere, on a ranch or in a mine, Piotr might also be a slave, and the only other option was death. He saw his son's shining face on this young man's shoulders.

Piotr was lost. In that sunny field, in this Indian's dark eyes, Nicolai again, but this time with finality, knew it.

There was a heavy silence as he absorbed all the lessons forced out of the ground on this hot, clear day. He shed skins, like a snake, removed blinders from his eyes. He saw so clearly that the world blazed painfully in the midday sun. He put his hand to his eyes, then let it fall into its habitual gesture of stroking his wild white beard.

And suddenly, his hand took on its own knowledge, taught a lesson of its own. He might cry for the Indians, for his own flesh and blood, but he had a mask, a white beard, Caucasian features, and for once, the mask and disguise and deceptions did not seem all bad. In fact, they seemed useful and purposeful.

"You are?" he asked.

The young man shrugged. "I'm called Jack."

"Did this rancher pay for you, Jack?"

The Indian shook his head. "He didn't have to."

"Would he take money for you? Sell you to me?"

For the first time, and only for a moment, Jack's eyes flared with interest, and Nicolai had a hint of how different he would look if he'd been allowed to be innocent. Then they dimmed and became suspicious. "Why?"

"Why not?" Nicolai said. "Do you have a place you want to go?"

"You mean I wouldn't be your—"

"Russians never had Indian slaves." An irrational wave of happiness warmed him. His gold was worth something for the first time. All these years the original sum for the land by the river had grown as Nicolai built sunny parlors, fancy cornices, and pretty peaked roofs, but only now did he have an idea of where it could be spent.

"First, I have to go to the reservation," Nicolai said. "I have to see for myself."

"You don't believe me." Without moving, Jack withdrew again.

"No, not that. First, I have to see about my—about this Kashaya, this Peter." He knew in his heart his son wasn't there, that if he had been, he would have been noisy and fierce, fighting the system before, or even while, it crushed him. People would have talked about him, and Nicolai would have heard. "Wait for me here. Don't go away."

Jack laughed again, a rasping, bitter sound.

Indian Pete turned out to be forty-five and a Wappo, not a Kashaya. It was true, however, that he was exceptionally tall, even lying down, dying of a fever. Nicolai left money to buy the man medication. He had known Piotr wasn't there, so he wondered why he was so disappointed nonetheless.

Everything Jack had said about the reservation seemed true, and worse. Nicolai hadn't been prepared for the blatant abuses, the grand and obviously expensive sawmill, the fat and happy white men selling each other whiskey and calico in a store built out of stolen funds, while outside skeletal Indians starved to death.

And worse was the way the men corrupting and destroying the place immediately accepted him as one of them, showing off their businesses, shrugging off questions about how it had all been done. Who cared?

He left with an ashy taste in his mouth.

Jack's owner was a suspicious bargainer, acting as if Nicolai wanted to steal his hard-won property. They argued, cajoled, wheedled. Nicolai pointed out Jack's scars, his narrow chest and puny size. The man insisted he was strong as a mule. They settled, finally, on fifty dollars, and the man never asked Nicolai for what purpose he was buying the Indian, where he was taking him, or for how long. It didn't matter.

"Things are better where I live," Nicolai said as the two men made their way south, taking turns on the horse.

72

"You said I could go wherever I—"

"Of course. But I think it's safer where I live, that's all."

"It's not safe anyplace for people like me. At least the Spanish and Mexicans thought we were human, had souls. But the Anglos—they think we're animals. No, something worse, something less, because they take care of their animals." He sank into lethargy and didn't say another word.

At dusk, they made a small camp in a protected spot. Nicolai divided his jerky and bourbon and they studied each other by firelight in the foggy dusk, as if through a veil.

"Why do you trust me?" Jack asked.

"Shouldn't I?"

"Why are you doing this?"

"Why don't you trust me?"

Jack looked at his hands. He seemed to seriously consider the question. "Habit," he finally said.

"You mean the reservation?"

He barked his unhappy laugh again. "That's just the newest part. I've been running for ten years. I'm from Clear Lake. You've heard of it? Of Stone and Kelsey?"

Nicolai shook his head. Ten years ago, he had been so deep in a virginal forest that he alone out of the entire world hadn't heard of the Gold Rush.

"Well, I'll tell you a bedtime story, Mr. Nicholas. I grew up hungry. Always. Every day. Stone and Kelsey wouldn't let us eat, wouldn't let us hunt or fish because it was their land now.

"One winter, about twenty old people starved to death, my grandmother among them. And four other people I knew died of whippings. My aunt was told to bring her daughter to Kelsey's house and she refused, so they beat her and tied her to a tree, and let her hang there for hours, her toes barely touching the ground. They liked doing that. Did it a lot." He stood up and paced in wide circles around the fire. "Stone and Kelsey," His voice floated out of the chilly darkness. "Demons. Devils. They—" He suddenly stopped, and Nicolai also heard the footsteps and saw, instantly, a flash, a torch swing through the night.

"Who is it?" a deep voice demanded. "Who's—what are you doing here, boy? This is my property and I take vagrants in for—"

Nicolai jumped to his feet. "He's mine!" he shouted. "I paid good money for him."

The man was all thick eyebrows and bulbous forehead above the lantern.

"I have a paper," Nicolai continued, walking toward the man.

"No need." The man's tone was completely different.

"We're on our way to my ranch. Near Big River," Nicolai said. "We started late. Thought to spend the night here before finishing the trip. If it's a problem . . ."

"No problem," the man said. "No problem." He looked at Jack again, then at Nicolai. "Startled me, that's all. I hope he's a good one, not one of the murderin', thievin'—well, he's your business. Just don't want any of them wandering around on my. . . . So I'll say good-night to you now." He walked on, until all they could see was the arc of the lantern, swinging in the distance.

They returned to the fire in silence.

Jack settled on his haunches, staring into the fire.

"You were telling me about your childhood. About your aunt and some men," Nicolai said.

Jack looked startled, then he remembered the lost thread of the conversation. "About Clear Lake. About when I started running. There was a high fence around our village and we were forbidden to go beyond it after dark, or we'd be tied to a tree and whipped." His voice drifted seaward, blending into the thick fog. He took deep breaths, as if steadying himself.

Nicolai waited.

"My mother was starving and sick. The white man had . . . taken her against her will and given her a disease. She gave it to my father. You understand what I mean? She asked my brother to go to our aunt who worked for the Stones, to ask for a handful of wheat, which he did. On his way home, he met Stone, who saw the wheat, took it, and shot my brother. I'm telling you so you'll understand why our starving villages hired two men, Shuk and Xasis, to kill—"

"Yes, yes, Stone and Kelsey," Nicolai whispered, urging him on with the story.

"No," Jack said. "To kill beef. But they had bad luck and lost the ox and they knew they'd be killed, so the whole thing turned around, and eventually those two and three others went and killed Stone and Kelsey. The food and cattle and horses were divided up for everybody, and we lived fat for a while.

"The government sent soldiers. The Indians greeted them in peace, but the whites started shooting. I climbed a tree, as high as I could go, and I lived, but I saw things I wish I could stop seeing even

74

today. I saw them stab babies and throw them into the water. Toss them off the ends of their guns. And mothers running screaming with their children. . . .

"I came out of the tree and ran, but a soldier caught me and another boy and made us climb the mountain going to the coast. We were barefoot, our feet bleeding, and a soldier told me to sit down, to wait, he had something for me.

"It was salt. He put it on all my wounds, on my cut feet and on my back, and he put cloth over the salt. I was nine years old, a long time ago, but I can still feel that pain, worse than being sliced, worse than hot daggers, worse than fire. The soldier and his friends laughed until tears ran down their faces while the other boy and I rolled around and cried and twisted, and they poked us with knives and put salt on those new wounds, too.

"Two days later, when my only wish was to be dead and burned, they let us go. I've been running ever since."

Nicolai lay awake the entire night rather than face his dreams. But even with his eyes open, the night sky filled with as many images as stars, with the greedy faces of the reservation men, Sutter's spitting Digger hater, the poor boy's wounds full of salt, and the otters, always the otters, all one long, bewildering nightmare, day and night.

"Only one thing," Nicolai said as they approached his house. "I've kept them safe from the world, and safe in their minds, too, because they don't know all the terrible things you and I know. Don't break either trust. Don't tell about them and don't tell them. We'll just say I met you, offered you a place to rest."

"Don't you think they should know what's really—"

"Please. That's my only request."

Jack sighed, but nodded agreement.

Jack stayed two weeks, eating almost nonstop, playing gambling stones with Ivan and Alexander, and teasing Helena. And then he said farewell.

"Where will you go?" Nicolai asked.

"I don't know."

"The men in town talk about the war a lot," Nicolai said. "There are parts of the United States that don't have slaves. Maybe you'd be safe if you could get all the way there."

"*This* is the United States," Jack said. "This is one of those parts. A free state. We don't have slaves, either. Not black ones, that is."

Nicolai gave him money to ensure some safety on his travels. He

felt as if he were sending him off the edge of a precipice, and he had grown very fond of the undersized, bright young man. "You can always come back, you know," he said softly. "We'll be here."

"I hope so," Jack said, and he left.

The following month Nicolai heard about a trader with a five-year-old "prisoner of war" for sale. The little boy was very expensive —two hundred dollars. "You'll get years from him," the trader said.

"What war is he from?" Nicolai asked. "Whose prisoner was he? How did you get him?"

The trader chose to ignore him. "I have someone else," he said. "A beauty. A comfort for your bed. Interested?"

Anna welcomed both children, although they spoke a tongue she didn't understand. However, their need was clear. She fed them and, when the little boy cried out in his sleep, she held him and sang to him and told him stories about Coyote and Spider until he dozed again.

"Where do you find these people?" Anna asked several times. "All so hungry, so thin. I don't understand."

"Well, you know, the white man takes their land, the way it is at Metini, and then they have no real home, and I find them." He was busy carving the last hoof of a small and delicate redwood deer for Helena.

"I can see meeting Jack," Anna said, "but this little boy isn't much more than a baby. You don't find a baby by chance." Nicolai concentrated on the deer's hoof until she gave up.

Nicolai put the boy and the young girl on his horse and walked alongside until they were back at their village. The tiny prisoner of war and the graceful young woman raced to a nearby grove of trees where women were filling burden baskets, and Nicolai, standing far back, felt his own heart swell at the commotion and joy their return produced. Then, before they thought to notice him, he turned and went back home.

He bought and returned three more captured children the following month.

And then the rains eased and were about finished and Nicolai was asked to build the town its first schoolhouse.

He tried to describe the enormous pleasure the project gave him. "When I was a boy," he told his family, "I couldn't learn. There was no school in the village or anywhere nearby. Not any school. None."

His family didn't find that particularly odd or wrong.

"Don't you see how important it is? The village priest who taught had never been to school, either. So now I look at that newspaper in town and to me it's wiggles, ink on paper like a drawing, but other men can find out things from it. Things they need to know. Important things."

They barely listened.

They had grown up so quickly. Helena, his princess, was eight years old. He could no longer hold her in his palms, but she was still a dark-eyed sprite, a wisp of a girl child, and it did seem that laughter would accompany her throughout her life.

He could understand why they felt no need for schooling. Anna and he had tutored each of the children in every survival skill they knew. The boys knew how to hunt and fish and the girls knew how to dig and weave baskets and cook. Nicolai had taught all of them to build and carve and to plant necessary crops. They knew as many of their parents' various legends and histories as there had been long quiet evenings by the large kitchen fireplace.

But they hadn't learned enough to know that what they had learned was not enough.

Nicolai sighed. It was too late for Ivan. He was a man, about to marry a girl from Metini, to join his brother Giorgi and sister Katerina in beginning a family elsewhere. Soon Nicolai would ride with him on his trip south, saying he owned him if threatened. But he couldn't do that forever or hope to accompany them on all the trips a life necessitates.

A voice inside him nagged. You have two other children. Will you really build a schoolhouse so that everyone else's children in Mendocino can be prepared for life—except yours because you are so afraid for their safety? Wouldn't they be safer being able to read the papers themselves?

Helena settled like a butterfly on the window seat beside her mother. They both wove baskets, although Helena's was a simple storage basket with a black lightning design banding it and Anna's was a decorative masterpiece, fine as a piece of dress fabric, soft and luminous with scarlet woodpecker feathers woven among the reeds.

Alexander, now as tall as his father, looked like a wire ready to spring. Sometimes the intensity of his steely eyes upset Nicolai. It was as if Alexander were always asking the question "Why?" His movements were quick and caged like a wild thing kept prisoner, as if there were no comfortable resting place.

But he was so bright. The brightest of them all. He had absorbed everything his parents could give him, listening with those strange eyes to their legends, songs, and memories. And he had added new skills of his own. He was the best trapper in the family. There was a large bearskin on the floor, thanks to Alexander's steady hand and eye. The unfortunate bear's head was in the stable, to keep the mischievous *domovoy* from bothering the cows Nicolai had acquired so that he could have milk and butter.

Nicolai had twice served as his son's agent, trading pelts for cash in town.

But as good as it was to be handy with a rifle, it was not enough to get him through life.

Nicolai felt his age settle into the marrow of his bones, and he knew that his strength and secrecy wouldn't protect his children for many more years. The world changed every day, and his children had to be ready to confront the new. The world was also closing in. More people moved north as more forests fell. Someday there would be a homestead next to his. And then another. Something had to be done.

He had gone around saving children, but he knew it was only for the blink of an eye because there was no place for them to stay safe. He had two more children to save.

That evening, Nicolai smoked a pipeful of the strong wild tobacco that grew nearby and he worked on another carving. It was an otter in a storm, paws over its ears. A doomed, deaf otter. Helena cooed and admired the little carving, which she would add to her collection.

"I have lots of otters now," she said.

"Be happy," he said. "You're the only one on earth or sea who does."

There was no good place left to hide, and no more point in covering one's eyes. The new world was here, the new people had been born.

No more Russians. No more Kashayas or Clear Lake Pomos or Wappos or Miwok. Instead of cowering in the woods, vulnerable because they were different, his children would have to stop being different.

They must become Americans.

7

The war stories continued. Nicolai kept his face flat and remote except when the news was of the distant, not local, war. Only when the War Between the States was the topic did he join barside arguments, disagreeing with James from Tennessee or Roger from Virginia, or throwing money into the hat to help the Union soldiers. But Yankee Bill, steady and boring as ever, read tales of bloodshed both at Bull Run and Northern California.

Neither Nicolai nor the others commented on casualties close to home.

Two hundred, mostly women and children, murdered in Humboldt Bay.

Three thousand children kidnapped and sold.

A man on trial bragging of killing sixty children with his hatchet at different slaughtering grounds.

Three to four hundred "bucks, squaws, and children" killed in Round Valley within three weeks.

This war was over, the enemy eradicated. The numbers floated silently like ashes through the warm room, which smelled of hops, men, and companionship.

Nicolai half listened, slowly downing his rum. He was here tonight

for his own reasons, and he was impatient to be done with the newspaper readings.

It might have been less a matter of brains and more the simple result of literacy and the possession of newspapers, but Bill always seemed the most informed of the lot.

After the last sale notice on the last page had been read, Nicolai bought Bill a drink. "You've seen the school?" Nicolai began.

Bill nodded. "Fine-lookin' place you built. My granddaughter's there a month now. Smart little thing she is."

Nicolai grinned. Then Bill knew the requirements, the necessary officials to see, the entrance tests and fees. "How did she get to go there? Did you see somebody? What did you need to do?"

Bill pushed his empty glass toward the edge of the bar and Nicolai offered him another. "Thanks," he said. "What's the matter, you're not satisfied with the way I read the news? D'you want to do it yourself? Hell, you shouldn't be ashamed of not knowing how. I can't read Russian."

Neither could Nicolai, but he didn't have to say so. "For my children," he said softly, suddenly timid, exposed and afraid, despite his resolve.

"Kids? I never knew you had any. You're one secretive Russian, Nick." Bill laughed, and then he told him how easy it was to go to the schoolhouse and enroll the children.

Nicolai continued observing the schoolhouse at recess and lunchtime, studying the children's clothing, ages, hairstyles, bags, and bookstraps.

He went to the dry goods store and bought fabric, shoes, and overalls. He took the cotton to a widow woman who sewed, and he explained his needs, and he carried the overalls and shoes home with him.

He spread his packages over the large kitchen table he had made of wood scraps years ago.

"What is this?" Anna asked, lifting the shiny, stiff shoes. "Why?"

He didn't sit down, needing all the advantage he could gather. Anna was small but a boulder didn't have to be enormous to block one's path. "Because," he said gravely and slowly, "Alexander and Helena must not look like savages or hermits when they go to school."

"Go to—" Her face played a hundred expressions, one bumping into the next. And then it settled on horror and outrage. "No!" she screamed. "No! You'd send them to the murderers?"

80

"It's a city, Anna, a proper civilized place, and now there's a school for its children. The men of Sonoma were a long time ago. They barely exist anymore, and you must forget them."

"And you think the new ones are better? Your new friends who kill forests and rivers? The ones who took Metini and have my children working for them? Why would I turn my last babies over to them?"

"So they can learn."

"Learn what? To ruin everything they find?"

"Learn to be Americans. They must."

She looked as if she might strike him, or herself. She stood across from him, gripping the edge of the table. "They've learned enough from me," she said. "Like the others. They know enough already. *I am American!*"

He nodded. "But they must learn to be like the new Americans."

She made a hissing noise and waved her hand in the air to erase his abominable suggestion.

"Anna," he said softly, almost crooning, "do you remember the story about the rattlesnake's children?"

She looked surprised, and then she lowered her lids and nodded. "That was long ago. I was angry and upset. I—"

"That doesn't matter. It's an old story, Anna. You didn't make it up. And it's lasted all these years because it has truth in it."

She smacked the table impatiently. "What of it? We're talking about the school in the city—"

"We're talking about the rattlesnake's children." His voice no longer resembled a lullaby at all. "They aren't you or me. The whole world's combining into something new here. Our children have to become a part of it because there won't be room for anything else."

"You want them to be like you!"

"I want them to live! We can't hide forever. They outnumber us." His voice dropped until it was a shadow. "They'll win, Anna. There's no stopping them."

They fought through the night, Anna clinging to what was familiar and Nicolai pushing, insisting, roaring, and demanding.

"They're my children, too!" he shouted at one point. "You forget that, over and over! Two of my children are dead. Three work as farmhands on land that once belonged to them. One was stolen. I have two left—let go of them, Anna. Let them be what they *are!*"

She cried and pulled her hair and threatened and even, at one point, screamed about poisoning him if need be.

And then, near morning, she capitulated, slumped in an exhausted

81

heap across the table, her face tear streaked. "They'll go, then, is that it?" she said bitterly. "They'll learn new ways, is that it?"

He nodded. "It's their only hope, their only safety." How many times had he already said that? He only knew that it was true.

The seamstress had Helena's dress and apron finished the same day Nicolai finally went to the schoolhouse. The teacher's dusty brown hair and sharp features reminded him of a field mouse. But her luminous eyes were kind and very human and she was so delighted to meet Nicolai and hear of more students that he soon forgot how plain she was.

She wrote down Alexander and Helena's names and ages, then passed the book to him. He signed his name in Cyrillic. "I don't know any American," he said. "I can speak it, yes, but not too good, but I can't write it at all."

"That's *all right*," she answered. "Look. I'll show you. This is what *Nicholas Ross* looks like in English." She straightened up. "Your children will teach the new way to you. You'll *all* be students, explorers, and pioneers together." She clapped her hands in delight.

"Pioneers," Nicolai whispered, committing it to memory. "My son," he said, "he's a big boy. It's not too late for him to come?" Maybe she wouldn't want a student who'd tower over the teacher.

"Of *course* not," she said. "There was no school, no *chance*, and there's lots of people who need to catch up. Not all of them bother, just the *smart* ones. Alexander won't be our only older beginner, believe me."

She made it so inviting and possible that Nicolai was tempted to be the oldest old beginner. He looked around the schoolhouse, which still smelled of fresh wood and high expectations. "I built this," he said.

"How *wonderful*, Mr. Ross! It's a splendid school."

He nodded in acknowledgment.

"Were you a builder in Russia, too?"

"I was a boy, then. But Russians are good with wood."

"You've come a long way," she said, closing the lined book that now had Alexander and Helena's names written in it. "So have I, but from the other direction. Have you heard of Philadelphia?"

"I'm sorry," he said, and then he grinned. "But you probably don't know my village in Siberia, either." Then he frowned, immediately fearful. Had he been rude to the schoolmistress, suggesting there was something she didn't know?

But she laughed. "You're right. Only you *should* know about Phila-

delphia. The name means The City of Brotherly Love, and it's known as the Cradle of Liberty, because our country's freedoms began there."

She was very proud of herself and her city, this brown mouse.

"That's where the Declaration of Independence was *signed*," she said.

He shook his head.

"*You* know," she said. She struck a pose, looking to the side and upward, as if for inspiration. She spoke slowly and dramatically. "'We hold these truths to be self evident, that all men are created equal, that they are endowed by their Creator with certain unalienable Rights, that among these are Life, Liberty, and the Pursuit of Happiness.'" She turned and faced him directly again, smiling as proudly as if she'd written the words herself. "Isn't it *lovely?*"

"It is," he said softly. He had listened so carefully he felt tired. "What, please, does 'unalienable' mean?"

"That it can't be taken away from you." She closed the enrollment register smartly and walked toward the door.

"Lovely, yes," he said again.

They stood in the doorway. "It's so *exciting* to introduce children to the story of this country! I congratulate you, Mr. Ross, for giving your children the *opportunity* for an education."

"Thank you." He wished Anna could hear her.

"It's the very *basis* of democracy. We have a government of *all* the people. That is how it was meant to be, that is how it *will* be when this terrible war is over. No kings—or tsars, isn't it?—telling us what to do, Mr. Ross. We rule ourselves, so we *must* be informed!"

He felt out of breath listening to her, the way she talked, banging on certain words as if they were gongs. He had no more worries about Alexander's being too large for his teacher. She was a whirlwind blown across the whole country. He thanked her again and then still once again and he rode home at a brisk canter, singing tunes from his boyhood.

They left early the next day, Anna wide-eyed and silent as the children mounted their horses.

"Nicolai."

He turned. Anna's head was bowed and he wasn't certain she had spoken at all, but then she spoke again. "Nicolai, I understand about the school."

He rode a long distance before his eyes stopped filming over and he

was able to see clearly. "Today," he told his son and daughter, "I'll come back for you after I finish work. After this, you'll go yourselves. Don't be afraid because you don't know all the American words. You'll learn them." He had taught them what he'd learned from the brides and the mill hands and the newspaper readings, but they spoke with a variation of his accent tinged with Anna's Kashaya sounds. "Other children also have parents who don't know so much American," he said.

The trip was going to be a long one each way, and this was a clear, crisp autumn day. When the rains made the river impassable, even for a raft, and the roads muddy slicks, how would the children manage?

They were at the schoolhouse before he had found the solution. All he knew was that they would, indeed, find a way.

Nicolai took his bandana and brushed off Helena's shiny shoes before he lifted her off the horse. Alexander stood tall, dusting off his trousers and bookbag, and then the three of them entered the schoolhouse.

The teacher turned toward the door, her large eyes warm and inviting.

And then her smile froze and her eyes grew glazed and hooded. She rustled over, hands up, signaling them to stop.

Students giggled and whispered.

"Mr. *Ross!*" the teacher said in a hard whisper. "*Please*—may I speak with you outside?"

Alexander and Helena looked at each other and stayed where they were.

"You two as well!" the teacher said.

Outside, her face registered open anger. "You never said!" she protested. "Never once!"

"What?" Nicolai asked. "I answered all your questions."

"About *them.*" She bit at her bottom lip so that her mouth almost disappeared.

Nicolai looked at his children. Their chestnut hair gleamed, their faces were scrubbed, and their clothing exactly what the other children were wearing. Even their nails had been inspected that morning.

"I told you everything," he said. "Their names, their ages, my name, my—"

"How was I supposed to know that they'd be *Indians? Half-breeds!*" She glared as if Nicolai had committed a crime.

84

"Half? What is half about them?"

She closed her eyes with irritation. "I'm sorry," she said. "I don't make the rules, but it's the policy of our schools *not* to admit native children. It is a regrettable truth, but half-breeds have the vices of both races and the virtues of neither. They are not a good influence on the—"

"On the what? The foreign children? Look at them! Look at my children! You said my children were welcome!"

"Not if they're half-breeds!" Veins stood out on her neck as she tried to keep her voice down and stay out of sight of her pupils.

Nicolai felt as if he were boiling and drowning. "Look at them!" he shouted. "They are *whole!*" More than whole—she had to see it. Alexander, saved from despair. The most beautiful of his sons, perhaps the most beautiful man in Mendocino with his slatey eyes and tawny skin and long, muscular body. And so smart, interested in so much, so that whenever Nicolai even looked at him, his heart swelled.

And Helena, the tiny laughing joy. She reminded Nicolai of Anna, before the village was raided and she lost her balance and laughter. She reminded Nicolai of good times everywhere, of songs and friendship and love. *"Look at them!"*

"Mr. Ross! You're shouting!"

"You're not listening! Not *seeing!*"

"It's official policy." Her petticoats and skirts swished as she turned away.

They could hear her inside. "Back to your seats, everybody. Back to your seats!" The entire encounter had been closely observed. A sideshow, a diversion for the young scholars.

Alexander and Helena stared at their new shoes, faces hot with unearned shame.

"You!" Nicolai shouted at the closed schoolhouse. "What of your unalienable rights? What of your all men are created equal! What of your democracy?"

He would pull down the teacher and her freedom for all and the building he had crafted with his two hands. He would smash the whole town of false-faced men and women, the whole state with its terrible twisted laws. The whole lying country, ripping itself in half, clawing at its own belly because nobody, anywhere, stopped the evil. What monsters were nursed in her cradle of liberty?

Heaven is high and the Tsar is far away.

"Stand tall!" he told his children. "They are wrong. They are the

halves. They are the old ways, the old world, and you are the new! Stop looking at your shoes and stand tall!"

And together, heads held high, they rode back to the house at the edge of the woods, to their fort, the only safe place they knew.

Nicolai stopped going to the saloon. He wanted no more news of the East's war, since he had lost his own.

He stopped accepting jobs.

He spent that autumn and winter near his house, planting cabbages and potatoes and carving his imprint on more and more surfaces. The kitchen mantelpiece was their history, the newel post a floral bouquet, and, around the entrance of the room that had begun as Alexander's birthing room, he created his own strange and mythical world where ocean and land merged and divided, and real and fantastic beasts floated and flew from one to the other. There were bears and tigers, griffons and long-eared jackrabbits, salmon and mermaids, horses and centaurs, Coyote the trickster, and a long-tailed fox.

"Why are you doing that, Papa?" Helena asked.

He shrugged. "Because it's here, in my head." His creatures had to be born because they writhed and struggled inside his congested brain.

His carvings made their way up one side of the door and down the other, and only what was to be the center portion that would fit above the doorway was left. It became a wavy, undulating surface with whales deep at its bottom, and on the waves, before his mind even realized what his hands were doing, otters.

"They're like my toys," Helena said.

He nodded.

"But what are they doing? Playing?" Her voice was squeaky and dubious.

He nodded. "They used to throw seaweed and catch it before it hit the water. They played with each other, and with their babies. Once I heard them sing."

"Animals singing?" She had never openly doubted her father's words, but she stepped back and folded her hands in a position that was a favorite with Anna in her moods.

"It's true. Back in the days of the fort, I heard a mother sing to her baby. A coo-coo-coo sound."

"Take me to hear them, Papa?" she said, her eyes enormous. "Please? I'd be very quiet."

He was working on an otter who sensed danger. It "stood" in the water, listening, sniffing, and soon, were it not carved of wood, it would dive beneath the waves and resurface a long time later, else-where. "I can't, child," he finally said, very softly.

"I know we don't have a boat, but people in town do. I see them from the tower, and maybe they'd let us—"

He put down his carving tool and pulled her close, surprising her. He put his old, tired white head next to hers and controlled the urge to sing in soft, cooing tones. She was fresh and undaunted, hopeful no matter what. He had seen the terrible toll the day at the school-house claimed on her spirit, so that for weeks she looked tied to earth, dragging her feet, stopping mid-motion with a perplexed ex-pression. And he had vowed to keep the rest of her spirit alive by going back to his old policy, by shielding her from truths that were poison with no known remedy.

"Can we?" she murmured, close to his heart. "I would love to hear the otters sing."

"Perhaps," he said. Perhaps. Perhaps there would be a miracle and the otters would be made flesh again and whole. There was no harm in hoping.

When spring began, he felt an almost intolerable need to take action and stave off the growing, encompassing sense of impotence, the numbing conviction that he made no difference, couldn't save anyone, and couldn't change anything.

He counted the coins in the chamois bag and set aside enough for staples. With no more income except from Alexander's skins, he had to be more careful.

But there was still a surplus. There was still enough.

"What do you buy with your money?" Anna asked. "You leave with gold and come back without it, but there's nothing in its place."

"I'll tell you someday," he said.

"Tell me now!" she insisted.

He had failed them all, repeatedly, despite his good intentions. How bent and crushed would she look if he told her he went off to buy and return stolen children?

"What do you *do*?" Anna asked again

"All right, then. I buy the services of women."

"Where? Who does such a thing?"

She really didn't know. There had been no such thing among her people and she had never seen the houses in Mendocino City, let

alone in every other town and hamlet in California.

"And afterward, I drink rum until I fall down dead drunk. And if there's anything left when I wake up, I gamble it away."

She put her hand over her mouth, to stop the protests and denunciations building up.

"Anna," he said softly. "I help people. People like us. Believe me."

She dropped her hand, exhaled, and nodded. He wasn't sure if she trusted him or was merely acknowledging that she had no real options.

This time he went to the Northeast, up toward the second Indian reservation in Round Valley.

The valley looked nothing like the hideous stories he had heard about it. A green and perfect bowl in the mountains, it radiated peace and security.

Until, that was, people began to speak. Then he felt as if he'd walked into a battlefield strewn with gore and ghosts and fury. From the whites, he heard stories of stolen cattle, attempted murders, and poisonings.

And from the Indians, those who would come near or talk to him, about massacres, rape, revenge, unfair accusations, and endless, relentless inequities. Their numbers were shrinking through venereal and infectious diseases inherited from their new neighbors, from war casualties and starvation, and now, as more and more adopted the white man's drink, from its evils, too.

Nicolai gave out money as long as he could, and then he left the reservation and the valley. He pulled his white man's mask back over his soul, and as he rode homeward, stopping for water and camping in fields, he let it be known that he needed workers for his ranch to the south. He couldn't save them all, but he had a few hundred dollars left and he could free a few of them, bring them to his house, or let them return to their families.

It was like fishing, building the dam and knowing the salmon and steelhead would find the opening and land in his net. A man approached. He had a peculiar accent and his left eye wandered. "Hear you need hands. I might be able to help. Young girl, twelve. Hard worker, too. Her mother's dead, she needs work. And she's real pretty."

She stood a few paces back, hands bound. She wasn't much bigger than Helena and she tried to make herself still smaller, pressing herself as far behind the tree as possible.

88

Nicolai nodded.

"Three hundred dollars," the man said.

"So expensive!" Nicolai protested. All he had.

The man shrugged. "Not so easy anymore," he said. "No more indenturing, so demand's up."

"No more indenturing?"

The man shook his head. "It's that Lincoln, you know? That Emancipation thing." He overstressed each syllable of the word, "Ee-mahn-see-pay-shun," making it long, loud, and derogatory. "You know about that?"

Nicolai shook his head.

"You live in a cave? No more slaves, he says. Back there, you know? The blacks. No more."

"No more?"

The man shook his head.

And yet here they stood, bartering for a young girl, no more than a child. Nicolai looked at her. Her skin was the color of rich honey, and she had the tattoo marks he had forbidden on his daughters across her chin. She watched him with absolutely no expression.

Perhaps she was the last slave, then. He'd buy her, despite the extraordinary price, because there'd be no further need to buy anyone. He handed the man his coins.

She shuddered as he approached.

"You understand American, girl?" he asked.

She froze like a wary deer.

"You understand?"

She made the suggestion of a nod.

"Then listen. Come to my house—"

She gasped, shook her head furiously, hugged herself for protection.

"Not that way! Not—" He ran his fingers through his beard and frowned. How could he explain? And why should she believe what anyone with blue eyes promised?

"Where is your home?" he asked gently.

She pointed to the east.

"Can you go back there?"

She looked at him sideways, doubtfully, waiting for the trap.

"I'll take you there. Then I'll leave." He could hear birds cry and grass sigh between each group of words. He could, he thought, hear her heart beat. "Do you have people left?"

"Grandmother," she whispered.

"Then let's go."

And all the walk to her village, and all the ride back to his house in the woods, the refrain played through his head nonstop. Let her be the last slave, please. Let her be the last. He had spent all he had.

His family had been busy in his absence. Katerina and Giorgi and their children had visited and promised to do so again when they moved further inland for the winter. Their lives, like the lives of all their ancestors except their father and mother, were lived in a cyclical series of dwellings, depending on the seasons. The house in Mendocino had been added to the various sites these last few years.

"Katerina says Metini is not so good anymore," Anna reported. "Nobody is happy there. Ivan's left already. There's a white man married to a Kashaya who's letting them all move onto his land."

"They could move here," Nicolai said.

"Aren't you listening? The whole tribe is moving there. They won't be alone, the way we are." She stopped and peered at him. "Are you well? You look tired."

"I am." He felt it in his bones. In his fingernails. In the strands of his hair.

"A hard trip?"

"They're all hard."

"All those women, old man," she teased.

"That must be it." He settled into his rocking chair, closed his eyes, feeling guilty of abandonment. "I'm too old for any more of it," he said—to Anna or the invisible accusers, he wasn't sure. "No more trips."

"One more," she answered.

He shook his head, his eyes still closed.

"I want to see this new place, this Haupt Ranch where Ivan lives and Giorgi and Katerina will move. Nicolai—Charlie Haupt is white—maybe we could all live like a village again. Alexander and Helena could have friends, husbands, wives. . . . Nicolai? Are you asleep?"

He sighed.

"I'll go by myself, then!" she snapped.

"Don't you dare!"

"Nobody bothers an old woman."

He opened his eyes.

She stood with her hands on her hips. "And maybe, if I like it, I'll stay. And you'll know where to find me, Mr. Ross!" He had told her

his Mendocino name, and it struck her as enormously funny. "Do you hear me, husband?"

He nodded. How could he not hear her? Her voice was excited and loud.

"The children will be here any day now, and then they'll go to Haupt's. Let's go with them."

"Ah, Anna, there's so much to do. Alexander needs to trade his furs, we need to ready the house for winter, and I'm so tired. I've been away all summer and—"

She pulled a rabbit-skin shawl around her shoulders.

"Where are you going now?"

"To wait for my children. Perhaps we'll all go off together on our own travels, the way you do. We'll go to the Haupt place without you, and you can come visit whenever you're not too tired."

"Perhaps," he murmured.

She left the house.

He rocked and dozed, a small smile on his face. He'd have a quick nap before Anna returned. She could be funny when she was in a mood to joke. He hoped she had a big meal planned. He was very hungry.

"Walk tall," Nicolai said a few days later. He and Alexander had left behind the enlarged, busy family—Anna, Helena, Katerina, Giorgi, their children and spouses, all still arguing about when, or if, Nicolai would accompany Anna so she could inspect this new white man—owned rancheria. Nicolai was completely disinterested in the project and each time the question was raised, he found work to do elsewhere. Today, Alexander and he had mounted their horses and returned to Mendocino City in search of staples and money for Alexander's hides.

They unloaded their horses and tied them up. "Rest," Nicolai told him. "Soon you'll have fifty-pound sacks to carry home."

"Mama seems angry about it," Alexander said.

"Oh, she's fussing about that rancheria. She wants to move there so everything makes her angry, even buying a year's worth of sugar. Don't pay any mind."

Alexander looked ready to protest, but then the work at hand occupied him completely until he was bent almost double under the thick pack of furs.

"Are you sure I can't—" Nicolai began.

"I'm not a baby, Papa. I'm strong." They walked together on the

91

wooden plank that served, unsuccessfully, as protection from the summer dust and, even less successfully, from the mud and muck it became in winter. Despite the endless millings, the light bouncing off the ocean gave the town a hard-edged gleam. Nicolai's intricate building trims and carvings took on a special clarity in the seaside air.

Across the way, the bluff was piled high with milled lumber. The tallyman called out as planks started down the chute to a ship bobbling on the waves below. Nicolai wondered what San Francisco, its destination, was like. He had always hoped to see it.

Alexander shouldered his bundle proudly. It was proof that he was the best young trapper in Mendocino County.

"Come, the fur broker's this way," Nicolai said a few steps later. Then he realized his son was no longer walking beside him. Instead, he was immobile, silent as stone, watching three young boys cross the wooden sidewalk. Each swung schoolbooks secured with a strap.

Don't care, Nicolai mentally signaled. Let it make you hard and fierce.

Alexander's slate eyes hungrily studied the schoolboys' swagger and style. How easily it had all been given to them, how easily they carried it.

Don't forget! Nicolai silently shouted.

Alexander snapped out of his slack-jawed moment. He shifted his burden so he could stand straighter and he walked briskly once again.

Nicolai nodded, satisfied. Alexander would never forgive and never forget.

"You'll have your own adventures," he told his son when they again walked in unison, as if they'd been interrupted mid-conversation. As if Alexander's thoughts had been written out and read to everyone by Yankee Bill. "Just as interesting as theirs."

Later, they walked beside horses packed with supplies for the winter. Alexander's coins jingled with each step, and from time to time he patted the little bag tied to his hip and commented on how rich he was.

A part of Nicolai smiled and acknowledged his son's justifiable pride, but most of him trudged along, brooding. He couldn't forget the "last" slave's face, or Alexander's that morning, watching the jaunty schoolboys. He felt as if he had eaten something tainted, and he needed to rid himself of it, but couldn't.

They crossed the river, passing a few tipis. The tribe was not Ka-

92

shaya, and wouldn't understand it if Nicolai tried to tell them they were fools to expose themselves that way, to believe the white man would not eventually want them or their tiny piece of earth.

It was time to turn off for home. How different the stubbled, bald hills looked since he'd first seen them. This country changes so quickly, he thought. Mill towns appear overnight and forests disappear by dawn. What would it all finally become?

As if being answered, terribly, he heard a raspy, strangled choke that chilled him.

Alexander stood so suddenly rigid that he looked like he might topple over backward. "There!" Now his voice was low and wary, almost a growl. "What is it? It looks like—" He didn't bother to finish his sentence. "What is it?" he cried.

Nicolai saw nothing except a moment long years earlier when Anna, not Alexander, had run. "What's wrong?" she had called out, swallowing the words as she raced.

His vision failed, his ears clanged and roared, and the cold thing he'd carried since that day, since Piotr had been stolen and he'd tottered under the first hard blow of his adopted country—that unnamed needle-edged cargo exploded, shooting ice through his body, freezing his fingertips and sealing his breath.

He forced himself forward, slowly, toward Alexander. Why should it be anything that concerned them? He told himself that Alexander knelt over a crumpled package of brambles and bark.

It was hard to see clearly but he was more and more certain that yes, it was brambles, the crimson of a dead rabbit. Half eaten.

Surely she wouldn't have really gone away without him—she'd been joking, she wouldn't. "You'll know where to find me," she said, but she wasn't serious, she—

Or perhaps it was a deer.

Yes. Large. Killed and not claimed, or dead of old age, or—

Because it could not be, it simply could not be. Even if it seemed that an apron or a foot. . . . He hadn't told her how dangerous this world was because she already carried enough sorrow. He hadn't warned her enough because he wanted to protect her. But surely she wouldn't—

Besides, the head—no one would do that to an old woman, hit her that way, with what? Only an axe could do such . . .

No.

He covered his eyes with his hands.

"Mama," Alexander whispered, but Nicolai heard it as a scream, a shriek, the sound of all the trees crashing and the world itself losing balance.

"Mama."

"Where are the rest of them?" Nicolai said, eyes closed, his hands over them. "Where's Helena? Katerina? The baby? Giorgi, the children—the rest of them? Where is everybody?"

Alexander said nothing.

"Where's Giorgi? He wouldn't let this . . . where is he?"

Giorgi was strong. Saleable still. As was his oldest son. And even the little girl. Dear God.

Nicolai had been so careful. He'd built a fort to protect them. This couldn't happen.

Where was Katerina? With that baby still at the breast?

And Helena? He thought his heart would squeeze itself shut. Helena, no bigger than a sprout—stolen? To be sold to some filthy. . .

And Anna, so bloody, so hurt because she fought them or because she was too old.

Eyes still covered, he saw the Aleut hunter holding the screaming otters on a spear. All gone now, as if they'd never existed. And not Nicolai's regret, nor art, nor love could bring them back.

"No," he said. "No, no. My God, no." Twigs snapped beneath Alexander's city boots, those shoes meant for the schoolroom. And then, for the second time, he heard his son's new and terrible voice, a quiet scream. "The baby," Alexander said in that deafening, hushed voice. "Katerina's ba—"

"NO!" Nicolai roared. "NO!" He cradled his head in his hands, covering his eyes, shaking his head. And then his whole body shook and darkness swallowed him, blackening his eyes, seeping into and filling him, hiding him from this world.

He would not look on it again. Never. Not ever again in this life.

PART II
1 8 6 0

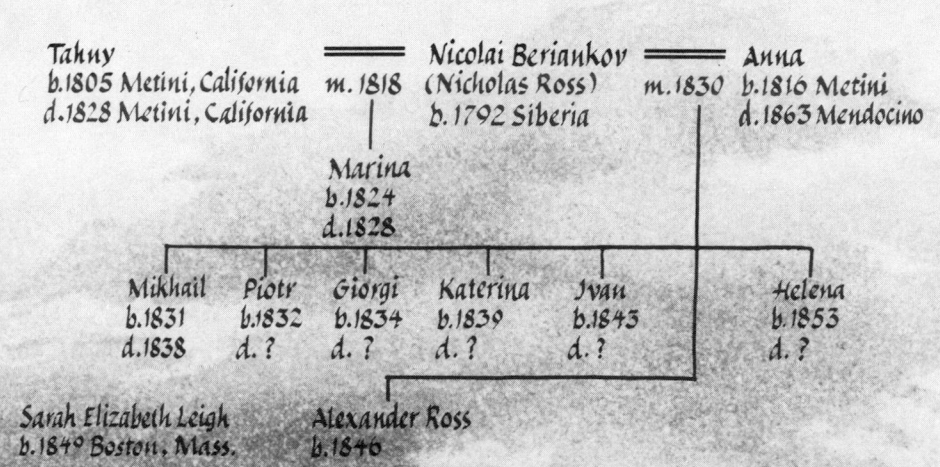

Tahuy
b.1805 Metini, California
d.1828 Metini, California

m.1818

Nicolai Beriankov
(Nicholas Ross)
b.1792 Siberia

m.1830

Anna
b.1816 Metini
d.1863 Mendocino

Marina
b.1824
d.1828

Mikhail
b.1831
d.1838

Piotr
b.1832
d. ?

Giorgi
b.1834
d. ?

Katerina
b.1839
d. ?

Ivan
b.1843
d. ?

Helena
b.1853
d. ?

Sarah Elizabeth Leigh
b.1849 Boston, Mass.

Alexander Ross
b.1846

8

"Sarah Elizabeth Leigh, Sarah E-*liz*abeth, S*arah* Eliz*abeth*, Sarah Eliz*abeth . . .*"

The wheels bumped below her and the rain thrummed on the taut canvas over her head, but Sarah stopped pretending there was music in her jolting progress across the prairie.

The wagon was musty from an overabundance of people, time, and distance; its constant motion was nauseating.

"Can't we stop and wait out the rain?" she asked the backs of her parents' heads.

Her father, normally the gentlest of men, sounded as irritated as Sarah felt. "Can't waste time," he snapped. "If we stop, we could get trapped in the snows in the mountains and never reach California. And you know that, child."

She knew it and hated it. Feared it and the fear itself that prompted it, that drove them on when they were exhausted, that made them abandon the weak ones and those who wandered too far and were missing when it was time to move on.

She sighed out of long, dull frustration and closed her eyes, willing herself away from the creaking wagon, back to her Boston bedroom. There were real windows, with ruffled curtains embroidered with forget-me-nots, and beyond the windowsill a comforting solid world of

houses and hedges. She heard the sounds of bells, hooves on cobbled streets, vendors, friends playing games, her mother downstairs at the piano. Perhaps she would join her for a duet for four hands. . . .

She loved the clean ways of music, as crisp and clear as the black and white keys. She loved the way a musical symbol stood for one thing and no other, the way all the emotions and longings that frightened her could be expressed safely through pressure on ivory and ebony. She loved hearing music, reading music, and playing music. It shaped her life and brought it joy.

And then Boston and even the memory of comfort were gone, shaken away by a violent lurch of the wagon.

This hateful journey would continue forever. Sarah had never wanted the "adventure" of gathering buffalo chips as cooking coals, of oppressive heat and swarms of mosquitos. The exhausting monotony was interrupted only by bad surprises: freezing nights, hail and wind and lightning storms, sickness and death from weather, cholera, typhoid, measles, lung fever, consumption, and the bloody flux. Or, worst of all, feared with every clump and squeal of the wagon wheels, with every in and out of breath and swallow—savages. Any speck on the yawning horizon might whirl closer and erupt into a howling, murderous Indian.

Indian. The word was the very core of her nightmares. Born the year of the Gold Rush, but three thousand miles away from it, baby Sarah had found her feet and balance in a world tilting toward the West. One of her first words had been "Cafforny," said with the enthusiasm and vigor she had heard in the voices of all the excited emigrants leaving for the far golden shore. "Cafforny!" she shouted, "Sarah want Cafforny!" She cried when the word proved less than magic, producing only laughter.

When she was ten and facing an unwilling exile from Boston, her father tried to encourage her with memories of her early, misguided enthusiasm. "You were born wanting California, Sarah," he said.

She'd bitten her lip and kept silent. Her father's only hope was that the California climate would clear his lungs.

Sarah's only hope was that Indians wouldn't kill them en route. The bloody prints of Indians stained all the bright tales of promise and plenty, and anyone hoping for earthly paradise or even clear lungs had first to run the gauntlet through their ranks.

More than the witches in her fairy-tale books, more even than the Devil himself, Sarah Elizabeth Leigh of Boston, Massachusetts, feared the half-naked, primitive creatures. The day she learned she

98

was going west, her nightmare Indian sliced his tomahawk through her skull, and ever since, her scalp tingled as if it had already been lifted off.

Her sister, Mary, interrupted her reveries. "Sarah's in a black mood again," she said.

"You're such a baby!" Sarah hissed. Mary didn't understand anything.

What Sarah needed was a piano. She would play away the hours and never hear the cloppety-clip of hooves and wagon wheels, never know or care where she was.

But how were they to take the piano? Adventurers did not have musicales.

Imagine unloading a piano every time the wagon had to be floated across a river. Imagine rafting it across, then repacking it. Imagine a piano in a downpour like this one. The canvas roof was already soaked through and Sarah, not for the first time, would be wet to the bone for days on end unless the wagon stopped and they all took last-ditch shelter in the mud beneath it.

No piano. No escape.

"I'm not a baby!" Mary said. "I'm seven years old! You're the baby! You sigh and sniffle all day long."

"That's better than singing stupid songs or playing with dolls or—"

"Girls!" Their mother turned halfway to face them from the front seat, next to their father. She moved her thick and bulky body with obvious discomfort. Although not a word had been said in the family about her mother's changed contours or slower tempo, Sarah had learned the amazing truth during a washday.

Along with several other girls, she'd been wading in and out of the creek, filling camp kettles to put over fires built on flat stones on the bank. A discouraging pile of grimy clothes awaited her. As much as Sarah hated the dirt and dust of the road, she dreaded the backbreaking attempts to remove it during their infrequent wash stops. By the end of their last washday, she had been so tired she put her camisole to dry on poison oak leaves. She'd been blistered and miserably itchy for two weeks.

Mustn't complain, she reminded herself. Everybody else worked just as hard. Her father, mother, and the younger children were busy reshoeing oxen, mending the wagon, drying out bedding, repacking provisions, and baking bread. At least being at the creek excused Sarah from hearing the "minister" who preached from the center of the corral while the necessary work went on. It was Mr. Whitmore

today, and his sermon was sure to be long-winded and annoying.

Still, that hadn't made her back feel easier or the day speed by more quickly.

"Do you hope for a brother or sister?" an older girl asked abruptly.

Sarah looked around, to see to whom she spoke. The girl, wearing her nightdress, as was Sarah, looked directly at her.

"Me?" Sarah's voice squeaked with surprise. "Why would I? I have both already."

"Surely you've noticed that your mother is . . . How old are you, anyway?"

"Ten and a half. Almost eleven."

The girl shrugged. "Thought you were older. Maybe I shouldn't have said anything."

Since then, Sarah had watched her mother with interest, not precisely sure what sequence of events to expect.

"I'm not a baby, am I, Mama? Sarah called me a baby!" Mary was still indignant.

"Don't fuss, girls." Their mother's voice was heavy and fatigued. "You'll wake William."

Their brother, aged five, lay curled next to a sack of flour. Their few remaining eggs were packed deep in its center.

"Why don't you write in your journal, Sarah?" her mother asked. "You haven't written yet today, have you?"

If her mother only knew how infrequently Sarah wrote! After the initial bustle and preparation had been recorded, after they had joined the other wagons and met their fellow travelers, what was there to write except "More of the same." She didn't care to catalogue the birds and flowers and wild animals spotted along the trail —or the roughly made gravesites.

More of the same. That's all there ever was.

"Can I sit up front with you, Mama?" Mary asked.

"Oh, Mary, it's—"

"I'll be very quiet. Please? There's nothing but Sarah to look at here."

"There's nothing but rain and oxen and prairie to look at here," her mother said, but all the same she gestured for Mary to come up.

Sarah sighed again—with annoyance, envy, frustration, or her familiar boredom, as endless as the landscape. Mary scrambled over their possessions, but Sarah ignored her, trying again to blot out the dreadful unending sameness, to return to Boston, to music lessons and hopes of the conservatory, and . . .

100

The wagon tilted and jolted.

Sarah's mother screamed, William awoke and joined in out of a blind, unfocused terror, and a third thin and distant shriek sliced the air and abruptly stopped, swallowed by the rain. Fear rose in Sarah's throat, but it choked her, left her mute.

The wagon shuddered to a stop. Her father scrambled down.

"What's happening?" Sarah shouted as soon as she could speak again. Indians. It must be Indians. Stay put, she told herself. Hide. But she pushed forward, needing to know.

Her mother shook her head. "No, no, no!" she said, denying whatever it was she saw. "No, no!" Her hands were fists, pressed to her heart. Her eyes, unblinking, stared at the ground.

Mary lay crumpled, wet and muddy and still as death. Her father carefully wrapped a blanket around her and Sarah pressed out of his way as he carried her into the wagon.

"Is she . . . is she . . ." She couldn't finish the sentence. She felt consumed with guilt. She had caused this. Her foul mood had driven Mary out, made her stand up front, vulnerable to the wagon's abrupt jolt over rocks and ruts. It might as well have been Sarah's hands that had tossed Mary out like a weed to be crushed under the oxen's heavy hooves.

She had killed her own sister.

"Our Father which art in heaven, Hallowed—" She stopped herself. He wouldn't listen. He must hate Sarah. Evil, evil girl.

"Mary, Mary," her mother crooned, heavy body bent over her younger daughter, wiping the mud and water off her body.

Sarah resumed her prayer, although her heart had gone as dead as she knew Mary to be.

And then Mary moaned.

"Praise God!" Her mother wiped gently at a bruise on the child's temple.

Mary groaned again, her eyes still closed.

"Oh, her leg." Her mother's voice was barely audible. "Dear Lord, it's . . ." She shook her head and could say no more.

"Forgive me," Sarah said softly, to God and Mary. "Forgive me."

For a week, Mary lay in the wagon, deeply asleep, but moaning and burning with a fever, and Sarah, without protest or complaint, applied fresh rainwater compresses to the parched lips and forehead, and prayed nonstop. She wrote a single entry in her journal: "Lord forgive me. Mary near death. I have killed her."

Then, after seven days, Mary's eyelashes fluttered like summer insects. And finally, her large blue eyes opened.

"Don't ever call me a baby again, Sarah," she said, as if their squabble had been interrupted a moment earlier.

That night, when the wagons stopped, neighbors congratulated the Leighs on Mary's miraculous recovery. "How lucky you are," the family was repeatedly told.

Mary's leg would never be normal again. It was twisted and stiff and caused her great pain, but the rest of Mary had recuperated, so they had been, indeed, blessed with good fortune.

When they next spotted a good tree, they fashioned a cane out of a long, straight branch, and from then on, Mary hobbled and half hopped to wherever she needed to be.

After a while, Mary's tilted locomotion seemed normal and unremarkable, echoing, in its own way, the rhythm and style of the heavy wagons crossing the endless plains.

One day when the sky was a hard blue shell encasing an unendurably vast world, the long line of wagons slowed, preparing to rest and refurbish.

Suddenly they heard a voice from ahead. "Look there!" someone shouted. "Beware!"

The grass needed by the livestock had been burned away.

"Indians," Sarah's father muttered, freezing her heart.

"Keep going, Papa," she urged.

He shook his head. "The oxen need food and rest. Besides, the Indians who did this would find us wherever we went." He conferred with the other men, and then the wagon train, with no other choice, divided up in search of fodder and thereby became even more vulnerable.

"Stay in the wagon, children," their mother whispered. "We'll be as quick as possible. Fill the time quietly. Sarah, why don't you write in your journal?"

Sarah stared at the paper for a long time. There were definitely things to say, but where would she find words to describe the tiniest portion of what she felt? The words she knew had been taught her in a civilized city with rules, with churches and orchestras and sweet-smelling women in pastel gowns. What would they mean here, now? Besides, how could she stay bent over paper when Indians might be circling the wagon, or riding wildly toward them, painted and violent and unpredictable? "I am afraid of Indians," she finally wrote. "I am

afraid of dying." She stared at the blank page surrounding her ten words, then she closed the book.

William had a wooden flute with which he amused himself. But at its first toot, his mother, father, and sisters shushed him, foolish as they knew that was. Why would a reedy note or two be needed to alert anyone when their lumbering wagon and oxen were so visible?

". . . Thy kingdom come. Thy will be done in earth, as it is . . ." Sarah barely heard the words anymore, she had said the prayer to combat so many terrors, so many times.

After hundreds of repetitions and several lifetimes had passed, the oxen were fed, and the wagon moved to rejoin the others. "Keep inside," her mother said again, which Sarah willingly obeyed. She let her mind unfold and float, let herself believe the threat was now behind them.

And then her father grunted, gasped, and her mother made a strangled, gagging sound. And Sarah, despite herself, pushed forward and looked into the final blaze of the day.

The family had been axed, shot with arrows, and burned. Sarah knew the girl on the grass. Her name was Lily and she looked so much like Sarah that people took them for sisters. Sarah stared at Lily's boots, so calm and normal-looking, because otherwise she would see Lily's head hanging loose from what was left of her neck. Nearby, on the grass, lay her sunbonnet, also like Sarah's. Their mothers always made them wear them, to protect their fine skin.

Vultures, circling, floating, waiting, cast shadows over the bodies on the grass.

Other wagons drew near, then stayed to dig graves and say prayers because it was the decent, the only thing to do.

But the prayers were whispered and hurried and there were frequent nervous glances, attempts to sift through the dusky light, to scan grass and rocks for half-naked bodies, tomahawks, and bloody murder.

After that night, the endless, forever trip blurred into a shapeless haze of unrelieved fear, as if Sarah had inherited Mary's fever. Life was a long delirium.

Still, work went on as usual. Sarah gathered sack after sack of buffalo droppings, and when it was too wet for them to ignite, she cooked the eternal beans, bread, and bacon under the wagon in ashy rock-lined pits. She lit smudge pots to keep insects away and swatted the millions who defied all deterrents, who lived in her hair, brushed

over her face, and were baked into the bread she kneaded. She ig-nored the dirt that lined her skin and clothing and dulled her hair between wash stops. Each morning, she milked the cow, then hung the churn from the wagon bow so that the bumps and lurches pro-duced butter balls and buttermilk by the noon meal. She endured the sickening rhythm of the wagon, its clammy dampness in the rain or thick inferno heat under the blazing sun. She watched with resigna-tion as another long rainstorm soaked through the painted fabric and ruined supplies.

Life went on.

Sometimes, even that wasn't true. Sarah cried, but from a bleary, feverish distance, when the little Beckwith boy wandered off and drowned. And cried again at another river, when a mule panicked and sank. It was mourned almost as much as Lily Williams or the Beckwith boy, it was so needed.

And then one day her father said her mother was ill, and he stopped the wagon train and summoned a neighbor who had seven children.

Sarah had almost forgotten about the baby. It had become, like the end of this voyage, an impossible, improbable, and altogether un-reachable promise of the future.

They were in a country of high bluffs, blind corners, and fear. People milled around their wagons, shuffled nervously about their chores, and glanced repeatedly at the horizon.

The baby obligingly hurried to be born. The midwife-neighbor called in Sarah's father, and after a while he reemerged. "This is Rebecca," he said, "your sister." He laughed and held up the tiniest, most miraculous creature Sarah had ever imagined. Her tension and lethargy left and she felt alive again, and safe. What a magical event. There had been nobody, just a clumsily shaped mother, and now there was life, a Rebecca fully finished and perfectly made.

Congratulations were kept to the minimum so that the wagon train could leave immediately. Sarah sat by her mother, who seemed happy but uncomfortable as they bounced inch by inch across the country. She was so charmed by her tiny sister she didn't even mind the onerous task of drying and scraping her diapers so they could be reused.

But Rebecca was frail and, after only ten days of life, her body was added to the trail of graves that lined their path across the country.

Her mother took a sharp knife and a flat slab of wood. "Please, traveler, protect this grave," she carved painstakingly. "There are

wolves," she told Sarah, who couldn't bear thinking about it. "She's so tiny."

Again they said quick prayers and moved on. They had to keep moving, had to cross the final mountains—wherever they were and if they indeed existed—before the snows came and trapped them. The feverish haze repossessed Sarah. She felt empty and wounded without Rebecca and didn't know what to do with the now-painful love that had arrived with her and outlasted her. Perhaps Rebecca had been a myth, a creature of her delirium, and now they were back to the unending, unbearable trek through the wilderness. She heard, but dully, as if through cotton, her sister's songs, her brother's squeaky wooden flute, her mother's voice reading from either the Bible or Mrs. Child's *The American Frugal Housewife*, the only two books on board. Sometimes her mother read recipes for ingredients they hadn't seen in months—tomatoes, breast of veal, cherry dumplings, gingerbread—as if touching and holding on, the best way she could, to favorite memories, reaffirming that somewhere there was a real world with familiar foods and comforts.

More often, she read the author's homilies and advice to persons of moderate fortune. "'The prevailing evil of the present day is extravagance,'" she began.

Mary listened attentively and embroidered linens, her stitches clumsy but constant, despite the wagon's erratic rhythms.

Sarah's sampler, a small house surrounded by flower beds, progressed imperceptibly. She hummed private tunes, softening the edge of her mother's words, which were, she feared, a warning and preparation for even greater hardships at the other end of the country.

"'. . . I would ask,'" her mother's sudden emphasis broke through Sarah's resistance, "'is it *wise* to risk your happiness in a foolish attempt to keep up with the opulent?'"

Sarah controlled the urge to ask what opulence or wealth had to do with their controlled surroundings, sparse rations, or the painful bangs and sways of the wagon. But her mother had moved onto the description of a foolish woman's overfurnished house.

"'. . . Brussels carpets, alabaster vases, mahogany chairs, and marble tables . . .'"

It sounded lovely, a mirage for the middle of the American wasteland. Real chairs with padded silk seats. Real tables with sleek veined surfaces. Tea in thin china cups with fine gold tracery at their lips. Mrs. Child was a stupid old witch who didn't understand anything.

"Mrs. Child is right," her mother announced one day, waving the

book in the direction of her daughters. "'The greatest and most universal error is teaching girls to exaggerate the importance of getting married; and of course to place an undue importance upon the polite attentions of gentlemen.'"

What did this mean? That husbands were yet another unavailable luxury?

"'. . . Two or three years spent with a mother, assisting her in her duties, instructing brothers and sisters, and taking care of their own clothes . . . is the way to make them happy, as well as good wives. . . .'"

In the corner, half hidden between a sack of corn meal and a nearly empty one of dried fruit to keep away the scurvy, William, exempt from years of kitchen duty, exempt from husband hunting and clothes mending, built castles of dried beans.

Finally, there was something worth writing in her journal. Sarah felt freshly remade, invigorated. Actually excited and glad. "Father says we will be there soon," she wrote. "Will California be as wonderful as they say?"

It would soon be a year since they had left the house in Boston. Sarah was eleven. Her body, refusing to spend the year in limbo along with her mind and soul, had grown so that her dress was high up on her calves and painfully tight across the chest. Her mother said she would soon become a woman.

Her father still woke her in the night with his coughing, but surely California would cure that along with all their other woes.

Her mother talked about the fruit pies she would bake in California, where everything good could be plucked from the trees and the earth. Her father laughed—between coughs—at the prospect of building them a house. "A log cabin, maybe," he said. "First I'll find work. There must be general stores like there were in Boston. They can always use a good clerk. Then we'll find land, and then . . ."

They dreamed and planned and moved through their days with energy and revived spirits. Sarah's mother's eyes, heavy and hooded since Rebecca's death, cleared and looked ahead, not into the past.

And then William, the good, barely noticeable little boy, vomited.

"Did you eat berries when we stopped?" Mrs. Leigh asked him. "What is it, William?"

But William grew glassy-eyed, disinterested in her questions. And then he bent over with cramps and his bowels ran like water.

"Dear God," Amelia Leigh said. "Dear God, no!" She gestured

wildly at Sarah. "The book—Mrs. Child! Quickly!"

They nursed him with laudanum, but the opium didn't stop him from wasting, and they had no other medicine save hartshorn for snakebites, a small bottle of rum, physicking pills, castor oil, and peppermint essence.

Mrs. Leigh combed through her book in a frenzy.

"Nutmeg!" she screamed, out in the wilderness. "Did we bring nutmeg, Jonah? Does anyone have it?"

"Why?" he asked, his voice hollow. Sarah noticed how dark the circles under his eyes had become.

"She says nutmeg—and cork burned to charcoal in brandy with sugar—is good for cholera. We have rum, maybe that will—"

"Nutmeg and cork won't cure cholera," Jonah Leigh said. Sarah had never seen or heard him cry—had never seen any grown man weep and barely believed they were capable of it—but her father's voice sounded like hers did when she was trying not to let a terrible wet sorrow erupt.

"Then ashes in cider!" Mrs. Leigh screamed, her finger pointing to a new paragraph of Mrs. Child's.

"Cider," her husband said, his voice flat and dead. "Will there be a miracle to produce cider now?"

"Then flannel with brandy—the Thomases have brandy—and cayenne pepper," she insisted, and she lay the wet compresses on William's stomach. William was inert and disinterested, barely there. His wooden flute rolled away and disappeared among the sacks and tins of provisions.

Another wagoneer said pepper in his drinking water kept his family from the cholera. Sarah's father said that was nonsense, too. Still, the other man's son didn't die, and William, in a matter of hours, did.

Sarah sat in a hollow of pain. Of all her fears, of all her complaints, none had been concerned with William, a loving, easy child born into his own self-sufficient world of music and quiet games.

This time, her mother didn't cry silently. This time, the entire wagon train could hear her grief. She pulled at her hair, repeating his name over and over, blaming herself for having no nutmeg. "Bury him deep, deep where the wolves can't find him, Jonah!" she cried.

Jonah Leigh was overcome with a coughing spasm. Friends from other wagons prepared the grave.

Sarah's mother, gestures and movement ragged, raced to them with a board in her arms. "We're so close—so close to California. I can't

bear for him to lie here forever, apart from us. Mark the grave so we can find him again, bring him home to us." She ran in wide, erratic circles, searching for stones to circle the grave, rushing back to tell her husband how to mark the wood so that they would recognize it, leaving abruptly to urge Sarah and Mary to find more stones and then more. Her movements were uncontrolled, full of fledgling bird flaps of her arms, nonstop urgings and advice. Numbly, Sarah lifted stones and placed them around the fresh grave, but felt the heaviest deep inside herself.

Finally, the grave was covered and edged with a double line of stones and marked, in lieu of a headstone, with a carefully notched piece of wood, and with a final prayer for William Leigh, they climbed back into their wagon.

The entire train had started once again when Amelia Leigh half rose from her seat. "NO!" she screamed into the afternoon sky. She grabbed her husband's shoulder. "Turn back, Jonah! You must turn back!"

He tried to shush her, to bring her to her senses, but her hysteria increased. "Let me off!" she cried. "Let me go back or I'll throw myself off the wagon!"

Tears ran down Sarah's cheeks. They were all dead. All of them.

"*Indians!*" Amelia Leigh wailed. "They'll see the grave markings. *They'll dig him up!*"

They had passed graves violated for the clothing of the dead. A night or two and many wild beasts later, all that was left was a small pile of bones.

"WILLIAM!" she screamed, edging off the wagon until her husband laboriously turned them around, creating confusion through the entire wagon train.

They scattered the carefully collected stones and rocks and tossed the notched stick into the distance and reburied William's poor small body so that Indians could never find and disrupt him.

Sarah's mother, frantically pulling at her arms, her hair, gesticulating to the heavens, watched, crying without sound, praying mutely.

William was laid in the earth on the trail itself and then their ox-team was led over him, turned and led over him again, pounding and sealing and obliterating the grave so that William was safe and secret far below. And forsaken to them forever.

And then, with no choice, they turned one last time, and, hooves and wheels pressing a last farewell to their son and brother, they headed west. California was near.

9

"If you're so upset about my leaving, then come with me, Sarah."
Mary put her hands on her hips and tilted her compact body forward
in a discreet but definitely argumentative pose that brought back
sharp memories of their mother. Sarah might have the maternal temperament and musical talent, but Mary had inherited all the rest of
the family traits.

"I have a job," Sarah reminded her. "I can't leave the children."

"Schoolteachers come and go," Mary snapped. "The last two married and left midterm."

"That's different." Sarah studied her large, competent, and unadorned hands.

Mary carefully smoothed the last item in her steamer trunk. "Don't
moon over your hands that way," she said, her voice just like their
mother's had been. "They'd have a ring on them if you weren't so
picky. Or maybe if you hadn't been saddled with sick and dying parents and a crippled sister."

"Don't talk that way! I wasn't 'saddled' with anything and I don't
want to marry anybody and get stuck in Mendocino City." Whenever
she passed Masonic Hall with its rooftop carving of Father Time
pursuing a young woman, Sarah kept her eyes on the ground and
walked briskly. The carving seemed a huge advertisement for rushed

frontier marriages and she'd have none of it. Not of Mendocino or of its men.

"Then come with me. San Francisco's a big city, a real city. I'm going to make tons of money creating fashions for rich women, you'll see."

"What will people think of you? A young woman all alone. . . ."

Mary laughed. "They'll think I'm wicked, I hope. Maybe that'll get me customers more quickly. I'll tell them I was made lame when my lover and I escaped from a—"

"Honestly!" Sarah walked to the window and looked out over a stable toward Main Street, full of saloons and dusty, rowdy lumbermen. San Francisco, she was sure, would be no more than an enlarged Mendocino.

"They have pianos in San Francisco," Mary said from behind her.

Sarah shrugged. "I'm going back to Boston," she said in a quiet and determined voice. "I'll have enough money in a year or so. Why not wait and we'll go home together?"

Sarah heard the steamer trunk's lock click, then the triple beat of Mary's walk—a soft clump of cane on carpet, a leg-drag, and a normal, almost soundless step. And then Mary's hands were on her shoulders. Gently, but insistently, her younger sister turned Sarah toward herself.

"We were little girls when Boston was home," she said softly. "Now we're women. The world has changed as much as we have these last ten years, and it won't change back. Stop dreaming about it. Stop waiting for our childhood to return, or believing we can go back and find it again. If you keep this up, you'll always feel as lost and misplaced as you say you feel now."

Sarah's eyes welled up. She blinked furiously so that her sister wouldn't see.

"Come with me to San Francisco," Mary said. "It'll be an adventure. We'll be partners. You're even a better seamstress than I am."

Sarah shook her head.

"We're all we've left in the world," Mary said. "I'll miss you so much."

"Then stay."

Mary shook her head. "We've been over this too many times. My only skill is my designs. I need a city for them. Besides, I need the adventure."

If Mary hadn't been lame, she would have climbed mountains, run races, hunted tigers. She was very different from her older sister.

110

"I don't want adventure," Sarah said. "I never did. You belong here on the frontier. I don't." She sighed, and gave up.

Mary pulled back, finally and fully separating herself. She adjusted her dress and thumped her cane on the carpeting. "Will you see me off, then?" she asked.

Even watching was frightening. Her sister was put into an open-topped box that dangled from a cable a hundred feet over the cliffs and ocean. Sarah's stomach lurched along with the flimsy-looking box as it made its descent to the schooner below. Finally, Mary was deposited like a plank of wood on the ship's deck. She waved up at Sarah, and Sarah returned it, but from then on she saw only blurs through such a watery, painful veil she felt as if she were drowning.

Every day, after her students left, Sarah spent a few moments at her desk, collecting her thoughts. She was reluctant to begin the long walk to the Peterson's house where she boarded. Roxana Peterson could be exhausting, reminding Sarah of how lucky she was to be with such a fine and prosperous family. She even claimed to have saved Sarah's life, because one week after she left the boardinghouse in which she and Mary had lived, it, along with twenty-four other buildings, burned to the ground. Somehow, Mrs. Peterson derived moral satisfaction from the event. In any event, Sarah needed time before she exchanged the noisy classroom for the noisy farmhouse.

The thoughts she collected settled around Mary, whose letters were as animated and enthusiastic as she herself was. San Francisco invigorated her, and after six months apprenticed to a dressmaker, she had opened her own tiny shop and was thriving. "Come join me," every letter invariably said.

Mary had been right. Boston was fading. Whatever she remembered and treasured of it from her childhood was gone—the house, the security of loving parents and a stable world, the future at the conservatory. Besides, it was terrifying to contemplate recrossing the country, even with the new trains. And even if she did, who would she be in Boston? A California stranger, as much an ill-fitting outsider there as she was in Mendocino City.

It was all baffling and depressing. How had they wound up in this backwater, anyway? Her father had heard about the north coast's special air—"You'll feel like you never breathed before," his informant insisted. But lovely as the crystalline atmosphere was, it was not given to miraculous cures, and the ocean air washed clean her father's grave, not his lungs.

Her mother, more remote with each death, refused to leave her husband's final resting place, and Sarah was certainly not about to abandon her ailing mother.

And that's how people wind up in Mendocino instead of Boston, Sarah told herself. For a host of wrong reasons.

She sighed. Time to get going. Mrs. Peterson appreciated her help around dinnertime. But Sarah was so full of people and places lost or imagined that she stayed in her seat awhile longer. Besides, Mrs. Peterson had a brother she wanted Sarah to meet and she was becoming more insistent about making arrangements. Sarah had seen the dusty, gruff brother at church and most emphatically didn't want to meet him, to be polite or civil to him, because in this woman-desperate town, the slightest encouragement would be the equivalent of an intense and long-term courtship.

She still dreamed, knowing she was foolish, of a Boston sort of man. Her height, her big bony hands, her nondescript pale hair and features wouldn't matter. He would see through to her secret heart and would sweep her away to a world of music, soft surfaces, and civilization.

"Ma'am?"

She gasped.

"Didn't mean to startle you. The door was half open, so I, ah . . ."

He stood silhouetted in the schoolhouse doorway, blocking the light from outside with his great height and broad shoulders. She scrambled to her feet, nearly toppling her chair. "Who are you?" she asked, straining to see him.

"Alexander Ross, ma'am."

"What do you want in my schoolhouse?" She made her voice as sharp and forbidding as she could manage, suddenly aware of how vulnerable she was in the empty room.

His only answer was a silence that lengthened and grew more ominous with each second.

She mustn't panic. Perhaps he had a child to enroll, even though he seemed alone. She couldn't see his face or tell his age.

Or perhaps he meant to harm her. She stepped behind her chair and grabbed its back, ready to swing it if needs be.

"Teach me." His voice had turned tight and thin.

"Pardon me?"

She heard him breathe deeply, saw his outline look to the right and left.

"Ma'am?" he said, his voice still barely audible. "Can I come into

112

the room? I could talk more easy if I wasn't in the doorway." He stayed in place, waiting.

"Yes," she finally said. "Only—leave the door open. For air." She continued to hold the chair back as he approached.

He was very tall. So tall she felt diminutive. Dainty, even.

And then she saw him clearly. She blushed and hoped it wasn't visible. His speech was crude and rough-hewn, but he was anything but. He moved gracefully and stood with an ease she envied. His hair was long and auburn, his features unlike anyone else's she had ever seen, with high cheekbones and a sculpted mouth, eyes a dangerous blue-gray contrast to his sun-baked skin. All color and contours. He made her think of burning autumn afternoons in the redwood forests, of stereopticon slides of statues she had seen when she was a child.

He made her think of things she wasn't supposed to think of at all—vague, unknown, impolite, improper, half-suspected, and beckoning things.

He was not at all a Boston sort of man.

She wanted to reach up and touch his skin, to see if it were as warm as it looked, to touch his mahogany hair, to find out if it were as silky as it looked.

She was frightened and flustered. Suddenly her black cotton stockings, her high-laced boots, her homemade cotton dress seemed both too plain and too constricting.

She wanted him to touch her.

It wasn't natural, right, or proper to feel this way. She couldn't imagine her mother or Roxana Peterson ever having these sensations, and Mary, for all her giggling and bluster and teasing, had never so much as hinted at this.

Sarah felt perverse and twisted, permitting thoughts and images that would never enter the mind of a decent woman. Particularly, unimaginably, about a complete stranger. And a backwoods man at that.

This was mortifying. If only there were somebody she could talk to. But Mary was gone and Sarah would never, ever risk telling the minister about this. His youngest daughter was a pupil of Sarah's— what would he think of the schoolmistress's depravity?

"I want to read." His voice was no longer timid at all. It was strong and melodic and determined. "Can you teach me?" He looked at her intently, waiting patiently until she regained her composure.

"Well, I—I am a teacher." The single sentence exhausted her.

"Then would you? After school, like now? Alone? I'd pay."

She should refuse. Should stop this right now. But of course she wouldn't. She wanted to hear that voice, see that face, be close to the long, lean body she'd seen outlined against the schoolhouse door. She was sure his body gave off enough heat to burn away fog. She wanted—she stopped herself, shocked by runaway, lascivious thoughts.

"Don't need to read fancy books. Just need to know what I sign."

"Did you just move here?" she asked.

"Born a few miles away. Why?"

"Because I thought—the school's been here six or seven years, and I wondered why you hadn't . . ."

His eyes turned hard and cloudy. He raised his chin pugnaciously, daring her, daring anyone to something she couldn't fathom.

"Will you teach me?" he asked. His posture and the timbre of his voice made it a challenge and a very special invitation.

She found his arrogance as attractive as everything else about him. He was dangerous. She would refuse him, pull away from his tug.

"Yes," she said. "I'll teach you."

His entire being relaxed, and he grinned.

Smiling, strong white teeth shining, he was even more a mass of contrasts, surfaces, and delights. She forced herself to be practical. "Would you prefer the texts I use with the children or the Bible?"

"What's a bible?" He looked suspicious, as if she were trying to cheat him.

"Mr. Ross! The holy book?"

He shrugged. "Never been to school, ma'am, like I said."

"Yes. Of course." Spare the man your surprise, she counseled herself.

"Then what is it?" he demanded.

"It's a book about God, the beginning of the world, and Christ, and, oh, Jonah and Moses and King David and the apostles and—you've truly never heard of it?"

"Oh, *God*, sure. My father talked about God sometimes. He wears a cross, from his childhood, and he explained it. But there's no church or priest for him here, and besides, he's been angry with God for a while now." He almost smiled at Sarah's obvious discomfort. "And my mother, she told us stories about the beginning of the world, about Coyote and—"

"What does an animal have to do with—"

"—but not out of any book. She had all her stories in her head."

"Didn't you ever go to . . ." She realized how ridiculous her auto-

114

matic responses were. This wasn't one of the State of Maine Presbyterians with church and customs transported to Mendocino. This wasn't someone she'd grown up with in the lovely Unitarian church on the green. She wasn't sure what this was, except godless, tall, incredibly good-looking, and uneducated.

"Go to where?" he demanded.

"I was going to say church, or Sunday school, you know, but of course, I didn't mean . . ." She tidied papers and stacked the few texts she had accumulated into a precisely matched pile.

"Sunday school? I thought school was school. Is this Monday school?"

She kept her eyes on her desk and shook her head. She would not witness this man's ignorance. "No matter," she said. "I only asked so you'd have a choice, since some of the schoolbooks are . . . well, since you're older than my other—"

"I want the real thing. The real thing you teach in Monday school."

The whole way home to the Petersons' she tried to rid her mind of images of how close they had to sit to read through the primer, of how excited he'd been with the idea of learning, of how quickly he had learned the sounds she'd taught him.

And how intently he had studied her mouth, shaping the sounds. And how she had blushed every time he looked at her that way, lavishing his attention and excitement on her. And how he had been so taken with her blush that once, spontaneously, he had reached out and touched her flaming cheek, as if to test it. And then had pulled back his hand and apologized several times.

Despite the cold and the fierce wind, she felt the imprint of his long, wondering, and gentle fingers on her face all the way home.

Mrs. Peterson took a particularly long time with the dishes. Sarah, oddly energetic, had offered to wash and dry, but Roxana Peterson, too, felt a need to pump and heat water and stand with her hands in soapsuds.

Sarah was not as alert as usual, her mind like Roxana's water with iridescent rainbow bubbles lazily floating through it. Monday school, she silently repeated, slowly rubbing a plate dry. How lovely. Alexander Ross . . .

Roxana Peterson cleared her throat.

And then again.

Sarah came out of her trance.

"Mind you," Roxana said, "I wouldn't say anything if you had family. You're a grown woman, a schoolteacher, and I know you've been through a lot, all those years you helped support your ma and little sister. And I'm not one for meddling or interfering."

Roxana Peterson was a virtuoso meddler and interferer, and if Sarah could have afforded to stay on at the boardinghouse without Mary, and if it would have appeared to be the proper thing, she would certainly have done so. Boarding with two or three families a year was exhausting and, in some ways she couldn't fully identify, humiliating.

But what could the woman possibly be up to? Surely she wasn't going to ponder the meanings of Mary's departure once more, or the pitfalls and dangers of the big city. Surely she wasn't going to discuss her homely brother's overlong bachelorhood again, was she?

"Mr. Peterson was in the city for supplies today," Roxana said, her eyes on the cup she scrubbed, "and he passed the schoolhouse. Late. After the children were all gone." She glanced sideways at Sarah before continuing. "Saw the half-breed come out of your classroom."

"The what?"

"Half-breed. Indian. You should know. You were there. Mr. Peterson saw you come out right after him. Child, you have a reputation to maintain. Everybody knows half-breeds are bad influences. He's a squaw's child. Too good for his mother's people, but not a whit bitter than them."

"He wants to read." Sarah's voice was husky and low. A half-breed? Glorious Alexander Ross was half Indian? He was what she had feared in all her childhood nightmares? Impossible.

"Little late for reading, isn't it? What's an Indian need with book learning, anyway?" Roxana sniffed.

Sarah thought of his wide, sharp cheekbones, the slight upward tilt of his slatey eyes, the rich deep mahogany hair. An Indian! For heaven's sake. So that's why he had never been to school, why the flare of resentment when she touched on the subject. They hadn't let him learn, had denied him his birthright. She put down the dried cup with a clatter, and had to catch it as it wobbled and nearly fell off the rack.

"I hope you don't mind my speaking this way," Roxana continued. "It's just you're living here, part of the family for a while, and it don't look good for a teacher to be with an Indian. If your own sainted parents were alive, they'd say the same."

Sarah didn't know what her parents would have said. She couldn't

think of her gentle, weak father and her reserved mother, of Boston and picket fences and rules of behavior, as having any connection with the strange new world that had birthed Alexander.

"He wants to read, Mrs. Peterson," she said softly. "And I want to teach him."

He arrived promptly each Monday, and each Monday she was surprised, completely, totally, all over her body, by how the combination of his parts and colors and movements affected her.

She would peek surreptitiously out the window a quarter of an hour before school ended, and there he would be, waiting, his striking features as impassive as stone. He never crossed the road until the last of the regular students had gone.

They had their lessons, sitting close together over the text, which was laughably infantile, although Alexander treated the foolish rhymes and stories with reverence.

> There once were two
> Sweet little girls
> Named Margaret and Kate,
> And every day
> They went to school,
> And never went too late.

"Good!" she said. "Very good!" In fact, it was amazing how quickly he learned, as if he absorbed and retained every word and idea that came out of her. He made her feel valuable and talented.

And his eyes made her feel beautiful.

Roxana Peterson made no further comments, except to raise her eyebrows and sigh heavily every Monday when Sarah finally arrived at the house.

One week Alexander paid his twenty-five-cent weekly fee, turned to leave, and then paused, pulling a leather pouch out of his pocket. "This, too, is money." He shook out a string of polished shell fragments. "For my mother's people. Pomo money." He stared at her, his features set and stern the way they were when he watched the schoolhouse from across the street.

"Yes," she said. "Pomo," acknowledging him, his past, her awareness and acceptance of it.

"To other people, people like you, it's a necklace," he continued. "I would . . . I would like you to have it."

Inside her head, Roxana Peterson and the entire town clucked in chorus, like disapproving old hens. She felt herself flush above the high collar of her dress.

What should she make of a shell necklace? What did it truly mean to Alexander? If it was jewelry, then how could she accept it from a man, from this man? And if it was money, it was even more unseemly.

But everything about them, except the primer and the alphabet, was unseemly, somehow out of bounds, and what did a man like Alexander know about propriety anyway?

She looked at the pale pink fragments, carefully smoothed at the edges. A string of challenges.

Alexander's smoky eyes bored into her, his features revealing nothing.

"There's no need to give me gifts," she finally said. "You pay for your lessons."

"I know. This is for you, not for the lessons."

She looked at him for a long quiet time. A few feet of schoolhouse floor lay between them, but it felt a chasm as deep and wide as the entire continent, as all history.

The little necklace waited on the desk, pastel and innocent, like a lure and a trap in a fairy tale. What about everything she claimed to cherish, to yearn for? What about Boston and music and tradition? Alexander would never understand any of it.

What about now? All the matrons whose children she taught? Roxana Peterson? "You be careful," she had been told the evening before while they washed the dishes. "Don't do to be alone with any man, child. Don't do to trust a one of them. Men . . . they aren't like us. They have ways, needs that . . ." Roxana Peterson shook her head. Then she cleared her throat and, staring at the dish she was drying, not at Sarah, she continued. "But Indians!" Her voice was near a whisper. "We're talking about savages! Savages! Do you . . . do you understand?"

She knew about savages, although perhaps not in the way that Roxana Peterson seemed to suggest. Still, whether or not that was what the woman had meant, Sarah would never forget Lily, the vultures, the sunbonnet near the severed head.

But Alexander had nothing to do with that. She closed off the portion of her that was tensed for Mrs. Peterson's scowl, the matrons' whispers and head-shakings.

She touched the necklace. "Thank you," she said. "I'll treasure this." She was out of breath, as if she'd just run a long distance.

A few weeks later, Alexander presented her with a lacy piece of wood. "How pretty!" she said, and then she realized it was not pure design. It was "Sarah Elizabeth" finely carved in script and polished until it was satin to the touch.

"You like it?" He sounded almost shy.

"It's beautiful. I knew you were a woodsman and a trapper, but I didn't know you were an artist as well."

He smiled broadly. His smiles came more often now. At first they'd been brilliant, infrequent shocks. "I'm not an artist," he said. "I'm a—what's the word you told me? A literate. I'm a literate now! So thank you, Teacher Sarah Elizabeth!"

She smiled, the familiar heat staining her cheeks. "You are an artist, nonetheless," she insisted. "This filigree is so delicate..." She shook her head, unwilling to speak the thoughts flooding her. So delicate I want to cry, to let you know I feel what went into its carving, what love your fingers held.

So fine, so feminine, and for me, a great oversized plain woman, all edges and pale colors and no grace. This lacy song made of my name.

"I learned from my father," he said. "Years ago, when I was a child. Russians are famous carvers. The best in the world." He shifted his weight and took a deep breath. "Perhaps..." Perhaps was one of many new and favorite words. He listened intently to every word that came from her mouth, repeating new ones and adopting them—and then using them until they were worn at the edges and truly his. "Perhaps you would like to meet my father? Perhaps Saturday? There's no Saturday school, is there? Perhaps I could bring an extra horse into town and take you to our house. I am sorry to make you travel, but my father never leaves his house. Perhaps it is a possible plan?"

The "Sarah Elizabeth" lay on the desk like a flower, a symphony crafted of her essence. "That would be lovely," she whispered. "I am honored."

She met him in town that Saturday, avoiding Roxana Peterson's comments and suggestions as to the behavior and choices of decent women.

119

"My father," Alexander said as they approached the house, "may behave strangely. He's old, blind, and deaf, so you must forgive his ways."

Sarah felt ready to forgive anything of anyone.

"He has suffered terribly," Alexander said. "It left him with a cankerworm in his heart. It eats at him, grieves him all the time.

"This is Sarah Elizabeth Leigh," Alexander told his father, a half-dead tree of a man inert in a rocker by the fire, muttering in foreign, impenetrable languages and refusing to acknowledge the existence of either Alexander or Sarah.

"This is my father, Nicolai Beriankov Ross," Alexander continued, as if they were all in a drawing room, bowing and curtsying and obeying every social nicety.

Nicolai Ross continued to rock in front of an enormous fireplace with an intricately carved mantelpiece. Sarah saw waves and fish, tiny houses, people, and forests. She wondered who had tried to fit a world on a mantel.

"He's blind," Alexander had said, but when the man's pale, pale eyes met hers, Sarah was positive they were sighted and intelligent, but defeated.

Alexander tended his father as gently as if he were a newborn infant. Later, they left the house and walked to the nearby redwood trees. "He's suffered more than a man should," Alexander said, as if it explained everything. Late afternoon shafts of sunlight punctured the heavy canopy above them. Alexander was suddenly outlined in light. He glowed from his russet hair to his high boots, at one with the massive trunks and silent beauty of the woods.

This redwood forest and this man were as far from Boston and piano lessons as she could get, and yet she knew at that moment that they had always been her destination.

She loved him. He had been no part of her dreams. He wouldn't comprehend her lost music or the conservatory or even what the words *Boston* or *city* meant. He was a backwoodsman to whom the dusty village of Mendocino City was the world's greatest metropolis. He had no formal learning except what she herself taught him from texts designed for children.

And he was an Indian.

No, Alexander, the most decent, gentle, and glorious man she had ever known, was as far from her dreams and plans, as wrong a match, as the most malevolent of marriage brokers might have planned. And

this wilderness of trees, rocks, and ocean was not where Sarah, child of cities and soft music, belonged.

Except that he was Alexander, and his place was Mendocino, this strange rambling house, and these wild woods. And she did, indeed, love him.

Later that afternoon, when they sat in a clearing flooded with orange and lavender sunset, Alexander told her what had happened to the rest of his family and her last misgivings dissolved. That he could love her, despite his memories of slaughter and of what her people had done to everything he loved, amazed her.

He was braver than she and much better at forgiving.

"Sarah," he began, "Sarah Elizabeth Leigh . . ."

"Yes," she said. "Oh, yes."

Alexander's forgiveness had its limits, she learned. She wanted to live in town, where she would have neighbors, streets, and closeness, especially when Alexander would go away to work the woods for months at a time. The village, while not Boston, looked enough like New England to provide a certain comfort, with its painted houses and squares of lawn, its churches, stores, hotels, and people.

But Alexander, gentle and smiling, had forgiven her race but not the village of Mendocino. "I will not live in a place that didn't want me," he said with finality. "You cannot imagine that day, with all the students watching, and that woman. No," he said, "we will live in my house." And that was that.

She thought of her mother, packing her household and following her husband, regardless of her own feelings, and knew she would do likewise. But surely, she told herself, she would find more happiness in the wilderness than her mother had. Surely.

It took Roxana Peterson half a day of spring cleaning and a great deal of throat clearing and false starts before she stood straight, looked Sarah in the eye, and said, "Well, then, if you're determined to go ahead with this . . . do you know—you being motherless and all—do you know what to expect?" Her face turned scarlet and she busied herself with blacking the stove.

Sarah didn't know how to answer. What she knew of marriage was what she had observed and been taught of its domestic rituals, but she was sure Roxana Peterson didn't mean that. She had a working idea of possibilities between males and females—only a blind person

could fail to notice the seasons and habits of the animals who shared the coast.

She knew there was more, wanted to know it, but wasn't certain that the pursed unhappy lips of Roxana Peterson would have been her chosen source. Still, this was a long-married woman, and the mother of four children, and certainly no one else had offered any information.

"Are you ready for marriage?" Mrs. Peterson asked, her back to Sarah.

"Well, I—"

"I don't mean your hope chest, or that fancywork you're doing."

Sarah stiffened. Her nightdress had been the subject of much commentary by the lady of the house, who inspected and critiqued each stitch on the fine white cotton gown, each small rosebud and lily she embroidered across its yoke and cuffs. Although it was never said openly, the message was clear that such finery was ridiculous for an Indian's bride.

Roxana stood straight and rubbed the small of her back. "I mean what happens. What men do. Did your mother tell you?"

Sarah shook her head.

Roxana sighed. "Didn't think she had. She raised you decent. Wasn't no point till now, anyway. Not proper." She sat down and sighed again. "It's like this," she said, her eyes wandering away from Sarah's face, to the floorboards, then across to the wall and up to the ceiling, where each rafter had been freed of cobwebs and spiders' nests earlier that day.

"It's how the Lord arranged it," she said, "so there's no cause for complaint, although I'll never understand why He saw fit to make it be so . . . but that's how it is, and we can't change it. And if you just . . ." She kept her eyes skyward, looking for either heavenly inspiration or missed webs. "If you think of something else, something pleasant while he . . . something like spring flowers or maybe embroidery for you, you like it so, or a favorite Bible passage . . ." She finally looked at her boarder.

Sarah nodded, quietly encouraging her on.

"If you do that, you'll hardly mind at all. And it doesn't take all that long, anyway." She stood up emphatically and brushed at her apron. Prenuptial instructions, to her obvious relief, were over.

Except for one addition as she left the room. "At least," she said, "that's how it is for Christians, for white people. Who knows what's to be said about savages!"

* * *

122

She was his wife now, their marriage reluctantly, but officially sanctified by the minister. Her wedding skirt and blouse had been replaced by her ruffled, tucked, and embroidered nightdress and she stood, watching her new husband build a fire.

This was the room he'd been born in, Alexander had said. Created for his arrival when the house had only one other room.

The room builder, the carver who'd created its overpopulated, unfinished door frame, slept upstairs in his tower. She tried not to think about him, reminded herself again that he was deaf and blind and no cause for nervousness.

She patted the sides of her hair, touched her long braid, smoothed the fine soft cotton of her nightgown. She wasn't certain if she should get into bed now, be under the covers when he turned around, or whether she was supposed to wait. There were so many things Roxana Peterson's advice hadn't covered. Then the issue was resolved as the fireplace gave off sudden heat, golden lights played across the walls, and Alexander stood up and turned to her.

He pulled her close, touching her cheek gently, almost reverently. With feather-light touch, he outlined her mouth with his finger.

"Be brave. I'll pray for you," Roxana Peterson had said that morning.

He kissed her, slowly, his hands on her face, then on her hair, the small of her neck, her back, making each part fresh-born with his fingers. Whatever he touched, he sanctified, so that when he put words to it and said, "You are so beautiful, Sarah," it seemed possible that he spoke the truth.

"Poor girl," Roxana had said, wiping a tear from her eye.

The firelight flicked over the carved headboard, made gauzy shadows of the two of them on the whitewashed wall.

"I want to see you," Alexander whispered. "All of you." He touched the top button of her nightgown.

All—all? She had never thought of this, had spent weeks fine-stitching the nightgown so that she would be as pleasing as possible. She had never dreamed—to have him see her? She had never seen her mother or sister naked, had learned to dress without exposing any part of herself, had barely ever seen herself, had been taught it was immodest and wrong. Was this supposed—allowed—to happen?

"Savage," Roxana Peterson had called him. "You poor child."

His hands worked at the tiny pearl buttons at the yoke, unwrapping her as if she were a gift.

Her heart beat double time, her cheeks burned, but while her entire past pulled and tugged at her, no words came of it and she did nothing to protest or stop him. This was probably not decent. Possibly not civilized. Definitely not ladylike.

Probably because he didn't know any better. She should stop him. Civilize him.

But she had chosen Alexander, not those proper ladies. She'd defied and deserted them and now they blurred into the woodwork, below the crackle and hiss of the fire. He lifted the gown up and off her until it fluttered to the floor, the ghost of who she'd been.

She was racing inside, blood rushing, and yet she was oddly calm, her only fear that he'd be disappointed by her pale angles and ordinariness. The room was still, except for the snap of wood burning. She dared finally to look up, to meet his eyes. He smiled, as if he'd been waiting for her to join him, and all she saw was pleasure and welcome.

He moved closer, ran his fingers over her shoulders, then slowly, luxuriously, undid her long braid, so that her hair cascaded over her bare back and nothing but her skin and Alexander's fingers and lips contained and defined her.

"Beautiful," he whispered, making it so. "Beautiful, precious Sarah." Under his hands, her hard edges softened and melted into him until she burned in the firelight and no longer knew what was Sarah and what was Alexander, only what they had become, and she had no name for that.

"Lord knows what savages do," Roxana Peterson had said again that morning. "Poor child."

Sarah didn't think about spring or embroidery or much of anything until the next morning, when she awoke in the massive carved bed and suddenly thought of Roxana Peterson, who didn't know what savages did. "Poor woman," Sarah whispered, with a smile. And then she turned on her side, toward Alexander.

10

Sarah had saved the water in which she'd boiled potatoes the night before and mixed it with flour, salt, and sugar leaving it to collect enough yeast from the air for her to begin baking.

Perhaps it was overambitious, planning to bake after a long day's washing, but the rains had stopped, the air was clean, and Sarah was impatient. She wanted fresh linens and fresh bread for Alexander's return. Besides, the helper girl he was bringing could change the hot coals in the bake kettle later while Sarah did the laundry.

Or she could do the wash while Sarah changed the baking coals. She couldn't decide which job was more onerous, which result— burned fingers and scorched dresses at the fireplace or backbreaking pain and muscle exhaustion at the washtub—was more to be avoided.

She had already made soap, the worst part of washday preparation. Sarah retched at even the memory of stirring the stinking kettle of lye and leftover household grease. Its steam and fumes nauseated her, ashes covered her arms and hair, and sparks burned her skirts and skin until finally the soap came and could be dipped in the soap barrel.

But it was over for a while and the soap barrel was full. There was comfort in that.

Her back hurt. She arched it, her swollen belly ballooning under her long skirt. She looked down and noticed it, as if it were a surprise visitor, and smiled. "Plenty of soap for you when you arrive," she told her unborn child. She thought of the baby waiting in its silky nest, waiting for the end of the winter storms so it could be born in full springtime. Then she forced her heavy body outside to take advantage of the first clear day in a week.

She built a fire under a kettle of rainwater and positioned herself so that the smoke wouldn't blow in her eyes. When the water boiled, she shaved a cake of her lye soap into it. She rubbed the dirty spots in the white wash on her washboard, pausing often to take deep breaths.

"Papa will be back soon," she told her belly. If she called Alexander "papa" and talked to the unborn baby, it made all the possibilities realities. Alexander would return quickly with the helper girl and become a papa to a baby who would live a long, healthy life. She knew it was selfish and foolish to grow attached to a baby before it was born—or after it arrived, or ever, for that matter. God took so many of them away. But it was hard to hold back, to keep one's heart in reserve while the child grew right under it, touching it, or after birth when it sucked, or smiled, eyes so intently on you, so loving and open. It was as if nature conspired against common sense, forcing the love onto you long before you knew if you could hold on to this one, if this would last at all.

She still ached with the pain of their first child's death and she often visited the small plot at the back of the land and talked to him. All the graves had redwood slabs that lay flat on the earth. That was the way graves were marked at Ross, Alexander said. Sarah didn't see the relevance, but she had no strength to quarrel. Now, very often, she visited the graves at the back of the land and cleared away the vines and grasses that wanted to obliterate all trace of death. "Nicholas," she'd whisper to the earth. "Nicholas."

They'd named him that, hoping to please Alexander's father. But the old man by the fire took no notice.

Until one day, as Sarah returned from milking the cow. The kitchen window was open and Sarah frowned at the plate of pancakes on the sill.

"For the *domovoy*," Alexander had explained. "And to please my father. Besides, maybe it does protect the house."

Pure nonsense, she thought, not for the first time. The birds would

be at those pancakes any minute. Her evaluation of the worth of pancakes and *domovoys* was interrupted by a noise from inside where infant Nicholas lay in his cradle near Nicolai. Surprised and worried, Sarah peered through the window. The old man was out of his chair, bending over Nicholas's cradle. Panic flared, but Nicolai simply studied the infant's face and stroked it with one finger. Then he began to sing a soft song in a foreign language. Russian, Sarah was sure. A lullaby. She stood still, unwilling to move a finger or breathe deeply. Nicolai's voice was rusty with disuse, but true enough so that his wistful melody filled her with a sharp, unidentifiable yearning.

And then the yellow dog that had wandered onto their land and into their lives barked, perhaps sharing her surprised reaction to the music and life in the house. Nicolai stopped his song immediately. Sarah moved out of sight. When she finally came into the house, Nicolai was back in his rocker, silent and remote as ever.

From then on, she made sure to leave the baby near the rocking chair when she milked the cows or boiled the grease and lye or collected eggs. On fine days when the windows were open, she heard scraps of songs and the metallic thrums of the balalaika. And once she heard a memorable duet of hearty male laugh and guttural infant chuckle as the namesakes entertained each other.

And then baby Nicholas died. Abruptly, meaninglessly, he coughed and choked, burned with a fever, stopped breathing, and broke all of their hearts.

Old Nicolai burrowed so deeply inside of himself there was no more of him left in this world. He was buried beside his grandson at the back of the land he had claimed and protected.

Sarah shook the image of Nicholas out of her mind and concentrated on her washing. She put the white clothing into the tub of boiling water and scrubbed the colored things. There was a long, thankless day ahead.

After her father died, her mother had taken in washing in order to keep them alive. All day while her children were at school, Amelia Leigh scraped, scrubbed, and boiled. After school, Sarah and Mary helped her, and at night they baked pies that could be sold to the lumbermen.

Sarah felt a rush of confused anger at the memory of her mother's hands—hands meant to play the piano, to gently, gracefully caress keys—raw-red, knuckles swollen, veins high on their backs as they wrung out a stranger's shirt or rolled out piecrusts.

Her mother's hands had never been still. When they weren't

washing or baking, they were stitching, darning, mending, embroidering, or piecing scraps of outgrown and threadbare clothing to make a quilt.

"It isn't fair," Sarah said one night, tired of everything: poverty, school, laundry, and baking apple pies. She hated herself for talking that way. Mary never said such things. But sometimes Sarah thought she would go mad with the injustice and stupidity of it all. "It's too hard and it isn't fair."

"Sarah," her mother said. "Please." She had become taciturn, as if words were an additional burden to lift during the exhausting routines of her days. She seldom offered more than basic instructions and necessary information. Pleasant conversation had been lost on the trail west along with her newborn daughter, her son, and her weak-lunged husband. Sarah's grumblings were usually met with disinterest.

But that evening, Amelia Leigh sighed, stopped stitching, and looked hard at her firstborn. "Sarah," she said in a gentle voice. "Look at the quilt I'm working. It's made of scraps and leavings, but I've given it a pattern, a measure of beauty. That's how it is. You're given things. That's your fate. But what you make of them, the way you put them together, that's what counts."

That quilt now hung on the parlor wall and one of Sarah's own design covered her marriage bed. And Sarah tried, through the long stretches while Alexander worked the woods, through the dark times after Nicholas died, to live by her mother's words. All the same, it was still nearly impossible to stitch something fine out of loneliness.

Sarah poked a broom handle into the kettle and pulled out the white clothes, grunting and straining against their weight. She put them first in the rinse tub and then into the flour and water mix that would starch them, did the same for the colored things, then washed and rinsed the rags, hung all of it on the clothesline Alexander had run from a tree trunk to the house, poured the rinse water into the flower bed out of habit, although it scarcely needed it after the torrential rains, and, finally, scrubbed the porch with the soapy water.

Then she stumbled into the house, breathing hard, her back a solid block of pain. She sat down on the bottom tread of the staircase, panting.

"But it's done," she told her belly, patting it as she spoke. The baby was oddly silent. Strange. That happened just before Nicholas was born, but it was much too soon to even think about that.

She must be imagining it. After all, how much movement could she expect to feel while she boiled and dragged wet clothing around?

She was absolutely imagining it. There was too much time, silence, and strangeness here. The house itself was peculiar enough to make thoughts skitter in odd directions. Part Russian, part Mendocino-Maine, and completely idiosyncratic and unpredictable, it winged off sideways and upward, with room after surprising room, built for a large family or a small village, not a lone and timid city woman. Sarah had tried to ease its wooden sameness, to domesticate its corners. She painted some of the woodwork, including the great and bulky door frame of her bedroom. She had enough of gleaming woodland eyes without inviting them to share her bedroom.

She removed an unsettling carving of Nicolai's—a saint, perhaps, with a halo and a spear in his side. "His icon," Alexander explained. It upset Sarah's Unitarian soul and she put it in the window seat.

She hung up her "Sarah Elizabeth" carving and worked on a quilt made of scraps saved for years. There was even a touch of Boston in it, with her mother's velvets and brocades, which seemed exotic and foreign in the silent woods.

She covered the parlor walls with calico, mixing a flour and water paste so it would stick, and she embroidered flour sacks and made curtains of them. Alexander laughed and asked whose eyes she kept out with her curtains. Perhaps she was afraid of peeking deer?

Alexander made a bookshelf, her pride, because it meant they were civilized. She had the Bible—which she and Alexander had read through together, and which he decided was the best of her storybooks. And she had her childhood texts that she had saved and used as a teacher and hoped to use to teach her own child. And finally, she had her mother's copy of *The American Frugal Housewife*.

It guided her, as it had guided her mother, in everything from the recipe for her wedding cake—which she baked herself—to the treatment for rattlesnake bite, which she had memorized. "Cut the flesh out around the bite, instantly . . . fill the wound with salt. . . . Drink sweet oil and spirits of turpentine. . . ." She wondered what had possessed Mrs. Child of rattlesnake-free Boston to put it in her book.

Nicolai had built a large chest inside the curve of windows. Beneath its fitted lid were odds and ends: a wooden ball, a nest of dolls, and a carved bear that could move his arms and beat a drum—both had been Alexander's playthings and then baby Nicholas's. After old Nicolai's death, in went his triangular balalaika that defied all of Sarah's attempts to create music from it and his teapot, his samovar, Alexander called it. Sarah liked tea made the American way. The chest also held an intricately patterned basket of reeds and feathers

that Alexander's mother had made, and some of Sarah's past, her ancient journal and William's wooden flute, which she had carried with her everywhere. One winter, she stuffed calico pillows with shredded corn husks to put on the chest and it became both a catch-all and a comfortable window seat.

The *domovoy*'s plate still sat on the sill, although Sarah wasn't convinced that the spirit or dwarf or whatever heathen thing it was did much of a job. "Why risk annoying him?" Alexander had asked, and she couldn't think of an answer.

Sarah was an able housewife. Nothing was wasted. The oldest of rags became rugs, the last of worn clothing patchwork. Drippings and ashes became soap. Old bones were pounded and fed to the chickens to produce winter eggs.

She was busy all the time and yet no amount of activity made up for the solitude.

Sarah had read about the lone woman of San Nicholas who didn't leave her island with her tribe because her baby was missing. She never found the child and lived on the island alone for fifteen years. Then, finally, she was brought to the mainland, but she understood no one, could not find any of her own kind, and she died. Sarah, not certain if she was alone on the island or alone of her kind, felt a painful kinship with that other dislocated woman.

Something was needed to counteract the eternal silence of the redwoods—aside from the night terror of panther screams and grizzly roars and imagined rattlesnake hisses and the morning's screeches when the wild turkeys flew down from the trees and the waiting coyotes ate them for breakfast. Something was needed to weigh against fear of the outlaws and bandits who hid in the hills, or of the wild boars that destroyed crops and people too, if they weren't agile enough to get away. Alexander said the pigs were souvenirs of the Russians. He made jokes about them. Sarah couldn't.

Often she found herself wishing for the companionship of music, the pure sound of a piano.

"You should have brought yours," Alexander said. She shook her head. "Impossible." She had heard a story of someone who tried. Now, they said, there was a ghostly piano on the plains, lying on its side like a skull, the lid open, keys like teeth in a last scream. One did not take pianos on adventures.

"Someday," Alexander would say when he saw her distant expression, "a piano for Sarah. My father told me that Princess Helena had hers brought from Russia, and if that is possible, then you, Sarah,

will have one brought from Boston, Massachusetts." He loved stepping around the name of her state and he always said it in slow syllables, with a wide grin, as if it were enormously funny. "What a shame the princess didn't leave hers. We could have brought it back for you from Fort Ross." He knew nothing about pianos and had no idea what years of neglect in an abandoned fort would have done. "You'll have your piano."

He believed it, too, despite all evidence to the contrary. He had never been rich and never would be. There were hard times all over the country and harder times in the woods, and when work was plentiful, loggers could barely break even after they paid back for their lodgings, food, work clothing, and tobacco. People said the lumber company reused one payroll forever, paying it out and getting it right back. Still, Alexander hoped.

And maybe it wasn't a piano that was needed so much as something human. If only Mary hadn't gone off to San Francisco. If only Sarah had gone with her!

Sarah felt immediate guilt. Alexander was here. How could she even think of such a thing! And Mary's move had been wise and definitely for the best. Mary now had her own dressmaker's shop, a husband, and a baby.

Well, then, if only Sarah had the money or courage to visit Mary. But her heart raced at the thought of being robbed or worse by bandits. Earlier this year, when she almost felt brave and lonely enough to risk the trip, Black Bart held up the stage. His name alone gave her the chills. She knew of him as everybody did by his signature "PO8" and by the poem he left at robberies.

> I've labored long and hard for bread
> for honor and for riches —
> But on my corns too long you've trod,
> You fine-haired sons of bitches.

And if travel by stagecoach was terrifying, travel by ship was even more so. She felt ill remembering Mary dangling from a wire, rocking wildly through empty space. And once on board, she would feel no safer. So many ships were smashed into driftwood on the cliffs and rocks. One year, when she was a child, ten ships had gone down in a single night.

Another time, the alarm had sounded and she and Mary had rushed from the boardinghouse to light bonfires on the beach so sailors,

confused and lost in a tangle of splintered ships and limbs, would know which way to swim. There was a large hole on the grassy headlands, the end of a tunnel that began in the rocky edge of the ocean. The blowhole was large enough to have supposedly once sucked in an entire ship. When the wind raced through it, screaming, Sarah hurried away, because the last agonies of the drowned were forever trapped in that blowhole, doomed to shriek for all eternity, reminding all listeners of the perils of the sea.

There was no safe route through the forests or away from the craggy coast. Sarah tried not to complain, not to be swallowed by months of silence while Alexander worked the woods, further and further to the north each year. But, to her somewhat guilty relief, Alexander finally understood her silent loneliness and decided to find someone to help with the chores and be a companion.

Then where were they? Where was Alexander?

Why wasn't the baby moving?

Where *were* they?

Sarah looked across the room, past the flower-bedecked newel post to the far window. The sky had become leaden and heavy. It might rain again. The clothes would need to be brought in, to dry slowly in the house, dampening the air she breathed.

More rain. The river was already high. It would flood.

She thought of Alexander and the girl stranded on its other side, then forced the picture out of her mind. They were probably already across it, on their way here. More to the point, she didn't have a crumb of fresh bread to offer them. Time to start.

And time to stop this shameful self-pity. She had been given so many fine pieces with which to work her quilt.

She remembered a little parable of Mrs. Child's, one of her "Hints to Persons of Moderate Fortune." Sarah's mother had been particularly prone to read it to her eldest. Mrs. Childs spoke of a slovenly, lazy woman who never stopped complaining for she had been raised improperly and was unable to handle life's harsher realities.

She had, in fact, "dressed in the fashion and learned to play on the piano." Sarah smiled bitterly as she recalled those words spoken by her mother, wryly, sorrowfully, but emphatically.

This was a good place, a good room. It was secure and strong, spacious, bright with the calico and the dark gleam of polished floorboard reflecting the fire. A cat slept on the rag rug, the yellow dog was equally contented at the opposite side of the room, and there was a basket of dried wildflowers in the center of the table.

No more of this whining. She wasn't alone and she wasn't that lady "taught the piano" who complained of being cheated her whole life through. What kind of mother would she be, otherwise, going about with a face that looked like what Mrs. Child called an "imbodied growl."

She meant to begin working, but instead, she walked—slowly, heavily—to her little bookshelf and again touched its small storehouse, as if each volume were an amulet.

How these books had made Alexander laugh! He was so clever, and he'd devoured the books in a matter of weeks. Their lessons continued after they were married, although more and more often he pulled down a favorite target and instead of studying it, mocked it.

"They teach little children such ugly things," he'd said, pointing at a picture labeled "A Chinese selling Rats and Puppies for Pies." "They don't do such things!" he said. "Do they?"

"Of course not." She wasn't sure if they did or not.

Alexander was further outraged by the illustrated spelling book. "Here we see a little boy shooting his sister dead; an accident which has occurred for want of proper warning."

"Your reading is excellent," she remarked.

"'Raise a child ugly, he grows up ugly,' my mother said. She knew more than this book," he answered.

The saga of "Mr. Tom Plump" ended their time with the primers. The unfortunate character vomited while sailing to California, grew thin out West, returned home, grew fat again, and then drowned when his bulk broke a bridge.

"Your bookwriters are barbarians!" Alexander said. "Maybe I wouldn't have learned to read if I had known how stupid your books are!"

After that, they relied on Bible stories.

There had been lots of good times. When Alexander was home, when they were together, Sarah's life contented her. Alexander said she had taught him to smile again, and she delighted in the way his slatey eyes crinkled at the corners, in his enormous laugh that filled every inch of the house.

She loved his joy in life, the way he broke into songs of his own creation and spun her around until she was light-headed.

And she loved as well what transpired at night between them. Each time he left, she felt herself harden and forget, but the sight of Alexander or the sound of his voice always brought back the passion of that first glance, that first night. Still, more and more often, those

bright times together seemed too brief and unsubstantial to balance the heavy dark times when she was alone in the woods.

She sat down on the window seat to rest, then stood again, lifted the lid, and, looking for a piece of herself, found her old journal. "I am afraid of Indians," she read. "I am afraid of dying." She had written so little, recorded almost nothing of her inner or outer life. "William is dead of cholera." "Papa died today. May God bless him." And later, undated, half an entry, familiar, if incomplete— "I am afraid of"—she was never to know what she had feared that time.

She took the journal to the table, found the pen and ink, and opened it to a fresh page. And what was she to write now? Only the same message. "I am afraid." No longer of Indians, but of wildness, of the unknown, of what happened to guiltless infants. She snapped the book shut and put it back in the window seat.

She hugged herself, shook her head. Alexander would surely be here very soon, before the storm broke. Meanwhile, Sarah had to get the bread and cake ready for him. The wash could wait. Sarah's back, a pulling, tugging arc of pain, hurt too much. Besides, the helper girl would be here very soon and she could pull the clothing off the line.

She awoke in confusion, cold and aching. Slowly, before she moved, the contours of the room around her took shape. The kitchen. A low fire glowed in the fireplace. Sarah slumped over the table, her head near three loaves of fragrant bread.

Her neck felt as if it had been axed. Her back was definitely broken.

But as fuzzed and dense as her mind was, something poked at it, something that was wrong, that had forced her out of her exhausted slump.

She sat up straight and strained to be awake, to locate what so bothered her.

It only took a second.

The wind moaned around the house. And it was a wet moan, a throaty, drowning sound.

Sharp sheets of rain whipped like waterfalls against the windows.

No Alexander. No helper-girl.

The wind rushed up from the ocean, down from the heavens, taunting her, filling the river, imprisoning her on this side, alone and ill and . . .

She must stop this destructive talk! She wasn't ill. She didn't feel well because she had washed all day and slept through the night with

134

her head on a table. God would punish her for always thinking the worst, for not trusting Him, for not making the most of what she was given, for—

She stood up and breathed hard. Every part of her felt swollen and beaten. But she had to face it. She reached for her cape, fur trapped by Alexander and thick enough to keep out the worst rain and cold. She reminded herself again what a lucky woman she was.

She opened the door. The storm-heavy night was thinning. She could sense dawn.

Her linens, bedding, and dresses sprawled like slovenly ghosts in mud, floated in puddles, twisted around bushes and ferns. The night-gown she had made so many years ago and worn so seldom through the night had blown onto the porch and lay like a shroud at her feet.

She wanted to howl, to wail, to curl up like the baby inside her, and hide, refuse to continue, refuse to be a part of this endless struggle.

Shouting, sobbing, she gathered the ruined wash into a streaked and stained mountain at the side of the porch, and stood above it, her belly protruding like a sister to the laundry pile. Nothing, not even the high Sierras and the threat of winter death years ago on the trail had ever looked as formidable and forbidding as the ruined wash.

The wind and rain pummeled the house, the earth, and the entire world.

She couldn't bear this. And wouldn't. She would lie down, sleep until Alexander was home and she was safe.

Except—the cows needed milking. She pulled her cape tight and turned toward the barn. If she didn't do it now, she never would. It would be like the wash, overwhelming and impossible.

She could not find a comfortable position in which to milk. Sarah's stomach seemed everywhere and she laughed at the sight of the swollen udder above her swollen stomach. "Two cows together," she said.

And then she gasped.

It had started. Too soon, much too soon, and Alexander wasn't back, and the cows still to be milked, and—another contraction seized her.

Too soon! What did this mean? How could the baby survive the world so soon? "Not yet," she cried. "Wait and rest, grow strong and big. You must live." She struggled to her feet, her arms out as if seeking, blindly, the safe place.

But the cows could not go dry, and she returned to the stool,

concentrating on her hands. Pulling, pulling, filling the milk pail, pausing only when a contraction knotted her into immobility.

She forgot her resolve to be brave and cheerful and remembered only the storm, the distance to the house, the miserable pile of wasted energy on the porch, the pain that ripped from back to front, wave after wave, the wrongness of it. And Alexander, far away with, she was sure, a wild and impassable river between them.

She was alone. The universe disappeared and there was only Sarah and her pain and terror.

She finished milking and left the pail there, to be kicked over. She stumbled and sobbed, splashed and fell in and through the rivulets and puddles that filled every crack and gap in the earth. She gasped for breath and leaned against a tree as a contraction froze her in place, then once again pushed with all her might against the wind and storm. The house receded with every step. But she would not deliver this baby, this baby that had to live, in the barn or on the wet ground. She pushed on.

She knew what the river must look like by now, swollen yellow and brown like a bruise, churning with mud and branches and roots. She remembered the mule struggling and flailing on the way west. Alexander would die if he tried to cross the river.

But he wouldn't—he wouldn't, couldn't know that this was an emergency. That something terribly wrong was happening.

And then, finally, she reached her door. A fierce gust hurled her in, then it swept around the room, twisted the curtains, blew the basket onto its side, and flung the dried flowers in every direction. The "Sarah Elizabeth" shuddered off the wall and crashed, breaking into pieces. The open door screeched and banged as the wind battered against it.

Sarah's eyes focused on some deep place inside herself. She put her shoulder to the door and pushed, then pressed her back against it until finally, straining, she locked out the storm, the wind, the world.

There must be something she could do, something she could find out to do. Mrs. Childs, she thought, but she had already looked. There were no entries for childbirth. Sarah had searched for that along with "confinement," "birth," "infant," "delivery," "newborn," but the book offered no assistance.

Because you weren't supposed to need a book for that. Mrs. Childs might tell you how to endure poverty, but even the most wretched

woman alive wasn't supposed to be completely alone while delivering her child.

There was no one and nothing except this vast, strange house, and even it looked different now, as if waiting for something. After the roars and crashes of the storm, the sudden silence overwhelmed her, an expectant, distant waiting, an engulfing yawn combining all the fearful silences she had known—the night her father's coughing stopped, the day on the plains when the other wagon had been stilled, her brother, her mother, Nicholas.

Oh, Nicholas! Now this one—this one she would not love at all until it was tall and strong and grown. This one—she gasped, and steadied herself against the door. Her sodden cape fell to the floor.

"I cannot do this!" she screamed. "I cannot—" The pain silenced her, slicing her through, then coating the halves so that she stood rigidly, afraid to breathe or move. Through a red haze she saw her filigreed name in pieces on the floor, dried flowers around it. Her name and marker, ruined.

It would never matter who she'd been. She'd live and die and make no difference, and only loneliness would keep her company in the end.

The contraction subsided. She must calm herself, must think clearly, must do what was needed. She took a deep breath, pushed herself away from the door, and slowly staggered to her room, the room with Nicolai's animals guarding its entry. Another contraction seized her and she shouted out in rage and pain and fury, banging her fist against the door frame. "No!" she screamed. "No! This isn't fair!" She pounded again, so hard the skin of her hand was scraped by one of the buried animals, but still she hit again and again, beating out her fury at life's betrayals.

She dragged herself to the bed. The little animals silently echoed her cries, howling and lowing and blindly following with their painted-over eyes as she lay down under her quilt. She touched a patch of emerald velvet and remembered a concert, a harpsichord, beautiful solemn notes like a fountain.

She put her hands on her enormous taut stomach, poised them for prayer. She would not scream again. There was nothing to fear. Alexander was on his way. There were no vultures circling, no savages behind a rock. "The Lord is my shepherd," she said. The rain pounded on the roof and windows. She clenched her hands into fists as her body worked to free the baby. All would be

well. This baby would live. She would not be defeated by this rain, this house, this life, this wilderness. "I shall not want. . . . He leadeth me beside the still waters. . . . Surely goodness and mercy shall follow me . . ."

PART III
1 8 7 2

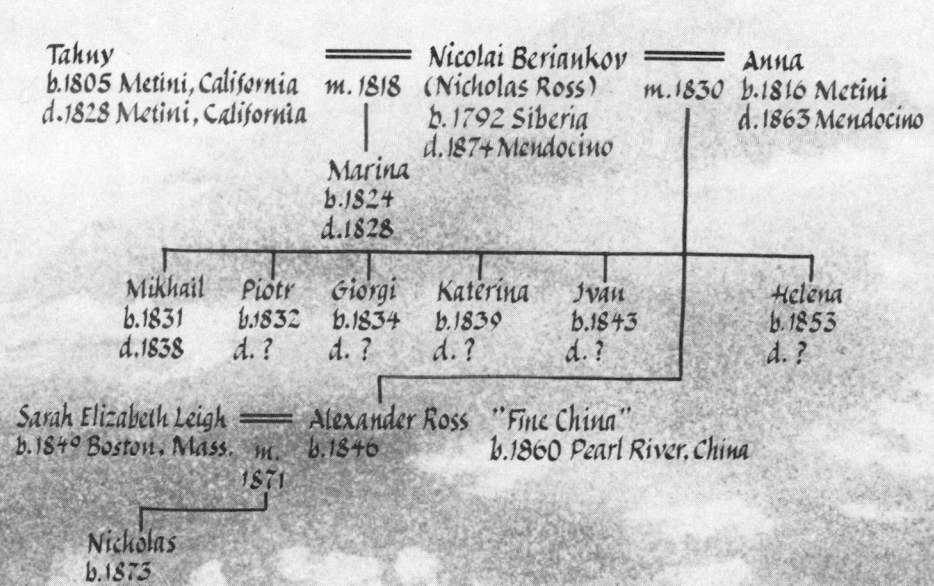

Tahny
b.1805 Metini, California   m. 1818
d.1828 Metini, California

Nicolai Beriankov
(Nicholas Ross)   m. 1830
b.1792 Siberia
d.1874 Mendocino

Anna
b.1816 Metini
d.1863 Mendocino

Marina
b.1824
d.1828

Mikhail   Piotr   Giorgi   Katerina   Ivan   Helena
b.1831   b.1832   b.1834   b.1839   b.1843   b.1853
d.1838   d. ?   d. ?   d. ?   d. ?   d. ?

Sarah Elizabeth Leigh   Alexander Ross   "Fine China"
b.1849 Boston, Mass.   m.   b.1846   b.1860 Pearl River, China
                       1871

Nicholas
b.1873
d.1874

11

"Such a little thing," he said. "Such a pretty little thing."

She looked down at the small carpet and pulled her shoulders in toward her body, trying to hide her shudder of revulsion. He was thick and burly, his whole torso furry.

She closed her eyes, blocking the sight of him, of his feet, hairy, white, and sickly like blind cave animals.

It did no good. She could still smell his sweat and whiskey stench.

Surely, if he put his beefy hand on her she would crumple, collapse in on herself and die.

But when he touched her shoulder, she stood there, head bowed submissively, pretending that her silk sleeve was protective armor. Every pore of her body closed against him.

She had seen what happened to girls who resisted. When she'd been in the Old Mother's house a short while, another new girl refused to service the men. She screamed and cried and begged for release, and all that her defiance won her was starvation and beatings. When the rebel was broken, the Old Mother made all the other singsong girls circle her. "Pay attention," Old Mother said in her piercing voice. "Listen well." She ended each sentence with a fierce smack on the side of the girl's head.

"You are finished with tears?" *Smack!*

"Yes."

"You are finished with refusals?" *Smack!*

"Yes."

"You are not a stone girl who has no place for a man?" *Smack!*

"No."

"You will do whatever a man wants whenever he wants it however he wants it until he is satisfied?" *Smack!*

There was one moment's hesitation. The watching girls saw the blur of flesh as Old Mother's hand thwacked with extra force.

"Yes! Yes! I promise!"

The Old Mother rocked back on her heels. She was a wiry woman with horrifying strength. "What happens if you break your promise?" she demanded.

The girl cowered, crouching on the floor. She had seemed so beautiful and strong only a few weeks earlier. "You will send me away," she whispered. "Lock me in a crib in the gold fields or the railroad camps."

"Where there are no women, just hungry men waiting to have you," Old Mother added. "And what else will happen?"

"The hatchet men will cut me. Or brand me."

Old Mother turned and circled the girls. She glared at each one in turn. "He'd do the same to all the rest of you!" she screamed. "Never forget it!"

China never had. Behind her eyes, she braced herself against the man, but her body stayed in place.

"They call you China, right?" The hairy man's voice underlined all the threats and loss and grief. She tried to answer him, but her throat constricted with fear.

"Shy, ain't you?" His breath was foul, coating her like decay. But it didn't matter, didn't touch her where she crouched deep beneath her skin.

The man chuckled, enjoying her discomfort, her smallness, her silent complicity. "How old are you?" he asked, and when again she couldn't answer, he shook his head. "What's the matter, no speakee English? You look nine, ten. A little young, maybe."

For a moment, her pulse accelerated with relieved anticipation. He looked as if he might actually back off. Then she realized how furious Old Mother would be.

"I'm twelve." Her voice was low and strained.

He clasped the silk that covered her small, new breasts. "Not a baby, then," he said. "Not at all." He began to undress her, roughly,

142

impatiently. He would rip the fine silk. Old Mother would be angry. China undid her own gown.

"Can't wait, can you?" His voice was the growl of a hungry dog protecting his meat. "Am I your first?"

He wasn't the first. The first had mud-stained clothing and wild black hair with streaks of gray. He had paid extra for the privilege and he had left bruises on her hips and arms and deep inside her.

Maybe she should lie. They all wanted to be the first, another girl had told her. Why? It had been terrible, so frightening and brutal and painful. Why did they want it, unless every awful story about white men was true—that they loved to hurt Chinese, wanted to eat their brains, boil their eyes.

She couldn't lie, anyway. There'd be no blood this time. Perhaps, by now, there would be no pain as well. The older girls said it stopped hurting, but it hadn't yet for her.

She shook her head.

He shrugged. "Don't matter," he said. "But you Chinks sure start early, don't you?" He pushed her onto the small bed, smothered her with his whiskey breath, his pale dead skin, his bulky hands. The only refuge she had was her mind, and she escaped into it. Away from this place, from this house, from this country. Back, back to a foggy memory of the Pearl River Delta, of a family so desperately poor they let their youngest daughter live only so they could fatten her for four years then sell her. How many times had China questioned the harsh first life that had shipped her to a new world in which she'd been reborn on a landing dock and renamed after the label on her packing crate womb. The customs inspector, amply bribed, let the four-year-old girl pass. And from then on, she was known as "Fine China, Product of Canton."

The man pushed and shoved inside her until she thought she would split into bloody fragments and die. But again, she did nothing of the sort. Neither did she cry out, or even whimper. It hadn't stopped hurting. In fact, the pain grew worse as each man hammered into her the inescapable facts of her life and destiny. She was here until she died, and the only relief was knowing that death came quickly to slave girls.

Would her family have sold her if they'd known she'd wind up a slave, a singsong girl? They had been told she'd be a rich man's servant. As she had been until a few months before.

It was the blood that ended it. China had screamed at the sight. "I'm dying!" she told the merchant's stern wife. After explaining

womanhood to the sobbing girl, the mistress of the house took a few hobbled steps back on her tiny feet and surveyed her servant. "Breasts," she muttered. She herself was one stout cylinder, like a sausage. "I'm selling you."

"No, please," China begged. "How have I offended you? Is my work not—"

"He'll notice soon enough and want you as a concubine."

China felt a rush of shame, as if she had done something wrong. She had seen the merchant eye her as if she were a steamed dumpling waiting on his plate.

"I'll tell him you were stealing," her mistress said. And two days later, while her husband was away on business, she took China to the barracoon, the selling room. It had been eight years since the first time she had stood there naked, examined like a piece of livestock and sold to the highest bidder, but every minute of the humiliation returned full force this second time.

Her price had tripled. She was a valuable, rare commodity. It was becoming harder and harder to smuggle women in past federal inspection, so prices had risen. Besides, she was no longer a risky small child. She was an attractive pale-skinned young woman, "ripe" as the Chinese doctor standing nearby and chanting out her health and primeness called her, even though she had big unbound feet. She wished she were hideous, deformed, so that she wouldn't sell.

She wished it again now as the man crushed her into the bed. Let her be a twisted monster no man would accept.

The man grunted. He had satisfied himself. But nothing was over. Downstairs, another hairy nameless man waited.

It was the monthly blood that had brought her to this house and it was the monthly blood that would keep her. Like every other slave girl, China had put her thumb print on a "contract" that day in the barracoon. In exchange for money, which she immediately gave to the merchant's wife, her seller, she promised to "prostitute my body for five years. If in that time I am sick one day, two weeks shall be added to my time and, if more than one day, my term of prostitution shall continue an additional month. . . ."

Every month's predictable "sickness" added yet another month's term.

Her contract bound her with unbreakable chains. "If I run away," it said, each word read to her in a hard voice by the master, and frequently repeated by Old Mother, "or escape from the custody of

144

my keeper, then I am to be held as a slave for life."

"Can't believe there are still slaves in this country," one customer had said. He was a kind man, more gentle than most. "Haven't you heard about Mr. Lincoln's Emancipation Proclamation? About the Civil War?"

"It is not for Chinese slave girls," she answered softly. That's what the master had said and he must be right, because the many, many slave girls were no secret. New shipments of girls were reported in the newspaper along with other imports. Fish, silk, shoes, and slaves, all with price tags. The police, lawyers, and courts all knew and looked the other way, just the way the inspector who considered her fine china had done. And, she noted, even this concerned gentleman who disapproved of her enslavement still came and used her.

Time passed. By her thirteenth birthday, China was much in demand. Her fine features and delicacy won many admirers and gifts so that now she wore a gold butterfly clasp in her piled-up hair, a ring of silver and white jade, another made of a small gold nugget, a bracelet of ivory carved into delicate floral filigree, and earrings that resembled golden bells.

She was very lovely on the outside with her intricate hairdo, her gowns of sky blue and apple green silk, and her jewelry. But inside, she felt herself unmade. She still disappeared, ran away to her mind, hid through the night in the safety of her imagination. No voices or threats broke through its walls, no foreign flesh impressed itself on her. There was nothing but sky, sun, space, and solitude.

Sometimes she felt as if she were going blind because so little that was human or real was allowed to pass through her eyes and into her brain.

There was one exception, a waiter named George Low who worked at the house. Through long-separated snippets of conversation, China learned that he had worked on the railroad, then been one of the thousands of abruptly unemployed men. He had planned to return to China, but had been robbed by a white man against whom he was not allowed to testify. The law, long forbidding Indians to testify against white men, had been amended, redefining the Chinese as Indians. All George had left after the robbery was his clothing and a permanent limp from the beating he'd received.

Now he worked as many jobs as possible, trying once again to earn passage home.

George Low was different from anyone she had known or seen. He

was young and slender, unlike her old master, the merchant. His skin was sleek, hairless, and smooth, unlike the men who filled her bed and body. The house was for whites only. "Chinese will start my girls on opium," the master said. "Besides, the whites wouldn't like it." So George was all new to her. Best of all, he was kind.

Not that any of it mattered. China was a slave, and even if she someday had enough jewelry to sell to earn her freedom, no Chinese man would touch her now that she'd been degraded by whites. But still, when George Low ran by with trays of drinks for waiting customers, keeping his eyes discreetly to himself, saying nothing, his very presence comforted her.

A few times each month, the Daughters of Joy were taken for walks outside along with Old Mother, the master, and highbinder guards, their razor-sharp hatchets hidden inside their wide sleeves. It was not safe for a Chinese woman to be alone on the street. Even a respectable woman could and had been kidnapped and sold—often after being disfigured—to service lonely men in the hinterlands.

They walked in guarded groups through the congested, narrow streets, taking the air. Sometimes they went to the theater, but more often, the walks were simple exercises, or lessons, as when they were led down foul, narrow alleys lined with crates the size of small rooms. The crates had slatted fronts, bars through which the "parlor" half with its few furnishings—a rug of sorts, a chest of drawers, and a mirror—were visible. A drape shielded the back half, but sometimes China caught a glimpse of washbasins and pallets on wooden door forms. Each crib held up to six girls, dressed in dark blouses and little else. They pressed against the slats and shivered in the chill and fog of San Francisco. Sometimes they called out to the highbinder or the master. "Chinee girl much much nice. Seventy-five cents for dooee. Twenty-five for looksee."

Their voices followed the group like an ugly song.

"See them?" Old Mother said. "Now remember what you saw. You want to live in a cage on the street? That's what happens to girls who don't cooperate. You have it good."

They turned the corner and Old Mother stopped walking so abruptly that China bumped into her. "I'm sorry," China began, but then she realized nobody was paying attention to her. Old Mother faced a tall American woman dressed in the hard fabrics of her kind. Half the people on the street stopped to watch the exotic outsider. China stared in complete and open fascination. This was her first

white woman. She was surprised that the woman was hairless, smooth and completely unlike men of her kind. Not that she wasn't strange enough with her tight hairdo, stiff skirts and bodice, and her large-boned hands. But she didn't seem as foreign, as much a different species as white men did.

Neither Old Mother nor the white woman said a word or made a move, but for a long, paralyzed moment, they glared at each other as if engaged in a bitter struggle.

Which they were, George later told China during one of their hurried hallway conversations. "No wonder Old Mother was furious. Must have been a missionary woman," he said. "The ones helping girls escape."

They heard footsteps and parted quickly, but George's last words had been enough. For days, for an entire week until they had a chance to speak again, China hid in the safe place in her mind, but now the words *escape* and *the ones helping girls escape* filled the space and expanded it so that she could hear nothing else.

"How?" she demanded of George.

"What?"

"How do missionary women help girls escape?"

He didn't know. But he left the bagnio every night. He had the freedom to explore, and he could find out.

It appeared, he announced weeks later, that there were two white church groups, Presbyterian and Methodist, who had buildings, rescue missions, where they gave refuge to slave girls. A dozen or more girls had already found shelter there, the first after being saved from drowning and refusing to speak to anyone but a "Jesus man." But it was dangerous to try, George said, and there were many pitfalls, ways escapes were unmade, bad possibilities.

China stopped listening. The word *escape* rang, reverberated, and echoed. The place she hid in her mind changed from a vague, sky-bordered space to a house in Chinatown, earthbound and safely guarded by a white woman in hard clothing.

Escape. Escape. She would tell no one, not even George. She trusted him as much as she could trust anyone, but even so, even if he turned out to be braver than he seemed, if he helped her instead of telling on her, then his life would be in danger for having told her. The streets were festooned with red paper ads seeking murderers to do away with specific and named victims-to-be, and she did not want George Low's name on red paper.

But how was she to do it? Even if she knew where the missions

were, she didn't know the streets well enough to find them. And when? Not in daylight, of course. Then after everyone left. Very, very late. But would the mission women be awake? Would they hear her knock—if she could find them? Did the highbinders guard the house all night long?

For the next several weeks, China, always with an excuse, wandered the house late at night. She had trouble sleeping, she said, tiptoeing across the soft carpets. Her stomach was upset. She thought there was another man waiting. She was hungry, or thirsty.

And she learned that even highbinders sleep. That even Old Mother, after enough wine, or perhaps opium, sat sprawled on a chair, eyes closed, mouth open and snoring, her keys rattling with each in-and-out breath.

One night George approached China in the hallway. He spoke rapidly and quietly. "I watch you at night," he said. "I understand. Let me help. I can wait outside and lead you there. Make a sign the night you choose—touch your throat as we pass." And then, almost as if he had said nothing, had never even existed, he was gone. Her heart raced wildly, insanely. It could happen. It would happen.

It could.

It would.

Five nights later, terrified by the idea of escaping and by the idea of not escaping, she passed George in the hallway and abruptly, without planning it, lifted her finger to her throat. He nodded and continued on his way so quickly, she wasn't sure he'd even noticed the signal.

The dozen or so times she had been permitted outside, Dupont Gai had been packed with noise and humanity. Now, a few hours before dawn, it slept in a blanket of fog, snoring in exhaustion in crammed boardinghouses or, drugged and oblivious, in subterranean opium dens.

It was almost quiet enough to hear her blood rush every which way.

China stood outside the building that had been her prison for nearly a year. Her hand remained on the door. The street and beyond terrified her. It wasn't too late to turn back, to creep up the stairs. Old Mother would still be snoring.

At least she knew the dangers behind the door.

What if any of the warnings had been true? What if the Methodist lady really did boil Chinese girls' eyes and eat their brains?

Her mind chattered, argued back and forth with itself.

Suppose, then, that her brains would indeed be eaten. Was that worse than those thick hands, the sweat, the smells? Would it hurt more than a slow death? Than the "hospitals" for sick and diseased slaves—cubicles with an oil lamp and a cup each of rice and water. Death by starvation was hoped for, but if it didn't happen quickly enough, then strangling was the cure when the supplies were gone.

Her heart pounded so loudly she was sure the noise echoed off the walls of the house and into the night. She had no idea which way to turn, where to go, what lay at the end of the escape if, indeed, anything did.

George hadn't noticed her signal. Or had, and had changed his mind.

Safer to return to what was known, however it was. She put her hand on the doorknob and silently pressed the latch.

Like a phantasm, George appeared and disappeared in the mist. And then he was solidly beside her. "Now!" he said, pointing. "Quickly!"

She swayed in place, pins of fear holding her fast.

"Now!" he repeated. Then, looking both ways for hidden high-binders, for hatchets whizzing toward them, he touched her hand where it clutched the door. "Let go," he said.

"I'm afraid."

"Of me?"

She nodded. Of him, of the unknown, of Methodists, of the city, of anything as improbable as a white savior. Of what was behind her, inside, and what was unknown around a corner, down an alley.

George looked incredulous. "China," he said, "in there is death. Out here is life."

He was right, but she was afraid to listen. She had no words to describe the pain inside her. She had heard women describe child-birth and she felt as if she, too, would explode with something need-ing to be born. She wasn't large enough to contain hope, let alone to permit it to breathe.

He didn't care. "Run!" he said. "Now!" He pulled at her arm until she let go of the door and the past, and she ran in terror because there was nothing else to do.

The cobblestones were wet and treacherous. For once she was grateful that she didn't have lily feet, that she could move swiftly and ably. And with each step away from Old Mother and the feel of that night's men, her tread was stronger, her back straighter, and the pain inside her softer, lighter, until it became buoyant and carried her up

149

the front steps of a house and lifted her arm to the knocker.

The woman wore a cap and a nightdress with a shawl around her shoulders. She didn't seem at all surprised by the pounding.

"Save me!" China cried, suddenly frantic and terrified that someone would see, that a hand would pull her back into the night.

"Child," the white woman said, waving them in. "No need to cry. You're safe here."

China meant to apologize for the sudden tears, but she couldn't control them and so she continued to cry and shake her head. The Methodist woman led her to a chair, all the while patting her shoulder until her sobs quieted. Then the woman turned and carefully scrutinized George.

China had nearly forgotten him.

"What do you want of this woman?" the Methodist woman asked.

"I wish to marry her."

China's lips fell apart. "But," she said softly. "But I have been with whites. I am . . ." She was fouled, disgraced, unworthy.

"Are you willing to wait the year?" the Methodist asked George, as if China were not sitting nearby, still sputtering in surprise.

George nodded.

"To pay her support? Five dollars a month?"

"Yes," George said.

"But I . . . a year? But . . ." China's gasps and protests floated around the spare room like wisps of fog, burning into nothing as they passed.

"Then you'll come here with a proper marriage license?"

Once again George nodded, and so did the Methodist woman. They had reached an agreement.

"Say good-bye now," the Methodist woman said. "You won't see each other for the year. That way nobody can suspect, nobody can harm either one of you." She pulled her shawl tight around her robe and busied herself with papers on a side table. She did not appear the sort of monster who would boil a Chinese girl in oil or eat her body parts.

"George." China spoke with relief, wonderment, appreciation for his many kindnesses, and a measure of unease, a fear that once again she had been an object to be bought and sold.

"Is it all right?" he asked, his eyes troubled.

He had handed her back herself. Her future hadn't been decided without her. "Yes," she said softly, and the creature inside that had insisted on birth and life expanded and filled her.

"I've never seen your smile before," George said. "It is lovely." And

150

then the Methodist woman turned and cleared her throat, and he left.

I'm safe, China told herself. Safe. It became a song, filling her. Safe, safe inside a large house guarded by a large-boned Jesus woman and clever regulations. Safe. And George Low is going to marry me. I will be respectable. A wife. She had never let herself dream of anything so improbably momentous, so preposterously grand. It was almost frightening to relax and allow joy and relief to pour into her long-frozen body.

Fog still blanketed the world the next morning. China awoke from a deep sleep and studied her room with delight. Her bed was her own and so was her night and her flesh. She luxuriated in the unbroken quiet, listened to the mournful warnings of the foghorns on the bay, looked out the window and saw misty colorless shapes and shadows. It was beautiful. Perfect. She stretched, and lay down again, smiling to herself.

And then she realized that something was wrong. There was noise below, angry, loud voices that didn't fit this house.

Chinese voices.

China left her little Methodist cot. She crept to the top of the staircase.

She recognized the voice of a waiter, Old Mother's close friend. "We have a warrant for her arrest!" he said. "She's a thief."

"A thief?" The Methodist woman sounded surprised—but possibly convinced?

Nobody could believe that of China. She had nothing but what she'd been wearing last night.

The waiter continued. "My mistress is missing several things: a gold hair clasp shaped like a butterfly, a silver and white jade ring, a gold nugget made into a ring, an ivory bracelet, and gold earrings shaped like small bells."

China's hand, the one wearing the gold nugget ring, froze in place on the stair rail. Then she ran forward, down the stairs. "No, missy, no. The rings are mine. The clasp is mine. They were gifts. They were—"

There was a policeman next to the mean-eyed waiter. He looked at China with impassive blue eyes and shrugged.

"I find it hard to believe this little creature is a thief." The Methodist woman was tall and bony, but she looked frail next to the policeman.

151

"Perhaps so, ma'am," he said, "but I have to follow the law." And with that, China was dragged out of the building, all her songs of safety left behind.

The jail was dank, fog seeping through every porous inch. China sat in misery, head in hands, waiting to die of chill and shame.

"You're in luck," the guard said, surprising her. "Bailed out."

It was not a luck to be desired. Old Mother and the worst of the highbinders stood on the other side. "You know what happens to girls who run away," Old Mother said.

It wasn't the Methodist woman with her sad eyes who would boil and eat the runaways, it was Old Mother and her cohorts.

"You're going to the gold fields," Old Mother said. "To a town with no other women, so you'll be busy in your little cage."

"I think maybe a few lines on that face might keep her from wandering again once she's up there," the highbinder said. "Besides, it's been so long since they've been near a woman, they won't care if she's pretty or not." He allowed his hatchet to be visible, and he stroked the edge of it to make his point.

"You're lucky girls are too valuable to kill," Old Mother said.

China tried as hard as she could to stay small and invisible and inside herself, to banish all thought, keep her mind clear, a small pond with one fish circling, again and again. But a whip of steel cut through her mental waters and then again, a memory of the deep scars she had seen on some crib girls, and tears seeped over her soon-to-be-ruined face.

She was upstairs in a room, guarded. They had taken the rings and earrings away. For some reason, they forgot the butterfly clasp, and China tried to think about it, beautiful in her dark hair, ready to flutter away to freedom.

She was very hungry, but didn't dare ask anyone for a thing. They were probably going to starve her. So far, nobody had touched her, except to tie her hands behind her. Her face was uncut and she was still in San Francisco, not on her way to the gold fields. Of course, no more than a few hours had elapsed, and perhaps it was only a brief reprieve, but even so, she was grateful and tried to stay silent and unnoticed.

She thought about her life, a confusing progression of jostlings, of arms lifting and repositioning her into worse and worse situations.

152

She could make no sense of it. The only thing she could do was endure, once again turn to stone, will her mind elsewhere and force her heart to sleep.

She wondered if George even knew what had happened.

And then, for the second time that day, she heard a racket a flight below. It was too early for customers, and besides, unless they were drunk, they didn't carry on that way, pounding and shouting.

Her guard became more alert, moved closer.

"We're sick of this business!" from below.

She'd heard that voice before.

"Every time a girl escapes, you people try a new trick! Last time you pretended your man was a husband. Before, it was false documents. Now it's a trumped-up arrest! Enough of this! Give her to me!"

It was the Methodist woman from the Asylum for Rescued Prostitutes. China had loved the name, rolled it around her mouth. Rescued Prostitutes. She'd been rescued. And then unrescued.

She heard scuffling, angry protests, hard footsteps on the stairs.

And then her guard lifted her as if she were a flour sack and ran up another staircase and then one more. He paused in front of a panel, pushed it, and China saw a tiny corridor, a secret room beyond.

The footsteps grew louder. "Where are you, girl?" the Methodist woman shouted. "China? China? Upstairs?"

The guard whipped a long knife from his sleeve. "Not a sound," he whispered, "or I'll put you down and slit you open." He looked into the secret room.

"Go up, then," the voice said from below.

Her guard deliberated, then made a decision. He took her off his shoulder, yanked at her tied arms, and pulled her, stumbling, behind him. Up they went once more, up and out through a skylight and over the rooftop. A man on the roof of an adjoining building stared at them impassively, as if this were a normal sight. The edge of their building was a foot or more from the next roof. China stopped all motion.

"Jump across!" her guard said. "Right now! Jump or I'll kill you on the spot." There was a clatter, loud clomps approaching. "Jump, girl!"

No, China decided. I'll jump, but not across. She looked down the narrow space between the buildings and took a deep breath. The fall would be quick, the end on the street five stories below immediate. It had been foolish to hope for anything better.

153

But the moment, the chance was lost. The highbinder grabbed her, half lifted her, and in one long leap pushed and pulled and carried her across the opening.

Stumbling all the way, she was propelled toward another rooftop door and pushed through it and down a series of fetid, dark staircases toward the bowels of Chinatown.

She was led into a dimly lit room no bigger than a closet. The highbinder closed the door, grunted, and settled down across from her. For several long minutes, his wheezy breath was the only sound breaking the dark silence of their cramped quarters.

Then footsteps resounded on the stairs. The highbinder inhaled sharply. Once again she felt cold metal against her throat. "Say anything and it's the last thing you'll ever say," he growled.

"Nothing's here," China heard. It was a man's voice. The policeman's.

"The man on the roof said they went down this skylight." The Methodist woman's voice was as strong as ever. "She's in here somewhere."

"The man on the roof lied." Old Mother's cranky voice was particularly shrill.

"Ma'am—"

"Don't the police help honest people, too?" the Methodist woman said. There was banging, shouting, pounding. And then their door rattled.

"Why is this one locked?" the Methodist said. "China, are you in there? Say something!"

The knife was icy against her. He clamped his other hand across her mouth. His breathing became fast and hard, like the men she serviced every night. If she bit him, freed her voice, no matter how hard she might scream, no matter how furiously the Methodist and the police might force the door, China would be dead before they could save her. No rescues. No asylum. And if she was to die, she wanted to choose it with her own hands, and not give her death like a gift to the excited man pressing against her. She held her breath and tried to back off, push against the wall and away from the knife.

The footsteps faded, then turned. They had given up. Her life was over.

There was a babble of protest in Chinese, a round of English. Then the combined noise moved closer. China barely breathed. Please, she prayed. Please, please.

And again, the Methodist woman's strong, undaunted voice. "And

154

I say she's in this building and I'm not leaving without her. What's in that locked room?"

More protests, confusion, and then shouts, footsteps, the crunch of wood splintering, the door giving, and the faint light of the dim hallway.

"China!"

The highbinder pressed harder against her throat.

"Do something!" the Methodist woman shouted.

Reluctantly, the policeman acted. "Drop it," he told the highbinder.

"She's a thief," the highbinder protested. "She's—"

The Methodist woman acted as if he were a tiny insect in her way. She bent and untied China's hands and hugged her as if she were her long-lost child.

This time the Asylum was a true fortress. Nothing penetrated it. One night, as China tried to sleep, she heard her name called harshly from the street below. "I put your picture in a coffin with a corpse, China," the voice screamed. "You'll be sick in a week—the spirit of the dead will come find you. You'll see. You're cursed, China. Already dead."

But China, warm in a clean bed, smiled. Once she had been cursed and dead, but now she was reborn. Every night she silently recited the story of the chase over the rooftop, the broken door, the rescue. That had been the day of her true birth. Now she was a little baby, learning the ways of the Jesus people, learning how to be a proper American and a proper wife. Why should she be afraid of curses in the night?

12

The iron was cold. China put it on the heating rack around the circular stove. She moistened her finger with her tongue, pressed another waiting iron, and, hearing the low sizzle, brought it back to her ironing shelf at the wall.

The Golden Mountain. The phrase had run through her mind like an ironic laugh all day long.

The Golden Mountain. California. George still, despite everything, sometimes called it that.

China put water from her bowl into her mouth, then expelled a fine mist onto the man's shirt she was pressing. Golden Mountain indeed. It wasn't the work that bothered her, although she was one of the only women working in a laundry. Or working at anything aside from prostitution.

Of course, she was one of the only women in Chinatown except for the rich merchants' wives, who managed their homes and were visible only on rare holidays or religious outings.

George hadn't wanted her to work. But he did want the two of them to return to China.

"This China can help us reach that China," she insisted with a smile.

"That's another thing." He shook his head. "It isn't right that you

carry a name from a packing crate. You're my wife, a woman, not a piece of merchandise. I'll call you White Jade, or Lotus Blossom, or Great Treasure. Yes, that's it, Great Treasure."

"It embarrasses me," she said softly. "Too fancy. Let me be who I am." Still, sometimes as she stood over her iron she liked to think of herself as George saw her. Great Treasure. She savored the words and pressed on the iron. Every penny moved them closer to passage home, but the pennies came slowly and painfully.

They lived behind the laundry in a sliver of the building divided into even smaller portions by thin partitions and threadbare hangings. To China, used first to the rich merchant's quarters, then the gaudy generous spaces of the brothel, and then to the clean, large Methodist Asylum, her cramped married "home" was cherished for what it represented, but not for its physical attributes. George, however, had come another route.

"Compared with the boardinghouse, this is a palace," he said. "Ten of us slept in a room there. My bed—my slab, really, my shelf, like the one we iron on—was this wide"—he held his hands a foot and a half apart—"and hard."

And before that, the railroad camps had been even worse. When he had first told her the stories, China had had trouble believing them.

"It took seven months to pay back my passage," he'd said one night shortly after they were married. "By then, I knew I wanted to leave the railroad, but if you did, they beat you and forced you to stay. Nobody but Chinese would do the work they wanted." His face, normally serene and forward-looking, turned inward and bitter. "And still they paid us less than the whites and worked us longer hours and made us pay for our food. All that so I could get in a basket, be lowered into canyons to plant dynamite. Sometimes it felt easier to stay down there and explode, end it once and for all rather than pull back up and face another day. But the worst for me was being kept prisoner underground a whole winter."

The Methodist women had taught her a great deal about America, all as magical and distant as their wonderful stories of Jesus and miracles, but even they had never spoken of cities under the earth. "Where can you live underground?" she asked. Exhausted as they were after the long days, as urgently as her body cried for sleep, she treasured and tried to prolong the times when they talked with each other, exchanging lives and ideas. At those times the world was both exciting and comfortable.

George laughed. "It was not exactly living. But you can survive

157

underground if Crocker makes you work Donner Summit through the winter of Sixty-Six. The camp was buried under snow. We dug chimneys and air shafts and burned lanterns all day long. That's what I most remember, the unending dark. It turned you strange, made you crazy for a glimpse of sky, of sun, the smell of clean air, of openness. All winter we drilled and blasted and hauled rock. In the spring thaw we could finally see the world. We could also see the bodies of the men torn away in slides." He shook his head. "'Coolies' they called us. Do they know it means 'bitter work'?"

And all that money, all those meager meals so that a few pennies more could be saved, all those snow-smothered winter nights dreaming of return passage, of becoming *gum san hock*, a returnee from the Golden Mountain, a rich man in his village. All those dreams that made the work and danger bearable, gone to the hands of robbers who knew they'd never have to fear a day in court if they chose Chinese victims.

And still George wasn't defeated, and his enduring optimism convinced her that they would, indeed, return to China someday soon. Perhaps she would find her true parents, although she couldn't imagine how. She couldn't even remember her given name.

The laundrymen spoke to each other while they worked, and the accumulated weight of their observations and fears hung like a storm cloud against the ceiling. The Golden Mountain was tarnished. San Francisco was not a good place to be Chinese. There was a whole different America from the one the Methodists described.

Old Lee was an unofficial and always depressing historian. He stood in small crowds of men listening to someone read the newspaper and so he knew bad stories near and far from home. It was no good in all of California.

"Shhh!" the men would sometimes say to Old Lee. China said nothing. It was strange enough to have a young girl work in a laundry, but she wouldn't shame her husband by chattering. Besides, she didn't want Old Lee to hush. She wanted to know.

"I've said so for years," he now insisted. He was able to have long arguments while pressing the finest and most delicate garments, and never did his vocal fury make his hand miss a fine turn of lace or an intricate pleating. "Since the Pacific Coast Anti-Coolie Association started."

"That's so long ago," another man grumbled. "Why don't you forget it?"

"Because *they* haven't!" Old Lee shouted. "How do you feel when

158

they march with torches against us? Protesting us? How do you feel paying special police because we can't be protected by the city? How do you feel about all the groups formed against us—the Knights of St. Crispin, the Industrial Reformers, the Workingman's Alliance, the People's Protective Alliance, the—"

"Names, Lee! We're sick of your names."

Old Lee folded the shirt and moved with fury and a red-hot iron toward the next item.

They were all trying to get back home, back to wives and children barely known. They had never intended to stay, but the Golden Mountain had withheld its treasures, and so they still worked in factories or fields or as domestics in a world short of women. Or they laundered and ironed. At least for that they were tolerated. Without them, before them, the men of the Gold Rush years had paid a fortune to ship dirty laundry to Hawaii or China for washing.

"I've seen it all myself, Lee," a sour man said. He twice had had his forty-dollar passage home and twice had lost it playing fantan. The fact that he was not alone in this pattern offered no consolation. "No point in dragging it up every day."

"But I tell you it's getting worse."

They stood in their blue cotton blouses, trousers, and stockings in the thick heat of the laundry. China felt sick and weak.

If only it meant a child was growing in her. She knew there was much to pity and lament in the world. She knew things were bad outside and growing worse. She knew there were laws passed against the Chinese every day and that an ugly undercurrent of violence charged the air. She knew their life was harsh and unlovely, and still the only thing that truly grieved her was her barrenness. She wanted to give George the son he deserved, the son who would assure him tranquility beyond the grave. The Methodists had taught her a great deal about Jesus, but that didn't mean she had to forget ancestor worship. Hadn't Mary had a son? A girl went to her husband's clan and was of no use, but a boy was forever. Still, a year, then another, and yet more slipped by with no child.

"You're young," George said. "And you work so hard. It will be fine."

But she was old enough and she worked no harder than her mother undoubtedly had on the river. Two years earlier, China had gone to the nearby joss house to pray for a child. Up and up the stairs she had climbed to the uppermost floor, where nothing used by human hands could come above the gods.

159

She bought her candle from the priest, clasped hands, and bowed in front of the god, lit candles and incense, and called the god by name three times.

When she threw the wooden pieces in the air, to her great relief, one fell oval side down and one fell flat side down, which meant the god wanted to listen to her. So she took the bamboo cylinder filled with the sticks of fate and shook them until one fell out.

The priest looked at its number and consulted his book. The god's answer was cryptic, despite burned offerings and additional prayers. "Eventually," the priest told her. "Eventually your prayers will be answered."

By now, she felt that she had waited through the eventuallys. She feared that her insides had been ruined forever, polluted by white men, that she was being punished for having let them enter her rather than choosing death.

Perhaps she should go back to the priest and buy a curse instead, let the priest burn it, exorcise it, call upon the devils who had poisoned her insides to be gone.

Except that every penny spent elsewhere, even to buy candles and incense, was a penny lost to their passages.

So time dragged on, punctuated by stacks of freshly pressed laundry inside and a growing and unclean miasma outside.

They survived the Cubic Air Ordinance, requiring each adult to have five hundred cubic feet of living space. Chinatown was seven square blocks and no San Franciscan would let it expand. If they even tried to walk out of the area, boys threw stones and called names. Nonetheless, although there was no alternative, it was now a jailable offense for a dozen men to be squashed on shelves in one small room, breathing each other's stale air. Until, that was, so many Chinese were imprisoned for their congestion that the overpacked jails were guilty of breaking the law.

The Panic of 1873 had hit all of the West, even their small and steamy workroom. The East's unemployed clattered to them on the brand-new railroads, and among their luggage was a growing hatred of the Chinese, who worked for low wages. The feeling was shared by the locals, who also faced hard times.

One day Old Lee had come in to almost gleefully recite what the *San Francisco Chronicle* had written about all of them. "Who have built a filthy nest of iniquity and rottenness in our midst?" the paper asked and Old Lee repeated. "The Chinese. Who filled our workshops to the exclusion of white labor? The Chinese. Who drives

160

away white labor by their stealthy but successful competition? The Chinese."

It wasn't fair, it wasn't true, and it wasn't even sane. When George and the other Chinese had protested their low wages on the railroad, had gone on strike, they had been starved out until they capitulated. Why now should the whites interpret the Chinese need to survive as some malevolent trick directed against them?

Why were they marching at night with those torches, shouting angry threats?

Even mild and optimistic George finally reacted. "You won't believe the new tax they created!" he shouted.

China waited patiently, in some surprise. George liked to pretend that events outside the laundry and their back room were not important or related to their lives.

"If," he said, "if your laundry employs a horse-drawn vehicle, you pay two dollars per quarter."

"But George, we don't have a horse or horse-drawn—"

"No, that isn't all. If you have two or more vehicles, you pay four dollars each quarter."

"But, my husband, we have no—"

"Yes!" he shouted. "I know! And that is the true white insanity, because if I have no vehicles at all, like most Chinese, then I have to pay fifteen dollars per quarter!"

She sat back, stunned. Sixty dollars a year! It was more than an entire passage home with some left over for gifts.

Old Lee was arrested for violation of the Cubic Air Ordinance, and as if that weren't bad enough, while he was in prison, the "Queue Ordinance" was passed, saying city prisoners had to have their hair cut to be one inch long. Old Lee's long braid was sheared off, and when he returned to the laundry, it was as if his manhood had been robbed away.

China and George worked harder, ironed more rapidly, more precisely, so that never did a portion need redoing. But still, the price of two tickets seemed overwhelming and impossible. China tried to eat still less, then worried that perhaps that was why no baby could take hold and be born.

And outside the world turned more sour. In 1875 the Bank of California failed and set off a financial panic that shook the already weakened state economy. Earlier, the stock market had plunged, and the price of silver had dropped. All of that was related by Old Lee in his angry iron voice. China could not understand what relevance it

had. She didn't even know what a stock market was, but suspected it was like the barracoon where she'd been sold like a mare or a sow. She was privately happy it had collapsed.

The next year, the wheat crop failed and fruit and cattle in California were affected by drought. Real estate slumped. Jobs were scarce. Tourists traveled east for the Philadelphia Centennial Exposition instead of bringing their money to California.

"It is not our fault that silver is worth less or that it doesn't rain or that people with money aren't making as much!" Old Lee shouted.

But his voice only reached the other workers' ears, and outside, the whites massed and joined together—the Anti-Chinese Union of San Francisco was formed, as was the United Brothers of California, both to drive out the Chinese and to discourage all employment of them. And it wasn't only in Chinatown that the cancer grew. In Gilroy the Order of Caucasians was formed. In Truckee, a Chinese house was burned and its inhabitants were shot as they tried to escape. Those arrested for the crime were acquitted with public approval.

And then the fury at home enlarged and took on a face and a leader. Denis Kearney, a drayman, seized the fears and forged them into the Workingman's Party. Their slogan was, "The Chinese Must Go!" Kearney said publicly that he'd fight until the streets of Chinatown held enough Chinese blood to float their bodies into the bay.

And, though San Francisco festered worst, it was only the ugly tip of an enormous boil. There were killings reported all over the state.

"We have to leave this country," China told George late one night in spring.

"Ah, China," he said, "this is a moment's insanity. We've done nothing wrong and they'll realize it. This will pass like everything else."

He was older than she and a man, presumably wiser, but no other evil she'd known had simply passed. People had to escape, fight, or die. Why didn't George understand?

She wanted to sell the butterfly hair clip, but George objected. "Something beautiful as that..." He shook his head, unable to find the right words. She thought she understood. Although she no longer wore her hair in the formal and elegant upsweep or decorated it with golden ornaments, it seemed important to hold on to one lovely and graceful thing, to remember the possibility of beauty, even if trying to forget how it had arrived to flutter and nest in her hair.

Besides, times were hard and much jewelry was being sold and the

162

buyers were not generous. The delicate gold filigree would bring almost nothing. It wasn't worth the loss.

Every night, while summer fog blanketed the streets and found its moist way into their dark, windowless room, China counted their money over and over, as if the pressure of her chilly fingers and the sheer intensity of her need could make it grow.

"Maybe," George said during one of her counting sessions, "I should answer a red poster. Become rich fast."

There were still advertisements for murderers printed on bright red paper and brazenly posted on Chinatown's streets. More surprising, the job was calmly described and the proposed victim named.

"One's up today. It pays six hundred dollars," George said. "A fortune for the rest of our lives in China."

"George!"

"Six hundred dollars, China! Imagine!"

The worst part was that she did imagine it. She saw them both on a gangplank, luggage and gifts in hand, two unimaginably wealthy people from the Gold Mountain embarking for the homeland in triumph.

"Ah, China, a highbinder has probably already done the job. I am not the type. And what would the Methodist women think of you now?" George had an odd half smile on his face.

"I said nothing!" she snapped. "I was thinking of . . . something else altogether."

"Such as?"

She searched her mind, thought about the laundry in the next room, about their tiny back room with its peeling walls, and low smoke-smudged door off a wet alleyway. She looked, sniffed, listened, in search of an excuse.

"Yes, China? What was the something else altogether?" He was grinning now, thoroughly enjoying her discomfort. "Or were you truly contemplating murder?" He laughed. "It's all right."

"No," she said. "No, George, I—"

He stood up and stretched. "But it is all right, my wife. As long as you don't really—"

"No, George," she said urgently. "Listen. Outside." She spoke in a low and frightened voice. Her ears had indeed found something that made her alert and wary.

He stopped his gentle joking and stood tensely, and then he, too, looked worried.

There was a growing roar of male voices. Low, growly voices, not

163

the cadence or peaks and valleys of their people's tongue. This was a white crowd, a mob. This was the nearing sound of white fury.

"What could it be?" China whispered. Even the terrifying parades, the men carrying torches and chanting, hadn't had this disorganized edge of madness. She opened the doorway and walked into the alley. There were already other Chinese standing there, silent and impassive, waiting.

She heard the sound of many feet, of malevolent laughter, shouts, encouragement one to the other. "Kill them all!" somebody shouted. "Vermin!" and "The Chinese Must Go!"—the Workingman's Party theme, Denis Kearney's refrain. Not until George put his hands on her arms to steady her did she realize she was shaking.

They heard female screams and pleas combine with the male rumble, and the noise was near, coming from the street in front of the laundry.

There were no groups of women in Chinatown except prostitutes. Why were they screaming? Why were they outside?

China edged away from the laundry's side walls until she could see the street that joined her alley. She saw backs, boots, broad shoulders—and then a glimpse of a silky bright pink, a leg, an intricate and ornate upswept hairdo. She heard a scream, a protest, a deep bass laugh, a smack, another male voice, another scream.

And then, through the legs and muddy boots of the Workingman's Party men, she saw what was happening. The men had emptied out the house of women and were using them, taking them, probably killing them, one man after another, right there in the foggy street.

"Get out of their sight!" George said, and, without waiting for her to respond, he pulled her back into the doorway.

Get out! echoed in her mind. Get out! They want you dead.

The fog in the distance turned a dark, thick pink and a gust of hot, acrid air hit them. "Fire," George said. "They're setting fires."

The men in the street waiting their turns with the women commented on their comrades' actions. "Burn them all!" one shouted. "Every damned laundry!"

The speaker was standing directly in front of one. George and China were behind it, trapped with no exit but the maddened mob in front. They held tight to one another, barely daring to breathe.

But as the minutes and then hours passed, while George and China waited, while the sky lit up in a dozen other smoldering pink outbreaks, the mob outside their particular building remained intent on destroying women, not laundries.

164

In the morning, Old Lee braved the still rampaging crowds. "There's a committee of public safety," he said. "They'll stop this. Bringing in the army, navy, and militia. A man told me. This'll be over in an hour."

His brief foray into optimism was ill-founded. Nothing was over in an hour or many hours. The military help was augmented by volunteers armed with hickory pick handles. But even the pick handle brigade, as the would-be riot quellers were soon called, couldn't control the furious mob.

Inside the laundry, the workers maintained a routine, although bursts of angry noise startled them into immobility so that they frequently stood like baffled statues, fresh linens or irons held high, frozen into place with no clue as to what to do next.

George insisted on making his deliveries. His white clients wouldn't understand the chaos in Chinatown and he couldn't afford to lose their business. When he came back the first time, his clothing smelled of smoke. "They've burned more," he said.

"More what?" Old Lee demanded.

"More laundries. Like last night."

China put down her iron with such force that the bone in her arm flashed with pain, but she said nothing. Neither did anyone else, so that George's words joined and darkened the dim misty air they breathed and filled their lungs and hearts with their poison. And then George filled his baskets, put his yeo-ho pole at the ready on his shoulders, and was gone.

When he once again entered the laundry, he was changed. He looked like a man under a curse, the subject of fables and warnings, a doomed man. His blue jacket was torn, and the skin it showed was scraped raw, slowly bleeding. His hat was ruined, the bamboo shattered, the palm leaves ripped. His face was streaked with soot. He didn't respond to China's gasp, to Old Lee's immediate questions. Instead, he turned and, almost carrying him, led in a man.

A half-man, half-dead thing. Head bleeding, crouching in pain, the man collapsed onto the laundry floor. George found a piece of clean linen and, after washing the blood from the man's face and temple, he carefully tied the bandage around his head. Only then did he look at the other workers and at his wife.

"When will it be over?" China whispered. "Will no one stop it?"

"I was near the wharf, near the Pacific Mail Steamship Company." George's voice was slow and weak, weighed by exhaustion.

They all knew the Pacific Mail. It had transported all of them to the New World.

"There were hundreds of them," George said. "Setting fires and then stoning the new immigrants getting off."

They all looked at the pitiable heap of man sitting dazed and in pain on the floor. George nodded.

"They threw stones all the way until we were at Kearny Street. He wasn't the only one bleeding, scalp wide open. Many were hurt worse, but nobody stopped the stone throwers, nobody arrested any of them."

"Welcome to the Golden Mountain," China whispered, half to herself.

That night, long after the new man had gone back with Old Lee to his boardinghouse, after they had eaten a hurried meal that could have been made of anything for all they could taste, George and China took turns as sentry. Now, George dozed fitfully as China sat listening and waiting.

Gunfire ripped through the night, and although it was at a distance, each barrage shot images of the vicious stone throwers, the men with torches, the destroyers, and their pathetic victims, marked by the shape of their eyes, by their long pigtails, by their language.

She didn't bother to count their money that night. She knew the sum and knew it was too little to buy them freedom. Furthermore, they had lessened it that very evening, giving the newcomer enough to feed him for a few days, for surely he wasn't going to be able to earn his rice bowl for a while. Besides, even if they'd had the necessary eighty dollars, hadn't the men set fire to the ship that might carry them away?

They should have gone long ago. She had known it deep inside her bone marrow and she should have found the strength to make George understand.

She fought the urge to cry. It would do no good. Still, her eyes smarted and filled, even as she cursed this weakness.

And then she realized that her tears weren't caused by memories or regrets but by the men with torches, by smoke curling toward their room.

"Fire!" she screamed. "Fire, George, fire!" She was already on her feet, gathering their few pots and dollars, their meager possessions, while George struggled out of sleep. She half-pushed him out the low door, into the alleyway, toward a back street.

166

They moved, automatically but fearfully. China had never been outside the small boundaries of Chinatown and the world beyond it was even more dangerous than the one she already knew. But there was no choice.

"Where?" George finally asked, his voice desperate. He shook his head as he walked, as if arguing inwardly with himself. "They massacred Chinese in Los Angeles. They drove us out of the gold country. Where, China? Into the ocean?"

She took a deep breath. She had thought about this over and over every night as she counted the money that would not grow. People could either move or stand still. If they stood still now, they would die. If they moved, there were only so many possible directions. To the west, they'd drown. To the south or east, they'd meet with more stones, more beatings, more massacres. There was only one way left.

"A long time ago, I heard of a place, all rocks and ocean and giant trees." When she'd first heard of it, in the House of Joy, it sounded like the place she'd created in her head. Sky, mountain, trees, sun, and water. Safety. "We'll go there," she said. "We'll go north."

They looked up at the sky, trying to find a bearing, but it was thick with smoky fog stained pink with fires and so they walked in the only direction they could, which was simply away.

"This place of trees," George said after a while. "What do they call it?"

She worked very hard to say all the many sounds she had heard years earlier. "Men . . . do . . . ci . . . no."

"Mendocino," he repeated softly in the dark, and in the fog and soot, fear and dislocation, that word promising a safe place to the north was their lodestar.

13

China's embroidery lay forgotten on her lap. Outside the window, below her, in every visible direction, Mendocino City busied itself. Even during these hard times, it was a compact, busy mill town. Fresh lumber ready to be loaded onto ships lay in great stacks near the headlands. Millhands, loggers in from the woods, and merchants pursued business and pleasure in the shops and saloons of Main Street. Up at the corner, wet laundry hung on lines stretched from the wash house.

She studied the town day in and out, observing women as they shopped for sundries and staples or tended their houses and lives. Their homes fascinated China, who had seen only the cramped dark streets of Chinatown and a blurred series of isolated farmhouses, furtively glimpsed in the dark during the flight north from San Francisco. Her image of home was a tiny, smoke-stained room, so cramped and airless that the cooking space was outside the front door.

But here, at her window, she studied the Americans' spacious houses, each set in its own square of land like a valuable jewel, then decorated with carvings, fancy swirls, and cleverly shaped windows and porches. Even the watertower that accompanied each house had fancy scrollwork on its deck rails. She wondered what so few people

did with so many rooms and watched what she could of their outdoor and public lives. Women swept away the ever-present sawdust, hung laundry—only, China assumed, to collect more of the dust on it— cut flowers from the vines and creepers growing against their fences, talked with neighbors, and tended children.

White women. Strong, visible, free. As fearless, she was sure, as their great long strides, uncovered smiles, and easy, outdoor lives suggested.

No one had ever crated or sold them. No one had threatened to float them out to sea in their own blood. Perhaps that was why they walked the streets with no apparent worries.

She and George had been trained differently, and had agreed that China should not travel around Mendocino herself. She was safe here in the boardinghouse, but as it was primarily populated by loggers, there was no one for her to talk to. There were Chinese in the county, hundreds. But their women, when they had them, were respectable and therefore invisible.

China was afraid of even meeting such a wife, fearful that she would unwittingly give evidence of her shameful past. She envied the other wives their blameless histories that had rewarded them with the most important thing of all, children. She sighed. Her lonely silent days underlined her barrenness.

She looked beyond the white women and men and their town and world onto the horizon, where the ocean rippled like a rich, wrinkled carpet.

Her days were spent by her window, marked by the shrieks of the mill whistle, by hope and anxiety. If George and she could save the impossible-sounding eighty dollars for their passages, if they really someday crossed that watery carpet to its other side, where, exactly, would she find herself? And who would she be? She would be as much a stranger and outsider there as she was here. She didn't know her family, would come to George's with nothing, not even a proper name. Perhaps she'd be considered American, a foreign devil. Perhaps those respectable matrons could see through her and know, like respectable matrons everywhere, that she had been the white man's singsong girl.

She sat so rigidly her green silk jacket was smooth and unwrinkled. Sometimes it matched the sea. Today, the Pacific was slate and silver, light-starved under growing clouds.

The dark sky set off another round of "what-ifs" and "what-thens." The rains would begin and the logging would end. That was good.

The boardinghouse would fill to overflowing with loggers "homing in" until the weather cleared. And George would be with her, safely out of the woods.

But it would also be bad, because what would they do for money? They could live off their meager and depleted savings like the rest, but then year after year they would be no closer to their two passages across the ocean.

Perhaps she and George would move south for the wet months, to Gualala, where someone said that Chinese ran the mill. Surely George could learn an easier, safer job than the one he now had in the woods.

They had fought about it. They had fought about almost everything.

"You don't have to do that. I can work!" China had insisted. "You know that. There's a laundry down the street. Or I could be a housemaid."

"No," he'd answered with equal firmness. "You cannot."

"But I know how to do those things, George. The Methodist ladies taught me. I am an *excellent* house—"

"My *wife cannot!*" His outburst startled and visibly upset him. When he continued, it was in a gentler voice. "I want you to rest. To eat. To become stronger."

I want a child is what he hadn't said, but meant.

"But water slinger!" The words were peculiar, as was the job.

"It's nothing. I'm used to a pole on my shoulders. So now it holds buckets of water, not bundles of laundry."

She shook her head. At first it sounded easy enough to run alongside ox teams throwing water onto the skids that made the logs' passage easier. But then she'd thought about George weighed down by a yoke with a five-gallon can of water on each end. And she thought about the size and fury of both the oxen and the enormous redwood logs. What was George compared to such giants? A wisp, and a lame wisp at that.

"We do it in turns," he said when she pressed. "While I refill my buckets, another man slings his water."

"But—"

"No buts. There are no other jobs, China! These are hard times. I'm lucky to have any work at all. The crews were already in the woods. Even if they'd let Chinese do it, I'm not trained to be a bull puncher, or a bucker, or a sniper, or a swamper—"

170

"I don't know about these things. I only know—"

He tried to deflect her by pretending she had asked a question. "A bull puncher drives the team. He has a stick with a metal brad at the end to help, to punch them with, you see?"

"You can't run back and forth with your bad—"

"The peeler's job is *much* more dangerous than mine. They peel off the bark and the fallen tree could be over a canyon, or on a slope. They wear boots with nails sticking out so they'll grab the—"

"Your leg, George! Your limp! How did they hire you with your limp?"

He looked ready to deny that he had any infirmity whatsoever, then he shrugged. "I stood still and they didn't see. It doesn't matter. Didn't we get here on our feet? I'll do the job the same way."

And for what? she asked herself. They paid water slingers less than anyone else. They would have almost nothing left of his salary once his room and board at the camp were paid.

"I have one last question, please," she finally said. "Why is this job available?"

"What do you mean?"

"What happened to the last water slinger? Why is there a job for you now? Please, I'm afraid for you, I—"

He was thinner than ever and looked much older than his years. He sat down on the edge of the bed. "This is where we wound up. And the thing this place has is woods and trees, a safe room for you, and a job, not a beating, for a Chinaman. I don't know if there's any other place that has that. When there are no choices, China, what's the point of questions?"

Since then, during his infrequent and brief visits back to the boardinghouse, they avoided the topic altogether.

And when he was not there, she sat in her isolation, watched the horizon, studied the movements of the town, and waited. Sometimes she was afraid to think what it was she waited for.

She looked back at the bustle of Main Street. And then her hand flew up to her mouth to stifle a gasp. Four men moved in unison, a plank between them.

And someone—someone still, someone unmoving—was on the plank.

She clutched the arms of her chair, shook her head, and looked away. It wasn't possible. It wasn't thinkable. It wasn't bearable.

She sat on her hard chair in this distant corner of the world feeling

171

hollow. Questions, like flying insects or demons, pushed and clawed at her cavernous insides. Her mind responded with a viselike clamp, smothering, silencing, squeezing the words to death, unanswered. There were no answers.

Hands shaking, she picked up her embroidery again. She had stitched flowers she saw from her window. She had been told the names of some—daisies, poppies, and the difficult two—azaleas and rhododendron—ungainly words hard to think, let alone say. Other blooms remained unnamed but equally lovely in lavender, yellow, rose, and orange. Suddenly, her handiwork seemed foreign and bizarre. For whom was it designed? What would China do with it? The imagined field of flowers sat in her hand like a reprimand. This pretty meadow was not her life. Her life was George Low, limping beside enormous oxen, trying not to clash with their heavy, lethal hooves.

She looked back at the gray sky, the sea that was like a wavy mirror of it, deceptively calm, hiding its violence and danger. She must control the fear, retract the dangerous assumption she'd admitted into the world. But the fear was a sharp cramp, clear and painful in her abdomen. She stared out to sea, neck rigid. If she refused to look at the men below, the men coming to the Chinese boardinghouse, the men moving with no rush because there was no life on that plank, the men carrying a man whose face she recognized—if she denied their existence, she would never have to feel what their mission meant, never have to live the rest of her life with that horrible knowledge.

He had saved her. That gentle, hard-working, loyal, and brave man lying crushed on a plank had shown her the way out of her cage and then been trapped himself. Why was she made so that she couldn't save him in return, no matter how many vigils?

She turned herself into stone, then bitterly laughed at the image. Stone women. That's what they called the ones who couldn't or wouldn't have sex with the customers. She never found out what it was that made them impenetrable. Maybe a gift, a magic talent. They were the only ones sold back out of slavery. If only she had been one.

Well, she would be one now. Stone woman. She set her jaw, lifted her head, and looked far, far out to sea, and even when the knock on her door came, she sat like a rock in her chair.

The landlord would have to let them in. She wouldn't. She couldn't.

*　*　*

172

She reminded Alexander of a bird in a windstorm, trying to hide when there's no hiding place, trembling all over, barely balancing.

Poor little thing, he thought. What'll become of her? It was hard believing she was Low's widow. She looked no more than a child, but there she was, speechless and shaking, eyes wild with grief and terror.

He looked away. Viewing her grief seemed an intrusion. It was one thing to be asked to carry somebody out of the woods, and something altogether different to face the survivors knowing there was no comfort or solace or even real help you could offer.

He was certain this girl was alone in the world. If she had family nearby, why would she be living in a boardinghouse, waiting for her husband's infrequent visits?

Still, he hoped he was wrong, hoped she had people. Alexander's memories of family were green and glowing. Until Sarah, his brothers, sisters, and parents had been the only safe island of the world, a cushion and shield against all the hard blows.

It was a childish concept, he knew, and history had easily and brutally given it the lie. In the end, his family hadn't been able to shield or protect even itself from danger. But still, the idea of family burned like the very light of life, and he was grateful for Sarah who, in her own Boston way, had eased his most bitter memories and restored whatever he remembered of joy. She had made his past and present bearable. Surely the new baby would be sturdy and the future would also open wide. And perhaps there would be more children until his house was once again full of life.

"Anybody speak Chinese?" Josef asked. He was an enormous Finn who thought he was whispering when he was close to a bellow.

The three others shook their heads.

Mrs. Low stared at her dead husband.

"We should leave. We done our job," Timothy said.

"Leave? What way is that to treat her, man?" Alexander glared.

"Maybe we're interferin' with her grief," Timothy said. "Maybe there's stuff they do. Private Chinese stuff. I don't know what good we're doing her."

"Maybe the landlord can translate for her," Josef said.

"What for? What's to tell her? The name of the bull that got him? How the whole team went over? How long he lay there, waitin' till there was wood to take out along with him?" Timothy was perspiring despite the overcast day. "She can see the only stuff she needs to know."

173

He was too engrossed in his own discomfort to notice the effect his words had on George Low's widow, but Alexander had noticed her wince as soon as the bull was mentioned.

"Ma'am," he asked softly, "do you speak English?"

Her eyes slowly moved from her dead husband to Alexander. But when they met his, they were blank and uncomprehending.

"Chinese women don't speak Eng—" Josef began.

"Yes," she said in a strangled voice.

"Ma'am," Alexander said, "we're sorry about your husband. He was a good man."

She nodded.

"The other men at the camp, they asked us to tell you, too. They all liked him and send their condolences."

"Thank you."

"Ma'am, is your family near?"

"I have no family." She stood straight, clutching one hand in the other as if holding on for dear life.

"Then, ma'am, I don't mean to pry, but what will you do?"

"Ross," Josef hissed, "this ain't our business."

But it must be. What if this were Sarah instead of a tiny Chinese child-widow? Would anybody take a moment to care about her welfare? And this girl didn't have a milk cow or a piece of ground with which to feed herself.

At least Sarah had the house, the land, a cow and sheep and horses. And the yellow dog for comfort. She had once confessed, half-laughing, half-crying, that often during the months Alexander was away, she'd lie on the floor close to the yellow dog just to hear him breathing, to have a response to her words. A cocked ear, a thumped tail, a wet nose on her arm meant that she wasn't the only living creature on the planet.

Poor, lonely Sarah. Dear God, let this baby live.

He looked again at George Low's wife, who didn't even have a yellow dog.

The two women held his attention, side by side, alike only in their solitude.

"He wanted to go back to China," the widow said abruptly. "That was all he wanted, and now how can I—" She buried her head in her hands. Her back shook, but she made no noise as she cried.

"Ma'am!" Alexander said, unable to contain his sudden excitement. "What if—"

174

She looked up, her hands still covering her mouth. Her eyes were puffed and pink, bruised deep within. She waited, tears balancing on her lower lids for what seemed an eternity. Then they spilled over and silently ran down onto her fingers.

What had he been thinking of? It was too soon. Who knew what this silent fragile creature wanted? And he hadn't even asked Sarah. But he would today, when he was home. And he was positive she would agree.

The other men were also waiting for his great excited revelation. Embarrassed, Alexander coughed, looking at his hands, and then realized there was something he could do. He turned around, dug into his pocket, and found his money, then counted out half of it. Sarah would have to understand.

When he turned back and she saw his hand, she shook her head.

"It's from the company," he lied. "For you."

Her eyes, dry for the moment, viewed him with complete distrust.

"They always do that," he insisted. "You don't think they'd leave a man's wife stranded and penniless, do you?"

She raised her head and he could see how regal and strong she was capable of looking. She said nothing, but she knew that the money was from him. As far as the lumber company was concerned, George was no longer their employee, and therefore of no interest. This woman knew it. And he could see that, yes, she considered the lumber company—and all white men and groups—capable of anything. Perhaps incapable only of kindness. He knew that view of the world, but it made him uncomfortable to know that she considered him part of the enemy camp.

"I'll leave it on the table," he said softly. "And, ah, the company's asked me to see how you're doing in a few days. See if there's any way else we can help." And, with a few more words of condolence, Alexander Ross and the three other loggers backed out of the tiny room.

"Look, George," she whispered. "Your ancestors are across that water. I'll get you back to them, I promise."

China sat on a large rock on a grassy seaside bluff next to her husband's grave. She had buried him on a pretty site facing his homeland. In spring he would be under a blanket of poppies that would put her best embroidery to shame. For now, the ground was spongy with recent rains and the sky was as winter-drained and bleak as her future.

175

In the week since his death, she had struggled with two questions —how she would ever afford to have George's bones sent home for their proper rest and how she herself was to go on living. So far, only wrong answers appeared. She was unwilling to approach the men who ran the local laundries for fear of being sold again, put to use as a prostitute. It didn't matter that she was now a respectable widow. Proper merchants' wives had been kidnapped in daylight in the streets of San Francisco and sold into slavery, so why wouldn't the same thing happen to an undefended eighteen-year-old?

She thought about the Methodist Aslyum with real yearning. No men but Jesus. But between Denis Kearney's men and the lethal highbinders, San Francisco was too dangerous to reenter, even if she could make her way alone down the coast.

She couldn't trust the Chinese and she wouldn't trust the whites.

And even while China wondered how she could keep paying her board after the money left by the white man ran out, her landlord made it clear that he wasn't comfortable with an unmarried female in his house anyway.

Her questions and problems had worn themselves into painful wires that cut across her mind. What could she do? Where could she go?

There was, indeed, no place on this earth for China Low. If she ran from one danger, she bumped into another.

"Ma'am!"

She was jolted out of her reveries. Except for the landlord, the only man who had addressed her in a year lay underground. She jumped to her feet.

"Remember me?"

How could she forget him? The tall one. White, but not terrifyingly so. Smoother, less hairy, easier in some way. He was the one who'd left the money, pretending the lumber company had provided it. She was ashamed of herself for taking it, but what should she have done? It had paid for George's funeral and for her room and board.

"Alexander Ross," the man said. "Your landlord told me where to find you."

She backed away.

He ignored the move. "I was thinking, ma'am," he said, "that you're in need of a place to stay. . ."

Her mouth grew tight. He wanted to take her home with him, to

176

make her another white man's singsong girl. And she had thought, for a moment, he was different, a kind man.

". . . and work, and I might be able to help out."

"Mr. Ross," she began in her most severe voice. She tried to imitate the Methodist woman's tone when facing Old Mother. "I appreciate your concern. However, I don't need help."

"But with no family, with no place, I thought—"

"Many men think all Chinese women—"

"I have a house outside town—"

"Especially when their families are not near—"

"It's pretty lonely, and—"

"Mr. Ross! I am a respectable widow who—"

". . . my wife needs a friend."

". . . will not tolerate being treated like a . . . your wife?"

He nodded. "Yes. She's expecting a . . . she's tired now, so it would be a real help if there was somebody there, and then, when the baby's born, she could really use some help around the place. We have a cow and sheep and the usual and—would that be possible? Help with the chores and the wash—all that. We'd pay room and board and a small salary."

She stared at him, unraveling all the skeins of misapprehensions that still crisscrossed her vision and confused her.

"Won't you say something?"

Was she to trust a white man? Travel to his faraway house? But the money—the money would pay for George's bones to be sent home.

"Maybe I misunderstood," he said. "Maybe your English isn't . . ." He cleared his throat and spoke again, very, very slowly, gesticulating, acting out his words in clumsy charades, pronouncing each one laboriously, separately. "My. Wife. Needs. A. Compan . . . a *helper*. She . . . you . . ." He pointed his finger at China, cleared his throat, and started up again. "You. Could. Could you? Do. You. Know. How. To . . . um . . ." He made the motions of sweeping, of scrubbing.

China covered her mouth to hide her smile. He was so tense and strained, battling for comprehension, pushing words and gestures around as if they were boulders. "I understand," she whispered from behind her hand. "I was . . . surprised. And yes, the Methodist missionaries taught me to keep house."

"So then," he said, "do you accept?"

His eyes were an unusual color. Bluer than the winter skies above the cemetery, but sharing their potential for storm and sudden

change. Blue enough to be dangerous. She shook her head. "I'm sorry," she said softly.

"Why not?" He stood up and paced around. "Why on earth not?"

"I can't explain."

"Why?" he asked again. "My wife's a good woman. She'll treat you kindly and fairly. And you need work and a place to live, so why won't you accept?"

He stared at her as if she were transparent, as if he could see into her very center. Maybe he could, and then he'd read the answer she didn't dare say.

"Are you *afraid?*" he asked, convincing her that he truly could see her heart pounding below her skin. "Of my wife? Of my house? Of the work?" He waited. His eyes, piercing her through, demanded an answer. "Of what could you be frightened, Mrs. Low?"

Nearby trees rustled in the rising wind and the tall grass rippled and billowed. Out at sea, storm clouds lay in wait. She saw that nothing but the truth was going to end this interrogation. "Of you," she whispered. "I am afraid of you."

He seemed stunned. "But why?"

How could he not know? Didn't he wonder what had forced George and her north? Didn't he know what his kind was doing to her people? She tried to think of ways to soften the truth, but there were none, so she simply blurted it out. "Because you're white." She tensed her shoulders and readied herself for a violent response. Perhaps he would solve all her problems by pushing her off the cliff.

Instead, he rocked back on his heels, his mouth half open. And then he laughed out loud, softly at first, then more loudly, shaking his head and wiping at his eyes. "White!" he said, breaking into fresh hard laughter. "You're afraid because I'm white!"

China edged further away, readying herself for flight from the madman who was still helpless with his laughter. She slowly turned, then ran, as fast as she could, back toward the boardinghouse. The earth was soggy, sucking her in with each step.

"Wait!" he shouted. "Wait for me!" He was up and loping after her, his long legs swallowing the grass between them until his hand was on her shoulder, stopping her. She didn't bother to scream. Nobody in this town would save her.

He laughed again. He took his hand off her shoulder, wiped his eyes, and calmed his expression. "I'm sorry," he said. "It's just that my

whole life . . . how do I explain this? Mrs. Low, please do *not* be afraid of me as a white man. Ask anybody in town. They'll tell you I'm not white at all."

His voice had changed abruptly. The laughter disappeared until it was so remote that there was not even a suggestion that it might ever have been present or possible.

"They'll tell you I'm a half-breed," he said, and the words were hard and painful.

"A half?" How could this enormous man be half of anything? Except, she had to admit, he was only half as ugly as most white men. Still, she hurried along.

"I'm half-Indian," he said in a low voice. He followed her easily, taking single strides to her several. "You know, according to the law, Chinese are classified as Indians as far as testifying against whites is concerned. So actually, you and I, we're the same breed. Except I'm half and you're whole."

She wasn't sure if he had said something important, made a joke, or simply produced a string of words to confuse her. Then he put his hands on her shoulder again, gently, and spoke kindly, and she was positive he didn't belong in any of the categories she had known before. Whatever "half" was, it was better than white.

"Look, Mrs. Low," he said, "we're two of a kind, you and I. I understand how you must feel. I've had times and reason to feel the same way. Now I'll ask you one last time, and then I won't bother you anymore. My offer is just what I said. There's no trap or secret or trick. I don't know what all's happened to you to make you so afraid of everything, but I never was or would be a part of it, and my house is the safest place on earth. I brought an extra horse back into town, hoping this would work out. We could leave anytime, but it should be soon, because the river was high when I crossed and the sky's looking bad."

As he spoke, a drop of icy rain hit her forehead. She pulled her cloak tighter. A fierce winter was coming and she was being offered a safe haven. "I accept, Mr. Ross," she said softly. Then she realized that the wind drowned her voice. "I accept!" she shouted. "Thank you!"

She put her hood on her head and pulled the cloak tight against the now-steady rain. The safest place on earth, she said to herself on the way back to the boardinghouse. The safest place on earth. What was it about the man that made her want to believe him?

* * *

179

"Two!" he gasped. "Twins!" He shook his head, reached out, not sure of what to embrace, his pale wife or his sons. Sons! He was suddenly a man with two sons. "I need three arms," he said, kissing Sarah first.

"They lived," she said. "We all lived." She said little more, leaning back on her pillows, dark circles beneath her eyes and fatigue marking every motion.

He introduced China Low, who seemed to materialize when necessary, emerging out of shadow, then disappearing once again when no one needed her. "Mrs. Low is here to help you now, Sarah," he said.

"Good," Sarah said with so little pleasure or true interest that Alexander felt a chill, then reminded himself that she had delivered alone and had cared for both undersized boys for the last thirty-six hours. She was exhausted. He kissed her again, then let her sleep.

China Low seemed to instinctively know how to tend babies. Alexander watched with fascination as she bathed and swaddled each boy, rocked and crooned them to sleep.

When they next cried in hunger, Sarah had to be awakened, and although she seemed startled, she accepted the boys at her breast. But still, she said little.

"What shall we call them?" Alexander asked the next day. "They need names."

Sarah nodded, looking at her sons with the remote, unemotional pride that was becoming familiar. "This one is Jonah for my father and this William for my brother," she said softly. "If you have no objections."

He shook his head. He had no objections to the names, but to the tone, the strange and formal distance from which Sarah now spoke. Where was she? Where was the passionate Boston-lady? He lifted her long-fingered hand, told her how he loved her, how he loved their new sons, how happy he was that they looked so like her, Jonah, with a sprinkle of light-brown hair, William, with something of her shape in his face, even now. How delighted he was in their lustiness, their appetites—even if they were small, he could almost see them grow day by day.

He spoke for a long time, and Sarah answered politely, but with no emotion at all. It was as if a stranger who knew their names but nothing of their true life had replaced his wife.

He sat in the parlor that night. He could hear China Low sing to his sons. As sharp-edged and foreign as her song was, it calmed the

boys until all he heard was her reedy voice, piping them into their dreams. Sarah had handed them over, once again, without a question, without interest, without a word.

Alexander's house was now brimful of life, but he felt very much alone and confused.

The door opened almost silently. China Low stood in the corner like a benevolent shadow.

"I have to leave soon," he said. "I don't know how I can—you were supposed to only help with the chores. With cooking, washing."

"I can do those things."

"But the babies, too. I don't know when Sarah . . ."

"It will be all right," she said, a disembodied voice floating across the room. "I will tend them."

He would lose his job if he didn't go back. Nobody had expected the baby—the babies—this soon, nobody had made provisions. "Are you sure?"

He turned, suddenly, before she answered and he felt even more panic. She couldn't be sure, couldn't be any more sure of anything than he was. Good God, she was the size of a ten-year-old child. He tried not to think about Sarah, wonderfully large and strong so that her embrace held the whole world, so that she could do anything, be everything. Except now, when she had gone numb.

"I don't know what to do. How can you do it all, anyway? There's the animals, the house, the babies—that was the whole reason for bringing you, for having both of you out here. Now Sarah, Sarah might as well—Sarah!" He put his head into his hands. How could this Chinese child understand the twists and turns of his life?

But her voice, always so soft he had to strain to hear it, suddenly crackled out of her corner. "Mr. Ross, this is not the worst thing to happen to a man. You have two healthy sons. Surely your wife will notice that soon. But even if she doesn't—you must—you have eyes and a heart, haven't you? Why aren't you giving thanks for them, for your immortality, for this most precious of gifts, which you don't seem to appreciate!" China's voice snapped with indignation. "Sons!" she said. "Two beautiful sons!"

He gaped at her, shocked by the fire she had kept hidden until now. "I'm sorry," he said. "Of course I appreciate them, of course I give thanks."

Her voice returned to its usual soft cadences. "I have heard," she said, "that this can happen. That sometimes women are sad after their babies are born. I do not understand why, but still, I have heard

181

it can be so." She paused. "But I have never heard that this is true for men—even white men. Never."

He looked up at her pale face in the half shadow of the corner. She had a smile so small it was a hint, a suggestion. "Rejoice in your gifts," she said softly. "Jonah and William will be fine. The house will be fine. And Mrs. Ross will smile again. I promise."

He wanted to tell her that she was a gift, a great, overwhelming one, but he was afraid she might misunderstand. Not, of course, that he quite knew what he meant.

14

"I can't bear this much longer, Sarah."

He stood in their room, his voice low, although he wanted to shout, to shake her until she reassembled her parts and became Sarah again. But the impassive woman who looked up at him from the bed was only vaguely interested in his discomfort.

"Raining again, isn't it?" she said dully. "I hate the rain. Hate it."

He heard the boys in the parlor, building and destroying small sloppy walls with their brand-new birthday blocks. He heard a clomp, a thud, and laughter, and sighed. "They're a year old, Sarah."

"It was a nice cake, wasn't it?" she murmured. "China is certainly a good cook."

She was pushing away from the subject, and he momentarily let her have her victory. "Very good," he agreed. "I particularly appreciate it after chewing through last year's bull team at camp. Toughest steaks in the world. But China's good. And she hasn't fried or boiled a single dog, far as I know."

Sarah managed a small smile. "Remember that dreadful book? China's learning to read it now."

He nodded, urging her toward the end of this side road. China herself had told him during one of the many evenings they spent

together while Sarah retreated to her bedroom. She, too, had found the passage about Chinese putting rats and puppies in pies, and had joked about it ever since, insisting that Alexander count the dogs before he entered the house, certainly before he ate that night's stew.

He had spent so many evenings talking with the tiny Chinese woman, she seemed an old friend who comfortably shared his memories. It surprised him to realize she had been with his family only one year. She knew his history, was very interested in news of the camp, in descriptions of what each worker did. She had examined the contents of the window seat, exclaimed over his mother's basketry, his father's carvings, the poison doll. It was China who left flat cakes on the windowsill for the *domovoy,* who tried in that and countless other ways to bring luck to the house and its people.

When Alexander came home, it was China who greeted him enthusiastically with tales of the children and the livestock, who prepared special meals and sat sewing and talking after the eating was finished. Through it, before it, after it, Sarah floated in a private, exhausting melancholy that blinded her to life. It was China who was, in effect, mother to Jonah and Willy, China and Alexander who were man and wife, everywhere save the bedroom.

And there, in the bedroom, Alexander had no wife.

"Sarah," he said, because he would not let another visit complete itself without forcing the issue into the open. "It's been a year since you and I, since we—"

A burst of anger or fear sparked her eyes, then sputtered away.

"I can't—I don't—what's happened to us?"

Sarah didn't answer him.

The doctor, reluctantly, finally summoned, had tried to explain her delicate constitution. "Your, ah, wife," he'd said, "suffers from neurasthenia. Perhaps hysteria. Many educated women are susceptible to it. It is most difficult to treat."

"But why?" Alexander had asked. "I never heard of . . ."

He'd looked at Alexander with barely disguised distaste. "Please don't confuse the strength of an Indian woman, of a squaw, with that of a refined white woman."

He suggested removing Sarah's ovaries, the cause of all female tempers and nervous conditions. Alexander asked about less drastic cures. The doctor chose bloodletting, leaving the leeches on Sarah until she fainted. And perhaps that had worked, because since then, at least when she took her tonic, her laudanum, her nerves seemed less inflamed.

But not enough so. "I don't know what to do," he said. "How to help. I don't know what you want."

She sighed.

"Can't you say what it is? We were—I thought we were happy. Don't you care for me at all anymore?"

Her eyes welled up, overflowed. Sarah cried easily, silently, and often, except when she took laudanum. "I love you," she whispered. "I do."

"And our sons? They're beautiful, Sarah, sturdy and bright. One year old, full of tricks and words, but you barely notice them."

She nodded, tears still wetting her cheeks. "China takes good care of them," she whispered.

He reached for the tonic bottle and poured some of the opiate into a teaspoon. "They're your sons," he said. "They need you. How can you keep so far from them?"

She swallowed her medicine, sighed, and looked at her long, pale hands. "I'm afraid," she said. "I don't want to love them too much. Not this time. And..." She touched her wedding band, twisted it around her finger. It looked loose. "I don't want more children. I thought, perhaps, they would make the fear go away, be company..." She shook her head. "It's worse. They're babies. Tiny weak things. It frightens me to love them, to hope to keep them, to..." She shrugged. "I cannot risk being your wife that way anymore. I'm sorry, Alexander. I simply cannot."

"But—"

She shook her head.

"Sarah, there are ways to not have children—"

"I don't want to want you, either, Alexander. When you used to come home, I would fool myself, let my mind forget how lonely I had been when you were away. It made your visits beautiful, but then it was worse when you left. Always a terrible surprise. I don't want any more surprises."

He was baffled and angry, remembering how it had been with them, confused as to what had soured. He was raw with need of her touch, her scent, and a love he could feel on his flesh and mind. "You have me and Willy and Jonah and China," he said, trying again. "Why feel lonely?"

She looked at him blankly. "You'll leave, Alexander. You always do. Babies leave, too. I still think about Nicholas. At night I hear the panthers. I hear creatures scream in death. I hear those trees."

"Trees don't make noise!"

"They do. A lonely ancient sound. A creak, a sigh, a sob. I see them in the night, enormous, dark, circling me like a prison wall. I hear the ocean, the ships smashing on the rocks." It was the most she'd said in a long time, but her voice was flat, devoid of all emotion, and she sounded as if the effort of speech drained her.

"We can't hear the ocean from—"

"I remember such sad things. People I've lost. Nicholas. My mother. My father. My brother. Mary."

"Your sister is in San Francisco! She isn't lost!"

"She might as well be."

He paced the room. Perhaps it was time for another consultation with the doctor. Perhaps it was worth the risk of surgery to cure the neurasthenia, the fatigue, the tears.

"I miss her," Sarah said. "I miss Mary."

He nearly tripped over himself. Mary. San Francisco. New sights, a sense of perspective. Who was it said that a change was as good as a cure? He was positive it was true. In no time, Sarah would be good as new, revitalized and refreshed. "That's it," he said. "A visit to Mary. A holiday. You'll feel brand-new and happy." A look of interest sparked her face, then disappeared. She had rejected the idea without a word.

A thick, boiling rage rose in him—she destroyed hope as if her only love and companion were melancholy.

Then he remembered her old fears of highwaymen and of the sea. "I'll go too," he said. "You won't have to take one single step alone. Mrs. Low will watch the babies. You'll be safe. We'll travel by land, together."

Sarah stared, disbelieving, as if he had suggested a trip to the moon, not San Francisco.

"Why not?" he demanded. "What's to stop us? The rain? Those trees you say imprison you? I'll get you past the trees, Sarah. Watch me. You'll see. By the time we come home, you won't remember why they made you sad. You'll be able to see how beautiful they are, how wonderful this place is."

She looked down at her fingers.

"Sarah, we were so happy, weren't we? There's no reason we can't be again."

Again she twisted her wedding band. He hated the gesture. "Then it's settled," he announced, since there was no audible opposition. "We'll leave as soon as you pack your trunk."

She looked at him directly, peering with some amazement. "Really?" she asked in a small voice.

"Truly. You'll be with Mary a few days from now. Won't that make you happy?"

"Yes," she said dreamily. "Yes." For once, there were no tears.

Sarah's fingers were finally warm, supple, and strong again. Each day of the past week she'd sat at Mary's piano—Mary's daughter Amelia's piano, to be precise—and tried, at first with tears at her clumsiness and then, slowly, with more and more ease and joy, to make music.

It had been so long. Decades. She had been a ten-year-old girl when last she played the piano, and now she was a matron.

Her fingers remembered almost nothing, but her heart and her mind had held on to everything and made up for the loss of dexterity. It was still in her, she realized triumphantly, the symbols, the shapes, the sounds. She could, very soon, catch up to where she'd been two-thirds of her life ago.

And then what?

She stood up and went to Mary's front window. Alexander was on one of his long exploratory city walks and Mary was at her store—at one of them, for now there were three Miss Mary Leigh's, managed by her husband, Hector, while Mary continued the designs and manufacturing that had built her reputation.

The stores' size and luxury stunned Sarah and made her suddenly aware of how primitive her clothing was, how unstylish and countrified her life. A Miss Mary Leigh design would be ludicrous in the woods, inappropriate and overstated even in Mendocino City.

But the dresses, coats, and hats belonged in Mary's grand home and in San Francisco. Sarah sat at the window like a child, dreaming out over the city that bustled in every direction until it boiled into the sea. Even the Pacific seemed more civilized here, eased into a sweeping and safe bay, unlike Mendocino, where it waged eternal war against the rocky land.

In the city, Sarah slept through the night, didn't wake to unidentifiable screeches and screams or clawings. The clamor of carriage wheels, clang and whirr of the cable car, abrupt and loud late-night street voices—none of that troubled Sarah's rest.

She and Mary had gone to a concert the day before. A full orchestra played music remembered from the best days of her life. Sarah had forgotten that such events existed, but the hall was full.

Now, sitting in Mary's parlor among marble-veined tabletops, rich carpets, and mahogany chairs, Sarah suddenly remembered her

mother's stern voice quoting Mrs. Child's dislike for ostentatious decor such as this. But this room, this house didn't feel overfurnished or wrong in any way.

It felt—and the feeling thrilled and terrified Sarah—like home.

"I can't go back."

She had said it once before, but he'd been positive he misunderstood.

"I won't."

Long-limbed Sarah looked small and frightened, but nonetheless determined.

"How can you possibly say such a—"

"I'm sorry, Alexander. Terribly, horribly sorry, but I never belonged in the woods. I loved you so much I thought perhaps. . . . And I did try. I tried for so long. But I can't anymore. I think of the woods, the house, and that terrible fatigue settles in my bones again. I haven't the strength." She sat down on one of her sister's overstuffed chairs and folded her hands in her lap.

"What about—what about our marriage? Our life?" How could she make him ask such questions? He hated asking and knowing her answer wouldn't soothe the tumult inside him.

"Please," she said, "stay here, Alexander."

He had spent a week climbing every hill of the city, intrigued but not attracted by its bustle and clatter. He could not, in fact, wait to go back to the woods, where only nature broke the deep silence he loved. There were too many people here, foppishly dressed with too much show.

"I cut redwoods. I'm good at it—I'm the *best*. What am I to do in a city?"

Her brown eyes were wide and sorrowful.

How could she do this? Even think this? A cart made its way down the street outside, poorly made wheels screeching with each turn, like a wild animal in heat. Why did she want this? "I would never let my sons grow up in such a place," he said, and meant. He'd seen fancy women before—used them, in fact, before his marriage and, in truth, this past year, as an edge against the loneliness and chill. But he'd never seen anything like the number and variety that San Francisco had to offer. Never seen anything like the opium dens, the endless saloons, the staggering drunk sailors swilling their earnings and liberty. And he was intelligent enough to know that he'd only seen the surface, and that there was more,

the real evil, buried behind walls. "Never," he repeated.

"Mary's children are growing up here. There're fine schools and—"

"Never while I have life!"

She looked down at her fingernails and sighed, choosing.

"You'd give up your sons? Your babies?" The woman dumbfounded him, astounded him—the woman did not seem at all the person he'd loved and married. This was a shell, a puppet, a dull and heartless doll-Sarah left by some malevolent spirit who'd stolen his wife. This one would give up her children for the blare of a city. This one had already given up her husband, had let their love dry into little more than a trickle, not enough to dampen the dust of their marriage.

"Please don't make me do that," she said softly.

"*Make* you? I'm not making you do anything! But you won't take my sons away. You don't care about them!" He paced the room, his strides too large for the congestion of furniture. A small three-legged table wobbled in his wake, until he turned and steadied it. "And you don't care about me," he said, his voice hoarse.

"I do," she whispered.

"We don't touch, we don't—"

"I explained."

"You explained nothing! What kind of craziness is it to renounce pleasure because pain might follow it? Because I have to leave you for a while?"

"Perhaps here," she murmured, "here, where you wouldn't need to leave, perhaps we—"

"Here where I cannot live!" He pushed through furniture with the air of an animal looking for an escape. "What are the new rules? I didn't come here with you when we married and then suddenly change my mind—I only want what we had. I want our life back! I'm the husband, Sarah! The head of our family!"

"Alexander, I'm sorry. I care so for you. I feel as if my heart is breaking. Why can't you understand?"

"Then what is it? The piano? Your eternal piano? I've told you we'd get one. I'll find more work, we'll—"

She shook her head. "That isn't it. I can't live there. It will kill me. Perhaps I'm not strong enough for that place. I didn't let myself admit it for a long time, but now . . . now I understand." She grew silent, but her head still shook. No, no, no, no . . .

Alexander felt as if the leeches that had bled Sarah were inside him, sucking, draining, destroying him while they fattened. He had

to escape while he could, because if he remained, remembering the touch and taste of her, her near-forgotten laugh, the urgency with which she'd met his passion, if he thought of such things and fought and hoped for their return, he'd go mad like his father.

No, no, no, no, her head kept saying.

Enough was enough. Sarah Elizabeth was the past. His sons and the woods were his future.

The war was over. Both sides had lost.

China kissed each boy's forehead. "Good night, my darlings," she whispered, feeling a guilty thrill along with her possessiveness. She looked at their ruddy cheeks, the small spray of freckles on Willy's cheeks, the light brown hair and round green-gold eyes, and still felt they were truly hers. Had been willed to her so thoroughly that China had hazy memories of carrying them in her womb.

She could not fathom Sarah Ross's willingness to abandon either them or this safe and hidden sanctuary.

Or Alexander.

China tiptoed out of the boys' room. Lately, when they forgot and called her "Mama," she didn't correct them. Perhaps Sarah Ross had not so much abandoned her life as bequeathed it to China.

"That was a fine meal, Mrs. Low," Alexander said. He stood up. "You're doing fine with the boys, too. Don't want you to think it isn't appreciated."

"It's my pleasure, Mr. Ross."

"I want you to tell me if it—any of it—becomes too hard for you."

She smiled. He still didn't understand that it hadn't been too hard for his wife, it had simply been too much and too frightening. China, having survived living, breathing demons, was not tempted to create any new and intangible ones. Particularly not here, not now. Every morning that she awoke in safety, every day that she walked freely, uncrowded and unchallenged, had enough food, enough sunlight, every night that she slept soundly without interruption, without fear, she thanked the *domovoy,* assorted gods, and fate for the gift of this place.

"I'll turn in early, then," Alexander Ross said. "Goodnight, Mrs. Low."

She worried about him, thought about him often, confused and troubled by the pressure her thoughts put on her temples, in her chest. He'd come back from San Francisco changed. The plates and bones of his skull had pushed forward so that he looked hungry and

gaunt no matter how much she fed him. She remembered how strong and sleek he'd once been. He'd needed Sarah's nourishment, and he'd been like a slowly dying plant ever since she stopped feeding him. The boys were a year and a half old. A very long time for a man to starve.

China took the Bible down for nightly reading practice, but her eyes refused to stay on the print. Instead, they pictured Alexander Ross in his carved bed, alone except for the door frame of animals standing guard. She returned the Bible to its shelf and went to her room at the end of the hall.

She had surprised and upset herself when she realized how often her thoughts turned to Alexander Ross's loneliness, how often she heard herself deciding—again and again—that no living creature was meant to be alone. Not if there was instead the possibility of comfort and closeness. God himself had created a woman for Adam, and Noah stocked the animals two by two.

But China was not God, and besides, she had surely comforted—against her will—more than her share of mankind and in return had been treated with brutality or indifference, and she didn't know which was worse.

The comforting of Alexander Ross was neither her job nor her concern.

Still, the angles and planes of his face became a map she memorized when he was at home and recreated when he was away.

She had never felt this way before. The men at the house in San Francisco were unwelcome invaders, despoilers, and her only escape had been to hold a part of herself as a separate country where she could hide. She had never looked upon a single one of them with welcome or interest, let alone invitation.

George Low had been a kind and gentle rescuer. She would be grateful to him for the rest of her life. She would respect him forever, would apologize nightly for not having produced his son. But, while his touch had never been repugnant to her the way that of the men at the house had been, neither had it been something she yearned for or missed when he was away in the woods.

Perhaps he'd happened too soon after the house. Perhaps they'd both been too hungry and tired and fearful to ever be free to feel much else.

But now, China Low, still a young woman, was strong and rested and healed through, and she thought about Alexander Ross every night of her life and much of her days as well.

If he ever emerged from his bleak lonely solitude, she knew she would be there, waiting and glad of it.

She prepared for bed, put on her night dress, unpinned her upswept hair, brushed, and braided it. Over and under and through went the triple strands, the way Sarah Ross had long ago taught her. And then China paused, hands still on the thick black braid.

Slowly, she unwound it, freeing a sheet of black hair that reached almost to her waist.

She stood barefoot and trembling, amazing herself with a decision that all the same didn't feel new.

She moved silently, barely creaking the floorboards, opened the smoothly hinged door to his room, and glided to the bed, her white nightgown billowing around her. For a long while, she watched him in moonlight, engrossed in his regular and deep sleep-breathing. Then she swallowed hard and eased herself onto the bed, under the patchwork quilt, slowly, slowly, until she felt his body's warmth and then, gently, she pressed close to him.

He sighed and shifted his weight so that she could more easily be encircled by him.

In his embrace, as unconscious and unknowing as it was, something in China untangled, loosened, and sought the light for the first time. She wanted to lie there, barely breathing, cradled by him forever.

He stirred, moaned softly, shifted weight again. His hand was on her hair, in it, and he pressed against her, pulled her in, and moaned again, and she felt already joined with him, easily and seamlessly meeting and matching his body however it moved.

And then his breath caught and his eyes fluttered open and his hands flew off her as if she were burning. His whole body pulled back.

She felt abandoned.

"My God!" he said. "My God! Mrs.—"

She clamped her hand over his mouth and held it there. "I want to give you pleasure, Mr. Ross. Let me take away your pain." She moved close to him again, then closer until each whispered word was a kiss.

"But this is—I can't—you're only a child. I—"

"I'm no child," she said with urgency. "I never was." He seemed frozen in his surprise, still pulled as far back from her as possible. Her own need collided with a sudden fear that he didn't, he couldn't, he wouldn't ever want her, and she would carry her ache and incomple-

tion to the grave. "I know it's wrong," she whispered, "but sometimes I pretend I'm your wife. When I bake your biscuits, when I tend your children, when I wash your clothing, when we sit and talk. And I've imagined this part of it as well. Haven't you ever thought about it, Mr. Ross?"

"I—but—I try not to, I—"

"If I don't please you, I'll understand, and if you want me to, I'll still care for the house and the children."

"It isn't that. It isn't that at all."

"Who will we harm?" She rose up on the moon-drenched bed and pulled her nightdress over her head. She sat back on her knees, black hair like a cloak. "Look at me," she whispered. "Am I so ugly that you can't love me?"

He groaned and pulled her close. "I do already," he said. "You're all the comfort, all the . . . I love when we're together. I love to watch you move. I was afraid you'd notice, be angry. I've imagined your hair this way, imagined this kind of time, but I . . ."

"No more, then," she said. "No more imagining and no more talk."

He sighed, he relaxed. He held out his arms. "Come here, Mrs. Low," he whispered.

She was already too close for him to see her smile. Surely it was time for first names. But that could wait. This couldn't.

15

China played nervously with her high lace collar. "I don't want to sleep here, Alexander."

"Oh, Ma," Willy said. Both boys called her that, although it angered Sarah, and on their rare visits to San Francisco, and their actual mother, they were careful to refer to China as Mrs. Low.

Alexander looked amused, as if she were a silly child. "Surely sleeping in a converted barracks would be more comfortable and warmer than on grass."

"It's not that it was a barracks."

"What then? My father lived here. It's a family tradition."

"Some man told Ma there's ghosts here," Jonah said. "A haunted chamber upstairs."

"Haunted by men from the Russian cemetery!" Pale Blossom seemed excited, not frightened.

Alexander looked down at his daughter and smiled. He always smiled when he saw her, doting on her and pampering her so much that China worried that the girl had already become too soft and self-satisfied for her own good. "Well, miss," he said, "maybe one of the Russians prowling the hallways is your grandfather, checking on what's happened to his old quarters. Probably not too happy about it, either, but he's nobody to be afraid of."

"No such things as ghosts," Jonah said. "That man was playing games with you, Ma."

China stood as tall as she could manage. The boys were already, at twelve, a head above her, and even Pale Blossom, only ten years old, was eye level. If people didn't look closely, they assumed that China was another of Alexander's children, and, she thought with a flash of resentment, even his real children, who knew who she was, behaved as if she were young, instead of small.

"I know what I know," she muttered. There were ghosts. But she also knew she was outnumbered, and that she'd sleep, or at least pass the night wide awake, in the haunted hotel.

"Actually, my father didn't live in those barracks," Alexander said. "Officials did. But my father told so many stories that I feel as if I were one of the officials who lived here." And indeed, he guided them around the fort with an air of familiarity, like a man retracing well-remembered steps. "Over there, that was the commandant's house. Very fancy, with thick rugs and pictures and even a princess. Your grandfather dragged the princess and her piano into half his conversations. I think he was a little in love with her!"

They picnicked outside the fort, on a grassy slope, and Alexander continued his tour, completely at home in the place. "My mother's people, the Kashayas, lived on the other side of that hill. That's where the family went after the Russians left. The village is gone, but I can see it in my mind so clearly, even though I wasn't born then. When I was little, my brother Giorgi always told me stories about growing up here." He paused and caught his breath, as if he'd suffered a sharp sudden pain.

He still grieves for Giorgi and all of them, China thought. And he says he doesn't believe in ghosts!

"I wonder what your grandfather would think of this place now," he said.

A public road ran through the middle of what had been Fort Ross. The barracks was a hotel, the north end a laundry, and the south end a saloon whose seats were pews from the old chapel, which in turn was now used as a stable. The fur barn had become a ballroom, the bastions were moss-covered, worm-eaten pigstys.

Outside the fort, nature reasserted herself, took revenge, Alexander insisted. A valley of redwoods, completely felled by the Russians more than half a century earlier, now sprouted tall young trees around the thick stumps.

"The forest will be back," Alexander murmured. "Good for it. But

Ross is falling apart and the Kashaya village is gone, so that someday there won't be a single sign that the colony existed. It'll be your jobs to remember, children. Your responsibility to tell the story of what happened here. Are you listening, boys? It's your story, too. How about you, Pale Blossom?"

"Please," she said abruptly, "don't call me that."

"Call you what?"

"Pale Blossom."

"It's your name."

"I don't want it anymore. It's *foreign*. Peculiar. Willy and Jonah don't have words, descriptions, as names. They have American names."

China's pulse accelerated. Everything in this new world—the redwood stumps, the fort, her sons who were not her sons, her husband who was not truly her husband, her miraculous, beautiful daughter who was not like either of her parents—perpetually whirled into new positions, pushing for change and redefinition. China, trying hard to stay in place, felt the instability like a fever. And now, while the rest of them were looking backward, her daughter was reinventing herself for the future. China was dizzy with head-spinning.

"Who is it you want to be, child?" Alexander sounded gentle and amused.

"Daisy," she said without an instant's pause. Obviously, she had planned for this moment and announcement. "A daisy, as you know, is a pale blossom," she added primly, fortifying her argument.

"And also very American," Alexander murmured.

The girl shrugged, as if that were not at all relevant.

China had lovingly, carefully chosen her daughter's name to reflect the fair-skinned new flower that she was. Besides, she couldn't see much difference between a pale blossom and a daisy, anyway, except that the former sounded delicate, exquisite, exotic, like her daughter, and the newly adopted one was hard-edged and ordinary.

"The other girls at your school," she asked quietly, "do they have these, ah, American names?"

Pale Blossom/Daisy's green eyes flared. "Yes," she snapped. "There's Matilda and Sally and Betsy."

China found that sad. "Americans" no more welcomed an eagerly renamed Sally or Daisy than they did a Jade Treasure or Pale Blossom. The public school where the true Sallys—and Sarah's boys—studied was as closed to China's child as it had been to Alexander. Nowadays it had nothing to do with Alexander's heritage. His twins

were easily admitted to the public school. There was no more Indian problem or agitation because, after near-extermination, there were almost no more Indians.

But the virulent anti-Chinese sentiment had yet to be appeased. Still, the Chinese had survived in a hostile world that claimed to offer universal education, so, when their numbers swelled sufficiently, a separate school was created for them, no matter how "American" their names.

"There is truly a Matilda?" China asked. It was a fitting name for many Americans, as thick and ungainly as they were, but why adopt it?

"Yes." Daisy put her hands back up on her hips and waited for further challenge. When none came, she relaxed. "Some are also named Snow Jade and Heavenly Perfume," she admitted.

"Or they were when you last saw them," China said. "But you were Pale Blossom then. Who knows what anyone will be when school begins again?"

Alexander's expression had hardened the moment his daughter's school was mentioned. He and China had waged hard war over the child's schooling. He wanted her fortified with reading and writing, but he was enraged by her exclusion from the regular school. He did battle with the schoolmistress, although the very sight of her in the school door made him a tongue-tied child again. But eloquence would not have bent the rules. His child by what the town perceived as his Chinese mistress was eligible only for the Chinese school.

He had stormed back to the woods and refused to let her attend what he considered a daily insult.

The battle waged for years. By the previous autumn, when Pale Blossom was nine, China was tired of waiting for either the schools or Alexander to relent. "She has to know things, to learn them the right way," China insisted. "She's not learning enough! You're in the woods most of the time and I know too little. Even in Chinese school, she can surely learn more than I can teach her. She can read books that don't tell her she's supposed to eat dogs and rats!"

"I don't care!" Alexander said. "I won't honor their hate, I—"

China was about to explode. "*I* don't care!" she screamed. "I won't go on this way, Alexander! We've fought over this year after year and day after day, but not one day longer! You're wrong, destructive, and I won't listen to any more of your arguments."

"You act like I'm your enemy," he said, spluttering the words, shock on his face.

"On this, you are." She took a deep breath. "You're holding that foolish pride of yours so close it's blinding you and it's hurting my daughter's future! Alexander, listen to me—I will never, ever, let anything or anyone, including you, harm my child."

Alexander gaped as if seeing her for the first time, and then he sighed. "I believe you," he said. Then he smiled. "And I pity anybody, ever, who tries to."

That had been a year ago. Now, Pale Blossom/Daisy had her first year of school behind her. Despite all the squabbling it had taken to win her a formal education, she proved an indifferent student. China wasn't surprised. The girl had been pampered and coddled by her father and now her head was filled with herself and bubbles and air, and she made the daily trek to town solely for the sake of the social life. Daisy was always able to describe the clothing she saw in town, the glimpses of privileged and comfortable lives, and the gossip overheard in the classroom. She learned those lessons brilliantly. Unfortunately, none of the other classroom activities engaged her mind at all.

"You see, there were no ghosts," Alexander said the next morning.

China smiled and nodded. Her dreams had been bloated with floating, faceless figures. But in truth, they were unknowable shadows from China's past and had to do with her daughter's change of names and identities, with the end of Pale Blossom, not with any former inhabitants of Ross. All night long she had reached for the phantoms, trying to capture and truly see them, but they slipped through her mind and grasp into the buried passageways of the past.

Daisy, China thought. I must think of her that way, call her that. Daisy. Who is this new person? She shook her head and packed her small valise.

Shortly before they were to leave, Alexander found and hired a man who took photographs, and the entire family stood in front of the hotel, posing in their best clothing.

Imagine, China thought, if there had always been such miracles as this. Imagine having the image of her mother and father now, across such a bridge of space and time. With that, there'd be no ghosts or bad dreams. Now there'd be no ultimate, final, forgetting loss.

The gentleman did not work speedily, taking forever to ready himself. Standing still in the heat was difficult for China, and seemingly impossible for the children. The boys' lanky bodies shifted and swayed, their feet tapped.

China wondered if their freckles would show up, and how their red-clay hair would look in sepia. And would Daisy glow on paper the way she did in the hot September daylight? The power of her beauty frightened China sometimes, but Daisy reveled in it, posing and preening, then oiling her skin with welcome glances until she gleamed even more. And that, of course, deepened her mother's concern.

The photographer continued his preparations. Only Alexander was unperturbed. His smile was not forced or a pose at all. He was a contented man, having finally made his pilgrimage to what he called "the place we started."

"Ready!" the photographer said, peeping out from under the black cloth. He burrowed back under and held up a hand. China looked at her family and saw, with a sudden clarity that had little to do with the glittering sunlight, their beauty and strength and solidity. She felt tears and blinked, rearranging her face so that she looked as thoroughly happy as she felt.

The daguerreotype would be wonderful, but she didn't need it, she realized. She would always remember this perfect, crystal moment when past and future fused and blazed, burned without consuming itself. She faced the camera directly, her wide smile still too small to contain her immense joy. She felt the five of them grow, fill the horizon and the world, become giants who were indestructible and permanent in ways only possible for gods and families.

Two months later, China was grateful for the daguerreotype. She lifted it from the mantelpiece and ran her finger over the carved frame Alexander had created for it.

There was one other photograph on the mantelpiece, also in the soft sepia tones that reminded China of her husband's skin by moonlight. Alexander, the best chopper in the woods, balanced high above the ground on a cutting platform. His partner stood on the other side of a tree that was more than ten times their combined girth, and both grinned proudly. China had always worried about the elevated platform, balanced as it was on springs and set above the bottom swell of tree.

"Why don't you stand on the ground, where it's safe?" she had asked him.

"Nobody wants the heavy butt log below," Alexander explained. "They don't even float to sea, just sink to the river bottom and clog everything up. Besides, half the trees have hollows, goose-pens at the

base, so cutting down there, not up on the platform, would be dangerous."

"But still—"

"China, why ask? That's how you cut those trees."

She was echoing earlier protests with George, and hearing, in return, echoes of his answer—with no other choices, what was the point of questions?

"Don't worry," Alexander insisted, "I'm good at what I do."

And in truth, he was sure-footed and agile until his last moments on earth. It wasn't the platform that killed him, but a branch knocked free by the plummet of a felled tree. A branch—they called those deadly and unpredictable hurtling clubs "widow-makers"— ended a man who had brought down giants. It made no sense.

For a second time, the hairy hands of white strangers brought her the lifeless shell of a husband. Alexander's beautiful face was ashy and shattered. She sat up all night holding his cold, stiff hand, already missing him and wondering how she and the children were to survive. Twice, men had rescued her, but there would be no more George Lows, no more Alexanders.

After Alexander was buried in the sunny space at the back of the land, she began talking to his photographs, finding some comfort in his image.

Every night she put his picture on the kitchen table, facing her. Together they grappled with the problems ahead. When she crumbled into fears and a sense of helplessness, she'd look at Alexander's strong and handsome face and the resolute set of his shoulders, take a deep breath, and sit straight again. Sometimes she opened the window seat and pulled out the assorted mementoes: a samovar, a basket of reeds and feathers, a baby quilt made by Boston Sarah, toys, Anna's peculiar poison doll, a wooden flute, the family Bible, bits and pieces, leftovers.

It wasn't much, but she held on to it for support. The children, the souvenirs, and the house were Alexander's complete legacy, so they had to suffice.

"We'll get jobs," the boys announced a few weeks after their father's death. "We're strong. We'll find something."

China shook her head. "You're twelve years old. Besides, it was your father's wish that you finish school, and you must."

"He never talked about this kind of time," Jonah said. "This is different."

"All times are different. All times are hard." She stood up and, on tiptoe, kissed each boy's smooth cheek. "You're good boys," she said. "But you must stay in school at least until you have beards."

"Then how will we live?" Willy asked. His voice was tremulous and unsure and not at all as adult as it had been.

"We'll find a way. We can plant more vegetables, raise more chickens. We have a cow for milk and cheese. We can . . . we can trust ourselves. Believe that the answer is somewhere right around us, only we're not seeing it yet. But we will. Soon." She realized she was speaking to herself, not the boys, but they nonetheless seemed reassured.

For several more weeks, China paced the house throughout the night, settling at the kitchen table with the accumulated souvenirs from the window seat and Alexander's photographs. Holding each object in turn comforted her. It was almost like holding a conversation with everyone who knew this house and somehow, through that knowledge, also knew and understood her.

Each night, she inventoried not only the dwindling supplies of flour and sugar, not only the unchanged collection of window-seat memorabilia, not only the condition of the house itself, but also the items, the facts, that felt relevant and unquestionable.

She had three children to raise and no money.

She was Chinese.

One of her children was half-Chinese.

It was unsafe being any part Chinese in this country. As remote from the world as she had been the past decade, she knew there was no place to be Chinese, or half-Chinese. There had been mass murders in Wyoming, lynchings in Idaho, men pushed into boxcars and shipped out of Tacoma, Washington. And in California, all over California, Chinese were shoved out, hounded, abused, and persecuted. There were terrifying stories near to home of men driven off cliffs and forced into the sea. Those who could sailed back to China. Others fled toward the East Coast.

This house was safe.

She must keep the house. She must keep all of them right where they were.

"We'll take boarders," she announced a week later. She had tested the idea backward and forward and felt confident about it. "Lots of people passing through, traveling, looking for work, selling things. Some houses won't take them if they aren't white, or whatever, but

201

we'll be a place for everyone. We'll put a sign down by the main road. 'Mrs. Ross's Boardinghouse. All welcome.' You'll see, people will come."

The twins looked at each other, discussing the matter in the eerie wordless way they had. Then they grinned and nodded. "We're pretty good sign painters," Jonah said.

"We'll make it big," Willy added, "so everybody can see it."

"And you'll stay in school," China reminded them. "You can help afterward and in summer. It'll work."

The three of them became so engrossed in their plans that they failed to notice, for a while, Daisy's prolonged silence and pursed mouth.

"What is it?" China finally said.

"A boardinghouse!" Daisy clung to her fine and fancy view of life, and while it angered and worried China, it was the child's absolute legacy from Alexander and there seemed little to be done about it. "She's never to feel ashamed of what she is, the way I did," he'd said countless times. "We're not less than they are, we're different. Special. New. She'll be as grand a lady as any of them, and I want her to know it."

Daisy knew it, perhaps too well. China glanced up at the daguerreotype on the mantelpiece. Well, Alexander, she signaled him silently. Look what you've left—a fine and elegant and penniless baby-lady. Now what was it you meant me to do about this?

"Let's move away instead," Daisy said. "Jonah and Willy have been to San Francisco, but I haven't."

"San Francisco!" What was China supposed to say? Had the fool child ever listened to her parent's stories?

"It'd be exciting!" Daisy's green eyes glittered. China could almost see the lavish images that danced behind them. "If I lived in San Francisco, I just know I'd become a famous actress."

"Sometimes you're really a baby," Jonah said.

"Why?"

China stood up. "No San Francisco. Not now, not ever."

"But—"

"Not another word!"

Daisy slumped into her chair. "But a boardinghouse! Strangers all over our house, people we'll have to feed and clean up after. No, Mama. There must be a better way. If Papa were alive, he'd tell you that—"

"If Papa were alive we wouldn't need to do it, you selfish, spoiled child! Papa would be ashamed of you!"

Daisy's eyes went wide with shock. She had been cushioned from birth with love and gentleness. She had listened to the stories of her parents' and grandparents' lives as if they were foreign, imaginative fairy tales. As if reality had nothing whatsoever to do with her.

China stood as straight as she could. "He left five things," she snapped. "The four of us and this house. We'd better make them add up to a life, because the only shame we can bring on ourselves would be to give in and give up. That's the heritage your father left. We have to survive and we will—or what's the point of it all?" She leaned toward her daughter. "Do you understand? You must. We have to save this—or *what has all the struggle been for?*"

"We could survive other places," Daisy insisted.

"No! This world is dangerous! Listen to me. There's a man up further, an Indian hunter. Papa told me about him. He has Indian scalps on his walls and chairs made of hickory and Indian hides. Skin that could have been your own father's. And he brags about it, shows them off to anybody who'll look."

"I don't see what that has to do with—"

"And in your precious San Francisco, little girls your age—little girls just like I was, pretty little girls, are forced to—" China stopped abruptly. Her daughter might be vain and a fool, but there was no need to corrupt her with knowledge of the possibilities of sin. "Daisy," she said softly, "you can't stay this young anymore. Try, try to understand." She sat down, exhausted.

Without a word, Jonah and Willy came to stand by her, one on each side. They patted her graying hair and glared at Daisy.

"I'm sorry," the young girl said after a moment. "I didn't understand, but now I do."

"Good," China said. "It's settled then. We'll have the house and we'll have each other, and that is all we need on this earth."

Two weeks later, her decision was thrown back at her, like a taunt.

"This isn't your house and they aren't your boys, and I want everything that's mine."

China had barely been able to regain her voice, let alone her composure, since she'd opened the door and seen the pale freckled woman. Sarah had arrived waving a letter from Jonah, as if she needed a pass. China, knowing of Sarah's many fears, was shocked

even before she heard the woman's declaration. "Sarah, why—"

"Mrs. Ross," the other woman snapped.

"Yes?"

There was a painfully frozen moment until finally China realized that Sarah had been correcting her, not addressing her. Sarah had been reminding them both of their accurate titles.

"Mrs. Ross." The words stuck in China's throat. For a decade she had considered herself the owner of that name. She mourned Alexander as his widow. "Forgive me, but I don't understand what you're saying, or why you're saying it."

"It's obvious, isn't it?" When last seen, Sarah Ross had been morose, withdrawn, and weak. Now, standing tall, she looked twice her remembered height, and her face had become stern and flinty. "I'm his widow, Mrs. Low. I am the mistress of this house and the mother of those boys."

"But you've been away a dozen years. You left!"

Sarah pulled in even tighter, her long slender body contracting on itself. "And you certainly made sure of that, didn't you? You worked it so that my separation was permanent, written in stone! You wrecked everything and every hope!" Her face mottled with red-pink patches.

China felt as if she'd been slapped. "What—what do you mean? Didn't I care for the twins? Did you see how fine they are? What have I done that was so wrong, Sa—Mrs. Ross? Why are you so angry with me?"

Sarah paced the parlor, then settled in the chair nearest the fireplace. She sighed, held her long hands in the position of prayer, picked at a stray thread on her elegant traveling dress and said nothing. When she finally looked up, her face was composed, but China saw the glints of tears pooled in her eyes. "If you hadn't—I thought he'd come back to me. Bring the boys. Live with me in the city. I thought—" She blinked, then dabbed at her eyes with a lacy square and took a few deep breaths before she continued.

"He loved me," she said in a low, painful-sounding voice. "Loved me in a way that couldn't have ended simply because I was . . . I was ill. And I loved him. It was this house, these woods, the fear, the— it had nothing to do with Alexander!"

China silently sat down across the room and waited, breath held, body tight, preparing for further blows.

"If you hadn't—" Her voice became thinner and higher with each

word as if it were stretching into a fine cutting wire that strangled her. "If you hadn't behaved like a *wife*—" She stood up, turned her back, wiped her eyes, then whirled around. *"He'd have come back to me!"*

She glared at China, then hung her head. "He'd have brought my sons! My babies! Do you think it didn't hurt me to leave them?" Her voice was lower now, rushed and barely intelligible. "But I thought I was dying . . . I thought I might harm them if I were alone with them any longer. I couldn't . . . I didn't . . ." She sat back down in the fireplace chair. "I did the only thing I could think of. I didn't expect it to be permanent. That part was your fault." She watched China impassively, like a judge.

All those years, Sarah had been building a case against her, hating her from afar, blaming her for the direction in which life had grown. China felt as numb and helpless as she had years ago when the policeman had arrested her on the false charge of stealing her own jewelry.

"I loved him, too," China whispered. "You left. We were both alone. We did no harm. You must understand. He . . . I . . . we . . ."

"You were my *helper,* not my *replacement!*" Sarah hissed.

The woman had become hard. All bones and brittleness. There was no point in trying to crack her surface with reason or love.

"I cannot change the past," China said in a cold voice. "What do you want now, today, Sa—Mrs. Ross?"

"Everything that's mine. My boys. My house."

"Your sons barely know you," China said softly. "They've just lost their father. Would you also take away the only home—and mother, too—they've known? Or do you now choose to live here?"

Sarah twisted her handkerchief and took deep breaths, and when she looked up, she no longer seemed cold or intimidating. "Help me," she whispered. "Please. I can't stand that I don't know them, that they probably don't want to be with me. I know that they . . ." She sighed once, twice, and wiped at her eyes. "They love you. Call you their mother. But I've missed them every day of their lives since I became well again. I knew Alexander wouldn't relent. They told me that it was you who convinced Alexander to let them visit me at all."

China said nothing. She listened with half her mind and with the other half looked ahead, terrified, to wandering the face of a bleak earth, Daisy tagging behind, homeless exiles until death.

"I've been punished for my weakness long enough. Please, help

them decide to come to me. They're almost men. I don't have much time left or hope of other chances. Please. They could come visit you. I promise."

Was it true, was there even a possibility that Sarah's sons and husband would have been returned to her if China hadn't intervened?

"China, do you remember when you were learning to read from the Bible?" Sarah asked softly.

China nodded.

"Do you recall Solomon saying he would divide the baby two women wanted? Can we . . . can we not fight over their bodies?"

"I love them," China said. It hurt to even consider their leaving, to think of giving them up, giving them away. Life without them would have large rips and empty spaces. But Sarah, for all her misplaced anger, was in so much pain and need that China accepted some measure of guilt—unintentional and perhaps undeserved though it was. And it was true that Sarah could give them a world forever closed to China. The boys' eyes were round. The world had been designed for them. Could China hold them away from what seemed their legitimate legacy? They could always come back. They could always make the choice themselves. But it would be a form of lying if she didn't encourage them to sample all that was available to them. She was sure, furthermore, that they would not require undue encouragement for this grand adventure. They had thoroughly enjoyed their visits to the city, and they were fond of their mother. If she didn't push them toward Sarah, she would be Solomon's mother, who would selfishly have cut up the child in order to keep it.

"I'll help you," China said. She took a deep breath. "But you must understand something. Alexander had three children. Jonah and Willy have a sister." Sarah stiffened and grew wary, defended, and China leaned forward, pressing her case. "No matter what you wanted to have happen, no matter what you choose to believe, you weren't his wife the last dozen years. I was. And Daisy is his child."

Sarah bit at her bottom lip, released it, almost looked as if she would speak, then reconsidered, nodded, and sighed.

After a long pause, she again opened her large traveling bag and pulled out a formal-looking document. Her face flushed and she spoke in a low, embarrassed, and rushed voice. "I never truly meant to take the house. I brought this to give you right away, no matter what you decided about the boys. But when I was actually here, in

this house I'd imagined for so long, and I saw you, I . . ." She waited a moment, collecting herself.

And none of them believe in ghosts, China thought with great sorrow. At least she acknowledged what haunted her.

"And I was afraid you wouldn't . . . I'm ashamed," Sarah said. "For a moment, I thought to barter for my sons, to use a piece of paper . . . I underestimated you. Forgive me." She handed China the paper. "This deeds the house to you. I know that's what Alexander . . ." She caught her breath and shrugged. "It was never mine," she said, looking around her once again, as if to confirm the strangeness of the house.

"Yes, it was," China said. "It belongs to all of us. Perhaps you can learn to love it. Perhaps you can come to the woods when the boys do."

Sarah looked surprised, then pleased. But she had finally noticed the framed pictures on the mantelpiece, and now she walked to them. She faced the fireplace, but China saw the tremor in her back, saw her clasp the picture of the woodcutter and hold it close, head bowed.

"Come back to visit," China said, and Sarah turned around and smiled at her.

"Yes," she answered. "To visit. And to remember. It would be terrible if any of us forgot."

16

"Foolishness," China muttered. She kept her voice low, so as not to awaken anybody. "But all the same," she said. She put a slice of leftover cake onto the carved plate on the windowsill. "My best recipe," she told the plate. Then she looked back at the kitchen table, on which sat the framed daguerreotype. "There, now. Is your *domovoy* satisfied, Alexander?" China grumbled about the foolishness of a Chinese woman caring for a Russian household spirit, but still, she kept the plate full.

Daisy complained about the *domovoy*, but then, she complained about everything and didn't believe in spirits or ghosts or much of anything aside from Daisy. "What sort of luck has he brought us?" the child asked. "The luck of cleaning boot mud? Of stirring stew until my arms ache, or of washing bed linens until my hands turn sore and red? Of milking—"

"Daisy—"

"Or of those people—all those people who come here? Is it the *domovoy* who made us so lucky as to know them, take care of them?" She stood regally, disdainfully, a young queen, disgusted by the peasants who had invaded her palace.

"Enough!" China stormed before her daughter's list continued. "Enough! Do you want him to be angry?"

"There's no such thing, anyway. It's just more of your ghosts!"

"Do you think the only things on earth are what you can see?"

"Well, if there's a spirit for this house, it's not doing its job."

"How do you know, little girl? There are worse fates than wash-days. Maybe the *domovoy* kept our misfortunes to what we could bear, and no more. We have our house, our food, our lives. Where is your gratitude? Where is your sense?"

From then on, Daisy kept her grievances to herself, and if she felt superior to the peddlers, itinerant workers, hops pickers looking for work after harvest, and the rest of the motley, rough-edged lonely lot who broke their migrations at her house, she kept that to herself as well.

And China kept the *domovoy*'s plate well stocked.

On this particular evening, she was very eager to please and appease whatever spirits she could. She put the plate with its fresh cake on the sill and rubbed her arms nervously. The hairs on her forearms rose, as if they were being tugged by tiny hands. It was a night to believe in spirits, but of the dark sort. She couldn't sleep and had been pacing her room until she pulled on her dressing gown and decided to use the time. The house swirled with dangerous currents, and China felt like the old, blind dog by the fire, sniffing the dark for signals.

"Alexander," she said, sitting back at the table with her mending. "Something's wrong. I'm worried."

Alexander looked back at her from high on his tree. How strong and wonderfully made he'd been. She sighed and shook her head, remembering. She was in her thirties, but she felt ancient, like one who'd lived many, many lives so that she was bent over with the weight of them.

Alexander's image consoled her. His stormy eyes, so well remembered, bored into her and she followed their path and, often as not, found her answers deep inside.

"Well," she said, carefully restitching the hem of a skirt, "it's probably nothing. Times are hard. It's easy to worry."

We've survived, she reminded herself. She had kept the idea and kept the name—Mrs. Ross's Boardinghouse had been in business for two years, ever since Sarah Ross gave her the deed. The word spread that travelers who didn't fit in, who weren't particularly welcome elsewhere—the Chinese, the Indian, the black, the Spanish—could consider China's their temporary homes. When times were good, the many bedrooms were full. When times were bad, like now, and there

were no men and no jobs, China and Daisy ate potatoes they grew and cheese they made. Sometimes there was venison or a ham from a wild boar.

Of course, there were still worries. Daisy had a head full of dreams, but there was no stopping that. She was twelve, still a child. There would be time to grow up. Still, China worried about her. Every man who sat at their table had to work hard to keep his eyes off of her—and Daisy, child or not, immodestly basked in the attention. She was a rare creature, green eyes atilt in a perfectly oval face framed with sleek black hair. More than any seasoning, Daisy's exotic existence spiced the dinner table, made the food delicious and the boarders expansive. Where would it lead?

China consoled herself with reminders that there were years before she really had to plan for her daughter's future.

But she smiled, wryly, remembering the bitter feuding over the child's schooling or lack of it, over what damage that would do to her. How much of China's life had been dedicated to preventing harm to Daisy? "I pity anyone who threatens your child," Alexander had said, conceding defeat.

"Look what it came to, Alexander," China said softly. "She had one year. And I don't know what it was she learned." Only one year because, despite China's hopes, it became necessary to have another set of hands at home, and besides, it was too difficult to make the trek to town in rain and cold without her older brothers as guides.

Daisy minded only the loss of gossip and parties. And even that loss would have been happily suffered if she could have lounged around the house like the grande dame she fully intended to be.

What on earth was to become of her? China snapped off an end of thread and frowned. Then she looked at Alexander on the tree, and then up to the mantelpiece, where the entire family stood in sepia tones like a small forest. How wonderful that sunny moment had been, but it reminded her that nobody could predict or control the future. She could only think about the present and feel proud that she had kept her home and kept her daughter away from the night-mare dangers of the city's hard-edged selling rooms. It would be worse later, when she'd have to keep Daisy from dangers that the girl her-self would create.

"We're safe," China murmured. "Daisy's safe." But there was some-thing about the night, about the way the air inside crackled and hissed as if whispering warnings. About the way the storm outside

enveloped the house and moved the rest of the world beyond the horizon. China murmured to Alexander's image, practicing her own Americanized form of ancestor worship, hoping that she could identify and conquer her fears.

Like a child clutching its favorite toys, she found herself once again gravitating to the window seat. She removed the calico pillows from its top and opened the box. Slowly, she carried its contents to the kitchen table. It would soothe her as ever to hold the house's memories, to think about the people who had treasured or used these things.

There was a loud creak from the next room. China gasped, then realized how taut she was. Houses creaked and moaned as they shifted in the night. It was nothing.

Still, her mind moved up the staircase to the lone current boarder, Emmet Mitchell. The man was trouble. She had smelled it on him the first time he'd stayed at her house, and she smelled it again this time, and she didn't mean his edge of stale whiskey or sweat.

Sometimes Daisy half-jokingly accused her mother of being a witch with a second sense, and perhaps it was true. There was a coppery breath to the man, a fiery glaze in the air around him that blended with his bright carrot hair, the orange freckles on his face. His eyes frightened her with their piggy wiliness. Too often, she watched those eyes slide onto her daughter, and she wished she could stitch them closed with catgut the way they did with wild cattle who wouldn't be herded. After their eyes were sealed, they stayed in line. So would he.

And yet Emmet Mitchell had given her no cause to ask him to leave. Besides, he was the only lodger they had at the moment. The winter rains had started, work was scarce, and few peddlers had the heart to ford the swollen river and trudge through backwoods mud in order to sell a paper of pins.

The house was silent except for the rain on the roof, the nightly creaks and groans of the timbers, and the low snores of the dog on the rug in front of the fire. He was called, as many of the house's dogs had been, Yellow, although he happened to be brown and white. He was also ancient, half-blind and deaf.

The steady, drumming rain one story above lulled her out of her amorphous discomfort and toward sleep. There was nothing to worry about. All was well. She stroked a tiny silk slipper she had embroidered for Daisy, when she had still been the infant princess, Pale Blossom.

211

And then, drowsy, she rested her head on her arms.

Creak, snore, silence. Night sounds. Nothing to fear. Her breathing slowed, her eyes grew heavy.

Creak.

She should go to her room, sleep in a proper bed. But this felt comforting, close to Alexander and all the others who had been here . . .

Creak, creak, creak.

She inhaled sharply. Her back tensed, stiffened. She sat up.

No house shifted and sighed in that rapid succession. No house made that sort of noise.

People made noises like that. Feet on a staircase. Yellow snuffled out of sleep and raised his head, ears back.

"What is it?" she whispered, but she knew. Her witchy eyes saw through the wall, into dark forbidding shadows.

She pulled her robe tight and tiptoed through the kitchen, into the parlor.

The staircase was empty, the room deserted.

A long creak, like a muffled scream. But where was it?

A startled cry from Daisy.

China ran, Yellow on her heels.

He hadn't even bothered to close the door behind him, to feel a moment's shame or need to hide.

"Leave her alone!" China screamed. "Don't you touch my child!"

Emmet Mitchell stood over Daisy's bed in long underwear that bulged obscenely. He blinked with drunken surprise at her entry. His regular whiskey stench had intensified.

"Get out!" China screamed.

"Out?" He blinked some more, weaving in place.

Daisy's hair was wild and she pulled the covers high around her neck. She looked half-terrified. But only half. The other half, intensifying China's rage and fear, was amused by the man's repulsive ardor.

"Out!" China screamed. "You *dare* to come into my daughter's room. She's a *baby!*"

"No baby." He slurred his words. "She's a woman. All night at dinner, I saw how it is with her. She's . . . look here." He yanked the edge of the covers and pulled at the neck of Daisy's nightdress. "Beautiful," he said, bending to kiss the child. Daisy screamed. Yellow growled. China lunged for him, pounding on his back, at the side of his head.

212

He brushed off China as if she were a gnat. With a drunken smile and lurch, he put his hand out, over Daisy's breast.

"Don't touch her." China's voice was low and flat. "Don't you touch my child."

Something in the tiny woman's voice stayed his hand. He sat on the edge of the bed, not moving. "Can't tell me what to do," he said, nonetheless.

"This is my house and I can tell you what to do, and I am. Pack and get out." China's heart swelled and pounded up, up, into her throat. He was so large, so foul, so thick. She hadn't been as aware of her size, or lack of it, since she was a slave in San Francisco. And she hadn't been as revolted by a man since then, either.

"Daisy, Daisy. 'S a nice name. Little flower, ready to be plucked. Oh, I saw how you was flirting over dinner, I saw—"

"Out!"

Yellow growled again, but China realized with desperation that the dog, lost inside his dimmed sight and senses, would be slower to anger than she was. Right now he looked confused. He was going to catch on too late.

Emmet Mitchell leaned down and wetly kissed Daisy's lips, muttering endearments. Daisy whimpered and moved away, but the wall blocked the other side of her bed.

The man chuckled. "No baby. A woman, I say. A real woman."

"She's *twelve!*" China screamed, and then she had to fight the urge to howl and scratch the eyes out of the world because twelve didn't matter, because this man was part of the same crude pack who had taken and hurt and used her when she had been only twelve herself.

"After some fun," he said. "Just a little fun."

In one long movement, China bent over, pulled up the oil lamp next to Daisy's bed and smashed its glass hood. She stood in front of the man, aiming the jagged glass at him. "I'll kill you," she said. "I'll cut you up if you put one finger on her. I'll cut whatever parts I'm near."

He looked at her with distant interest, as if trying to remember where he was and what was going on.

"You'll bleed to death, right on this floor," she said, glad that the dark and his drunkenness hid her shaking.

"Bitch."

She moved her weapon closer, let a needle-sharp tip graze his hand.

"Chink bitch." But he backed off.

She followed him, the glassy dagger in front of her. Followed him up the stairs to his room, so he could pack and find no counter-weapon. Followed him back down to the door and the stormy night.

But he turned and faced her before he opened the door and the look he directed toward her was not bleary at all. "Ain't right turnin' a man out into the rain," he said. "I'll show you. I'm coming back. I'll have her. And maybe you, too. I'm comin' back whenever I want, over and over again. You're just a little bit of a woman. If I wanted to, I could knock you down and take my pleasure wherever I liked."

"Out," she screamed. "Out of my house."

"No, it ain't." His sloppy wet chuckle turned her stomach. "It's my house now, lady."

"Mine," she hissed.

He shook his head. "Ain't nothin' you can do about it, Chinawo-man. You can't be a citizen or own no property. It's the law. Since your man died, this house is up for grabs, and I'm gonna tell those people in town when I get there and I'm gonna claim it myself. And claim whatever else I want, too." He put on his hat and opened the door. "See you soon," he said.

She heard his laugh for a long time, until it blended into the rain. And then all she could hear was the pounding of her heart and endless, wailing questions.

After China had comforted her daughter and then in stops and starts, embarrassed to be dealing with the exhausting subject of men's urges and behavior, tried to explain why the girl had to be more discreet, more modest, and after her words had been met with sullen incomprehension and yawns, she went back to the kitchen mantel-piece.

"What do I do, Alexander?" she asked the photograph. "Sarah's deed is no good, he says. Not legal. He says he'll come back and take the house and, worse, take Daisy. If I tell the people in town about Emmet Mitchell, they'll take the house away. And without the house..." Without the house, without a single welcoming safe spot on the entire earth...

She knew with bone-center certainty that Emmet Mitchell would come back, perhaps with friends. She had a gun, but what would happen if he wasn't alone, if someone heard the shots, if the law came and found out that a Chinese woman—not even Alexander Ross's legal widow—claimed ownership? They would say she had stolen the deed.

She would write to Sarah. Sarah could tell them that she still

owned the house, that Emmet Mitchell couldn't have it.

No. She couldn't. Sarah and the boys were on a long trip back to Boston. There'd be no way to reach them until it was too late and didn't matter.

And what good would that have done in any case? Emmet Mitchell could still come and steal her daughter, dishonor and humiliate her the way so many men had done to China.

She had to settle this now, and on her own. Not man nor law would side with her. She was completely, unbearably, alone.

She held Alexander's picture close to her. "What will I do?" she whispered. The contents of the window seat were still on the table, and there they'd have to stay a while longer. She lacked the energy to put them away.

"Alexander, what should I do?"

She couldn't risk jail. She had a child to raise, a house to keep. She couldn't even risk being found out.

The rain smacked the windows in great windswept splashes. China lit an oil lamp to push away some of the dark. The tabletop became a glowing island in the quiet room. She saw that one of the embroidered silk slippers had fallen to the floor, and she put it back with its mate. It pleased her to have already added to the window seat, to be a part of the accumulated history of the place.

When she took out the ragged-edged treasures, she liked to replay their stories through her mind and imagine how her additions would be described in years to come. She wanted, needed to believe that there would be years to come and storytellers still unborn. "Your great grandmother," she heard a voice say in the unimaginable future, "embroidered these shoes for her baby, who she called Pale Blossom. But the little girl hated the name and so one day, wanting to be a proper American, she changed it to Daisy, and then . . ."

Then what? Would there be any future after Emmet Mitchell came back and had his way?

She opened the nesting dolls, the Matryoshka Alexander's father had carved for him years and years ago. A heavy peasant woman contained a soldier, a young girl, a priest, a hunter, and a baby. China put them each on the table, populating it.

The rounded, painted hunter wound up next to the primitive little figure made of an oak ball and a forked stick.

"And this was my mother's," she could remember Alexander saying. "This is a poison doll, and this is what you do . . ."

Neither of them had taken it very seriously, of course. But still, she

remembered what he had said. She remembered all his stories and songs. After they had read through the Bible several times and the silly-funny textbooks, it was their own stories that filled the nights.

"Semen is the strongest poison to use against a man." Alexander had said that with a raised eyebrow and she had giggled and promised that she never, ever meant to poison him.

She stared at the poison doll, then closed her eyes and thought about semen as strong killing medicine, about allowing Emmet Mitchell to touch her, to enter her body the better to poison him. The idea was repugnant, but she had once known how to become a tiny speck that could hide in the middle of her mind—the one place they couldn't reach—while men moved around her body. Was one more time worth it, even if her skin crawled at the thought?

No. She couldn't let him back in the house, couldn't allow herself to be vulnerable, and certainly couldn't allow him near Daisy. There were other alternatives. Other bodily fluids.

She lifted the awkward doll with its heavy head, its bead eyes, and crease mouth.

The charms didn't work as well with white men as they did with Indians, Alexander had said. But Anna had crafted this one for a white man spotted in the woods, so she obviously had been willing to try it and so would China. She sat still, remembering every word Alexander ever mentioned about the evil charm. Then she carried the doll upstairs, into the room Emmet Mitchell had occupied.

There were hairs on the pillow and on the edge of the washbasin. She carefully picked each one up and put it into a small leather sack that had also been part of the window-seat trove. Then, controlling the urge to gag, she pulled out the chamber pot and dipped the stick body into Emmet Mitchell's urine.

At dawn, wrapped in an old fur cape of Sarah's, China went out into the rain to find a pine tree. By the time her daughter awoke, she was sitting at the kitchen table sipping coffee. She felt pregnant with justice and evil. Inside her apron pocket, inside the little leather pouch, the poison doll waited, beady eyes alert, its head smeared with pine pitch and strands of Emmet Mitchell's carroty hair.

Two hours later, she heard the shot. It came from a distance, but not a very great one, charging its way through the unending low roar of rain and wind. China looked outside but saw nothing except the dark shadow of the tall trees and the saturated, mucky ground.

Still, her bones felt the gunshot and knew it as a warning. He was

announcing his return. She sat in the big kitchen with her rifle in one hand, the poison doll in the other. In the past two years she had brought down a decent number of deer and Emmet Mitchell was much easier game, she told herself. He was slow-witted and stumble-footed. And then she told herself all of it again, because her self-confidence tottered and slipped between each beat of her heart.

The second shot came minutes later and was closer. She imagined she could hear the man's wet laugh through the storm, could feel his evil excitement.

"What's that thing you're holding, Mama?" Daisy asked. "The stick man from the window seat?"

China nodded.

"Mama!" Daisy's jade eyes were incredulous. "You don't believe things like that, do you?"

"I believe whatever I need to believe." China's voice was a monotone. She was listening, attentively, and repeating, inwardly, the curse Alexander had taught her. She chanted the strange foreign words first, "Boxa elya midok stuk djuke," and then their hard, literal translation. "West-water it you pull-under will-happen." They were the only words she knew to say with the doll, a drowning curse, meant for the ocean, but whether or not they applied, their solid power helped her.

The third shot was close. China took a deep breath.

"Boxa elya," she murmured. Daisy stood behind a chair, watching her mother as if she were a wild beast.

"What are you doing?" she asked. Her voice was unusually quiet.

"Stay in the house," China said, rising out of her seat and walking toward the door. Boxa elya midok stuk... "Don't look outside. Don't go outside."

"But I'm afraid, I—"

China couldn't loosen her concentration long enough to look at her daughter. She thought only of the death she was bringing Emmet Mitchell, thought about it so hard and thoroughly she saw it and felt its molten weight in her hands. She moved like a sleepwalker. Boxa elya...

"Mama, don't go out there—"

China was already outside, closing the door behind her. She saw him in the distance, walking. Where was his horse?

It didn't matter. His horse may have slipped, or left him for shelter. Or he may have traded him for whiskey, if Emmet Mitchell had even gone far enough away to find another human being.

217

In any case, the horse was gone and China took it as a good omen. They were more evenly matched on foot. Except that she had revenge magic, the house, and history on her side.

He lurched toward her, clothing plastered to his body and covered with mud. "Welcoming party?" he said, managing the words with great difficulty. "Why the gun?"

"For the same reason you have one."

"Mine's saying *welcome.*" He tripped over a root, but caught himself. "Welcome home," he said.

"Then mine's not the same as yours. Mine's saying you're going to die."

"You're goin' to shoot me?" He looked amused. "Little tiny Chinawomanthing like you?"

She shook her head and held up the hand with the poison doll. "This is what will kill you," she said in a level voice, and as she spoke, she knew she held the truth in her hand and a great calm strength possessed her.

"A stick?" He laughed. "A little stick and ball?"

She despised the wet laugh that came from an ugly bog inside him. She held her hand higher. The rain ran down the inside of her arm, chilling her, but she ignored it. *Boxa elya . . .*

"This some kind of Chinese curse?" he sneered, but he'd stopped advancing.

"The house's curse," she said. "Very, very old."

"It's a dumb piece of wood," he insisted, but she could feel the porousness of his voice. There were spaces she could enter, and she did.

"It has your hair on its head and your urine on its body, and after you're dead, I'll burn it, and you and your memory will be gone forever."

"You're crazy," he said in a hard whisper. He took a step backward. She took two forward.

"Why'd you have a gun, then, if your little stick's so deadly?" Another step back as she advanced. "Why?" he demanded.

She didn't answer. She held the doll like a torch, believing in it with such force she knew he must as well, and must die. She walked toward him, and although she was afraid of tripping over rocks or sliding on the slick muddy spaces, she kept her eyes on Emmet Mitchell's, as if her glance alone could destroy him.

"You're crazy, lady. Twigs can't hurt a man." Suddenly, and she could see it in his eyes, he remembered that he, too, had a weapon.

She saw his slow, stupid mind work hard toward a decision, and before he could, she rushed toward him, headlong, waving the poison doll.

She felt herself lifted safely above the muck so that she flew toward him with no fear of falling or failure. Many hands supported her, many voices promised victory in languages she didn't recognize.

Mitchell's eyes looked like a horse's in a fire. He raised his rifle. "I'll kill you, lady," he shouted. "I swear I'll—"

"You won't! You can't! You're already dead!" Closer, closer China came, flying, whirring, propelled by her ghosts, waving her arm above her head so he had to see it, had to understand the force she carried.

"Dead, dead," he muttered, walking backwards as he cocked the rifle and took aim. "I'll show you dead, I'll—"

"DEAD!" she screamed, racing now so that he could feel the doll on his flesh, he could burn under its power. "DEAD!"

He forgot his aim, held up his hands to protect himself from her, from the twig figure.

She laughed. He knew now. He believed. "Touch him!" she screamed through the storm. "He's you, dead man! *Boxa elya midok stuk djuke*—west-water it you pull-under..."

"Shut up!"

"... will-happen... *Boxa*—"

"I swear I'll—"

She never knew his threat because the bead eyes glaring into his drove him further backward. He was already too drunk or frightened or poisoned to hear the rush of water behind him, stronger even than the water pouring down from above. Once again he retreated, but this time he found no footing, only the slick bank of the engorged river. This time he stepped into space and a roar engulfed and over-powered his flailing and screaming until he was silent.

When it was quiet again on the riverbank, China dared to look down at the water. Emmet Mitchell was pressed between two rocks, half-submerged, face down. Her muscles relaxed, one by one. She lowered her hand. Slowly, she loosened her cramped fingers from around the stock figure and stared at the grotesque face. Its slash of mouth was almost a grin. "The magic works," she said. "Even for white men, if they believe it can."

"Yes," she heard. It was a woman's voice. But when she turned around, she found no one. And no traces of the strong arms that had carried her.

"Anna?" she whispered. "Are you there?"

She filled with a fierce rage and pride in herself, and in all of them. They were truly kin now, she and Alexander and Nicolai and Anna, a family united by the survivors' blood that ran in their veins.

"Saved," the wind in chorus whispered through the high branches. "Safe," the raindrops in a babble of tongues splashed onto the river.

"Thank you," China whispered. "Thank you all." It was bone-chilling cold and wet, but she still felt their warmth and strength as they surrounded, protected, strengthened, and saluted her.

PART IV
1 8 9 7

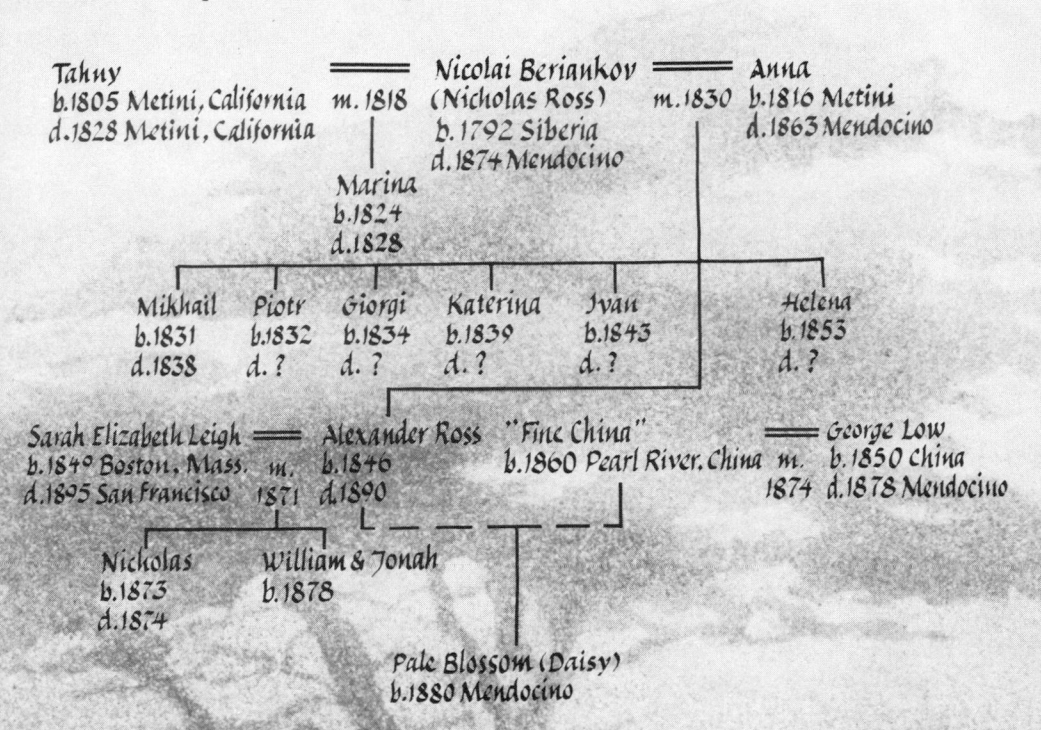

Tahuy
b.1805 Metini, California
d.1828 Metini, California

═══ m. 1818

Nicolai Beriankov
(Nicholas Ross)
b. 1792 Siberia
d. 1874 Mendocino

═══ m.1830

Anna
b.1816 Metini
d.1863 Mendocino

Marina
b.1824
d.1828

Mikhail
b.1831
d.1838

Piotr
b.1832
d. ?

Giorgi
b.1834
d. ?

Katerina
b.1839
d. ?

Ivan
b.1843
d. ?

Helena
b.1853
d. ?

Sarah Elizabeth Leigh
b.1840 Boston, Mass.
d.1895 San Francisco

═══ m. 1871

Alexander Ross
b.1846
d.1890

"Fine China"
b.1860 Pearl River, China

═══ m. 1874

George Low
b.1850 China
d.1878 Mendocino

Nicholas
b.1873
d.1874

William & Jonah
b.1878

Pale Blossom (Daisy)
b.1880 Mendocino

17

There were two things Daisy Ross loved to watch. One was the distant horizon and the other was her own reflection. At the moment, she was enjoying both.

She was upstairs in the octagonal stair landing. She called it the tower because that sounded exotic, a place in which a princess might hide until swept away by a determined prince.

She spent as much time as she could in her private world at the top of the stairs. Sometimes she brought up an old musical instrument she'd found in the window seat, but while it seemed that her sessions in the tower deserved sweet plaintive accompaniment, her fingers could never find their way through its three strings into music.

The light hit one of the panes in a way that let her see her image, which she viewed with great pleasure. She wore an apricot dress that showed off her curves, and her black hair was swept high on her head. She smiled at her reflection, then turned her attention to the other panes of glass and to the horizon.

Not that anyone who could be mistaken for a prince was likely to charge through the redwoods and recognize her special destiny. Their lodgers were tired and ordinary men. She enjoyed their company — or, more accurately, enjoyed their enjoyment of her company. Sometimes they gave her samples from their cases — bits of lace or fancy

trim to tie in her hair. One even gave her enough organdy for a blouse, but her mother made her return it.

Her mother watched her every move, balancing Daisy's emotions like a scale. If Daisy laughed at a salesman's joke, her mother's face grew tight and serious. If Daisy smiled, her mother frowned. Her mother understood nothing. It was hard to believe she had ever been young or had even an idea of what happened between men and women.

Once Daisy had gone to a dance and that memory was as enchanted and dear to her as her fairy tales. All Mendocino had been there. The hall had been full of faces remembered from errand visits to town. Young people. Fresh people, not like the men who trudged to their doorstep for food and rest. These people were alive, dancing and eating the whole night long, their babies parked on benches and mattresses around the room. Then, at dawn, when the party was finally over, Daisy had walked the seven miles home, back into her life. She hadn't even felt tired until her mother forbade any more such expeditions.

Daisy was allowed into town for necessary marketing, and those trips were the high points of her life. She loved Mendocino's noise and movement, the colors of the women's clothing, the rich arrays in the shops, the miles of lumber stacked on the bluff ready to travel the globe, the ships, the buggies, the staggering loggers drinking up their paychecks, the screech of the mill whistle—all of it was exciting and splendid.

On her last trip into town, she'd shared the road with a herd of cattle being driven to market. She had stood and wondered over the peculiar wrappings on some of the cows' hooves until the cowherd explained it to her. "Those are barley sacks, ma'am," he said. "Their hooves start to hurting, then they wander off looking for soft earth and, likely as not, step off into the soft blue air, over the cliff and into the hereafter." Then, with a small bow, he went back to work and was soon lost in the enormous cloud of dust stirred up by the animals' cushioned feet.

While Daisy was still brushing off her skirts, the water wagon appeared to wet down the road and with it a crowd of children who gleefully played in the new-made puddles. Daisy, on impulse, unlaced her boots and joined them, splashing and laughing.

Such extraordinary ordinariness. That's how it was once you were out of the woods—surprising, exciting, full of life and adventure.

She tried to explain it to her mother. She told her about the

224

cattle's barley-sack shoes, about the water wagon, but her mother fretted and worried, talking about panthers and bears, but truly fearing only human beings. Fearing, still and forever, more Emmet Mitchells.

He had marked them, and even after all these years, he haunted them, disguised as the bad symbol of all men to her mother.

Five years earlier, her mother had reentered the house, mud-stained and soaking wet. She had thrown her little stick figure into the fire and stood so rigidly she seemed in a trance. The only sounds were the dripping of her skirts onto the floor and the crack and snap of the fire as the wooden body was consumed. And when it was indistinguishable ash, she turned to her daughter. "Emmet Mitchell is gone," she said. "He will not bother us again."

Daisy had seen it all from her tower. She'd seen her tiny mother advance like a madwoman, the stick-figure doll pointed as if it were God's own finger that could accuse and destroy a large armed man. And it had. It had.

Days later, when the rains ceased, her mother had given Daisy a make-work chore that would keep her inside, then, tight-lipped and determined, she'd left the house. Daisy rushed up to her tower and watched China Ross, so small that unwise men treated her like a youngster or a toy, drag the bloated corpse up the bank. Daisy almost rushed to help, but knew that her mother needed to believe she acted secretly.

The process took hours. Her mother dug a grave above water level, pushed the man into it, and repacked the dirt. That day's actions were never mentioned. But even now, when wild lilacs and sword ferns blurred the outlines and filled in the raw space, Daisy knew what had caused the slight bulge of earth, and she walked in wide arcs to avoid it.

Outside her tower window, the enormous dark wings of a condor made the breath catch in her throat. It, too, seemed part real, part legend, too oversized and overwhelming to be completely true as it rested, suspended on an invisible bank of air.

When it moved out of sight, Daisy returned to the work in her lap, a sampler showing off her needlework. She had copied a pattern she'd seen at her one dance, her single play party, but her family tree had mostly empty leaves. It had been a foolish project; her family was limited and unknown. Her mother didn't even know the names of her parents or her own given birth name or day.

Still, Daisy felt compelled to embroider the thing because that was

what girls did—at least the lovely girls in Mendocino City with their petticoats, fine homes, and ladylike skills. Not girls like Daisy, who found themselves misplaced and surprised, milking cows, churning butter, and rubbing their hands raw on washday. But the true Daisy, the girl who would someday be discovered, embroidered elegant bed linens and charming keepsakes for her trousseau.

She was certain, however, that city girls not only had servants, parties, and fine educations, but also leafier family trees. Certainly the girl at the play party had. Her tree had gone back to England and Finland and forward with sisters, cousins, uncles, and aunts. Daisy enlarged and fluffed her own tree with the long-gone Sarah Leigh Ross, Willy, and Jonah. Daisy missed her half-brothers, who'd made the isolated woods noisy and entertaining and who'd told her so many of the stories they'd been told in their school. They'd promised to write and visit, but so far they'd come only a few times and written almost never. She'd heard that Sarah Ross had died of a fever and the boys had gone to the Yukon in search of gold and adventure. She wondered if she'd ever see them again.

She added yet another leaf, a rather brown-edged one, for the descendantless George Low.

The sampler was still top-heavy. With no known ancestors, her family tree began in California and was shaped like the redwood—a mile high of solid, branchless beginnings, and then a canopy of late-arriving leaves.

Daisy's name was up high and all alone, and she feared that there she would stand, isolated, protected, guarded by her mother, the mountains, the woods, and wild ocean, until she, too, withered at the edges and died.

She had heard the story of the Russian nobleman Rezanov, who came to California before even the fort and colony began. And there he fell in love with patient, loyal Concepcion Arguello. In order to marry, he had to seek permission from the Tsar and the Pope. He never reached either, but died in Siberia after a fall from his horse. Unaware of his fate, Concepcion waited until her youth was gone and her chances ended. Then she became a nun.

Daisy hated the reverence given Concepcion, who'd squandered her youth and beauty. She also feared the story because she could see her life imitate those calm patterns—without, however, even a day's true love or glory with her very own Rezanov.

On Daisy's trips to Mendocino City, she always looked intently at the roof of the Masonic Temple, at Father Time and the maiden.

Even wooden statues said that time could soon run out for young girls. She was seventeen, a woman. Trapped in a tower.

"Daisy!" The sharp voice knocked her back into the present.

She turned and faced her mother, who stood at the top of the stairs, holding the bannister and looking tired. "I called you twice!"

"I didn't hear."

"What do you do up here?"

"Look outside. Think."

"She thinks!" China said with a snort.

Her mother often conversed with an imaginary listener. Daisy was positive she was pretending her father was still around, aware and responsive. "Well, then think about this," her mother said. "There's a tired man downstairs and his room isn't ready." She turned and slowly descended the stairs.

Another tired man. Another bed to make.

Daisy walked across the hall in a sulk. She shook out a sheet and tucked its ends under the mattress. Nothing but a servant girl. Cinderella. So unfair! She could see what was in the mirror. She could see what was on the men's faces. Daisy Ross wasn't meant to make beds and stews and cure hams like a drudge. Scrub chicken houses. Render lard. Churn cream and salt butter. Stuff pig's entrails for sausage. Empty chamber pots and dish out fried potatoes and wash strangers' bed linens. Unfair, wrong, a serious mistake that somebody had to rectify.

"Someday," she muttered to herself. It was almost her only prayer. She didn't know what was going to happen, but something had to. "Someday," she promised again, making sure the dresser top was clear and clean. "Someday."

"Beg pardon, miss?"

"Some..." She turned, her mind fuzzed with unnamed hopes. And before she had even stopped turning, the man in the doorway replaced all her faceless dreams with clarity and finality.

"I startled you. I am sorry." He spoke with great precision, nervously handling the language. There was a soft foreign edge to his words. "I am Antonio Silva. This is, perhaps, my room?"

She nodded, so awkward suddenly and silent she didn't recognize herself. Antonio Silva. The name ran into her center. The man glowed, as if everything about him had been heated and was on the verge of melting. His skin was dark gold, his dark eyes moulten, his lips full and curled at the corners as if he were ready to laugh. Or love.

227

"I have not interrupted you? Caused you trouble?"

She shook her head, taking deep breaths to control her flush and lightheadedness.

He bowed. "Then I am very pleased to meet you, Miss . . ."

"Ross. Daisy Ross."

"Like the flower." He smiled as if her name had been a carefully selected gift for him. "Very, very pleased to meet you," he repeated.

He understood how things were without being told. He knew they had to be careful, had to avoid China Ross's eyes. The morning after he arrived, Tonio was waiting inside the barn when Daisy entered for the milking. He watched her with interest and amusement.

"In the Azores," he said, "our pasture was far from the house. Five miles at least. You had to leave the house around midnight to get the milk at daybreak. When I was eight, it was my turn. I was so afraid of walking through the woods all alone, I made all the noise I could, singing at the top of my lungs. Mile after mile, hour after hour, until it was daylight. My voice was so rough and hoarse all the time, my parents thought it was changing early and they teased me about growing a beard."

He lounged against the doorway and didn't make a move toward her, except with his eyes, until it was time to help carry her milk pails.

Later, he was standing by a redwood, a bouquet of wildflowers in his hand, ready to accompany her at least part of the long walk to town. He explained what being "Acoreano," from the Azores, meant and tried to teach her enough geography to pinpoint the islands off Portugal. And, more significantly, he took and held her hand while they walked. He didn't ask permission or hesitate, but behaved as if he and Daisy were the foregone conclusion to a story both had heard a long time ago.

She was being claimed.

The next day, when her mother was outside, Tonio walked through the open door of Daisy's bedroom. She was fully clothed, sitting on a chair, mending sheets, but she was still shocked by his boldness. And delighted.

"This is a fine bed," he said, pressing on it. "On my island, I had a bed of corn husks and moss."

She felt as if he were waiting for a response, but she didn't know what it should be.

"Here," he said with a smile. "I'll show you how my island is." She watched in confusion as he moved her pillow to the center of her

bed, under the sheet and quilt. "This is Pico, see? High in the center with villages around the slopes, near the water. And another peak here"—he pulled the bedding into a lump on one side—"for the volcano. And all different color patches like this quilt from corn and wheat and barley and grapes." He stepped back from the bed and regarded it. "Makes me homesick."

It made her another sort of sick, a nervous, giddy, lightheaded, and fearful sort. She didn't see any island. All she saw was her rumpled bed and a very handsome man who had claimed it casually and now seemed a part of it.

She had lived as if she were a removable piece of her mother, another set of arms and legs. Now she had her own separate limbs, her own secrets, her own life.

But as much as her life was now her own, it was also only a fragment. Tonio was the missing part, her kindred soul.

"I had no school," he said. Then he shrugged. It didn't matter, not to him, not to her. "If you read and write," he continued, "you have to vote, and politics is for *fitzadas*, for witches."

He believed in bad luck brought by women. He spoke of *bruchas*, active, evil witches. He explained that women weren't allowed to board fishing boats because of their potential evil. He formed a *figa*, holding his thumb between his second and third fingers to ward off evil spirits.

In turn, she told him about the *domovoy* although she barely knew why they put cookies and biscuits on the carved redwood plate in the bay window, and the *domovoy*'s supposed magic was puny compared to Tonio's *bruchas*. Still, it was another link, another way to say she understood him.

And he understood her, because he leaned over and gently, tenderly kissed her lips, and it was like every daydream she had ever allowed herself to feel, all those long afternoons in her tower.

She hid the remaining sulfur matches, then offered to buy a can of them in town. On the way, she and Tonio walked to the beach at the end of the river. Daisy never tired of the sea's changing texture and promise of distant shores. It was better still with Tonio, who had ridden those waves halfway around the world to be by her side. They looked for shells, talked of shipwrecks and sailors' lore, and held hands all the while. She told him about digging abalone when the tide was low. "You pry it off with a bar," she said, "or the abalone

could clamp your hand and trap you, and when the tide comes in, you'd drown. One man saved himself by cutting off his hand." She shivered at her own story, and Tonio pulled her close and kissed her.

"We'll dig abalone together," he said. "So we can save each other."

She breathed in his scent, spicy with memories of hot distant shores, and wished she could breathe all of him in as well.

When they finally reached town, it churned and danced around them, pulling miracles out of its top hat. There was even a medicine show at the end of Main Street, funny skits and snake oil cures. Pure magic. The whole world had been designed and arranged for Daisy and Tonio's delight.

They paused on their way back to the boardinghouse and sat on a hill covered with wild mustard.

"Why did you leave the Azores?" she asked.

He ran his fingers over her face. "It's very poor there. And crowded. Everybody divides the land, more and more, for all their babies. Here, a man can breathe. Besides, in the Azores, all men must go nine hundred miles away to Portugal to serve in the army for eight years. You can't escape unless you're rich enough to post a bond and leave it."

"But you—"

"There are backdoors. My father left on a whaling ship, years ago."

"He's here?"

Tonio nodded. "In Monterey. My brother, too. They fish. My father has sent for my mother now. I have family here, too."

"In Mendocino?"

"My uncle. On the other side of town, where the Portuguese live."

Daisy felt queasy, less sure of the story she was weaving around the two of them, but she couldn't say why.

"I was on my way to my uncle when I stopped at your house. And then, seeing you, how could I leave? You are very different, Daisy. So . . . American." In his smile she felt the heat of all the generations that had lived on his sun-baked islands. His kiss, his embrace confirmed her dreams. She never tired of him, couldn't be close enough, long enough.

"If you permit," he said, "even when I go to my uncle, I will come back and visit you. We can be together then, too."

She would permit anything. They were destined to be together for all time, combined as one creature. There was no room for cowardice, doubt, or questions.

* * *

"He's white!" her mother hissed after seeing them exchange a smile. "Never trust a white man! They'll eat your brains or your eyes."

Her mother was going mad. The last thing Tonio resembled was a cannibal. "My brothers are white," Daisy said.

"Half-brothers, and when you last knew them, they were boys! Who knows what they became, what they learned to be in that accursed city!"

"My father was white," Daisy said.

"That's different. They didn't think he was white, only half of him was, so he understood."

Her mother was becoming peculiar. The only sane course was to ignore her and stay out of her line of vision.

Each morning Daisy rushed through her chores so that each afternoon she could meet Tonio in what had become their own sheltered clearing far from the house.

Her mother grumbled and complained about her inability to find Daisy, about chores half-done or never begun, but Daisy scarcely heard, because inside her head there was a joyful din, a glad noise like a song or a waterfall, or both. She wished she could tell her mother or a friend—anyone—how she felt, how Tonio was unlike any other man.

She knew the difference. She wasn't as much a child as her mother wanted to believe. She remembered Emmet Mitchell standing over her in his pajamas and she had known, even then, what it was he planned to do. But he had revolted her, disgusted her, and his hand on her chest—she hadn't truly had breasts then—had been loathesome, like one of the blind and monstrous subterranean creatures that sometimes crawled above earth.

And that's why she knew that Tonio was different and right, because the idea of his hand on her naked breast didn't upset her at all. In fact, her flesh required it, felt starved for it.

At night, alone in her bed, she touched herself and imagined the hands were Tonio's and nearly wept for wanting him. And when they were together, as carefully as she dressed and primped for him, her clothing became a fussy barrier, a choking constraint that made no sense.

For two afternoons, they kissed, they spoke, they held hands and stood close.

For two nights, the voices, the singing, and the wanting kept Daisy awake.

They were so close, but still not enough, and the distance that stretched between them made her ache. They were meant to be joined, had to be joined and committed to becoming one.

"I want you," Tonio said. "I want you so much I burn for you. I cannot think of anything else."

Tonio had made a nest, soft as a feather bed, of pine tree limbs all lying in the same direction. They lay close, talking, while she studied his profile, the great dark eyes and moustache, the sensuous lips.

His hand was at her neck, playing with the small top button of her dress. She could feel her cheeks burn and her whole body heat by a force other than the sun breaking through to their clearing. "Do you love me?" she whispered, opening her arms, pulling him toward her.

"I ... Daisy, Daisy, my heart ... you are so beautiful, so ... I, oh, God, Daisy!"

She didn't hear clearly, didn't know if he'd answered her, and didn't care because they were so close then, his hand in her hair, pulling it free, his hands undoing the buttons, one by one, fumbling with the tiny pearl circles. She heard both their breathing, hard sounds in the silent forest, and then she heard her own moan as he touched her breasts, then buried his face in them, kissed them while his hand moved, claiming all of her, finding the flesh beneath her skirt and petticoats, above her boot, riding up her leg to her thigh, where only her hands had ever been.

She gasped with the pleasure of his touch. She wanted his hands and lips to be everywhere, wanted to be completely pressed against and around him, feeling him in every part of her being.

He moved over her body, kissing her, telling her how beautiful every part of her was, calling her his American princess. There was a moment's shock of pain, then Tonio pulled back.

"I thought—"

"Shhh," she said, pulling him close until they moved beyond it, deep into the center of the whirlpool, and there were no more questions.

The trees circled and shielded them so that the world beyond their one spot no longer existed.

Later, as if from a great distance, Daisy looked at the tangle of their bare arms and legs. Her skin was tawny, but forest pale. His had

been painted with amber. Their fleshtones blended and complemented each other.

"Daisy, my little daisy," he murmured. "The most beautiful flower in the world. You have made me the happiest man on earth."

She lay on her back, still half uncovered, letting the sunlight wash over her. She was newly made, a different creature than she had been all the other, drab days of her life. She had entered the mystery and been transformed.

"You're smiling," he said. "You're happy. Good."

He was the one she had dreamed of who would take her away, out of the woods and the dark places into the glitter of sun off sea, of large families and easy laughter. Of cities, fine dresses, and elegant hats. Adventures. And love, of course. Love forever.

"You are so beautiful," he murmured. "You must be the most beautiful girl for miles and miles. You would surely be the Pentecost Queen," he said.

His admiration melted her so that she was no more than floating liquid, evaporating in the sun. And yet she was also intently aware of herself, of every pore and sensitive spot.

"If, of course," he added, "you were Portuguese."

Her mind stumbled as if his words were pointed rocks sticking out of their meadow. Nonsense. She returned instead to the safe, soft sentences that had preceded it. Loving sentences. About how happy she'd made him, how beautiful she was. The Pentecost Queen. She had seen the parade the year before with its fresh-scrubbed children dressed in white, carrying red banners with white doves on them. People lined Main Street to watch. The queen wore a crown and was radiant. Very splendid and intense, but Daisy had no idea what it celebrated or honored. That, then, was a safe question, unlike a dozen dangerous ones that prickled her mind.

The sun shifted so that they were in partial shadow.

"In the thirteenth century," Tonio explained, "because of a miracle, Queen Isabel won a day of jubilation and feasting from the king. She found roses in January, an impossibility. To celebrate, the nobility honored and waited upon the poorest of the poor."

"Roses in January," Daisy said. "Lovely."

"That is what I thought when I saw you the first time—a miraculous flower. I was so tired, walking day after day up from Monterey. All I wanted was a place to sleep. A real bed. And instead I found a

daisy blooming wild and all alone in the woods. Truly as much a miracle as a rose in January."

She listened carefully and to her relief, he didn't say "as much of an impossibility."

Her mother began to stalk Tonio as if he were dangerous prey, and even after he was asleep or in his room for the night, she sat in the kitchen mumbling to her photographs. "He was tired when he came here, I know," she said one night when she and Daisy sat mending. "Walked up the coast. But by now he should feel fine, should move on. How long does that man plan on lazing around?"

Daisy felt a jolt of surprise. Had it been a long time or a short time since Tonio arrived? It seemed decades, centuries, and brief as an eye blink. She couldn't remember a time before him, a life without him. Perhaps for outsiders, living in ordinary time, there were still clocks and calendars, but not for Daisy Ross.

"What are his plans?" Her mother sounded crackly, old, and annoyed.

Daisy tugged too hard at her needle and the thread pulled out. She busied herself rethreading it.

"A grown man, healthy and fit, doesn't sit around a boarding-house."

"He doesn't sit around," Daisy muttered. "He leaves. Sees people."

"How do you know? When do you talk? How much do you really know about this man?"

Daisy said nothing. She was surprised, relieved, and mildly disappointed that her mother couldn't see his imprint on her flesh. Certainly Daisy still felt the afternoon all over her, inside and out. I know him well, she could have said. And he knows me. But if her mother couldn't see and celebrate the magical change in her daughter's life, then what business was it of hers? Why this obsession with Tonio's plans? She was so suspicious, so full of mutterings and warnings and old-fashioned superstitions. She didn't understand this new world, the way people were today. And she certainly didn't understand love.

A few days later, Tonio moved to his uncle's. It grieved Daisy, but since it put her mother off-guard, it seemed for the best. She still rushed away with a new excuse each afternoon to meet him in the woods.

Once, when Daisy was supposedly picking berries, Tonio borrowed

his uncle's buggy. They rode into the valley and picnicked on apples and cheese near a strange rock formation.

"It's called Squaw Rock," Tonio said. "I was told the story on my way to you. An Indian girl's betrothed married another. He and his bride were sleeping under that cliff and Sotuka, the betrayed, stood at the top and saw them. She grabbed the largest stone she could lift and sprang off the cliff and onto her victims. They all died here. Like that."

"How sad," Daisy said. "For everyone."

Tonio thought about it. "Yes," he finally agreed.

"Daisy, Daisy." As always, it sounded soft and exotic when it passed through his mouth. "Dassy, Dassy." She lay in his arms in their meadow, floating on his voice. "You have made me such a happy man."

Her eyes were closed. She loved what they did together and she loved remembering, reliving it afterward while the sun washed their limbs.

"My American girl . . ." he said, and the words made her smile, as always. Her tawny skin and tilted eyes were his image and definition of American. What would the people say who didn't agree at all, who wouldn't let her go to their school with their American children? What would Emmet Mitchell and his laws have made of that?

"So beautiful . . ." It was he who was beautiful, who filled her with his beauty.

What a glorious child they could create someday.

Or perhaps they already had. The idea flooded, frightened, and enchanted her. She touched her abdomen, low, wondering if her body was capable of such serious magic.

She half-dozed, thinking of the future. Did Tonio know that schooner captains could perform weddings? She wondered if they had any rules about half-Chinese brides. If not, they could run away, sail to San Francisco, and become man and wife. Eloping sounded right —wildly romantic and practical—because it avoided both her mother and his family's probable objections. She imagined their honeymoon, one night cradled in a tiny bed aboard a rocking ship.

". . . will always remember you . . ." Tonio's voice was grave and, she belatedly realized, had been for a while.

It was difficult, but she left the schooner dream, sat up, and pulled on her blouse, hastily buttoning it. What was he saying? He'd always

remember her? No—because what could that mean? Perhaps he'd said he'd always remember this time, this special day's lovemaking. What did he mean and why couldn't she dare ask him to explain, to back up and fill in the spots her daydreams had left.

". . . You are so merry, so carefree, so generous and loving."

She twisted a long blade of grass around and around her finger.

"I will never forget you."

"Why?" she finally whispered.

"Why? Because you are not like anyone else I have ever known."

She shook her head. "Why would you have to forget me?"

He looked confused.

"Where are you going, Tonio?" she asked, surprised that her voice was calm, showing none of the unbearable strain she felt in every tendon of her throat.

"To my family, as I said."

"But you're already with your uncle. I don't understand. Won't you see me anymore?"

"Dassy, you weren't listening."

She looked down at her hands and heard his deep sigh. He wasn't coming back. He was going to stay with his family. Without her, without taking her to them. She remembered when he'd said she could be queen of the festival if only she were Portuguese. It wasn't enough to be his American. She had to be like him, cook his food the old way, share his memories, go to the *chamarita*, dance with his countrymen. She put together scraps and bits of their conversations and saw all the ties that still bound him to his origins. He'd join one of the *irmandades*, the brotherhoods of Portuguese men. He'd go to mass, pray in ways she'd never heard.

But she could learn, couldn't she? Why wouldn't he give her the chance? How could he kiss and touch and love her so and not give her a chance to be all the things he wanted? "Don't you care for me at all anymore?" she whispered.

"Oh, yes," he said with all the heat of sincerity. "Oh, yes, much more than I would want to, my laughing Dassy."

There was one more scrap left to pull up and hope it would cover her.

"If only you were Portuguese," he said softly. "If only this were years ago. If . . ."

"But nothing's different. Nothing's changed. You can come back here, back to me." But he had been saying he'd never forget her. Never. Not a word for short separations. She shook her head, trying to avert his answer. Better not to know.

236

"No," he said nonetheless. "It would not be good, would it? My wife would be very—"

"Your wife?" Daisy stood up, buttoning her skirt, stammering and hopping as she laced her boots. Then she stopped and leaned against a tree. Let him say she misunderstood. Let him say something that fit the pure sunshine of what had been a golden day.

"Have you heard nothing I've said? Maria will be here soon with our son. This is why I came up from Monterey. She sails with her sister, whose husband is here, so they both will arrive soon and . . ."

But Daisy's mind had stopped somewhere around "Maria" and "our son." Unconsciously, she touched her lower abdomen again. She was afraid she would faint, and she turned away and held on to the tree.

"I did not think you'd be so upset," he said, coming behind her and putting his hands on her shoulders.

"How could I not be? How could you think that?" She was glad she couldn't see him, gladder still he couldn't see the embarrassment, rage, humiliation, and terrible, wrenching pain that translated into tears.

"You are so carefree," he said. "So bold and full of pleasure. So different. So American and new."

"You should have said you were married."

"I didn't think it mattered," he said. "You never asked or seemed to care or stopped me or—"

"You should have told me!"

"But why?" he asked. "You didn't think that I'd—" He came close to her, touched her, then pulled his hand away. "Dassy, I could never marry somebody like you. Somebody so . . . different. It's not only that you aren't Portuguese. You're beautiful, perfect, but my mother, my father, my uncles, they'd be . . . Dassy, you must understand. I thought you always did. I never lied. I never said I loved you, or would marry you, did I?"

"Go away." She pressed her face to the tree trunk.

"But Dassy, I'm still here, the sun is shining, there's time for—"

"For nothing. I can't look at you again."

She heard his good-bye and the soft rustle of the grass.

Then she turned and watched his retreat, pained by the sight of his broad shoulders and dark hair. Her prince, her deliverer, walking, with no white steed and no special gait. Just an ordinary married fisherman who had done the most ordinary thing with a poor country girl. An easy, half-Chinese country girl. More than anything, more than disillusionment and more than fear of what lay ahead, she recoiled from the ordinariness of the big adventure of her life.

18

Somebody was rocking his bed. Gideon James groaned. He was too tired to get up.

He opened one eye. Not even light out yet. God, but his neck was stiff, and the noise—what in all that was holy roared and shook in the middle of a forest?

He sat bolt upright.

He was in a forest. Alone. There were no beds to rock. No hands but his.

He scrambled to his feet. The earth heaved again, violently. He didn't know whether to run for a clearing or stay put, whether it was more dangerous to navigate moving earth or to stand where trees might crash. But these trees were so large he couldn't run free of their range in time.

Before he finished his deliberations or pulled on his shoes, the shaking stopped.

Just as abruptly, the deafening accumulation of sound ceased. No more rustle of fern fronds, protests of giant trees, bellows and howls of distant animals, din of bird cries, grunts and sighs of heaving earth. The startling silence pressed in on him as loudly as if it had been a scream of terror.

"Mother of God," he said. "A quake."

He couldn't see much damage, and as soon as he was finished with fear, he became, in truth, disappointed. He wanted his terrifying awakening justified by catastrophe, disaster, cataclysm, the splitting of the earth, the swallowing of the redwoods. But despite the roars and cracks, the trees still stood. Nearby, the river ran brown with soil ripped from between stump-littered banks.

The ground beneath him was not only intact, but still covered with shamrock-shaped leaves. Gideon picked some of them to include, along with news of a genuine earthquake, in a letter home.

He wouldn't say it had been only a mild and boring quake. He'd make it more what they'd expect back in New York. He could see his mother reading the letter in her favorite chair near the window. She'd put her hand to her heart and close her eyes. She didn't mind Gideon's wanderlust unless his travels exposed him to something truly new or different. Then, on hearing of it, she'd shake her head and ask his brother, Sean, what in the name of God Gideon wanted. And Sean would stay quiet, knowing that Gideon wanted the whole world.

Gideon waited, but the quake was so completely over, it might as well never have happened. The forest had shifted back into its own deep musings. Gideon packed his few belongings.

Should he pick shamrocks for Isobel as well? Maybe not. She was satisfied with so little, she might consider a letter and some dead weeds a promise he wasn't ready to make.

Besides, his mother would surely inform her of Gideon's latest exploits. Anything to keep Isobel's ladylike and quiet flicker of interest in him alive. He could imagine Isobel's eyes widening in surprise and fear when his mother told her about the earthquake. She did have those enormous blue eyes, a tiny waist, and a sweet womanly air. He remembered her in a pale flax-colored dress that matched her hair, bent over the fine needlework with which she stocked her hope chest, a patient, soft-spoken, good-hearted woman.

He didn't know why the thought of her made him uneasy. Isobel was a logical, easy choice, an extension of his mother and sister. Isobel was the right thing to do.

He was almost twenty. Old enough to think about taking a wife.

But not right now.

The forest reminded him of St. Margaret's with its high columns, naves, and silence. The beams of morning light turned the vaulted canopy of leaves into green and gold stained glass and the mossy, pine-needled ground into a shifting mosaic. "'There is a pleasure in

the pathless woods; there is a rapture on the lonely shore,'" he recited. Never, when he'd memorized the words of Lord Byron, had he thought to feel them, wish he had written them, but they so perfectly fit this spot. Gideon felt at peace, a single celebrant of the power and majesty that was palpable, visible here. This was his cathedral.

If his mother, his brother, his sisters, or Isobel could read his thoughts, they'd be horrified and urge him to confess his blasphemy.

He wasn't like them. This idea made him uneasy, but it didn't change reality.

Now he was even less like them. He'd been through a quake, been initiated. Now he was a true Californian.

He walked carefully, realizing with a grin that the early spring flowers, the hot poppies and nasturtiums and the purple and yellow irises, he passed were in more jeopardy from his boots than from the recent upheavals of nature.

They'd have to beware. He was eager to be on his way. He knew he must be near the places where men took on these giants.

It was obvious from the state of the riverbank's stumps, sprouts, and debris that loggers had come and gone here before modern machinery made clearing and hauling logs easy. The early loggers took only the trees that could easily slide into the river and be transported to sea. Here, a narrow strip of riverbank had been logged, and that, partially. Nowadays, nothing at all would be left. He had passed some "clean-logged" sites that looked like Atlanta after Sherman marched to the sea.

He walked purposefully into an ancient untouched grove, feeling like the first and only man on earth.

A scream shattered both the illusion and the solemn quiet of the woods.

"Hurry!" somebody cried. "Nicky, no! Get the—"

Gideon strained to hear more clearly, but all he caught were fragments.

"—on *fire!* Can't you—*please!*"

He broke into a run, dodging trees as he raced.

"—here—*no!*—More, go get—" Broken commands, advice, pleas, all with a terrible undertone of tears. "How can I—Nicky, don't go there, don't—"

"Ma'am!" He burst into the clearing.

She screamed and dropped her bucket. She looked like a witch. Her black hair was wild and tangled, her dress ripped at the shoulder, and her face and arms streaked with soot and old tear tracks.

"My water!" she wailed. "Spilled! Now I'll never—"

Gideon picked up the pail and raced down the slope to refill it at the river. There was a pump down there and a water barrel on a sled, but it would take a horse to drag it up the slope, so Gideon dipped the bucket and ran uphill toward her.

"It's the house!" she cried.

He never broke stride, but loped toward a large, strangely shaped house. She ran behind, redirecting her torrent of directions and explanations at him. "The kitchen—the quake broke the stovepipe and it fell over and set fire to—"

He wondered where the undependable Nicky had gone.

"I was milking the cows and everything shook so, it was so noisy, then I came back and the stove fell and—"

He sloshed water on the smoldering rag rug. The floor nearby was littered with glass and splots of fruit preserves and vegetables the jars once held. "It'll be all right," he said. "You've taken care of most of it yourself." Scorch marks showed where flames had licked the floor and wall. "You have no well?" he asked.

"Broken. And now the rain barrel split in the shaking."

He rolled up the rug and dragged it outside, then raced back to the river, disapproving of such a poorly maintained house. And where was Nicky?

She ran beside him. Both carried buckets down and back up the hill, splashing their contents over the floor inside and the braided, blackened rag rug outside until it was soggy.

"Where is he?" she asked abruptly. "And where's *she*? How can she sleep through this?" She glared at Gideon with strange eyes that glowed green against her sooty face. She looked untamed, filthy, and frightening.

"Ma'am, I have no idea who or where any—"

Her eyes stayed on him, but she didn't see him, he realized. Then she looked toward the house, took a step, and turned back to him. "Something must have happened to her. Come with me."

This demon-woman needed to be reminded that he had already put out a fire in her house without so much as a word of thanks. He didn't know her, let alone owe her any further favors. Besides, why didn't that ne'er-do-well, Nicky, help? "Ma'am!" he said in protest.

She stopped at his call and turned to face him, looking surprised, as if this were the first time she'd truly noticed him.

Her green almond eyes flashed. She had fine, if angry, features. He had never seen anyone, anything like her. Perhaps the earth had

241

shaken her loose this morning, a dangerous wood nymph sprung from beneath the roots of the trees. "Yes?" she asked. "What?"

"Nothing." He felt mesmerized. "Beg pardon."

He was surprised by her house's sprawling size and fine workmanship. He would have envisioned this woman in a tree stump or cave. And where was the family large enough to warrant such a place?

She stopped at the top of the stairs in an octagonal landing. There were wooden benches under windows from which Gideon could see the ocean on one side, the mill town at its edge, the mountain on another, and the river at yet another angle. The whole place was like a fortress, or a lookout post.

How odd.

The woman peered outside. "There he is," she muttered. "Daydreaming. Always forgets what he's doing." Visibly annoyed, she turned and gestured Gideon along.

Like an obedient dog, he trailed behind and waited as she opened a door.

"Oh, no!" she screamed.

He, too, gaped.

A heavy branch, thicker than a man's torso, had crashed through the roof onto the bed.

The witch-woman seemed rooted in place as if she wanted to keep the broad segment of tree between her and whatever evil it had committed. "No," she whispered. "No. She can't be . . ."

Gideon took a deep breath and walked toward what needed seeing. Thin light from the gashed ceiling revealed a tiny hand, a wrinkled and bloody face. "Ma'am," he said gently, "the branch hit her forehead."

"Is she . . . is she . . ."

"My condolences, ma'am."

The sob from the foot of the bed was so loud it almost drowned out the groan from the other end.

"She's alive!" he cried.

Another groan.

"The tree—help me with it!" The woman pushed so forcefully her face turned purple. Gideon also strained and tugged until he lifted the heavy limb while the witch rolled a tiny old woman out from under it and then, along with Gideon, wrapped her in a quilt.

"We'll take her downstairs. To my room. She'll—"

A high-pitched voice interrupted her. "Mama? Who's that man? What's he got there?"

242

"Nicky!" Her voice was back to the worried, irritable tone he'd first heard. "Where *were* you?"

Gideon lifted the old woman, carefully maneuvered around Nicky and the witch, and made his way down the stairs, cradling his bundle as if it were a baby in its bunting. His mind, however, stayed upstairs on the landing. Nicky looked seven or eight. The witch's child.

He felt unaccountably depressed.

They came clattering down, squabbling all the while.

"But, Mama, I *got* the water—"

"*Finally!*" she snapped. "It doesn't matter now! You *know* you shouldn't wander off!"

"But, Mama!"

"The fire's out, no thanks to you! And now a tree came through the roof, and grandma's bleeding and—"

"Mama, I—"

"Not another word! Open my door. She'll stay there until we fix the roof and she's better. I'll be right back."

Gideon lay the old woman on the bed. Her closed-eye silence and near weightlessness seemed touching, pitiable, as if she didn't matter at all.

After a quiet, awkward time, during which Gideon and the child eyed each other and said nothing, the witch returned, carrying a broom dripping with spider webs. "Barn's full of them," she said. She carefully pulled them off the straw one by one and applied them to the old woman's bloody forehead.

Gideon watched with horror. Next would be bats and toads and strange spells.

The witch looked up, saw his expression, and stood straight, hands on hips. "Stops the blood," she said.

He was disgusted by her primitive superstitions until he realized that the old woman was no longer bleeding.

Gideon felt awkward and useless. The woman ignored and annoyed him. He wanted nothing further to do with her. But abandoning a family in visible distress was not at all the right thing to do.

He shifted his weight to his other foot, then sighed.

The sigh was echoed at thigh level.

The little boy looked up with enormous, heavily lashed eyes. "Mister?"

"Yes?"

The woman put her finger to her lips. "Shhh!"

Gideon stiffened. No acknowledgment, no thank-you for putting

243

out her fire, carrying her mother, staying when asked. What a crude, rude backwoods wretch she was! He turned and left the bedroom.

"Mister?" The little boy was at his heels. "Can I show you something?"

Gideon shrugged. "Why not?"

"Not here," the boy said. "Outside."

The boy rushed ahead, disappearing down the slope toward the river, and suddenly Gideon was tired of this family's nonsense and not at all sure how he'd become embroiled in it. "Wait!" he called out. "Hey, Nicky!"

The little boy turned.

"I changed my mind. I can't stay," Gideon said. "I'm late already. The day's half gone and I haven't made one mile's progress, don't you see?"

"No."

"I'm heading north. To the logging camps, or to where they work the tanbark. It's peeling time. I've been traveling for days, by ferry and train and stage and foot. All the way from San Francisco, you see."

The boy shook his head. He didn't see anything except his own bare feet, which he studied. He said nothing.

"I need a job," Gideon said. "So I can keep moving. I plan to see the whole world."

Nicky kept his eyes on the ground. "Couldn't you look at this one thing first?"

Gideon sighed. "Is it far?"

Nicky was again all animation. "At the river. Not far." He waved Gideon on.

A few moments later, Nicky's voice piped high with excitement. "See?"

Gideon saw only a hacked continuation of the same tableau he'd already seen downstream. Enormous stumps, slender young trees, and, at the river's edge, raw-edged splits in the earth. Man and nature had chewed the place up.

"Over there," Nicky said. "Look!" He broke into a run.

"Wait!" Gideon called. "Watch out! You'll fall into—"

But the child stopped himself, averting a slide into the river. He looked self-important and proud, a discoverer, a conqueror. And still Gideon saw no reason for the boy's excitement. Perhaps it was the great chunk of dirt, ferns, and shrubs that had fallen into the river?

244

The open scar was interesting, but not worth a frantic race from the house.

"Don't you see it?"

Gideon followed the direction of the boy's intent gaze and pointed finger. And saw it.

A bony hand, wrist deep in earth, pointed back. A dozen inches away, a half-submerged skull grinned mirthlessly. Its chin was buried or missing, and it had a single tuft of rusty hair. Gideon unconsciously touched his own forehead and scalp.

"Skeleton," the boy whispered. "Dead thing. I seen lots. Deer, once. Raccoon. Skunk. Once, a bear. But that's a hand. A person's skull. Never saw that before."

Gideon stared. Who had it been? And why buried in such an awkward place? The tuft of hair suggested that the skeleton had not died long enough ago for nature alone to have slowly buried it. Somebody had helped, planting the corpse uncomfortably on an incline above the river. Planting the corpse hastily, secretly, because there was something wrong, suspicious about its death. Planting it here, in a remote area where almost no one lived. It must have to do with the house up the hill.

He turned to the boy. "Where's your dad, Nicky?" he asked.

The boy shrugged.

"He work the woods or the mill?"

A slow shake of the head.

"Where is he, then?" The skeleton had rust-colored hair, more kin to Gideon's head than to the boy's shiny black mop. But who knew what burial did to color? Besides, the mother had black hair, so it didn't matter.

The boy looked at him blankly. He obviously had no idea where his father was. Did the witchy one know her husband's whereabouts? Was she waiting for him to return? Had he been accosted on his way home, robbed, murdered, and hidden by bandits, and did she keep a candle burning, say prayers every night, and hope in vain? Was that why her face turned bitter so easily?

Or had she herself murdered him?

Should he inform her of the corpse's existence? Accuse her of killing it? Or pick up his rucksack and leave?

The last suggestion brought such a wave of relief he had his answer. Let sleeping dogs—and dead men—lie. He had no business here and he'd have no more of the place.

"Can I tell her now?"

"Who?" Gideon asked.

"Mama. Do I still have to wait?"

Gideon had no idea what her rules might be at any moment. "I'll walk you up the hill," he said. "Tell her if you like, but I've got to go."

"Nicky!" she shouted from the window when she saw them. The boy was fairly dancing. Gideon trudged. "Grandma's awake. She's talking. I think she can see, too. Hurry!"

Nicky raced inside.

Not a word of acknowledgment for Gideon. Was he invisible? A gnat she could ignore? He changed his mind. Damned if he'd miss the show, whether or not she wanted him in there. He stomped inside, uninvited, eager now to see her expression when her son announced his discovery of the corpse. To see if she was indeed a murderess—and he was suddenly sure she was—and then to decide what to do about it. He positioned himself outside the open bedroom door where he could watch and hear the three of them but not be very obvious himself.

"What's on my head?" the old woman was asking.

"Sliced potatoes, for your headache."

"Where's my bed? My quilt?" The old woman's accent made it hard for Gideon to understand her.

"A branch hit your bed. Your quilt ripped. I'll mend it. There was a quake."

"Is Alexander fixing our bed?" the old woman asked.

"He isn't here. You know that." The young woman's voice was softer, slower than it had been all day, but tense still.

"Is he still in the woods?" As she asked the question, the old woman pushed to sit more upright, gasped, and lay back. "Oh," she said weakly. "It's all blurred but when I moved it turned darker. I'm dizzy. I . . ."

"Rest, please. You hurt your head."

"Where *is* Alexander?"

The young woman clamped her lips together.

"Grandma." Nicky's voice was strong and resolute. "Grandpa's dead."

Gideon felt sick. Had the boy recognized the rusty hair of the skeleton, then? And was he really bringing an injured old woman such horrifying news?

246

"Dead?" Her voice was incredulous. The black-haired woman, on the other hand, didn't look at all surprised.

Gideon's revulsion grew. She knew. Had she, then, been the one who put him there? Killed her own father?

"I just saw him," the old woman insisted. "He was playing with the baby. With Pale Blossom."

"I'm grown up," the witch said. "And I'm Daisy now, remember?" Her voice climbed higher with each word.

"But Alexander?"

"Gone sixteen years," Daisy–Pale Blossom–witch said. "Since I was ten."

She was older than he'd thought. Maybe that was why she had dismissed him as if he were no more than a child, because of a few years' seniority.

"I have my own baby," she continued. "You remember your grandson, don't you?"

Gideon looked at the three generations, each with a completely different face. How unlike his family. When he was a child, walking with his grandfather, people would laugh at how similar they were, from their russet hair down to the shape of their noses. Here, in this room, entirely separate worlds combined and redefined what a face could be.

"You do remember Nicky, don't you?" the woman insisted.

"I *found* something," Nicky said on cue.

"Nicky!" the old woman said. "Of course. Beautiful Nicky! Is that you? Come closer. It's so dark here."

The light was perfectly fine.

Nicky pressed on. "We saw a . . ."

"Who? Why do you say 'we'? Who was with you?" his mother demanded.

Gideon felt tired and no longer cared if they would ever get to the point. Why should the corpse's identity or story matter to him, anyway? He had to be on his way. He had a world to see. But first he would remind her that he did, indeed, exist.

"The man who was here," Nicky said as Gideon rapped on the doorframe. "He saw it, too. The skeleton."

Gideon stepped into the room.

"Down by the river!" Nicky shouted. "With hair. Red—"

"Oh, no," the young woman said. "You dug him up."

"I didn't dig up anything," Nicky said. "The quake—"

Nobody noticed Gideon. "Ma'am!" he said, announcing himself.

247

The woman turned with an astonished expression. He, too, was surprised. She had washed and transformed herself. She was smooth, clean, and clear. He felt a brand-new tug, a second, different spell thrown over him.

At the same moment, there was a frenzy of action on the bed. The old woman screamed, one hand flew up to her chest, and the other pushed at the air. "You're dead! I burned the poison doll. I buried you—get back under the earth!"

"Ma'am," Gideon said as gently as he could, given the circumstances, "I don't know what this is about, but I won't bother you any longer in any case. I . . ."

"*Dead!*" The old woman spat her words. "Can't hurt us." Again she tried to push herself up, to have at him. But she groaned and sank back. "I remember," she said, her voice cracking. "I remember *everything.*"

Her daughter came to the edge of the bed and gently touched her forehead. The old woman pushed away her hand and kept screaming at Gideon. "Trying again, are you? In the very same room! Listen, Emmet Mitchell, listen: *Boxa elya midok . . .*"

Gideon suddenly yearned for New York, no longer a cage that trapped him but a place where the wildness had been smoothed over. He remembered its tidy corners, organization, the precise intelligible language of his family, the symmetrical streets that didn't shake and unearth corpses, and Isobel with her blank blue eyes and few words, spoken quietly. How had it ever seemed boring?

"*Boxa elya—*"

"Mother!" The woman called Daisy raised her voice, trying to break the old woman's chant. Was it Chinese? There was something terrifying in the adamant syllables, each one hurled like a rock or a bullet.

Nicky, bellowing with his own frustration, was the third part of the screaming trio. "A *dead* thing!" he shouted.

Gideon backed away from the bedlam. Good-bye, he said silently. Good riddance. At least it would make an interesting letter. A quake, a corpse, a fire, a tree trunk, an insane old woman cursing him in a foreign language, a witch—

"*STOP IT! LISTEN TO ME!*"

"*Boxa elya—*"

"*There's a hand sticking out of the mud and—*"

"*HE ISN'T EMMET MITCHELL!*"

The old woman's voice cracked and stopped. The boy squeaked,

then he, too, became silent. Gideon stopped backing out.

The young woman's arms hung limply at her sides. There were tears on her cheeks. "He helped us. He's not trying to hurt us. He's nothing like Emmet Mitchell." She looked up at Gideon and her face was no longer witchy or frightening, but young and fearful and apologetic.

And beautiful. Absolutely breathtakingly beautiful, once she unlocked her tight expression.

"Even his hair's a different shade of red," she added. She looked directly at him.

Well, then, she had noticed him after all. "Is that who's down by the river?" he asked. "This, um . . ."

She nodded. "He drowned." She spoke with great precision.

"*I killed him!*" There was satisfaction in the old woman's every crackly, accented word.

"He drowned," her daughter repeated. "He was an evil man."

"Wanted Daisy," the woman said, "and my house. Didn't get either one." She made a sound of disgust. "And you—you look just like him. You his son? What is it you want? Do you eat eyes? Will you boil our brains?"

"Mother!"

"Don't tell me about white men," the old lady said. "I know—"

"Mother, this is—" She stopped. "Who are you?"

"Gideon James, ma'am." He made a small bow. He'd show her he was no child. He was a city man, old enough to cross a continent alone. He deserved respect. "And you are Daisy . . . ?"

She seemed dazzled by his words. When she responded, her voice and face were newly soft. She barely resembled the harridan he'd helped earlier. "Daisy Ross," she said. "I'm glad to meet you. This is Mrs. China Ross and this is Nicholas Ross." With each repetition of the last name, her face regained some of its bitter armor, confusing him.

"Pleased to meet all of you, to have been of assistance. I have to be going now," he said.

"Young man!" This from the bed in a surprisingly strong voice. The old woman must have been fierce before she was knocked silly by the redwood branch.

"Ma'am?"

"Daisy says the roof is broken. Can you fix it?" Her voice weakened as she spoke, grew ragged. She ran her hand over her eyes. "Too dark," she muttered.

"I . . . I . . ." He'd never fixed a roof before. It didn't sound particu-

larly difficult—or particularly appealing. Still, how would these three get their house in order without him?

"Can you?"

"Suppose so."

"Come close."

He bent over the bed. She pulled his shoulder with her tiny hands. Only when his ear was next to her lips did she whisper. "Take care of them."

He pulled back. "Beg pardon?"

She tugged at his ear. "They need somebody. Daisy isn't strong."

"Ma'am, she seems—"

"Not that way. Take care of her."

"Ma'am! I'm not the one who—"

"There's nobody else. Take care of them."

"I'm afraid I can't."

"You must. You can. That's why you came here."

"No, ma'am. I was merely passing through. I'm off to see the world."

"Stay. This is the world. A little country of its own, and a good country, too. You won't find a better place."

He said nothing, hunched over the bed, her tiny hand clamped onto his ear. He felt lost in a feverish and quietly frightening dream, but at the same time something inside him eased.

"I can tell you're a good man," she whispered.

He knew she'd been blinded by the injury, but she seemed to have supernatural light that could peer into the center of his heart and see something he only hoped was there. He was the youngest of ten children. The baby. Always the baby. But this old woman knew he was a man and her words made his maturity authentic, his solitary travels and plans less frightening. He had forged his way across three thousand miles on his own, half the steps taken not because he wanted to, but because he needed to prove he could.

"Care for them," the old woman said.

And Gideon James felt himself take on the solidity she believed he already had. This was the way being knighted by a queen must feel.

Even so, the situation was ridiculous.

He looked up. Daisy Ross and her child stared back with their amazing eyes. He remembered a doe and fawn he'd startled a day earlier.

The old woman grabbed his ear more tightly and pulled him closer. "At least the roof," she gasped. "Will you fix it?"

He looked at Daisy again.

"Will you?" She pinched his earlobe.

"Yes, ma'am," he said. "I'll fix the roof."

She nodded. "And bury that red-haired—"

"Yes, ma'am." He felt a fool, bent over double, but at least he had agreed only to two do-able chores, not a lifetime's caretaking.

She released her grip.

Gideon straightened up and looked at Daisy and Nicky with complete confusion.

"Mr. . . . Mr. . . ."

"James," Gideon said to the old woman.

"One more thing."

He bent over. "Yes, ma'am?" he asked warily.

"Don't eat their eyes."

19

There. The last shingle was in place. Gideon sat on the roof and surveyed his handiwork. It was his roof now, with his imprint all over it. With, in fact, more imprints than he'd have wanted, since he'd had to pull out and redo much of his work as he learned how to do it.

Now he knew how to repair a roof, and didn't particularly want to use the knowledge again. He intended to leave his mark on grander things than shingles.

It was definitely time to leave. They'd have to understand. It wasn't as if he were abandoning them—he was merely continuing on his course.

The old Chinese woman's fingers still clutched her quilt and life, even though her mind wandered in and out of the present. Sometimes she summoned him, specifically asked for Gideon James. And then, likely as not, she'd confuse him with her dead husbands or beg him not to steal their house or, when her mind was truly gone, implore him not to eat her daughter's brains.

Her daughter.

Daisy Ross entered Gideon's thoughts with surprising frequency. One moment he'd be placing a shingle, and the next the wood was gone and he'd see not so much Daisy but an essence, a hint. A tilted green eye, a slender arm, a way of watching him from a distance, an

intensity based in fury or pain or something he couldn't yet guess.

He reminded himself that Daisy was older than he, she had been or still was someone else's wife, someone's mother. She boiled with angry unshared wisdom and undoubtedly thought he was an overgrown child. He tried instead to think of Isobel, young, fresh, patient, and loyal, but all he summoned were saucer eyes. Blue ciphers.

Besides, he was off to see the world and all such thoughts were irrelevant distractions.

Definitely time to leave. He had already lost three days. The old woman could return to her own bedroom now without fear of rain or wind. He'd repaired the walls and a window frame, and even though they were still raw and unvarnished, that surely wasn't his concern or obligation. He gathered his hammer and the remaining shingles. The job was over.

From his perch, he watched Daisy and her son walk toward the river, carrying buckets.

Damn fool house without water. Broken well, and now there wasn't even a watertight rain barrel. Easy enough to fix things, so why hadn't the woman done something about it? Her mother was right—Daisy Ross wasn't completely grown up. Her eyes always watched the horizon, interested in someplace far away. She seemed misplaced, an enchanted princess in the wrong woods.

He kept watching her. She had an unusual walk, graceful, but jaunty, as if at any moment she might break into a dance, or run away.

Maybe he should fix the rain barrel. Varnish the old lady's room. Think about fixing the well. Then he'd absolutely leave.

"This ham's delicious, ma'am," he said. "You cure it yourself?"

Daisy nodded. The pig had mystified and tormented her all its life and given her pleasure only in its killing, and now, translated into slabs of bacon and succulent ham, she still had to fight rage at the sight of it.

"Aren't you hungry, too?" Gideon asked. "Won't you have some?"

"I've already eaten," she said, lying. She had killed it with savage pleasure, but it had the last victory, sticking in her throat and choking her whenever she tried to eat it.

One autumn morning, many seasons earlier when Nicky was toddling, she had gone to milk the cows and found the piglet. It sat pathetically in a rough, open-ended crate. There was no sign of its donor, no message explaining its presence.

Her mother said it was probably from a boarder who hadn't been

able to pay for his room. She never turned away a hungry or tired wanderer, and this was a mark of gratitude from an embarrassed traveler.

Daisy was certain Tonio Silva had left the pig.

He had been gone from Mendocino since before Nicky's birth. She had searched for him, her bulging belly speaking volumes even though she did no more than ask his whereabouts. But surely, somebody had told him about her, about the belly. Surely he knew he had a son in these woods. Surely he worried in his fashion about his son and Daisy's welfare. Surely he was repentant. And surely he was about to return.

The pig was his messenger, a first step, a symbol as strange as any in a fairy tale. She must treat the pig properly in order for it to work. There was no other possible explanation for its appearance.

She built it a sty and fed it the best scraps and leavings. The pig inflated, expanded, and lost whatever charms it had ever possessed for her.

Tonio Silva did not reappear.

The bloated creature stared malevolently out of tiny eyes, pig-grinning contempt for her naïve optimism.

So she killed it. When she put the gun to its head, it was Tonio Silva's ear at which she took aim. When she scalded the great beast, it was Tonio Silva's skin she burned. When she bathed it in brine, sawed it into hams and steaks, she did so with a great deal of dark-edged pleasure.

And now it satisfied her profoundly to have Gideon James chew the last of it into shreds and pulp.

"You're from far away, aren't you?" she asked. No good would come of talking about the pig. The man already looked at her strangely. He probably thought of her as an old, worn-out madwoman, even without hearing about a magical pig. When it had been just the three of them in the woods, she let herself tangle and crumple and didn't care, and rare travelers passing through stared with reason. But since Gideon James had arrived, she'd taken special pains with her hair and her clothing, and still he looked at her peculiarly. Tonight she was wearing her best dress, the one from the Sears, Roebuck catalogue, but his expression still made her uneasy.

"I'm from New York City," he said.

"Is it much like here?"

He shook his head and helped himself to more ham. "Not many trees. Tall buildings packed with people."

She sat down across from him, imagining how it would be to grow up where there were other easily reached houses, friends to share secrets and games, voices answering your own. When she went into Mendocino City, she knew that her life would have been different if she had been part of the rows of shops, the buggies and horses, the mill noise and sawdust, the rowdy hustle of carousing lumberjacks, the sedate hum of houses behind painted fences. Her life had grown like a creeper vine, taking hold wherever it could, but in a town where nature had been subdued into tidy patterns of streets and corners, she, too, would have found direction.

The familiar acid taste of defeat and finality pulled the edges of her mouth. Her mother blamed her bad moods for the declining number of boarders, which was unfair. Mendocino was on the down. Times were hard.

Nonetheless, she tried to be polite. "It sounds interesting," she said. "Exciting. I can hardly imagine it."

"Interesting, maybe," he said, "but you feel cramped there. Packed in. At least I did." He stopped eating and looked at her. "Have you been to a big city?" he asked. "Have you been to San Francisco?"

She shook her head. "I once thought maybe I would. I have half-brothers who . . . only it didn't work out." She felt ashamed of having revealed how small and drab her world was.

"There are some wonderful things in cities," Gideon James said.

"Like what?" She pulled closer, waiting in the same position as she had in school when the teacher announced story time.

"Automobiles," Gideon said. "Ever seen one?"

"Once. I'm glad I did, in case I don't get another chance."

"Why wouldn't you?"

"They say they'll do away with them, they scare the horses and cattle so, and cause accidents. Even with that man."

Gideon James looked confused. "What man?"

"The one who beats the frying pan to warn teams that a car's coming."

He smiled. "They don't have that in New York. Automobiles are pretty popular, and there aren't lots of cattle to scare."

"You probably have real roads, too."

He nodded.

She sighed.

"How about telephones?" Gideon said. "Ever talk on one? Or use electric lamps?"

255

She shook her head. "New York sounds splendid. Your life must have been very grand."

"Oh, no, not really."

"You're modest."

He looked embarrassed.

"Why would you ever . . . why did you leave?" she asked.

"To see the world."

"And have you?" There was an enormous pressure in her chest, her forehead, as if she might explode, but softly, sadly.

"Not yet," he said. "Not the world. But I've crossed this whole country, mostly walking, so I've seen a great deal."

"And now you're here."

"For a while."

"Why here?"

He grinned and looked even younger. "You know what Horace Greeley said?"

She shook her head. She knew nothing, nobody. She had never been in an automobile, spoken on a telephone.

"He said, 'Go West, Young Man,' and I did. But I got to the edge and still didn't find my fortune, so I kept going."

"You're looking for it *here*?" She covered her mouth to hide her smile.

"The trees, ma'am." His skin seemed pinker and even his hair flared more than usual.

"What about them?"

"People need lumber. I'm strong. That's how it is."

"So you'll work where?"

"Wherever they'll take me. Further north, I suppose."

"Maybe you noticed the stumps by the river," she said. She realized her voice had become bitter, and she took a deep breath.

He shrugged. "Noticed new sprouts, too. They'll grow back."

She still felt belligerent and wasn't sure why. Let him move north, chop trees wherever he wanted to. It was no business of hers.

"There are trees enough to last a million years. And after that, I'll move on. Keep seeing the world." He smiled engagingly. "That was the best ham I ever had."

She offered him apple pie. "My father was a cutter," she said drily. "I never noticed him making a fortune."

"Well . . ." Gideon James obviously saw no relationship between ordinary men like her father and himself. Her lips pressed hard, one

against the other. Once upon a time she'd found that sort of confidence—or arrogance—attractive.

He stood up and paced, as if it was hard for him to sit still even for a short while. It wasn't only his hair that seemed on fire. The man was a fidget like Nicky. "Maybe I'll learn the woods, then the mills, then open my own company," he blurted out. "Maybe not. Maybe I'll keep going, sail around the world. Always wanted to see Egypt."

She thunked the plate of pie on the table without a word and, like a chastised child, he silently resettled in his place. "You don't think I'll find my fortune, do you?" he said, half worried, half challenging her.

"I know nothing about fortunes or how to find them."

"But do you think I can do it?" His eyes were very young and blue. She softened momentarily, and was frightened by the easing, the new looseness inside her.

"What do I know of such things?" She snapped back into the bitter envelope of all she would never have a chance to know. All she had and knew was Nicky. He was dear, he was beautiful, he was hers—and he had cost her every other possibility. "I'm a backwoods woman. I have no education, no knowledge of the world. I know how to milk a cow and run a household and that is that."

"You know how to make a fine apple pie," he said. She cut him another wedge, which he devoured. And then he smiled in a way that made her feel balanced on a dangerous edge.

She leaned forward. "Do you miss your family?" Her voice was sharper than intended.

"Sometimes."

"Who?"

"Ma'am?"

"Who do you miss?"

"My family. My mother, my sisters, my brothers."

"Your wife?" Her voice was pinched and shrill. She cleared her throat.

"Don't have one to miss."

She sat back. Suddenly she remembered how powerful she had once been, pulling and holding the boarders' eyes on her as often and long as she liked. She remembered how it was to know she was special.

He had no wife.

"Not yet, that is. Although, of course, I am no longer a child, so

257

I'll most likely, well, you understand, don't you?" He chuckled and looked uncomfortable.

"You have an intended." Her voice was as impersonal as she could manage. She was a thousand years old, an aged crone who could ask such questions because she was not and never could be anyone's betrothed or beloved.

"Don't know if I'd say that." He shifted weight. "Not really." He shrugged and reconsidered. "Well, perhaps," he admitted.

Perhaps, indeed. Inwardly she snorted and turned her back. She was not surprised. And would he have ever mentioned it had she not asked? Did any of them?

"And you, ma'am?" he asked. "Where did you grow up?"

She was flustered, floundering in the middle of an angry torrent. "Here, of course. Why?"

"I don't know... you asked about my hometown and I... I thought maybe this was your husband's house."

Her heartbeat doubled. She took a deep breath. "My grandfather built this house sixty years ago. His name was Nicholas, like my son."

He nodded and smiled, encouraging her, but she said no more.

She carried his plate and fork to the sink her grandfather had carved out of a redwood log. She sloshed the plates in the water and kept her back to Gideon James.

"I was thinking maybe I'd varnish the wood in Mrs. Ross's bedroom before I moved on," he said. "So her room's really ready and finished."

She swished the water and pressed down, scouring the plate.

"And fix the well and the rain barrel. It must be tiring carrying every bucket of washwater from the river."

"Nicky's father's family lives in Monterey." She scrubbed furiously as she spoke. It wasn't a lie. Nicky's father's wife, his father's other son, and his father himself were there. That was surely family. More than enough family.

"Ummmm," Gideon James said from behind her.

"They're fishermen. So is... so was he."

"Oh," Gideon said. "I'm sorry. When did he, ah, pass away?"

Her eyes stung as if she'd scrubbed them with the harsh soap. Good thing he couldn't see her face. "He... left us. Before Nicky was born." Her voice was barely more than a whisper. The truth, no matter how twisted, how presented, how interpreted, still hurt.

When the dishes were done and she finally turned around, he was studying her with such an intent expression she froze, trying to see

258

through it, to read him. He snapped his head back a bit, and seemed embarrassed to have been caught scrutinizing her.

And what had he seen? An old, red-eyed, red-handed ignorant country woman, lying to cover her shame and humiliation.

"Thank you for a fine dinner, ma'am." He stood up hastily. "I'll say good-night now. Tomorrow, I'll go into town for supplies and take care of the room and the well."

She heard him go outside before bed and after a long while she peeked through the parlor window. He stood on the porch, his back to her.

Studying the trees, she decided. Contemplating what world he would conquer. Looking away from the house and from her. That was all that mattered. Or in truth, if she'd think clearly, she'd admit that none of it mattered at all.

When Gideon returned from Mendocino City the next day, his news completely overshadowed his purchases or plans. He paced around the old woman's bed as he spoke. "The quake," he said. "The quake shook up the city, and Fort Bragg, too. The mill's closed. Its chimney's down—the bricks are all over. In fact, all the chimneys in town are down. Lots of ruined roofs—I could stay busy fixing them for a long time, if I wanted." Daisy, Nicky, and the old woman listened to his every word. "The hotel parlor's up six feet from its foundation—and it moved five feet south. Railroad bridges collapsed, the track's a mess, Big River Bridge lost a span. What else . . . ?" He paused to refresh his memory. The trio of listeners didn't make a sound.

"Earth's split open in the fields, the high school's off base, every store's damaged, and all the cemetery monuments were thrown from their foundations." He paused, and viewed Daisy's shudder with satisfaction. Then he took a deep breath and presented them with the biggest item of all. "And San Francisco's gone."

"San Francisco? But it's so far away! A hundred, a hundred and fifty miles."

"Gone," he repeated.

"The whole city?" The old lady had been silent until now. Gideon had thought she was off again, lost in her memories.

"Up in flames. Burning for days. Water mains broke in the quake, so they're using dynamite—and even wine—to fight it. It may still be on fire. I swear, you can smell the smoke in town here." He sat down heavily on a chair in the corner. He had thought retelling the news would make it less confusing and unsettling, but he still felt as if

259

he'd been spun around and dropped on his head. His tiny woodland quake had been massive. The world had fallen apart and he hadn't known a bit of it.

It was hard—close to impossible, in fact—to believe that the solid wonders he'd seen a week earlier were smoldering ruins. That the elegant San Franciscans parading in their Easter Sunday finery, the men he'd envied and determined to equal, were sleeping in Golden Gate Park with no more to their names than the nightclothes they'd fled in. "President Roosevelt said it was this country's worst catastrophe ever," he said. "Congress is giving money. More than a million."

He didn't know if they wanted more information, but he was carrying so many heavy pieces of it. "I was at the Cliff House last week," he said. "The enormous place overlooking the Pacific? Don't you remember—I told you about the sea lions."

Daisy and Nicky nodded.

"They say it fell into the sea."

"And Dupont Gai?" the old woman demanded. She still lay on her back, unable to move or to see.

"Pardon me?"

"Dupont Gai. Dupont . . . Dupont . . . *Street!*"

"Gone."

"And the rest?" the old woman asked.

"Of the city? Most of it's—"

"Of Chinatown!"

"Gone. Burned to the ground."

Her sigh was so ragged, so harsh, it seemed to come from her toes.

He couldn't envision this tiny white-haired woman knowing any of the denizens of that filthy, congested area. "A cesspool," someone had called it in town. "The one good thing about the quake is that Chinatown's gone and they'll never let them back in again."

"You have family in Chinatown, ma'am?" he asked gently.

The old woman said nothing, so he dug back into his bundle of earthquake news and pulled out another item. "They're shooting looters on sight, and—"

"My family is in this room," the old woman declared. "My ghosts are on Dupont Gai."

Gideon looked to Daisy for explanation, interpretation, but Daisy was looped in on herself, silent except for an occasional sharp reprimand to Nicky.

"It hit Monterey, too," Gideon said loudly. He waited for Daisy to

260

show a sign of recognition, to wonder about her dead husband's relatives, but he seemed to be the only one who made the connection.
Daisy stood up, blinking blind eyes. "Dinner," she said in a choked
voice. "I must see to it," and she ran out of the room.

She seemed as muddled and disturbed as he was, but he didn't
know what they could or should say to each other. He left the house
and prowled in search of nothing he could name. A few days ago, the
quake had seemed a morning's minor excitement, extended only by
the unearthed skeleton.

Now Emmet Mitchell was back in the earth, but everything else
had shifted and unsettled. Gideon stared at the man's lumpy grave
mound and moved on. Even in daylight it was cool and dark and
silent in the canopies made by the trees, but as the light ebbed,
Gideon was shrouded in a blacker, deeper night than he'd known
anywhere else. The tree columns no longer reminded him of cathe-
drals, but of sentries, and he wasn't sure if he were friend or foe.

Time to leave this place, but everything except his mind protested.

I don't even know her, he thought. I don't understand any of this.
Still, lines of Marlowe's had played through his head many times in
the last few days.

> It lies not in our power to love or hate,
> For will in us is overruled by fate...
> Where both deliberate, the love is slight;
> Who ever loved, that loved not at first sight?

Was it advice, truth, a warning, or a dirge?

He walked through the trees, down and back to the river again,
and then the growls of his stomach led him back through the night
into the house.

An empty plate—Nicky's, no doubt—was still on the table. The
kitchen was fragrant with her cooking, but Daisy Ross was anything
but the picture of contentment. She slumped over the table, her
head resting on her arms, eyes closed.

He cleared his throat.

She remained inert, seemed dead. "Daisy!" he shouted, rushing
over and grasping her shoulders. "Are you all right?"

She gasped and straightened up, then jumped to her feet, smooth-
ing her dress and her hair. Her eyes were red.

He backed off. "I'm sorry," he said. "You were so still—I was

afraid, I thought something had happened to you." His cheeks heated. He had called her Daisy, had touched her as if he were her familiar. What would she think? Why had he done it? Why didn't he ever think before he moved?

"I'm ashamed of myself." Her voice was subdued, unfamiliar. "I'm sorry for the people who died, lost their homes, everything they owned. But all the same . . ." She shook her head as if impatient with herself, and furiously wiped away a tear.

"All the same what?"

"I'm too ashamed to say." She busied herself with the stew, then turned to him. Her beautiful face fought emotion, then cracked and opened to reveal someone very new, frightened, and young. "It's gone and I'll never see it now! I hoped that someday I'd see San Francisco, see some of the things you've seen and talked about, things I've dreamed of my whole life." She sat down again, her hands on the table. As she spoke, she studied them as if they could make things different. "Now, the door's clanged shut. Locked me in. Took away my chance. I know it's selfish to say this, but I can't help it." She quickly wiped away another tear, then looked up shyly, nervously, as if fearful of his response.

When he'd heard of San Francisco's destruction he, too, had felt locks turn, but in the opposite direction. The earth had opened and swallowed his past and he was newly minted. He respected the foundations that were still there, but he liked the rubble, frightening as it was, because it meant he could choose what to reconstruct. Perhaps it would look nothing at all like what the rest of his family might have built. He felt sad, confused, and free at the same time, and he wished he could tell her.

But she would laugh at the pretensions of a youngster with nothing to his name but enthusiasm.

Still, he reached over audaciously and took her hands. She tensed, almost withdrew them, and then she relaxed and kept them motionless.

"They'll rebuild San Francisco," he said. "It will be just as splendid. And I'll make sure that you'll see it and everything else. You have my word."

"You?"

"Don't mock me, please. I'm young and penniless, but I'm going to find my place and fortune. I—"

"I wasn't mocking. I was surprised."

"May I hope that you might someday... that I might someday, after a time..." He couldn't finish, wasn't even sure what he wanted to hope for. He tried a new tack. "Mrs. Ross... asked me to take care of you and Nicky. I would like to honor her request. I would very much... do you understand?"

She glanced down at her hands in his, then up to his face. She took a deep, shuddering breath and freed her hands. "I am not who I said. I am not what you'd want. I was never married. I was ruined."

Yes. Well. It made sense now, didn't it? For a moment he recoiled, deafened by a chorus of voices from his childhood, of his mother's outraged pronouncements on sin, his older sisters' shrill condemnation, Isobel's ready echo of their disdain. Then he remembered that the earth that separated them had shaken and remade itself. Daisy Ross hadn't been ruined. Not ruined at all. Nor was the gold-skinned, black-eyed boy, so unlike red-haired, freckled Gideon at any age, but also somehow kin.

"Nicky is not a ruin," he said gently.

Her hands still in his, she closed her eyes and cried silently.

"I've misled you, too, or let you believe an untruth. My mother was in service until she married," Gideon said. "A servant. My father broke rocks and built canals, sired ten children, and died when I was two. It was a hard life. Sure, I was in New York, but as far from its wonders as you are, and I was wrong to let you think otherwise. I wanted you to think I was rich, special, not some little boy you could ignore."

"Nicky's father's family *is* in Monterey," she said. "That part was true. Perhaps they were hurt in the quake." She looked so hopeful about it, Gideon laughed, and finally she joined him.

Then Daisy sighed and switched to a serious expression, her old mask almost back in place. Red nose and bleary eyes notwithstanding, she took on a regal stance. "And what of your intended?" she demanded.

He shook his head. "Not my intended. My mother's intended. Part of my intended life. To work and live as my father did, as my brothers did and do, in a box with other boxes above and below and beside me. No. Especially not now. Not after you and the quake. Everything's different now."

"Well, then," she said.

"Yes."

They considered the table, the dark outside the kitchen window,

their hands. "Is this really because of the promise you made my mother?" Daisy asked after a long pause.

"No. This is a promise for you and for me."

He would leave in search of his fortune as soon as the house was back in shape. He wasn't sure where his travels might take him, but he was certain that they would end with this woman in this house in Mendocino.

PART V

1 9 1 8

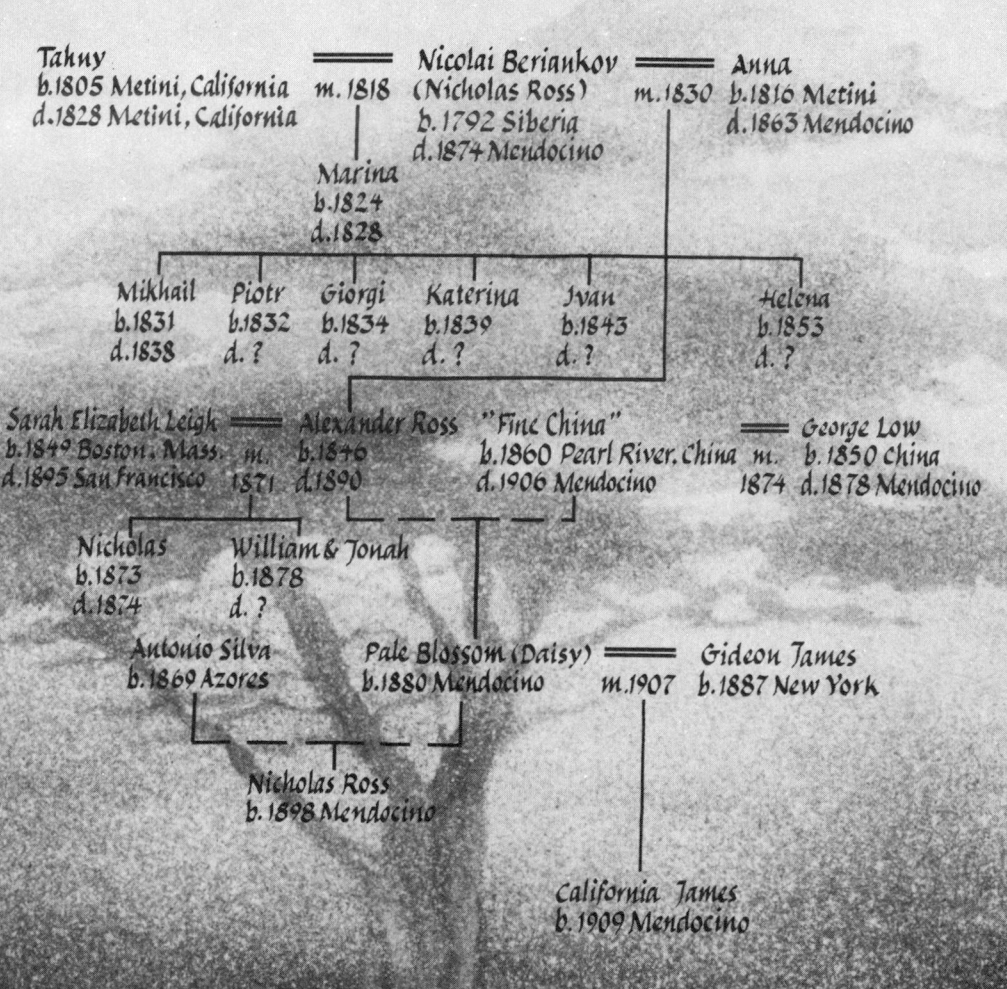

Tahuy
b.1805 Metini, California
d.1828 Metini, California

m. 1818

Nicolai Beriankov
(Nicholas Ross)
b.1792 Siberia
d.1874 Mendocino

m.1830

Anna
b.1816 Metini
d.1863 Mendocino

Marina
b.1824
d.1828

Mikhail
b.1831
d.1838

Piotr
b.1832
d. ?

Giorgi
b.1834
d. ?

Katerina
b.1839
d. ?

Ivan
b.1843
d. ?

Helena
b.1853
d. ?

Sarah Elizabeth Leigh
b.1849 Boston, Mass.
d.1895 San Francisco

m.
1871

Alexander Ross
b.1846
d.1890

"Fine China"
b.1860 Pearl River, China
d.1906 Mendocino

m.
1874

George Low
b.1850 China
d.1878 Mendocino

Nicholas
b.1873
d.1874

William & Jonah
b.1878
d. ?

Antonio Silva
b.1869 Azores

Pale Blossom (Daisy)
b.1880 Mendocino

m.1907

Gideon James
b.1887 New York

Nicholas Ross
b.1898 Mendocino

California James
b.1909 Mendocino

20

Daisy sank down at the kitchen table, too tired to do more than unbutton her coat. The day in town had been exhausting, and she had a headache to boot.

Nothing was right. Absolutely nothing.

There had been no mail again today. No news, no reassurances that things would ever right themselves.

"Callie!" she called. "I'm home!"

She was worn out. Too much worrying about the war, about Nicky off in some trench in Europe, about Gideon, stuck on the other end of the country with his sick and demanding mother.

Maybe she'd fry some onions, make a hot poultice, drink the juice. Or maybe horehound syrup. One of them would drive her cough out, make her feel better.

Not so very long ago, life had finally seemed right and logical and in place. Gideon had fit himself into the best of Daisy's stories, returning after only one year of wandering to claim her hand, be her long-awaited shining prince. He and Daisy and Nicky, and then baby Callie, had been a true family, secure in the woods even when Gideon was off working the tanbark trees or when he sailed away for long stretches to the far corners of the earth.

They had such fun, too. A dance where the floor was a gigantic

redwood stump. Bicycle rides up the coast. Picnics at Russian Gulch and bonfires on the beach. Movies—Theda Bara, Charlie Chaplin, William Desmond, and Pauline Frederick.

Now nothing was fun. Everyone was scattered, the movies were closed because of all those people sick with the flu, and Daisy was too tired to do more than resent the world for falling apart.

Tea might help. She put the kettle on, forced herself to hang up her coat and put her hat and gloves away.

"Callie!" she called again. Her throat was dry and scratchy from the dust of the road. Where was the child? She could be such a dawdler and daydreamer.

Well, she was only nine years old. Daisy's irritation lessened as she remembered her own long-ago afternoons in the tower, full of fairy tales. Callie wasn't like that at all. She'd been born with a level, no-nonsense way of taking on life.

Perhaps she was asleep, as unlike the child as that would be. Or engrossed in her daily letter to her brother. Every single afternoon, Callie wrote, describing, among other things, the scarf or sleeveless sweater or even the washrags she knitted during school recess. She had every hope that her handiwork, thus described, would be the one Nicky would choose to keep his neck warm while he fought the Huns.

Daisy climbed the stairs, pausing at the landing to catch her breath, but her daughter's room was silent. She went back to the kitchen. The water was near the boil. Daisy tapped her foot impatiently, then went to the door and called out, as loudly as she could with her throat so dry and her voice so foggy.

No answer.

She reentered the kitchen, poured boiling water over the tea, and, leaving it to steep, once again went outside.

The afternoon sun slanted through the redwoods, heightening the blaze of color on the forest floor. Pine needles and redwood droppings painted the earth a bittersweet orange lit from within. The color, shocking, dramatic, and warm, reminded Daisy of Gideon's hair, of Gideon. And it reinforced the idea of Callie, who had inherited her father's flaming mop.

But where was she? "Callie!" Daisy called through the woods. "California James!" The tea would soon be cold.

Daisy already was. She shivered in the afternoon shadows and tried not to remember all the whispers and scraps of anxious conversation in town, the gruesome statistics piling up as the disease claimed more

and more victims. She was fine—just bone-weary from all the worry —and now Callie was adding to it. She hurried back to the house.

If there had been a letter at the post office, the day wouldn't seem as bleak and discouraging and probably Daisy would have more energy.

Not that letters came often or even said much. Particularly from Nicky, although she didn't begrudge him his writing habits. He was, after all, at war.

When one of his rare letters arrived, it said almost nothing. He always said that he was well. That he missed them. That he hoped and believed the Huns were about destroyed and that the war was going to end very soon. That he loved them all. And that was that.

But then, even before he'd gone off to fight, he hadn't been exactly talkative when it came to himself. He was a mysterious one, all hidden springs and deep silences. So unlike Callie.

Even his going to war was a surprise. At eighteen, he was under age for the first draft, and such a solitary type, Daisy didn't dream that he'd volunteer. It was Gideon she'd worried about. He was two years over the thirty-year-old cutoff, but she was afraid his patriotic fervor and need to make things right would push him into the middle of the fray.

And perhaps it would have, if Nicky hadn't beaten him to it.

They'd seen him off for training camp, in a crowd of a thousand or more people doing the same for the other boys. Gideon's mood shifted wildly from wistfulness to impatience. "I feel old and useless," he'd said. "I envy them."

"Kaiser hunters," they called the boys. The cheers and music and hullabaloo made their departure romantic and exciting, but it didn't ease Daisy's heart. There was a popular song called "I Didn't Raise My Son to Be a Soldier," and Daisy could have written it. The words rose in her of their own will, day after day, an insistent dirge.

Why, when the enormous struggle for survival seemed over for her family, did there still have to be battles and wars to fight?

"I didn't raise my son to be a soldier." The melody played through her brain again.

But what had she raised him to be, or had she raised him at all? He was such a puzzle, his dark eyes always watching, amused but distant. Had she ruined him by not wanting him? "Raise them ugly, they grow up ugly," her Indian grandmother supposedly had said, and Daisy sometimes worried whether her misery had made her raise Nicky "ugly" those early years. She couldn't remember. Couldn't remember much

before the earthquake that changed the world around, crushing her mother and unearthing a skeleton and Gideon James.

If only Gideon would write, soon.

His mother was very ill. Dying, his sister had written, and she yearned to see her youngest child once again. She had never reconciled herself to the idea that he had settled three thousand miles away from her, nor had she considered visiting him in what she believed to be the wilderness.

She'd been lingering on her deathbed, holding Gideon's hand for months now. Not that Daisy wanted the old woman to die—although she had no fondness for her. How could she?

When they were first married, Gideon had paid a photographer to take their wedding portrait, and when the old woman received it, she responded not with thanks for the picture, not with good wishes or a wedding gift, but with questions about why the bride was so "peculiar" and "foreign" looking. Gideon laughed over it, but Daisy's heart went cold and the old woman did nothing in the intervening years to warm it up. The creature didn't even care for her own flesh and blood, for her granddaughter Callie, and she certainly had no interest in Nicky, even though Gideon treated him like his own.

Daisy suddenly ached so for her husband that she went to her room for his last letter. She'd read it many times because it consoled, confused, and frightened her with its hard intimations of great changes ahead.

She sat on her bed and read slowly. Her eyes were sandy and watery and unwilling to focus. The letter was loving and concerned, but inconclusive, as all of them had been. His mother was critically weak and he thought it would be a matter of days, but in the meantime, one of his sisters' husbands had been sent home from the front injured from some sort of gas he'd inhaled and Gideon was sorting out their affairs. He was also helping yet another sister's son decide his future and seeing a lot of his older brother Sean's widow. Thank heavens, he wrote, that the clean air of Mendocino would keep away this flu, but his sister Bridget and her husband both had it, so he was helping with their children and their nursing.

It was as if the family were willing all their troubles to Gideon, and with so many of them, Daisy feared they'd never run out of problems to keep her husband on the other side of the country.

At least he was working at the shipyard, doing his part for the war—and slowing the dwindling of their funds as well as helping

with the care of his mother. He'd enclosed a money order.

"I wish it were more," he'd written. "I wish it were the fortune I thought I'd make someday, but that does not seem to be likely to ever happen, and I no longer care. Other things matter more. I think about waste and excess, about boys dying over there, or coming back ruined by gas or bullets. I look at this city where nature is lost with no trace, covered by concrete and brick, and then, when I miss Mendocino, which I always do, I think about the ruined forests, about the oaks I stripped for the tanbark, leaving the rest to die, about the redwoods I helped destroy, about the bare earth running into the rivers and killing the fish.

"I refuse to be part, ever again, of desecration. I am tired of wanting new things. I've traveled most of the world and what do I have to show for it? Soapstone carvings, brass, Chinese porcelain. Trinkets and trash. Now it seems important to save what we've already been given."

She put the letter down, still unsure of what Gideon's great change of heart would mean for their future. Perhaps nothing. Perhaps it was a mood, as wrong as his opinion that nobody could get the flu in Mendocino.

Everybody was. That's all people talked about, how victims were dying up and down the coast. There were so many sick, there was an emergency infirmary in town. Daisy shivered again. Thank heavens she was fine. A good night's sleep and a few letters and she'd be herself again. She coughed and put her husband's letter back in her dresser drawer. Tonight, she'd write him, even though all she wanted to do was curl up in her bed. Perhaps she'd wait until she felt better. Besides, she was always afraid her letters revealed how little schooling she had, and how little she truly knew or had to say.

Tea. She'd forgotten all about it and it would be cold by now. The kitchen seemed so far away.

She must think of something to tell Gideon. She'd tell him about how Callie was going to be New York State in the Apple Fair. The grammar school float was going to have "Columbia" surrounded by the forty-four states, and California James had been given her father's original home state. Daisy had stitched her a fine white dress for the occasion.

She wouldn't tell him there was talk of canceling the event because of the flu.

She wouldn't tell him she was worried about money. Worried about

living alone for so long, with only a little girl for company. Instead, she'd write about how she and Callie were part of the "Do-With-outs," helping the war effort by cutting back on meat, wheat, sugar, and fat so that more could be sent to the front. She was also buying as many war-savings stamps as she could afford, and she'd tell him that. Twelve bought a helmet, seventy-eight a rifle. She saw Nicky, bare-headed, empty-handed, before each purchase, even though by now she was outfitting some other mother's child.

And she would definitely tell him about the delicious, wheat-saving, sugarless bread she'd perfected. Daisy's Victory Bread, she and Callie called it. She considered the delectable loaf her great triumph, the one truly imaginative and special thing she'd ever done, although she'd never admit that sort of thing to Gideon.

There was no other news. Daisy was waiting, holding on until her shattered family reassembled.

She must not think about how dreadful she felt. Must not think about the influenza. She couldn't be sick.

There was no more family to spare, not to war, not to illness.

Still, her limbs were so heavy, so tired. It was exhausting to breathe. Her muscles ached.

Please, God, no, she silently begged, but she felt terrible, and all she wanted to do was to lie down and float in a feverish dream.

She was sick. Let Gideon believe what he would, the Spanish Influenza knew its way into the backwaters of the country. Into Daisy James.

Her eyelids dropped. Give in, her body urged. Curl up, wrap the quilt around you, put a warm brick from the fireplace near your toes . . . give up. The silence of the house was broken only by the soft tick of a grandfather clock Gideon had installed in the parlor.

But where was Callie? The sunlight slanted at a dangerous angle. It would be dark soon. This wasn't at all like the girl.

Perhaps her room held a clue. Perhaps her schoolbag had a note, a project that necessitated a long hike. Something missed in the earlier, quick scan.

Once again, Daisy dragged herself upstairs, holding on to the bannister as if it were a lifeline. Callie's room was innocence itself, filled with books, rag dolls, puppets, figurines, and all the whatnots Gideon had collected on his merchant ship travels and disparaged in his letter.

There was no bookbag.

In a feverish blear, Daisy made her way downstairs and scanned the

spots where her daughter customarily hurled her schoolbag. They were untouched and pristine.

Callie had never come home.

Daisy nearly fell down under the weight of her fatigue. A cough ripped through her lungs and tore apart her throat. Her daughter was lost. Missing. But they had a telephone now. If she were all right, she would have let Daisy know where she was.

Then she wasn't all right. Something had happened that didn't allow her to phone.

The house engulfed Daisy, the nearby trees dwarfed her, the mountains and the ocean, the cliffs and the endless Pacific stretched to all sides, hiding Callie and making Daisy minuscule, insignificant, and terribly alone. She needed someone. Gideon again, charging out of nowhere to set things right.

But there was no Gideon, and she had to do something. She forced herself forward, pulled on her coat and gloves to ease the chill in her bones. She was half out the door before some portion of the deadweight of her mind roused, and she turned back and took the rifle. She wasn't much of a shot. After her father died, boarders sometimes presented her mother with venison or bear meat, or they made do with eggs, cheese, chicken, and fish. Then there had been Gideon and Nicky to bring down deer when necessary.

But deer didn't attack little girls, and if something else already had, then what use would the rifle be? If a hungry or sick mountain lion or bear . . . Daisy stopped her thoughts before they defeated her. She carried the rifle, heavy as it was.

She paused outside, wondering which way to go, then decided in favor of the route from school. Callie might have tripped, gotten tangled in roots, hurt herself. Daisy stopped her mind from thinking of any more, any worse, possibilities.

"Callie!" she cried at the top of her lungs. She had to stop and control her coughing. "California!" How they'd argued, back and forth, about that name. They'd begun with family names, "China" ("But she's not that at all!" Gideon had said), "Catherine" for Gideon's mother ("Never!" Daisy had declared), "Alexandra" for Daisy's father, and "Michaela" for Gideon's father, then they wrangled over names of movie stars and Biblical heroines and all of Gideon's aunts and cousins and sisters. When they hit "Bridget," Daisy stopped making countersuggestions. "I want an American name," Daisy said. "Not Irish or Chinese or Russian."

"You're right." Gideon seemed surprised, then excited. "This

child's brand-new, like nothing that's come before. She's not anyplace else, not the Old Country or the Old World. She's California,
and that's what she'll be called."

"*California!*" Daisy screamed and coughed, over and over, staggering and controlling tears both for her missing daughter and for her
own body, which was drained and empty of everything except fear
and illness. What was she to do? Why didn't she ever know what to
do?

"Callie!" It would be dark soon and the woods went on forever.
"Callie!" Her throat was raw and pulsing with pain. "*Callie!*" The
rifle pulled at her shoulder. But she didn't, she couldn't stop moving
and calling.

After what seemed forever, she realized that something besides her
own voice was trying to make its way through the trees. She turned
back and forced herself into silence, hoping she really had heard a
noise toward the river.

"Mama! Mama!"

"Callie!" She ran in a haze, tripping over ancient roots and dense
ferns, talking in a husky, rapidly disappearing voice. "Don't move,
I'm coming. Are you hurt? What happened? Is it..." And then,
finally, she saw the familiar flame of hair, a blazing beacon, a torch in
the forest. But up high, as if Callie had become a giant.

The girl stood on the stump of a redwood. At its base, a wild boar
guarded his prey.

Daisy froze in place. The boar eyed her daughter obsessively, react-
ing to her calls, to her slightest move. He was a bloated messenger of
death with his hide like dried clay and his double-dagger tusks. Daisy
felt too weak to do more than weep. What was she supposed to do?
What could she do?

Callie and the boar flickered and shimmered as if she were dreaming them. Yes, that was it. They weren't real, none of this was real.
She was making it up, dreaming. She didn't have to do anything
except sleep.

She ached so in body and mind that she began to cry, quietly.

She was ill, freezing, burning, shaking.

"Mama?" Callie's voice came from much farther than the old tree
stump. It came out of a newly hollowed place inside the child.

It was real. Images ran and congealed. The beast, the enormous
hog, was real and it wanted her child. Its bulky shape in the growing
shadows looked as if it weighed three hundred pounds, at least.

"Mama?"

It was so big, so fierce, so hard to see in the dusk. If she missed or only wounded it, it would turn and charge, goring her on those tusks. And she was dizzy, unable to see anything clearly. It was sad that she had never learned to be a marksman, but it was too late now and she was too ill to do anything. There was no point, no hope. Maybe it would leave on its own.

"Mama? Make him go away."

She understood how Callie saw her, just as Daisy had once seen Tonio, and then Gideon—someone come to save her.

Oh, how wrong, child, she almost said, but her throat was too scratchy. I'm small and weak and sick. I can't do it. And nobody really rescues you, anyway.

"Mama?"

And then she remembered that children can be rescued. That she herself had been. From a feverish distance, from her tower window, she saw her tiny mother fight off a different beast. But she'd had magic and Daisy had only a rifle.

"How were you so strong?" she heard herself asking so many years before. China Ross had looked annoyed. She didn't like to speak of that night. "Please?" Daisy had asked until it was obvious that it was an important question. "How were you suddenly so strong?"

"Because I had to be," her mother had snapped.

Because I had to be . . . because I had to be. . . . Daisy stopped shaking and felt memory clear her vision and toughen her. "I have to be," she murmured. "I have to be." She cocked the rifle and aimed.

"If it comes after me," she called, "run home, Callie. Stay inside. Call for help."

She remembered Tonio's soft pig, who had welcomed her and the food she brought. It had been so easy shooting it cleanly in the ear. She let the memory calm and flood her, concentrating on it alone until this pig became that one, moving close as the first had done. There were no more ferns and distance between them. This pig's center was no further away than the last one's had been. No less accessible. His ear expanded, became enormous, a crater her bullet could easily enter.

She pulled the trigger. The recoil knocked her backward.

"Look out!" Callie screamed.

The boar whirled and came for Daisy. She had missed.

But she couldn't have—the ear had been there, surrounding the rifle. There was blood pouring out of it.

Yet the beast kept coming toward her.

Daisy didn't stop to think. She pulled another bullet out of her pocket and reloaded the rifle blindly. Perspiration beaded her forehead and her head banged so that she barely heard the next shot.

Garlands of blood exploded on the pig. It ignored them. It was invincible.

Even in the dim light, Daisy could see the fury in its eyes. She could see the hair on its back. She could barely move her fingers, she was so weak and tired. She reached for another bullet, felt it slide out of her fingers. A sob left her lips. She was going to die here, at the base of the trees.

"You *have* to!"

The voice filled her head, leaving no space for excuses. With her last strength, Daisy pulled out another bullet and reloaded, wondering who had shouted. It hadn't been Callie's voice. No matter. Cock the rifle, watch that skull, that snout—and pull.

This time the recoil was too strong for her. She couldn't hold on any longer, no matter what. The rifle dropped onto the sword ferns with a thud. "Run!" she called hoarsely. "Save yourself!" She lifted her head to meet her doom with dignity, eye to eye.

But the boar, looking surprised, rolled his tiny eyes until they were lost, stumbled, and crashed to the ground.

Daisy, crouching, watched his death throes so intently she didn't realize for a moment that her daughter had joined her, then she pulled her close. "Are you all right?" she whispered. It was nearly impossible to speak. She patted her child, stroked her glorious hair, wiped at tear streaks on her cheeks.

"I was there since morning," Callie said.

"On the stump? All day?"

"I was going to school and he—he wouldn't leave. He came running and I couldn't think of what to do. I threw my lunch at him, and he ate it, but then he came at me again. I was so scared. Did you see his tusks? I climbed up the stump. Oh, Mama, I knew you'd come. I knew you'd find me."

Daisy's teeth chattered. Every bone in her body felt broken. It hurt to breathe. Her daughter floated in and out of focus and spoke a half-familiar language that Daisy had forgotten. She staggered forward with Callie until they were inside the house.

"You're truly all right?" she asked in a raspy whisper.

Callie nodded. "What's wrong, Mama?"

"There's food," Daisy whispered. "You must be hungry. Eat it. Be brave. Brave feels good." Daisy's eyes flooded.

Poor Callie. Her father was away, her brother was at war, and her mother was going to die. But that was the way of things, wasn't it? She had been saved and her mother had tasted bravery. Perhaps that was enough.

And then, almost blissfully, rewarding herself, Daisy James sank down onto the parlor floor as if it were a feather bed.

"How are you today?" Callie asked almost a month later.

"Quite well," Daisy answered, still surprised by the fact. "Much stronger."

She had been shocked the first time she opened her eyes in her familiar bedroom, on the tiny animals framing the doorway, on her daughter. She couldn't remember anything of what Callie informed her had been three weeks, and little of what had preceded them, except that she had expected to be dead.

However, she was not only alive, but had even become strong enough to walk around, resume a few light chores and ease her daughter's burden.

"Good," Callie said, "because today we're going into town."

"Oh, no," Daisy said. "It's too soon. I couldn't."

"It's important," the child insisted.

"But there's so much to do here," Daisy answered. "Although you certainly have done an amazing job of it." The child had managed the house, the cows, the garden, and a deathly ill mother. Daisy was awed by her offspring's abilities.

"Don't you feel well enough?" Callie asked.

"It isn't that. It's that Papa's on his way home and I want every-thing—"

"Please, Mama?"

And so they were going. It would be good to be in the fresh air again, and Callie would drive the buggy. There had been no school for weeks now because of the influenza, but when Daisy looked at her daughter's achievements, she wondered if there was anything that Callie didn't already know or couldn't learn all by herself.

"Make sure your mask's on tight." Daisy, too, wore a gauze mask. She hated the way it closed in the world and made her aware of every hot breath. But they said it could keep Callie safe and prevent Daisy's getting sick again.

"I've been wearing it for weeks," Callie reminded her. "Ever since the doctor said to."

Daisy settled onto the buggy and sighed. She still tired too easily

and coughed all the time, but it was pleasant rejoining the world.

"Am I too pale?" she asked.

Callie shook her head without even looking at her. She must have asked the same question too often. The fact was, she was too pale, but she didn't want to begin painting her face. Gideon wouldn't like it and he was due home any day now. She smoothed her best mail-order dress and held her head high. He knew nothing of her illness, nor did Nicky. Her men had other battles to wage and didn't need to worry about something they couldn't help. She held a handkerchief at the ready for her long, wracking coughs. The flu and pneumonia were gone, cured, she was certain, by her hot flaxseed poultices, not the doctor's medicine. She was glad she hadn't gone to the temporary infirmary. It had meant additional trouble for Callie, but the other way, Callie would have been completely alone in the woods. The good air of home had cured her, even if she still coughed and needed to sleep half the day away.

"Maybe I was wrong. Maybe you should have stayed home and rested," Callie said through her mask.

"I've spent too much time resting already." She patted her daughter's hand. "Besides, I've got to find out your big surprise, why coming to town is so important today, don't I?"

"Maybe you came because you're hoping to see Papa on his way home."

"I'm glad I didn't bob my hair," Daisy said abruptly.

"What?"

"Bob my hair. Like the ladies in town and the magazines. Papa wouldn't like it." Gideon loved her hair puffed and piled high and so it would remain, even though the exertion of arranging the elaborate coiffure tired her and produced coughing spasms.

"You look beautiful, Mama," Callie said.

Daisy looked away, embarrassed. "And if you see Papa first, on the road or in town, you won't—"

"I won't tell him you were sick." Callie looked as if she wanted to say more, perhaps object to the secret, perhaps admit it was a foolish one, since anyone who knew Daisy would require no more than a glance to know the truth. But the girl said nothing.

They could see the headlands and the town. Callie drove the team smartly. She had certainly become good at it during Daisy's illness. "Did you come into town often?" Daisy asked.

Callie shrugged. "Pretty much. For the doctor. For medicine. To go to school once, except then I found out there wasn't any. To see

278

about the Apple Festival Pageant, before I knew that was canceled, too. And for other things."

"Poor Callie." Daisy patted her hand. "You handled so much. You deserve a treat. How would you like to go to the movies?" She stopped and considered. "If we have enough money." She shook her head and lapsed back into silence. They'd be true "Do-Withouts" soon—without anything more than their potatoes, milk, and homemade cheese. Gideon had to get back home.

"The movies are still closed," Callie said.

They rode in silence until they reached town. "Ready to be surprised?" Callie asked.

The town looked more alive than ever. Daisy feasted on the sight of so many people. She still hadn't traveled any further from home than her childhood trip down the coast to Fort Ross. But the lack of comparisons made the little town the entire world, and its sight and sounds all the more exciting.

Callie pulled up in front of the hotel. Surely they couldn't afford to eat here. Nonetheless, her daughter helped her down and then marched her into the lush dining room.

"Callie," Daisy began. "This is sweet of you, but—"

"Don't worry, Mama."

"Ah, yes!" The hostess looked delighted and winked at Callie. "Glad to see you well again, Mrs. James. And it's always lovely seeing you, California. Please, do sit down."

"Thank you very much," Daisy said, surprised and confused that the woman knew their names. "But we really can't—"

Callie, however, sat down and tugged at her sleeve. "Please?" she begged.

Daisy sat down as well, but only so that she could settle the matter less obtrusively. She leaned over. This was embarrassing. "I know you mean well, Callie, that you want to surprise me, but this place is too—"

"We're delighted to have you with us today, Mrs. James," the hostess said. "I'll be right back with menus." She turned away.

"Callie!" Daisy hissed. "I have twenty-five cents with me, and it's for a thrift stamp. We can't—"

"Mama, it's free."

Daisy pulled away, studied her daughter's face. "Why?"

Callie smiled again. "That's the surprise."

The menu had been carefully printed in an exquisite hand. And near the bottom were the words "Daisy James's Victory Bread."

279

Callie's grin nearly split her face in two.

"What does this mean?" Daisy whispered.

"I told you it was the best in town. Now everybody knows it. You're famous."

"I don't understand."

"Well, most of the time while you were sick, you slept. So I made some loaves the way you had, and when I went for your medicine, I took them around."

"And the hotel bought them?"

"They paid me and gave me the next batch of flour and rye and everything. Now that you're better, I knew you'd find out, so I wanted to surprise you, and they said to do it this way."

Daisy didn't know what to say first, or if she could say any of it at all. Below the wild red hair, inside her unformed, gawky, spindly limbed daughter lived a giant of a woman. Who was it made her so large of heart, so brave, so wise, so generous? Callie was the one who had thought of the idea, baked the bread, carted it to town, and sold it, and yet she called it "Daisy's."

"You aren't angry, are you, Mama? Your bread was so good. And we needed the money."

Daisy stared at her. Of course. You couldn't dig medicine out of the ground along with potatoes or squeeze it out of the old cow. "You're amazing," was all she could say.

Callie made a face. Daisy knew that expression. Her daughter had been convinced from birth that she could do anything anyone else could do. No matter that she was younger, or weaker, or a girl. She had followed her adored older brother everywhere, listening to his stories, imitating his bravado, stopping only when he went off with his friends to places even he shouldn't be.

She had told her mother that she, too, would like to be alongside Nicky, killing Huns from a trench in Europe.

"You're so strong, Callie, so brave, so—" She was silenced by noise that came from every angle and intensified by the second.

The mill whistle shrieked, church bells clanged, people shouted.

Daisy held her breath. What was the alarm about? An invasion, a disaster? But two waitresses suddenly hugged, then they spoke to a man nearby, who also became all smiles.

Instantly, Callie was up and over to the informed gentleman's side. She pulled down her mask. "Please, sir, what's happening?" she asked.

Daisy was tempted to call her back, remind her of manners, but

she was more tempted to know what was going on.

He was a stout man with a flushed face. "Little girl," he said, "it's about the biggest news possible."

"I am not a little girl! I'm—what news?"

"The Armistice!"

"Armi—" She looked confused, but Daisy saw her daughter set her jaw and look like a knowledgeable person who merely wanted to verify information. "What about it?" Callie asked in a dignified manner.

"They signed it today. Isn't that the best news, little—"

"I'm not a little girl!"

He nodded and smiled. His face was very pink. He was drinking beer, and from where she sat, Daisy suspected it wasn't his first of the day and certainly wouldn't be his last. "Right," he said. "Well, little lady, what else is there to say? The war's over!" And, with a loud burst of laughter, he held out his glass. "Want some beer to celebrate, madam? Soon we'll have whiskey again, now that soldiers won't need the grain anymore, and that'll be the second-best thing to celebrate!"

"Will the soldiers—will they come home soon?"

His pink cheeks jiggled with his emphatic nod. "Can't think why not." His voice grew more serious. "I got me a nephew over there. Sister's son. Like my own. I . . . well . . ." He took out a handkerchief and blew his nose, then spoke in his jolly boom again. "Like I say, lots to celebrate."

"Thank you," she said. "Oh, thank you!" She rushed back to tell her mother, but Daisy had already heard. Her mind filled with Nicky, with a house full and complete. The day was enormous, overwhelming. Her family would soon be under one roof, all well, all together. The war was over, the flu was over. All their battles were over and everything was going to be just the way it used to be.

"Have you heard?" the waitress said.

Daisy and Callie nodded, too happy to say much.

"They're building a bonfire on Lake Street," the waitress continued. "Going to hang Kaiser Bill after dark. Celebrate all night. Stay around. It'll be a party you'll never forget."

They nodded happily and the waitress left to spread the news.

"Good thing I wasn't hungry anyway," Daisy said. Then she realized that Callie's smile had disappeared. "What's wrong?" she asked. "What could possibly be wrong?"

"Oh, Mama," Callie said in a mournful whisper. "They won't need your Victory Bread anymore."

Daisy laughed and coughed and laughed some more. "It was lovely being famous for a minute," she said. "But I'll be happier back in the woods with everybody home. We'll save a menu, if they'll let us. That'll be enough." She was flooded with joy, with warm remembered images.

"Things are going to be right again, exactly the way they were," she said at the same moment that Callie, looking excited and flushed said, "I bet Nicky and Papa—and everything—will be so different!"

Daisy felt a moment's trepidation, but she pushed it away and returned to her happy, floating world. Why should anything be different or changed? What could Callie possibly know? She was only a child.

21

"Just this once, Callie, please?"

Nicky was the picture of innocent need, and Callie had never liked disappointing her handsome brother or missing whatever outings he'd allow her to join. Still, it had been a long time between adventures, and she didn't feel at all easy about this one. She sat further back in the upholstered chair and lit a cigarette to give herself time.

"My," Nicky said, "aren't we daring? When did this begin? I heard talk that my baby sister was pretty wild, but I never dreamed she smoked! Do you also guzzle bathtub gin?"

Callie shrugged.

He stood up. "I think this woman-of-the-world business is an act. You haven't even bobbed your hair. You're my same baby sister, innocent child of the woodlands."

Innocent, perhaps, but hardly a child. In fact, she had barely ever been given the chance to be one. She saw her life in two halves, a firm apple sliced neatly down the center. The knife had been The Day of the Pig, and it had ended her childhood.

She had come to believe that people were given one special chance to be their best selves. Her mother's chance had come facing a pig, gun in hand.

Then, less than an hour later, because of the way of things, because of war, because of disease, Callie had become the adult. Luckily, she had a talent for it.

Or maybe because she lacked her mother's fragile, helpless beauty, she also lacked the rest of the package—a belief that she could wait passively for someone else to take action. In either case, for either reason, Callie had had no choice but to grow up quickly.

"Or are you still too vain about that hair to cut it?" Nicky asked. He stubbed out his cigarette and paced the room, picking up and putting down ashtrays and carvings without pausing to look at them.

"Of course I am. Insanely vain. Everybody knows that." They probably did. Callie James didn't see the point in lying. Besides, her hair was her best asset. She was small and slender with pleasant features that were easily forgotten—except for the titian curls that cascaded down her back. "Besides, everybody else has bobbed hair. Why follow the crowd?"

Nicky paced, no longer interested in her smoking, dancing, or coiffure. "Will you do it?" he asked. "There's not much time. I need to know now."

"Nicky, there's talk about you—real talk, not like about me. Even mama worries about where you get your money."

"You mean Gideon worries. Mama doesn't think about things if they worry her."

For a while, when they were both little, Nicky had called Gideon "Papa," but after the war, he had abandoned the term. Nicky had come home changed in small ways on the surface, but Callie sensed deep shifts below. He seemed so uncomfortable that he essentially reinvented himself. One of the changes was to drop the "Papa" and any claims on either side that went along with it. He moved up the coast, had a string of beautiful women, a job in Fort Bragg at a dry goods store, and too much money.

There was a lot of talk about him.

"They're both worried. I'm worried, too," Callie said. "Rum running, bootlegging's dangerous."

"Come on," he said. "*If* I were doing it, what's so dangerous about a fine?"

"And jail?"

"Almost never."

"And being killed?"

"You sound like all the frightened dopes. Who'd kill me? Everybody wants the stuff, everybody loves the supplier. Let me tell you,

half the people on the North Coast are involved. You know how many potatoes are turned into whiskey? How many hay wagons and trucks hide five-gallon jugs? I know a guy hauls pigs to market, except they've got bootleg jackass inside instead of guts. Don't act like I'm the only one."

"Nicky, there've been bodies on the—"

"Shipwrecks," he said. "Drownings. Imagination."

"They say they stuff their corpses into blow holes."

"If you're afraid, say so. I'll find somebody else."

"I'm not afraid!" She was angry at the suggestion and angry that she was constitutionally unable to ignore his bait.

"Good, then . . ."

"But that doesn't mean I'll break the law for you. Or with you!"

"You're getting to be an old man like Gideon. Preachy, self-righteous. It's hard to believe."

"I am not! He isn't either, Nicky. Why are you so hard on him?"

"Cal, when I met him, he was going to make a fortune, see the world, have adventures. He saw the world, all right, but the rest—is saving the damned redwoods an adventure?"

"He thinks so. I can understand. He said when he came to the coast it was beautiful, and the old ways seemed fair, cutting trees one by one, by hand. He said he once thought the trees were forever, for a million years, but after he saw what the new machinery did, he—"

"I know what he said, what he says! For chrissakes, haven't I heard it over and over again?"

"Then why should it annoy you so much? All he wants to do is save something special, that—"

"But that's all he wants, all the time! That's all he does! Write letters, sign petitions, start petitions, go to meetings, to San Francisco, to Sacramento, lecture—ladies' clubs, senators, you, me. Mostly me. And what difference does he make? Nothing changes for the redwoods, but meanwhile, everybody in the United States of America gets rich except Gideon James, who is too holy to work the woods or the mill anymore, who is the most stubborn damned—"

"He says exactly the same thing about you! Besides, why be angry? He's not doing anything wrong!"

"He's not doing anything, period! Would Mama have a single decent thing if it weren't for you and me? Look around!"

There was truth in what he said. The Edison phonograph and the tall mahogany radio were Christmas gifts from Nicky. In the kitchen, the new gray-and-white Wedgwood stove was Callie's contribution.

But still, that didn't mean her father's choices were wrong.

"And you—you're just as high and mighty and god-awful serious about life as he is! Soon you'll be just as boring, too, and I always thought you'd turn out special, not some dried-up old maid!"

"Old maid! I'm not even twenty yet and I'm not—"

"Look, Cal, you love the old family stories. This is traditional. Nobody in this family was ever exactly in the middle of things. We're all kind of rebels and outsiders."

"But not lawbreakers."

"How do you know? Sometimes it was against the law for them to be alive. Besides, why are we fighting?"

He sat down across from her. "Callie," he said softly, "if I don't show up tonight, if I don't deliver, I'll be in big trouble. All I need is a lookout. You'd sit in the car while I get the stuff."

"What stuff? Where? No more mysteries. Say it."

He looked directly into her eyes, almost angrily, then he sighed. "This is between us, no matter what you decide, right?"

She nodded.

"Whiskey. On the beach."

"So the rumors are true." She had so wanted to believe that the dangerous edge she saw in Nicky was an illusion, that he wasn't knee-deep in things that didn't serve him well.

"I never heard the rumors, so I can't say. Anyway, that's the job."

"And after you get the whiskey, however you do that, what then?"

"Then I get it to somebody who pays me a lot of money, and I give some to you, and we celebrate."

"If anybody sees me, I'd lose my job," she said.

He waved away the idea. "They need typist-stenographers in jail, so your talents won't be wasted."

"Nicky!"

"No Prohi's ever—"

"What?"

"No Prohibition Officer is going to bother us."

"Don't do it," she said softly. "It's too—"

He stood up again and she felt they were back in their old roles—the little girl who literally looked up to and idolized the daring big brother who provided most of the fun of her childhood: picnics, abalone hunts, her first view of the blow hole in the meadow up at Russian Gulch. Who gave her his prized collection of clay marbles and taught her how to make a baseball of cork and twine.

Her brother, who took her on secret missions, swearing the two of

them to a blood pact, nicking index fingers and pressing them together. Who took her to see where he'd once found a redheaded skeleton. Who told her about the Chinese grandmother who had confessed, right in front of him, to murdering and burying the man. Who showed her the graveyard at the back of the ground and told her sad, bloody, exciting stories about the generations buried there. Who drove her down the coast over dirt and fields all the way to San Francisco, too fast, and then gave her the wheel most of the way back, and laughed when she drove the roadster into a mud hole. And kept laughing when they cut brush and filled the hole and still were stuck so that they had to hire a mule team to pull them out. Who poured her first, very illegal drink. Who managed, even while keeping his own love life private, to know of each and every beau of hers and to make sure she knew what he thought of them. Who lavished extravagant gifts on everyone. Who almost never finished anything he began.

Perhaps Nicky, like their mother, would never fully grow up, but even so, those Nicky times were the days her memory held tight, the days she would have called her true life. Almost all the responsible rest swirled into a long blur.

"Okay, Cal," he said. "This is it. You in or not?"

"I'm in," she said for form's sake, because neither one had ever really doubted her decision.

"Our secret," he whispered, pressing his index finger against hers.

She tied back her hair, pinned on her good luck charm, her grandmother's gold butterfly hairclasp, and pushed everything under a cap.

She certainly didn't want to look like a girl, like Nicky's little redheaded sister. She put on pants that had been used for gardening ever since Nicky had outgrown them and an oversized sweater she'd knitted before she was very good at it, and packed a small bag with a dress and dance shoes—for the celebration afterward. Then she raced downstairs. Nicky would be back in a few minutes.

"Where are you going in that getup?" Her mother's voice could be surprisingly sharp, no matter how fragile she appeared.

"Why I—why I—you startled me." They weren't supposed to be back yet.

"I startled you?" Daisy James held her pale hands to her chest. Her heart had never recovered from the Spanish Influenza and the pneumonia that had followed, and she sometimes seemed no more substantial than a memory, or a ghost.

"Your mother and I had become used to having a daughter." Gideon helped his wife into an easy chair. "Instead, we come home to a rather sloppy little boy."

"I'm sorry," Callie said. "I thought you were seeing a movie."

"Mama's too tired. But that doesn't explain your costume."

"I thought I'd dress warmly. I'm going for a ride with Nicky," Callie said defensively. "My hair blows around in his car. Besides, I'll wear a duster over this."

"Nicky?" Her parents flicked looks at one another.

"My brother, remember?" Maybe Nicky was right. They'd become too stuffy and boring for words.

But they suddenly looked old, both of them. Her mother was quite gray and her father's posture had changed so that he was less towering. How had that happened, and when? She softened as she read the creases on their faces and between their eyes as justified concern for her welfare. "I won't be late," she said, deciding to postpone whatever celebration Nicky might have planned.

There were two short honks outside.

Daisy James gasped. "I'll never get used to that sound," she murmured after she caught her breath.

"Isn't he coming in?" Gideon looked disappointed, but Callie knew it would never occur to him to go outside and see the young man he considered his son. Two stubborn fools.

"He must not realize you're home," Callie said.

"But our car—" Gideon began.

"You know how distracted Nicky can be." She kissed her parents good-night. "Don't worry," she said again.

Her mother took both her hands. Her eyes were large and glittery green pools, ready to flood. "Give him our love," she said.

Nicky pulled off the road into a small grove of trees that almost concealed the roadster. She saw a farmhouse on a short, dark bluff, and beyond it, nothing. Black night and ocean. The air felt thick, impenetrable, with only the smallest sliver of new moon.

"Here?" she whispered. This looked so ordinary, so uninhabited.

He nodded and put a finger up to his mouth as he looked around. "Okay," he said after a moment, "I'm off. If you hear anything, or see anybody—anybody, even if they look harmless—start the motor, honk twice the way I do, and drive off."

"Leave you?"

"Then circle back and pick me up at Twin Rocks in a half hour or so."

"But Nicky, what'll you do for that half hour while I—"

"I'll get to you. Besides, it isn't going to happen. Gotta go—" And he was out, disappearing into a cleft in the cliff's edge and then down to the beach below.

She sat in the car, straining for every sound, anything, but all she could hear were night noises—the sea, the wind through the leaves, a cat's howl.

Bloated, empty time filled the car, a shapeless inert blob. Callie sighed, crossed her legs, recrossed them, hummed a nameless tune, and peered toward the blank Pacific. If only there were a moon, but of course, if there were, neither she nor Nicky would be here. Too easy, then, to see the ship head for the cove, whiskey barrels pushed overboard and floated in to be emptied into jugs and sent back to sea.

And then what? Surely her brother and whoever else was down there weren't going to carry one after another five-gallon jug up that cliff face?

She continued to wait. It felt as if months had passed, as if surely the sky must be ready to lighten, as if, indeed, it should already be midday.

Finally, she heard muffled sounds, steps, fabric rustling, and she was able to decipher two figures coming through the narrow split in the cliff. They ignored her, moved low to the earth, busied themselves around an enormous, twisted tree, and, in a silence broken only by an occasional grunt or deep breath, hauled their booty up the cliff.

That meant there were at least three of them, she realized. Someone was down there tying new kegs or jugs onto the rope pulley.

There was nothing to look out for. No one approached, no one interrupted. Callie floated on a dark cushion, drowned in night. Now and then she heard the slap of surf against the rocks below, low male whispers, a night bird.

And then she realized something had been subtracted from the low register of sound. No matter how hard she squinted into the night, she could no longer make out any movement or sense of men at work on the bluff.

They were gone.

Finishing up, she reminded herself. Inside the farmhouse. Be patient.

But patience had never been a virtue she particularly admired. She was tantalized by a thin slice of light on the bluff. At least one of the windows must be partly uncurtained. What harm would a small peek be? Her singularly uneventful lookout job seemed well and truly over. Indeed, what would there be for anyone to see or be suspicious of now? The night silence was unbroken, and surely a sleepy farmhouse was not going to alert the Prohi's.

That decided it. She had come for the adventure, and she was tired of sitting on the sidelines, speculating. Leaving the car door open so as to make no noise, she quietly made her way around to the oceanfront side of the farmhouse. As she approached the window, she crouched low, almost crawling until she was at the sill. Then she pulled up, inch by inch, until she could see into the room.

There was a heavy table much like the one at home. A back that looked like Nicky's facing it and somebody else beside him. And at least one other man in the far corner. He held a gun, but absently, as if it were a good-luck charm he unthinkingly tossed around.

There was money on the table. Stacks of it, enough to make her gape. Counting it out, handing bills to her brother, was a man who was like none of her fantasies of gangsters or bootleggers. He was . . . normal. Somebody who might go crabbing or dancing with her.

A criminal, distributing money, guarded by an armed watchdog, should not look ordinary. It twisted things around and felt perverse and frightening. She pulled higher for a better look.

And then speculation stopped. The black night exploded into shock waves.

Something hard and metallic pressed the back of her neck.

"Get up," a voice said. "Hands up."

"I'm—I'm—"

"Shut up. What the hell you think you're doing?" he whispered, but so fiercely that it came out a low growl. "This isn't a public meeting. What do you want? Who sent you?" He didn't wait for an answer or allow one. Instead, he grabbed the neck of her sweater and yanked her away from the window, moving the gun around so it aimed at her heart.

She opened her mouth to scream, then clamped it shut, afraid that noise would get all of them outside after her, or put Nicky as well as herself into jeopardy. But it didn't matter what she decided, her throat was dry and closed and she was mute.

"I want to know who you are before I show you to Mr. Nelson in

there," he said. "Or maybe I won't bother. He'd just get mad. Maybe you'll just disappear over the cliff."

The night clamped on top of her head, sealed her up, inked out her sight. She was going to be one of the people who disappeared, one of the unreported whiskey murders.

She had an image of her mother and father waiting for her promised early return home, and then the darkness swelled still more and she let go inside of it.

And caught herself. *Swooning?*—California James? What kind of habit is that to start now? Save yourself, dammit!

She took a deep breath and yanked. The sweater neck stretched like an elastic band. She yanked again. Her captor hissed, pulled back, pressed the gun closer, but she was sure he wouldn't pull the trigger until he knew who she was or what her business had been.

She yanked once again, harder.

And her cap flew off and landed at her feet. The pins loosened, hair tumbled. Instinctively, she put her hands to her head, then put them back up heavenward, as directed.

"Jesus!" the man said. "You're a . . ." He bent down, craned to see more clearly, held a strand of her hair close to the window. "I know who you are," he whispered. "What the hell you doing—excuse me, miss, I—but what are you doing here?"

He was bluffing—he didn't know her and she wasn't going to get Nicky in big trouble.

"Does Nicky know you're here?"

So much for a theory of bluffing. On the other hand, he relaxed his grip on her sweater and put his gun back wherever he normally kept it.

She nodded. "I'm supposed to be in the car. Please, don't tell him I left it."

They both heard end-of-business noises from inside. Chairs scraped, the talk became scrappy sounds, and Callie's guard sighed. "Okay," he said gruffly, "if he trusts you, I trust you. Get back in the car. I won't say anything about this, but maybe you ought to think hard before you ever do this kind of thing again."

She thanked him and raced away, then sat in the car, her heart still doing a quick-step.

Nicky got in, grinning. "See?" he said. "Nothing to it." He counted bills and handed them to her.

She shook her head. "I didn't earn it."

"Of course you did. Take it."

"No, I don't feel good about it. I—who is it you're dealing with, Nicky? Who paid you? What kind of people are they?" Who was the Mr. Nelson she had been almost forced to face? What nightmare acts would he have committed, or ordered committed on her? How could Nicky be friends with people who threatened to push other people over cliffs?

"What do you mean, what kind of people? They're like you and me." She slid over and he started the car. "What image do you have in that backwoods mind of yours?" he asked. "Some kind of monster? I'll tell you something funny. The guy who's the head of it, who pays me, is called Baby Face. Shows you how fierce my business contacts are. Baby Face. Does that scare you?" He chuckled. "Take the money." He put the bills on her lap.

She didn't touch them. "I can't celebrate," she said finally. "I promised to be home early."

"Just as well. Another boat's coming in."

She swallowed hard. "Don't do it, Nicky. Please don't."

"Let me tell you something, little sister," he said in the most serious voice she'd heard from him in years. "This is my chance. This man's important. I think I impressed him. I think I can get somewhere with him."

"But you shouldn't want to! He's bad. Those people are criminals."

"They're business people, providing a necessary service like the men who own the lumber company or your boss at the mill."

She sat up straight and a twenty-dollar bill fluttered to the floorboard. "My boss isn't afraid to work in broad daylight!" she snapped.

"I should have moved away after the war," Nicky said. "I meant to. I planned it the whole time I was in France. I knew I couldn't come back here. They wouldn't understand that everything had changed, especially me. I wanted different things, different ways. If Mama hadn't been so sick, I would have, too."

"Why? What changed you?"

"How could I come back as if nothing had happened? Settle into the littlest backwater village and follow a lot of rules that were killed over there. It changes you, facing death, never knowing what's ahead. I hated it and loved it—loved the tension, the excitement of surviving. How do you go from there to here?"

"I still don't understand what's so wrong here."

"There's nothing but trees, Callie. I could cut them down or saw them up, drive Gideon wild, and still wind up a poor man. I have to

make my mark. That's what this country's about. That's what's happening everywhere else and there's no way to do it here. You know what I remembered yesterday? I remembered another one of my Grandmother China's stories."

"She was my grandmother, too," Callie said. She was jealous of Nicky's years with the story-telling grandmother, resentful that she only heard the tales filtered through him. Her mother, it appeared, hadn't paid nearly as much attention as the very young Nicky had.

"Yes, but you didn't know her," Nicky said, emphasizing the edge he had on her, as he always did. "Anyway, she told me that the first Nicholas Ross, my great grandfather—"

"Mine, too," Callie snapped.

"—the one I'm named for, said he came from a village in Siberia that was so far away from everything else it never knew what had happened until years later. They called it a deaf village. That's what this place is, Callie. This is an American deaf village."

"That's stupid," she said. "This is a wonderful, beautiful place. There are good people, and jobs, and—what else do you need? A fortune? Why? Because Pathe News shows you flappers, champagne, and 'flaming youth'? Because you hear some man in New York say that everybody can be a millionaire? Why is that what the country's about? Who *cares* what anybody else says it's about? Everything that's important is here, if you'd look. Why don't you think about all those people you tell stories about—*your* grandmother and *your* great grandfather and all the rest who lived good lives here."

"That was then. The world's different now."

"Nothing's different! Important things don't change. Nicky—"

He interrupted. "You don't understand," he said with finality. "It's different for you. You're a girl."

They drove up the bumpy dirt road that led to the house. "Give them my love," he said.

"Come in and tell them yourself."

"I have to get back."

She put her hand on his forearm. She would try once more, convince him not to push his luck. Remind him of what the papers said about the new hoodlums, remind him of the homegrown variety who killed in order to steal from one another and eliminate competition. Remind him . . .

But he understood her intent before she said a word. He shook his head. Then he smiled and his boyish, brilliant charm flooded the car. "I nearly forgot," he said as he put his hand into his shirt pocket.

"Look what I stepped on when I came out of the farmhouse." He passed her a filigreed gold butterfly hairclasp. One wing was mildly indented.

Her hand shook as she took it. "Amazing," she said. "I have one something like it at home."

"So did my Chinese grandmother."

He leaned over and kissed her forehead. Then he lifted her hand, kissed her index finger, and pressed it to his. "Our secret," he said softly, winking.

Her fears for him were pebbles she carried in the back of her mouth. It became impossible to swallow as the pebbles enlarged. She remembered the rare times it had snowed in the hills and how she and Nicky had rolled pellets into icy balls. All night long, her anxiety rolled icy bits of stone around, and now they were the size of boulders.

"You're not eating your cereal," her father said.

She was surprised he noticed. He had a stack of papers next to his plate, his eternal correspondence as well as the draft of a speech for some garden group. Most of the time he interrupted his chews and swallows only to tsk at a misspelling or to lift and dip his pen and make notations.

She had once told him, gently, and with love, that she believed he was obsessed. He had responded with a thoughtful smile and, eventually, a nod. "Nobody ever saved anything important without being obsessed," he said quite happily.

He was already back at his speech, wrinkling his forehead over a troublesome line.

Her mother looked more delicate than usual, more transparent, almost ready to dissolve into invisibility. "Is anything wrong?" she asked in a soft voice. And, as if anticipating a problem, any problem, she breathed deeply and pressed her hands to her chest.

Callie shook her head. "Not hungry, that's all." She felt so fidgety. "Mama," she asked, "do you remember the day the war ended?"

Her mother's hands fluttered toward her lap. "Of course. How could anyone forget such a time?"

"Remember the hotel? The church bells and the car horns and the mill whistle?"

Her mother nodded. "And our masks. We took them off to shout and celebrate. Very daring of us."

"And you said that soon the family would all be together again,

just like we once were, and that nothing would have changed?"

Her mother lifted a spoon half full of cereal. "Did I say that?" she asked mildly. "I can't remember."

But Callie remembered, and recognized that she had known as a child that nothing would ever be the same. And so had Nicky, who was part of the change.

The grandfather clock ticked in the parlor. Gideon's penpoint scratched on the paper. Daisy lifted spoonfuls with delicacy and grace, slowly, waiting.

When the telephone rang, it was no surprise. Callie stood up calmly and walked to the wall and lifted the mouthpiece, but she didn't need to. Whatever the particular words would be, their meaning would be the same. Things were forever, irrevocably changed.

She recognized the voice from the dark. She'd never know what he looked like, and it didn't matter. She heard the important words. Gunshots when the barrels were coming in. Rivals. Nicky's car, parked in the little grove of trees, still unclaimed. A body sighted on the predawn beach, gone by sunup. No sheriff's report, no mention of it at all. "I thought you should know," he said. "I'm sorry."

She replaced the receiver. She hadn't said a single word after "Hello."

"Dear God," Daisy James said, clutching her heart. Her face turned as gray as her hair. "It's Nicky, isn't it?"

Callie nodded, because she had no words and because her mother couldn't possibly understand that it was Nicky and much, much more that was gone.

Nicky would have understood, but he was gone.

22

Callie stuffed her stockings into her shoes and left them toe to toe on the path leading to the bluff while she went off, barefoot, in search of seabird's eggs.

Not that she cared if she found any. Not that there was anyone who wanted to eat them. She didn't want them and her father survived on air, his endless save-the-trees campaign, and a potato now and then.

But searching for hidden nests was something to do with a long Saturday and a way of remembering Nicky and her mother. They'd both been gone three months now, dead within days of each other, and life was eroding the sharp edges of memory. Callie wanted a quiet time that they alone could fill.

She walked to a lone rock jutting high out of the water and carefully climbed, avoiding slippery spots and pools of ocean water.

The sun-warmed rock and the fresh ocean smell provoked the desired memories. She remembered a time years ago when she and her brother had defied parental orders and climbed here. They'd been so proud of their find—a dozen captured eggs—until they realized they couldn't take evidence of their disobedience home. Years of Gideon James's frugality intensified the dilemma—they'd been trained to abhor

waste, so they couldn't simply throw their take away. What, then, to do?

Callie suggested returning the eggs to their nests, but according to Nicky's intricate, impenetrable, and flexible code of honor, that would be cowardly. Furthermore, he insisted, a mother bird wouldn't accept an egg with human scent on it. The only honorable course was to eat the eggs as planned. He downed six of them, raw, and dared Callie to follow suit.

Of course she did, gagging and feeling overwhelmingly guilty at swallowing an uncooked generation of gulls, ospreys, and pelicans.

"Hey, you'd better get off there!"

She looked down, around the edge of the rock face, at the beach, at a man pointing up at her. He wore a skimmer that shaded half his face, a blue and white shirt, and flannel slacks rolled up. Rather dandified, she decided. Overfond of himself.

"Talking to me?" she demanded.

His sweeping gesture at the empty beach clearly said that of course he was talking to her. He looked at her as if she were dim-witted.

"Then may I emphasize that my whereabouts are none of your business!" Callie snapped out her words so they'd hit him like sticks.

He shrugged and walked off.

Arrogant creature. She didn't want to be up there anyway, but she'd wait. As soon as he was out of sight, she'd climb down, but not before, not while he'd think her descent was because of his directives.

He turned around. "The rocks are dangerous!" he shouted from his distance.

"I know!"

"There's waves, enormous, sudden ones, and you could be—"

"I *know*," she repeated. "I've been here before." She tried to turn her back to signal the end of this conversation, but her foothold was too narrow for major gestures. She stayed in place, suddenly as weary as if she were holding up the bluff and the town that perched on top of it.

"I know," he said. He was closer now, edging back toward the foot of her rock.

"What do you think you know?"

"I know you've been here before. I've seen you around and . . . never mind. Anyway, since you know the beach so well, what are you doing up there? Even without waves, those rocks can be slick!"

He acted like a schoolmarm. She planted herself more firmly on her ledge.

"And... and I'm annoying you, am I right? I apologize. Good day." He tipped his hat and walked off.

She waited until she was sure he wasn't coming back, then she eased around, looking for the best way down. But she stopped in place, momentarily forgetting her purpose.

She was surrounded by dazzle, a happy prisoner in a crystal ball. All around her, life blazed. A rush of joy filled her. She wanted to embrace it all. The winter air, washed to brilliant transparency in recent storms, shimmered above undulating blue, green, turquoise, and deep purple. It bleached the sand and deposited some of its glitter so that light flashed from below and above, from the beach and the ocean.

An osprey with a fish in its talons rose out of the water in a great triumphant sweep. And then, like a watery exclamation point, there came a spout from a gray whale on his way home from Baja.

Callie sighed with pure pleasure. How had she not noticed all this earlier in the day? She edged her way down the rock until she found a narrow perch just above the water line. She eased onto it, and sat, tailor fashion, absorbing the world. The rock behind her back radiated stored sun.

If only she could save such times, capture their color and glory, remember and preserve their power and effect. Then others would feel them, too. They would be hit with the same force she had been and they'd understand each other without words.

If only she knew how to paint what she felt, then she could have made Nicky understand that he wasn't locked in or trapped. Look, she would have said, holding up her canvas. See how open it is? The world floats around us, connected by that vast roll of moody ocean, always changing, rearranging itself. How could it bore you?

And if he felt unmoored, too exposed, too uncovered by its vast openness, she would have found a way to make him see the refuge of the deep, dark forest pockets.

Being on the edge didn't mean you were shoved aside. Other edges faced you. It meant you were free, at a jumping-off place—if you had any desire to jump. If you thought jumping was an adventure.

Neither Nicky nor their mother had found their imagined worlds of adventure, and now Daisy was buried steps away from her birthplace and Nicky's bones lay in some anonymous grave.

Callie hoped they both rested peacefully, finished at long last with yearning.

Her father was also driven by dreams, but at least his were definite, attainable, even if difficult. He wanted trees that had survived fire, earthquake, and storms for the milennia to survive the white man. The single issue directed his days. Of course he mourned his wife and Nicky, but the fragility of all life, he said, intensified his need to preserve what he could of it.

He believed he was moving toward something. Callie couldn't believe the same of herself. For the last three months, she had felt like a metal windup toy on a track. Off to work, back to home. Off, back. Sometimes there was an evening or weekend picnic with what Nicky would have called a swain, but she didn't call them much of anything. She could barely remember their names.

"Be patient," Daisy James had always said. "One day you'll be swept off your feet, and there will be your prince. The one you've dreamed about."

"A prince? In Mendocino?"

"A figure of speech, dear. The wonderful man who'll arrive to save you."

"Save me?" Callie said indignantly. This was the twentieth century and Callie wasn't a damsel in distress. "I haven't been locked in a tower or kidnapped by an evil witch or asleep for a hundred years, Mother. Save me from what?"

Her mother looked surprised. "Why from . . . well, you know. From being single. Alone all your life. Lonely."

How was Callie supposed to answer, ever? Aside from one moment facing a pig, her mother had spent her life waiting to be saved. Given any dilemma, she fluttered and waited and leaned on the strength of those around her. That was her honest view of a woman's role in life, although that helplessness had forged a very different sort of daughter, the sort who lacked one iota of interest in waiting for anything, least of all something humiliating, like being saved.

She didn't know if women aside from her mother had also entertained such foolishness, but if they had, their daughters didn't. Even in Mendocino, the new generation was different.

She had shown her mother Mr. Fitzgerald's book, *This Side of Paradise*. By the time a co-worker had loaned it to her, years after publication, it had long since stopped shocking anyone except Daisy James, who insisted that it was not realistic. Surely "normal," "de-

299

cent" girls didn't kiss dozens of men—did not in fact kiss anyone but their "prince" and future husband.

Callie considered her mother's generation—and certainly her mother—hypocritical. After all, Daisy Ross James had kissed one prince too many, hadn't she? But Callie wasn't cruel, and she was more generous about mistakes of the heart than her mother seemed to be, so she never mentioned it. She read and adopted Mr. Fitzgerald's book. "Oh," she'd murmur, quoting a favorite line, "'just one person in fifty has any glimmer of what sex is. I'm hipped on Freud and all that...'" She also read Mr. Freud himself, but she didn't attempt to share any of that book with her mother.

She had long hair and didn't use rouge, but she wore thin dresses with short sleeves, sometimes rolled down her stockings, and never wore a corset. She danced to saxophone music, smoked cigarettes, and drank gin. She had none of her mother's dreams.

Still, she wanted something more than what she was offered. The youths she met didn't seem to be flaming, no matter what the press thought. Their cars were too often shinier and more exciting than they were, and nights with them hardly felt like breaks from her tedious daily routine. She missed Nicky's company, imagination, and thirst for adventure.

She needed to break the loop of her days, but she was afraid she would instead drive Nicky's roadster up and down the same dusty road at the same hours her entire life.

"I want, I want," she murmured. How boring, how selfish. Still, she was twenty. Time to finish that sentence. "I want, I want, I want..."

And then the words and Callie were engulfed, swallowed by a wide-jawed wave, tumbled off the ledge into space, into nothingness, toward the whale, toward the heart of the ocean.

Callie gasped, choked, flailed, tried to right herself, find a sense of direction—of up, of down, of shore, of deep sea.

The freezing water numbed her and increased her confusion.

She was tugged under a wave, tossed back up, flipped, and rolled again. For one brief blink, she saw the bluff and the town above it. And lost it again.

Her arms pulled at the water, legs kicked as hard as she knew how toward the memory of land.

Arm over arm, kick after kick, but the ocean knocked her sideways, dragged her down, and fought to undo her every move. And it

was so cold, so enormous. She could barely feel her limbs or make them move.

She pulled handfuls of water in imaginary tracks, hoping she was close. She couldn't tell. When she lifted her head, salt spray blinded her.

It grew more difficult to pull and more difficult still to hope. She reached with her left arm, over and out with her right, and . . .

Her head jerked back, her body flipped faceup and whipped around in the opposite direction. She resisted, fought, insisted, churned water in an attempt to turn back. With her last strength, she clamped her mouth shut so as to contain her rising panic and twisted to regain direction.

Something punched her. Hard. Pulled her back, the wrong way, nearly drowning her. Shouted unintelligibly. She flailed, thrashed, and lost. She had no more strength.

She hurt all over. She shook with an icy chill that was far beyond skin deep.

Then her skin burned and felt raw. She was shaking and aching, but immobile. On firm sand, out of the ocean.

"Of all the stupid—! Can you sit up? You're all right now, aren't you?"

She shook even more.

Hands clasped her shoulders. "Come on! Show some life!"

It took a while to make sense of the words, and even then she did nothing. She was showing enough life to satisfy herself. She was breathing.

"Come on!"

She reluctantly opened her eyes—and gasped. His face was no more than an inch away, lips almost brushing hers. He pulled back.

"Alive, then," he said.

Him. The dandy, as drenched and wretched as she was. She swallowed and nodded.

"Sorry I punched you," he said. "I couldn't think how else to stop you from making it worse. You wouldn't listen. You acted crazy. You nearly drowned."

She coughed and spit out seawater.

"I grabbed your hair," he said. "Hope I didn't hurt you, but it was all I could catch hold of. Good thing you don't bob it or you'd be halfway across the Pacific by now."

She remembered the yank, the about-face that had terrified her.

Her scalp felt raw, as if all the hair had been pulled out. Her skin did, too, as if he'd dragged her the final distance over pebbles and rough sand.

"I warned you about those rocks. I can't believe you stayed there. Lucky I came back or you'd have . . ."

No. She shook her head again. She would not have!

"You were heading out to sea!"

No. She would have found her direction. She was not like her mother, she was not a damsel in distress. He had interrupted her, disoriented her.

"You're the most stubborn, obstinate, wrong-headed girl!"

He sounded just like Nicky now. But of course he wasn't at all like him. He waited. He thought she was stubborn, but he kept on waiting, even though he had to be as cold and uncomfortable as she was.

"Fine," he said. "You weren't drowning."

She nodded.

"I interrupted your bracing swim. I should have kept walking and stayed dry, right?"

He was rather attractive, now that she could see more clearly. He had olive skin and rugged features that were softened, just enough, by long-lashed dark eyes.

"I take your silence as agreement," he said. He stopped crouching over her and stood up, brushing sand off his hands. "Guess the only fair thing to do is throw you back in like a bad catch, which I'm beginning to think you are." He lifted her.

He wouldn't.

"Now you can prove that you don't need anybody for anything," he said.

He couldn't.

But he walked into the water, ankle deep, and kept going. "When you dry off," he shouted, "learn some manners."

And he dropped her.

She landed with unpleasant force on her rump and sat, stunned, while the water churned around her. Then she summoned the strength to stand up and turn around, stumbling.

He was already on the beginning of the path off the beach, his back to her.

"Wait!" she said. "Wait!" She burst into tears.

He stopped, turned, then raced back. "Are your hurt?" he asked. "Did I . . . I didn't mean to hurt you."

She stood immobile, sobbing, wavelets lapping at her ankles. "I was drowning," she wailed.

"I know."

It was difficult saying the next words. The detritus of too many tensely self-reliant years piled up like rubble blocking a tunnel. She squeezed around it, her voice dwindling. "You . . . you saved me," she finally managed. She recognized why the words were so difficult to say. Was her mother on a celestial observatory, laughing and saying, "I told you so! We all need saving sooner or later!"

"Yes, I did."

"Thank you."

"You're welcome," he said solemnly, "Miss . . . Miss . . ."

"James." She allowed a tentative smile. "And you are Mr. . . . ?"

"Prinz." He made a mock bow.

Prince? If, as an angel, her mother allowed herself a little more vigor than when alive, she had now dropped her harp and was crushing her wings as she rolled around on a cloud, incoherent with laughter.

Callie, dripping, sneezing, hair wet and tangled, clothes sodden and clinging, looked at him with open-mouthed awe. "Are you really 'Prince'?"

"Not unless you insist," he said. "Prinz," he repeated. "With a *z*. Spanish-Portuguese and who knows what else. Also, Rafael, with an *R*."

Callie giggled, sneezed, giggled some more. "Not only that," she said, "but I was literally, truly, swept off my feet. Everything she ever said and I disagreed with in one afternoon!"

"How's that? I'm afraid I don't understand."

She shook her head. "Some other time," she said.

"Agreed." He put his hand up to his head, then looked around. His skimmer was gone. He didn't seem overly disturbed by it, and she revised her earlier decision that he was a dandy. He was actually rather enjoyable. Good-looking and well-dressed, and there was nothing so dreadful about that. Besides, who was she to argue with her mother, fate, or princes?

Gideon James rubbed the tiny whiskered face. The detail work was amazing. He wondered who had done the carving and who in turn had covered it with paint so that all the fine woodworking was obliterated.

Another otter. Odd how many of them there were on the doorway.

303

All the other creatures were one of a kind, and then the carver had switched to nonstop otters, as if he couldn't get them out of his mind.

Or maybe that's just what he saw. They said the ocean once teemed with them.

He put down his rags and paint remover and rested, but the otters stayed on his mind. Seas once full of them, land full of trees and Indian villages. Now no one had seen an otter for a hundred years, the Indians were dead or all but invisible, the coast was ravaged with clean cuts that left no anchors, no root systems, so the earth ran into and destroyed the rivers and the salmon and steelhead that had filled them. If somebody didn't cry halt, soon only barren rock and empty ocean would be left.

His own daughter thought he was peculiar. One-track mind, she said. Gideon had hoped that she would be his ally and co-fighter, but perhaps more had to happen to her before she could comprehend the true size of the loss.

He didn't think that would be for some time. She was certainly taking a long vacation from ideas, grimacing when he became too serious. She'd gone frivolous, into a real tizzy since Rafael Prinz arrived on the scene. It was good seeing her look alive again, end her mourning, but she'd gone too far, kicking up her heels day and night. And now, before she even took a breather from dancing, she was marrying the fellow. Like that. June 23, three months to the day since they'd met. Their honeymoon would be longer than their courtship.

Gideon knew he was hard on the fellow. Prinz was nice enough, if a little too deliberately modern. Shiny, as if he polished himself every morning. And mostly surface. And what was that stuff he practiced? Couéism? Reciting, "Every day, in every way, I am getting better and better." Convincing Callie that it was the secret of everything, the brightest thing she'd ever heard. She called her father obsessed, but lately she never stopped talking about the power of the mind, about Freud and psychoanalysis. She even suggested that had her mother practiced autosuggestion by reciting Coué's jingle, she could have healed her body's ills. As if the Spanish Influenza had been something Daisy imagined!

Well. No matter. When he was their age, he also had thought his parents' generation were fools and that he was something completely new and different. He had planned to see everything there was in the world and make a fortune to boot. And now none of that mattered. He had once been so ready to waste, and now all he wanted to do

was save. The thing that made him saddest was that apparently each generation had to learn the same lessons the same hard way on its own.

Certainly his future son-in-law wasn't interested in Gideon's philosophy or causes. He was polite enough, but his impatience with Gideon's projects was barely concealed.

"You have to be practical," Prinz said.

"I am," Gideon answered. "As Teddy Roosevelt himself said, 'There is nothing more practical than the preservation of anything that appeals to the higher emotions of mankind.'"

Prinz was not interested. What he meant by being practical was getting rich. It appeared that everybody in the entire country was doing it except Gideon James. Prinz had a broker—"my" broker, he called him—up in Fort Bragg. It was his broker, not his job as a clothing salesman, that accounted for his wealth. To Gideon, it sounded a little shady and suspect, like Nicky's money, which had turned out to be from bootleg.

But Prinz, like a revivalist, thumped around, preaching the word. "Buy on margin," he'd insist. "A hundred dollars buys a thousand dollars' worth of stock. Then, when it's worth ten thousand, you sell it, pay back the nine hundred you borrowed, and you're still nine thousand ahead."

Gideon shook his head, annoying Callie and Prinz. "It would make me uncomfortable to spend what I didn't have," he said.

But Rafael Prinz had done it and accumulated enough to marry, to spend a summer in Europe, buy a handsome house in town, a very fancy convertible cabriolet, and fine clothing. Prinz even gave a generous contribution to Save-the-Redwoods, so how could anyone complain?

Gideon knew that if he, too, made a "killing," he could do more, save more. He would think about it. But he felt more comfortable living the way he always had, dull as he knew it made him sound. He had everything he needed anyway.

Frankly, the frantic dance Callie and Rafael were doing made him uneasy. Indeed, the whole world seemed on a wild tear, so intent on grabbing the new that it forgot to hold tight to anything.

But this was undoubtedly the doddering of a foolish old man. He should be happy his daughter had picked such a go-getter. And it went without saying that Prinz was lucky. California James was special. His eyes misted at the thought of her as a June bride with that gold-red hair against white lace. His California was the best of every-

thing, the old and new combined. The way it all should be.

If only her mother were here to see her.

He grew tired of his disjointed thoughts, picked up his cloths, and decided to free another paint-covered otter.

The champagne bottle opened with a loud pop. Rafael laughed and wrapped a towel around its neck.

"To us," he said, handing her a fluted crystal glass they'd bought in France. "To our anniversary."

It was their October anniversary, four months since their wedding, seven months since Rafael had saved her from drowning. They had lots of anniversaries, lots of celebrations.

She pinched herself often, and still she couldn't believe that this life was hers. Callie James had never dreamed of sailing across the ocean, of sipping champagne in Paris, dancing the night away in London, seeing paintings—the *Mona Lisa*, buildings—the Colosseum, of touching, smelling, and tasting a thousand other impossible, unavailable things. And coming home to a splendid, sparkling house within walking distance of the beach where they'd first met. Obviously, California James had been an overly serious creature of little imagination, much more old-fashioned than she'd realized. California Prinz, however, was modern, a brand-new person who understood enjoyment and who was handed miracle after miracle by a husband who acted as if this were the natural order of things, the way life always should and would be. He was so carefree, the best of Nicky the adventurer, but without criminals and guns and fear.

Rafael had opened her eyes and her world. Before they left on their honeymoon, he'd quit his job so that he could travel freely. Callie would once have been horrified by such an act, but of course it was the right thing to do. Why taint enjoyment with a deadline? Rafael had earned his travel. And everything would work out just as well ultimately. It was taking him a while longer than expected to find a worthwhile new position, but it was nothing to worry about. She was learning to be less nervous, less insistently practical about everything. Less dull. She was learning to have a good time.

She looked at her shining fresh house, crisply painted and papered walls waiting to embrace a happy, exciting new life. Rafael had already surprised her with a washing machine, a refrigerator, a beautiful radio console, and a phonograph, and he'd given her a free hand in selecting furniture. Each time she opened the refrigerator door or even passed it, she thought of her childhood, of keeping food cold in

the river. Right now, she wished her mother could see how it had turned out for Callie so she, too, could thank fate and her daughter's generous, clever husband.

"Why are you smiling?" Rafael asked.

"Because I'm happy. Because I have everything—twice everything —a person could dream of. I want to keep saying thank you, thank you."

"Don't thank me," he said. "Thank New York Central, Montgomery Ward, Electric Bond and Share. Thank this wonderful America of ours."

She kept smiling and quietly touched her lower abdomen, silently thanking nature as well. The small sunny room next to theirs would be a perfect nursery.

The three of them, or more, would live happily ever after, just as her mother had promised. Why hadn't she ever believed the poor woman?

What a stick Callie had been until Rafael removed everything mechanical and predictable from her life. All over the country, tracks and fences had been falling away for years, but Callie hadn't truly caught on until Rafael explained. And this was so much more fun!

"It wasn't timid people who built this country," Rafael said. "Now we're building a new age, and again it's not work for cowards. This is the end of poverty, Callie. Anyone with sense and daring can have a good life."

And then he kissed her, and kissed her again. And told her how he'd known from the instant he saw her balanced up on that rock refusing to come down that she had the courage and will and heart to take on life and conquer it, to be a part of the new day coming. He had the bold blood of adventurers and conquistadors in his veins and she had the style to match his own.

So the two of them—with baby making three—toasted a future as buoyant and airborne as the champagne bubbles in their glasses.

The next day she didn't feel well. Morning sickness, or a hangover, she wasn't sure. She pampered herself and stayed in bed, drifting in and out of sleep.

A few hours later, Rafael woke her up. He sat on the edge of the bed, his face ashen, strained and unfamiliar. Glasses from the night before, a pool of champagne in each, stood on the night table. The smell of the flat wine nauseated her. Rafael told her, in the voice of a stranger, that something had happened to the market and that the

enormous pile of money on which they'd bounced around the world was gone. He seemed like one more dream in a hallucinatory day. He had to tell her several more times before she understood.

"They've called the margin, and I don't have it," he whispered, his voice buzzing through Callie. "We don't have any money, Callie." His stocks were no longer worth enough to let him pay back all he'd borrowed on margin.

They had no money or job. What they did have were debts and a baby coming.

"Of course, things may right themselves yet," Rafael said. "And I'm sure I'll find a job soon, somewhere. Maybe . . . maybe I'll try the mill." She looked at him closely. The day had unraveled him, turned him around. He was diminished and uncertain, as if not only the market, but Rafael Prinz as well, had crashed. "Meanwhile," he said, "we could stay with your dad. Until things straighten back out."

She nodded, slowly. Her head felt full and heavy.

Tears welled up in Rafael's long-lashed eyes. Callie had never seen him cry, never even imagined it. "I'm sorry," he said, his head muffled in his hands. "I'm ruined. Ruined."

"No," she insisted, holding him as close as he'd allow. "We have each other and the baby. Remember who we are? We're still brave and daring and smart. All those things you always talked about. We'll be fine."

His eyes were empty. "I've lost everything," he said.

"You haven't lost me."

His eyes were still empty.

Then she truly understood. The past seven months hadn't been a new life, but rather one small segment of her life. The early Callie, the responsible, self-reliant one she'd made fun of and thought an old-fashioned, outgrown skin, sighed, shook itself, and stood back up.

PART VI
1 9 4 1

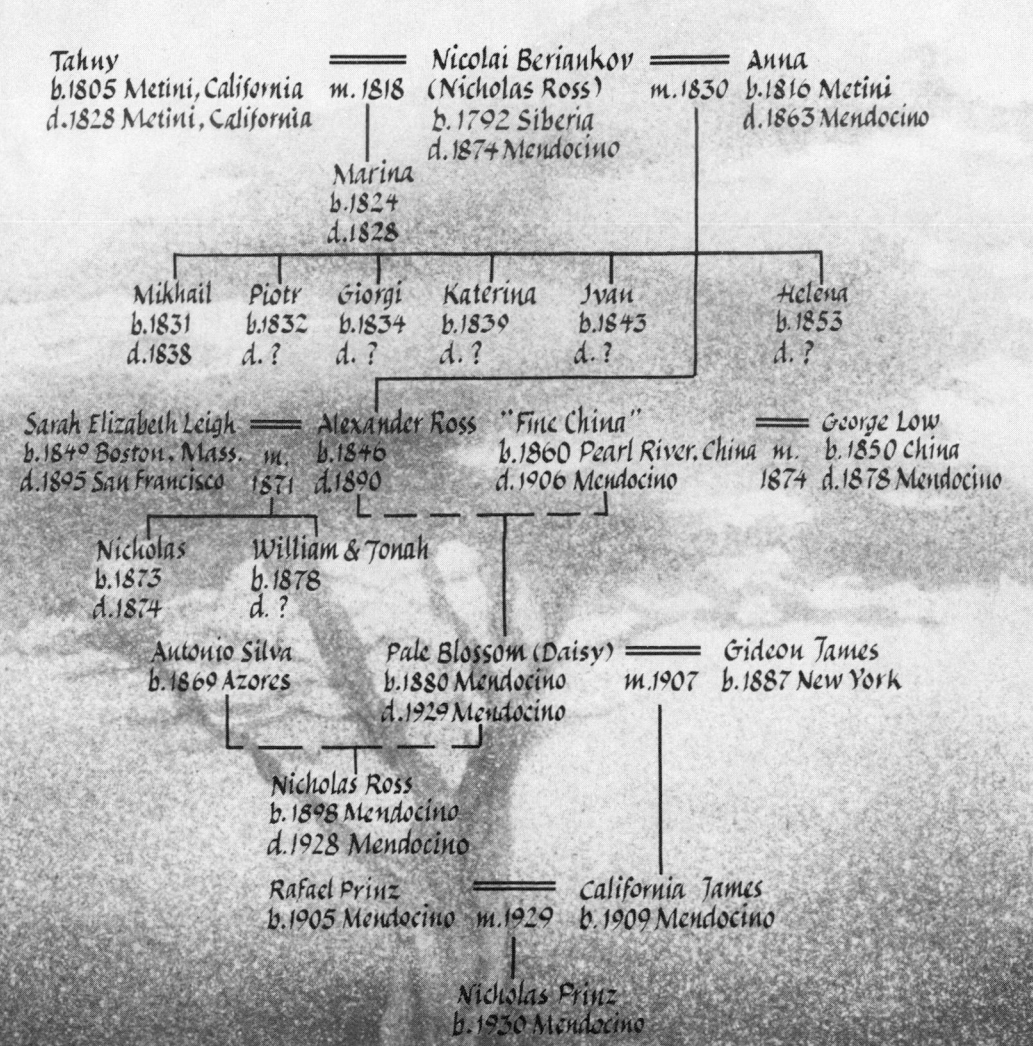

Tahny
b.1805 Metini, California
d.1828 Metini, California

m.1818

Nicolai Beriankov
(Nicholas Ross)
b.1792 Siberia
d.1874 Mendocino

m.1830

Anna
b.1816 Metini
d.1863 Mendocino

Marina
b.1824
d.1828

Mikhail
b.1831
d.1838

Piotr
b.1832
d.?

Giorgi
b.1834
d.?

Katerina
b.1839
d.?

Ivan
b.1843
d.?

Helena
b.1853
d.?

Sarah Elizabeth Leigh
b.1849 Boston, Mass.
d.1895 San Francisco

m.
1871

Alexander Ross
b.1846
d.1890

"Fine China"
b.1860 Pearl River, China
d.1906 Mendocino

m.
1874

George Low
b.1850 China
d.1878 Mendocino

Nicholas
b.1873
d.1874

William & Jonah
b.1878
d.?

Antonio Silva
b.1869 Azores

Pale Blossom (Daisy)
b.1880 Mendocino
d.1929 Mendocino

m.1907

Gideon James
b.1887 New York

Nicholas Ross
b.1898 Mendocino
d.1928 Mendocino

Rafael Prinz
b.1905 Mendocino

m.1929

California James
b.1909 Mendocino

Nicholas Prinz
b.1930 Mendocino

23

"Put your shoes away, Nico. People will trip over them there. Take care of things. Be considerate. And look at them! All muddy and scuffed! They have to last. Ruin them and you'll go barefoot."

The boy never paid attention or remembered. Didn't understand the worth of anything. Never wondered how it was to count every penny, scrounge, and make do to feed and clothe them all and run a boardinghouse to boot. Tossed his shoes around as if they were pebbles skating the river and never thought how she felt walking miles to buy her own poorly made pumps that had to do because they were on special for forty-nine cents.

"Don't drag your bookbag. You'll ruin it. Put it on the table, if you're doing your homework here. Dinner won't be for a while." Callie stirred and tasted the gravy.

"Stew again?" Nicholas Prinz at eleven was a haphazard collection of elbows, knees, ears, and nose. Parts bumped against one another and pushed for space. "We had stew yester—"

"Lucky there's food," she snapped. "Lucky your grandfather's a good shot. Lots of people in this country would gladly change places with you."

He sighed, bit into a crisp apple, and cracked the spine of his textbook.

"Take care of that book!" Callie said, automatically. "You'll ruin it."

"Who cares?" Nico said. "It's a stupid book."

"I care if you don't take care of things. Dad cares if we have to buy a whole new math book. The person who has to use it after you would care if the pages fell out. Your teacher would—" She suddenly heard herself, truly heard sound after harsh sound as she grated her anger and frustration into words. She recoiled from her own voice, from a woman who, wrapped in the virtuous cloak of necessity, did nothing but quibble, criticize, chide, remind, warn, correct.

But there was always so much to do, and redo, so many potential disasters, wastes, or foolishnesses to avert, and no one to do any of it but her. And once the doing was finished, so was the day, with no time left for pleasure. Years ago, even while the Depression was new and staggering, she had enjoyed evenings full of talk and popcorn and making sketches of her family, especially her always fascinating young son. Now her drawings, curled at the edges, were fading inside the window seat, and there never seemed time or spirit for any more of them or for any kind of ease. Life was fragments, brief glimpses and rush. Sawdust and shavings, no juice.

She remembered champagne corks popping, bands playing, a red-headed flapper dancing on shipboard. Maybe that woman had been made of fluff, bubbles, and ignorance and maybe she was no great loss, but in some ways she'd been bigger than her successor, and she'd had a vitality, an excitement about being alive, that this Callie missed.

She remembered the day on the sun-warmed rock, the day the whale had spouted and the world had unfurled around her. Except for Nico's birth, except for moments with Nico, she hadn't felt that pure, spontaneous elation in nearly a dozen years. She'd become a dark-spirited drudge.

She remembered days when Nico had been a toddler, when they'd played by the river's edge. She could still see him naked and laughing as he splashed in the dappled light, grabbing for dragonflies.

She remembered foggy mornings when there somehow had been time enough to take her son outside and repeat stories her father had told her of how the trees ate fog for breakfast until there was none left, only sunshine for the rest of the day.

All that was left was the fog. Those mornings, that child, and that woman were gone. Even the land had changed. Most of the forested acres that had stretched around the house had been sold to pay a few

dollars' worth of taxes. It broke all their hearts, especially Gideon's, but it was the only way to save the house.

"Gone," she said out loud. "All gone."

"What?" Nico was only half-interested.

"Everything." Time, laughter, stories, pleasure. Even something as simple as her drawings. She felt pressure in her chest as the truth of herself drilled home. She saved paper, string, and pennies, and squandered her life.

Yes, but times and the whole world had changed. Callie was what she had to be—a practical woman keeping a family alive. Her father had picked coastal redwoods, not human beings, as the species to preserve. He considered the Depression catastrophic mainly because the seedling program had been canceled. He still had his dreams, his campaigns for protected lands, national parks, his favorite poems as consolation and encouragement, and so long as he kept his concerns and his world limited to his single vision, he was content.

She could hear him in the parlor reciting "Inversnaid." His audience, as always, was the Misses Emily and Laura Stevens, Callie's boarders since their father "passed," as they put it. Gideon's voice was strong and confident as it repeated the familiar words of Gerard Manley Hopkins.

> What would the world be, once bereft
> Of wet and of wildness? Let them be left,
> Oh, let them be left, wildness and wet;
> Long live the weeds and the wilderness yet.

The old women politely applauded. They were an irritating pair, noisily gargling with saltwater at the kitchen sink, reading *Ivanhoe* to each other every single night of their lives, interminably reminiscing about their papa. But they were the only boarders, they paid on time, and they were Gideon's best audience. He loved to preen and strut for them.

Callie set her lips. Poetry and dreams weren't enough. Nico needed shoes for school. Life had been hard and frightening since the crash and it grew darker daily with news of the war in Europe. There were no more popping corks, and only fools and madmen were giddy.

All the starch in her collapsed. The rims of her eyes prickled and she blinked hard.

Because so what if times were hard? These were her times, the only

times she would ever be offered, and she was crazy not to find the buried pleasure in them.

She couldn't be like her husband. The man she'd married or imagined was long since gone, missing and lost without his money, convertible, home, and broker.

When there was money for gasoline, Rafael drove Nicky James's ancient roadster into Fort Bragg on futile hunts for work. When there were no extra pennies, he walked the woods, or wandered down to the ghostly streets of Mendocino City. He once admitted to spending half a day staring at the house they had lost.

Callie herself went to town as infrequently as possible. The day before, however, there'd been a special she couldn't resist—two pounds of coffee plus a pound of rice for sixty-five cents. Mendocino City made her want to weep. It stood quietly, somewhat embarrassed, like a pretty, faded maiden lady with no future, its curlicues and lace turning yellow. The winds of change had blown away the mill, the town's center and reason for being. The town's shine and most of its people were gone. Sad, abandoned houses and stores rotted like teeth in an ancient jaw. Grass grew high through the boardwalks, and as Callie hurried through her errands, her footsteps echoed hollowly. She remembered so many crowded days and nights on these streets. The Apple Festival, the Fourth of July parades, the Pentecost celebrations, the night the war ended. More ghosts than people populated the town.

And how ironic that now, finally, Mendocino was connected with the rest of the world by a highway. Cars no longer had to bump over corrugated dirt roads or spin and sink into glutinous mud.

At first, the new roads seemed godsends, opportunities for employment and ties with the rest of the country. They turned out to be neither. Rafael tried to work on the road in from Cloverdale, but so had hundreds of other unemployed men, and their fury was so terrible, they threatened to dynamite the project. Armed guards eventually forced them to leave. After that, Rafael was even more sour and half-hearted about finding anything.

The roads were also supposed to produce a new industry. Smooth roads would surely attract tourists to Mendocino's fresh air and spectacular scenery.

Except that tourists and vacations were early casualties of the Depression. There were summertime campsites along the river—one dollar for the entire season—and they were filled, but mostly by people stretching money by living under the trees. Sometimes Callie's

kitchen worked overtime feeding the campers, and that brought in a few dollars, which was good. But it was never enough.

Thank heavens for the house. She said or thought the words many times every day. Thank heavens for the vegetable garden, the chickens, the good, fresh water that kept them alive no matter what.

There were not too many other things to be thankful for. The old radio crackled out terrifying news. Europe was turning to ash and the United States was anemic and weak after a decade of dreary promises that had turned into lies. The "era of fear" would end. Prosperity was just around the corner. The Bank of America ran weekly ads in the *Beacon* urging Callie to open a "California Prosperity Account," as if she were being petulant, selfishly continuing to hoard cash and prolong hard times. As if her window seat were filled with money instead of the only valuables the family had, souvenirs.

Her gangly son worked at his math homework. He grew so fast she could almost hear the pops and pulls of his ligaments. She had named him for her always-missed brother. But then she'd worried so that he'd turn out like Nicky that she squelched even normal laughter and frivolity. The only time the solemn rules were down was when they scraped together a few extra cents and went to the movies. Scratchy silent films had been her mother's escape during her frightening times and now Nico and Callie were soothed by lush, expensive fantasies about rich and clever people who wore smoking jackets, spoke wittily, and had never heard of poverty.

But once outside the theater, Callie pulled on real life like a drab, raveling sweater, almost as if the people on the screen were real and alive, and she and Nico were short-lived inventions who slinked back into the shadows when the lights went on.

She remembered the dragonfly days by the river, but Nico couldn't, and since then, she'd worried so about food and shoes that she'd forgotten to give him any gifts of laughter.

Callie felt disoriented and confused. She had to change. If she didn't, she'd miss her son's life as well as her own. "Let's have tea," she said. She put her special mix of dried mint, lemon grass, and herbs into the teapot and added boiling water. "We have sugar, too." Thirty-nine cents for ten pounds and she hoarded every grain.

"Didn't mean to be so scratchy," she said when they were both sipping the sweet, fragrant brew. "Especially about shoes."

Nico shrugged. "It's okay."

"I remember when I was little, I lost my shoe. And my mother carried on—I stopped listening, just the way you do."

Nico looked surprised, then he grinned.

"The river was wild and I lost my shoe crossing it. My mother was so angry—I could have drowned and I thought she didn't even care. Really, she was sick and my father was away and she was scared about everything. Then she told me *her* shoe story, how her mother once bought two left shoes from the peddler and she had to wear that uncomfortable pair for the whole year or go barefoot."

It didn't matter that she'd told him all this before. Stories were important. History was important. Stories and the house were his inheritance, and she could repeat herself if she needed to. "So my mother spent a year with a sore right foot and I spent a long while barefoot until we could buy another pair. Those were hard times."

"That's what you and Daddy say now."

"Guess it's true again."

"Were there ever easy times for this family?" Nico's tone was slightly superior, as if he were a cut above his shabby, luckless stock.

"There were times that seemed that way. They just weren't very long, I guess."

"But the bad times were." Nico spoke with a disdainful, removed air that clearly said their drabness disappointed him.

"Not necessarily bad. Just not easy. There's a difference."

Nico shook his head, disagreeing.

"Depends what you decide is worthwhile, what constitutes good times. Your grandpa could be rolling in money and be unhappy if the trees were being destroyed. On the other hand, no matter what else is happening, if he wins some tiny victory, then everything's great."

"I didn't mean Grandpa, not that kind of thing." Nico returned to his homework. Even mathematics was more interesting than his grandfather's obsession.

"I used to feel that way," Callie said, half to herself. "I thought maybe he was a little crazy." Her father was still reciting for the ladies in the parlor. Now it was Byron on the pleasures of the pathless woods. They both listened for a moment, then Callie continued. "Nowadays I think saving what you love is a pretty fine way to spend your life."

Nico added more figures. She had probably said all of this before and he had probably not listened or cared that time, either.

She patted his hand and took his empty cup. "I hope your times will be good and easy. Maybe you'll wind up someone splendid, someone important, like..." She couldn't say exactly what, but she had dreams of his becoming solid and serious, of his moving into the

center of things. A lawyer, perhaps, a teacher. A businessman.

He looked at her, licked his upper lip, took a deep breath, and spoke. "Like an actor," he said. Then he blushed, grimaced, disparaged his own ambition, and appeared to be mesmerized by his homework.

An actor! Who ever heard of such an ambition? But she remembered his face as he watched a film, enraptured. It was her own fault—she'd made those hours at the movies the only ones worth living.

She took the dishes to the sink. "Maybe you can act in college plays," she said in a very cautious voice.

"Mom, we can't afford college."

"Things'll get better. But even if they don't, you're going. I was the first in the family to graduate from high school. You'll be the first college graduate."

He shrugged, his usual way of punctuating, emphasizing, or discussing anything. "Anyway," he said, "there probably won't be time. Soon as I can, I'll enlist."

"Enlist? In what?"

"The army."

"No," she said. "This isn't your war. It isn't America's war." She was surprised by the depth of her bitterness. "My brother fought in a war they said would make the world safe for democracy. It didn't do that, did it? But what it did do was change him forever. You can be a casualty even if you aren't killed or wounded." Nicky had said it. You couldn't see what soldiers see, do what soldiers do, and come home the same person.

She remembered how annoyed she'd been when her mother sang "I Didn't Raise My Son to Be a Soldier." Callie had been so young. She'd thought Nicky's uniform and the war were glamorous. She had thought her mother was unpatriotic and foolish, but her mother had simply been a mother.

"Anyway," she said, "this war will be over long before you're old enough to go, so do your homework and let's not even think about it."

But of course it was America's war and they all had to think about it. The bombing in Honolulu sent shock waves to the remote Mendocino coast and into Callie's house.

"I'm going," Rafael said the day after Pearl Harbor. "I'm joining the navy."

317

"Why? You don't have to," she said. "You have a wife and a son."

"It's my country. My duty. A matter of pride. Of patriotism."

She knew that it was also a matter of finally having a definite job, of not standing in long lines and turning back empty-handed at day's end, of not relying on the possessions, savings, and vegetable patch of his father-in-law and the industry and energy of his wife, of feeling part of something besides despair, of not looking into Callie's eyes and seeing the reflection of somebody very different from the man he'd started out to be. A matter of ego. He'd been at war a long time. This merely channeled it and gave him an acceptable enemy. He seemed more alive and excited than she'd seen him in years, his posture straighter, his shoulders squarer. Even his old, carefully preserved clothing looked less pathetic.

She worried over his departure, she wept. She also felt relief.

The war repopulated the house with the remnants of other disrupted households. A woman with a colicky infant son rented a room while her husband fought in Europe. A quiet elderly man whose son and support was now a marine took yet another room. A young, very quiet widow moved in with five cartons of books. The Stevens sisters, delighted to have new audiences for *Ivanhoe* and their memories of their father and childhood, remained.

Between Rafael's military pay, the boarders, and Callie's frugality, there was a surplus of money for the first time in a decade. After expenses, taxes, and war bonds, she put every spare cent into an old leather drawstring bag she'd found in the window seat, and then she hid the bag in the dented samovar. Nico's secret college fund grew. Knowledge of it almost made up for the fact that, if anything, life was even more rushed and cramped, and she still spent her hours and energy cooking, cleaning, changing linens, and snapping out the same nonstop warnings and reminders. There was no breathing space, no little window to unlatch and release the building pressure. Sometimes, late at night, she ignored her body's cries for sleep and forced a moment of solitude into her day. She brewed her special tea, removed her apron, and made herself comfortable in the window seat, pillows plumped against the small of her back, bare feet curled under her. She sat, sipped, and let her thoughts ramble out to where ideas, memories, formless hopes bumped against one another and disappeared into the black-on-black shadow layers. Somewhere, in the trees, in the house, in the past, in herself, there was something she needed desperately, but she never found it, not even in those silent moments in the sleeping house.

One afternoon, when everyone was away, her floor scrubbing was interrupted by knocking.

"Hello, please, I am Mr. Hiro Nakata. Can I stay here?" a man asked when she opened the door. "It says room and board." He pointed in the direction of a sign she had posted on the mailbox.

He was a well-dressed bespectacled man carrying a large valise and a square package wrapped in brown paper.

Callie nodded and ushered him in. He would fill the last vacant room and would mean even more cash in the samovar's secret belly.

Mr. Nakata was delighted by the airy upstairs room that would be his and even more so by the tower. He exclaimed over each window's special view. "I paint," he said with a half-bow, almost as if apologizing. "This is beautiful. I see all the way to the ocean, to the town, and into the forests. Could I—"

"Work up here? Yes, of course." She felt a peculiar stirring that was both pleasurable and upsetting. "It must be fine to paint. Did you bring any of your work?"

He nodded.

"Could I . . . would you show it to me?"

He was so small and frail, she expected sparse, delicate drawings, but inside the brown-paper parcel were canvasses with bold strokes and strong colors, heavy watercolor papers with lush washes, and line drawings that often interpreted the same scene in a completely different manner. Scenes of San Francisco brought back the hills, the houses, the clang of cable cars, and smell of bay breezes.

He had captured life, made the feel of it visible. That's what she had wished she could do, years ago, that day on the rock. "They're wonderful," she said. "You're so lucky. I wish I had talent."

"You have painted?" He had a very soft voice.

She shook her head. "I've drawn, but . . ." She raised her hand and waved it vaguely at the house, and then she let it drop. "There's so much else to do, and I wouldn't know where to begin, anyway."

"I'll teach you."

"Me? To paint?"

His smile was broad. He nodded vigorously.

Exhilaration, fear, and recognition filled her. This was it. The something that would make the difference, the thing she'd tried to find or remember those nights by the window, the suppressed longing that had been forced deep inside, where it smoldered and choked her.

She felt a rush of embarrassment and anxiety. "Oh, you couldn't,"

she said. "Thank you anyway, but I have no talent. I'd waste your time."

"You have desire. Try. I have taught before. Little children. Big people." He nodded, emphasizing his words.

"Where was that, Mr. Nakata?"

"San Francisco." Another nod. "Many pupils. Nineteen-twenty-two until twenty-nine, even thirty. But then hard times..." He shook his head sadly. "No money, no pupils. I work as shrimp farmer, as grocery clerk, then in the nursery." He sighed, then his expression brightened. "Now, I teach again. I teach you."

Outside, the sky was a boggy gray, seeping into the ocean. There was little light, although it was midday, and the landscape was drained and colorless, marked only by tree silhouettes drifting in and out of the foggy mass. She mentally translated the pearly gradations into pigment and paper.

She caught herself. "I have no money," she said. She thought of Nico's college fund, then pushed the idea out of her head. "I'm sorry," she said. "I can't take lessons."

He smiled again and bowed his head in acknowledgment. "I have no money," he said. "Not much. My job is"—he tossed an imaginary ball over his shoulder—"gone. I worked now in a nursery, for plants, but..." A heavy sigh. "An exchange, perhaps?"

An exchange would add nothing to the college fund, and might subtract. How much farther could she stretch her stews?

But she also knew, without thinking about it, that if there were one hour in the day—or the week—when she could spread colors around, try to speak through her fingertips, have a chance to breathe slowly and truly look at life, then her endless round of chores would be easier and she wouldn't need to snipe at her son, jealous of his future, or at her father, jealous of the freedom he had to pursue his dreams.

"All right." She shook his hand. "An exchange."

"Sir!" a voice said gruffly.

Callie and Mr. Nakata turned to the staircase where Gideon James, returned home, stood wiry and stern.

"Sir," he said again, "have you citizenship papers?"

"Papa!" Callie said. "Mr. Nakata is renting a room. He's been in this country for years, teaching in..."

"Sir?" Gideon James demanded.

Mr. Nakata shook his head. "I am *issei*. Born in Japan. Cannot be

citizen. My son, he was born here, so he was citizen, but it is not permitted for me."

"Then I'm afraid, sir, you'll have to stay with your son."

"Papa!"

He waved away her protests.

"My son no longer lives," Mr. Nakata said softly. "But I understand. I will leave now."

"No!" Callie said. "Please!" She turned and, hands on hips, faced her father, opened her mouth to speak, then reconsidered. "Please, Mr. Nakata, enjoy the view while my father and I excuse ourselves for a moment."

Gideon finally complied when her glare became explosive.

"I have never been so embarrassed!" she said when they were downstairs in the kitchen. Her father sat down at the table and she headed for the window seat, distancing herself.

"Callie," Gideon said, "he's a Jap! We're at war with them!"

"Not with that timid, peaceful little man!"

"Your own husband is on a ship risking death to defeat them."

"Not Mr. Nakata!"

"I know why he's come here all of a sudden," Gideon said. "He's not allowed in town anymore because it's west of the highway."

Callie shook her head. "I don't understand."

"Don't you read the paper? Axis Aliens aren't allowed west of Highway One. They don't want spies on the coast, sending signals, but here you are handing him a lookout, a tower. Bet he's pretty excited about his find!"

"Because of the view! He paints!"

Gideon stood up, took a few paces, then faced her, pointing his finger accusingly. "I will not harbor an Axis spy."

"That's ridiculous. Look at the man, would you? Papa, please . . ."

"He'd be like a prisoner anyway. Even east of the highway there's a curfew and restrictions—he can't travel more than five miles away from here. I don't care how much money he offers." Gideon's face flushed with feeling. "Or whether you need it for that college fund of yours."

"How do you know about my—"

"The stews are getting too watery, girl. Nakata has to go. Besides, it isn't up to us. They're evacuating the Japanese. Relocating them further east."

"Who is? Who are 'they'?" Curfews, forbidden lines, restricted

travel, then forced moving? "What's 'evacuation' mean?" The conversation might as well have been in Japanese. "Where could they possibly relocate them? Are there houses sitting empty somewhere? Where? How can they do that? Where could they put them? Who are 'they'?"

Gideon put up his palms. "None of that's our problem. Nakata is."

"He's going to teach me to paint."

Gideon tugged at his earlobe, a sign of impatience she had always respected before. "Callie, you're wasting my time and his. He has to leave."

"No. He has to stay. He needs a house, a place to live." She stood up slowly, as if pulling weights. Her father remained motionless, watching her.

The window seat's cover squeaked as she rose, but nothing else made a sound. The room—the whole house—seemed to hold its breath and wait in judgment. When she spoke, her voice was soft and tender. "Papa, he's an alien because he wasn't allowed to become a citizen. And calling him an Axis Alien—that's somebody's new definition. He's Mr. Nakata. Besides, he isn't the issue. We are, this family, who we are."

"The law says . . ."

"It's a bad law. Think, Papa. Think about my mother, who couldn't go to school with the white children. Think about my grandmother, who nearly lost the house because she was Chinese. And my grandfather, the half-breed. And his father and mother. You must remember how Mama's old stories called this house the safe place, even—especially—when the laws were wrong."

"That was different. We weren't at war."

"We were always at war."

Her father said nothing.

"He has no money, either," she added. "You might as well know right off. We're bartering art for room and board."

"It's wrong," Gideon said.

She spoke very gently. "I've learned from you, Papa. Saving what needs saving is worth it, and people are surely as valuable as redwoods."

"This isn't like you, Callie. You're a practical person."

She came closer. "You taught me again. Remember? 'Teddy Roosevelt said the most practical thing was the preservation of anything that appeals to the higher emotions of mankind.' Remember how often you said that?"

"I never thought you were listening." Gideon sat down. "Callie, this is dangerous."

"Maybe that's why it's important. Besides, we can make it so that nobody knows he's here."

He sighed, ran his fingers through his thin red-gray hair, and stared at the table's grain. "It's illegal," he said, shaking his head. "I don't like breaking the law. Maybe I don't like everything this country decides to do, but still, it's my country. No," he said, "I won't . . ."

"That's it!" She spoke so abruptly, so loudly, her father flinched.

"What?" he asked, his face cross. "What's what?"

"Remember? Remember the first day you came here? The day of the quake?"

"Yes, of course. What of it?"

"Didn't you tell me that Mama's mother told you to stay, that this house was a little country of its own?"

"I don't see the relevance of any of . . ."

"Because in that case, this country can have its own laws." She looked toward the ceiling, as if she could see through the boards to the man sitting patiently by the tower windows. "Therefore, it's not unpatriotic of us—it is in fact the privilege, right, and obligation of our little country to grant Mr. Nakata citizenship."

"Ah, Callie," he said. "She was using a figure of speech and you're playing games."

She sat down across from him. "No, I'm not, Papa. Not at all."

He sighed and shook his head. "I don't see how, anyway. It isn't as if the two of us are the only people with eyes in this house."

"Let me try. That's all I ask. I'll think of something."

"People will be coming home any minute."

"I'll think fast!"

He stared at her for a moment. "Well," he finally said, "you always were a resourceful child."

That night, Callie rang the dinner bell with mixed emotions. *If* things went well, then tomorrow she would paint. She could almost feel the hours open and the days stretch to accommodate her. *If . . .*

Mr. Nakata was the first to the table. "Now remember," Callie whispered. "Let me introduce you."

He looked worried, shook his head. "Mrs. Prinz, everyone will know. Chinese and Japanese don't look alike."

"Trust me," Callie whispered. "You have an artist's eye. You notice things." More important, she knew that a person had to care about

you to notice who you were, to separate you out from other foreign or exotic beings. She smiled at the Misses Stevens as they walked in. "What a lovely new hairdo," she said to Emily.

Once everyone was seated, and before she brought any food to the table, Callie cleared her throat. "I would like to introduce a new guest," she said. "This is Hiram Low, my great-uncle from China. He doesn't speak a great deal of English, but I assure you he is very happy to meet you."

"From China?" The Miss Stevens whose hairdo hadn't been complimented sounded doubtful. "I thought maybe he was . . . your uncle? How is that possible?"

"Great-uncle," Callie said. The rest of the boarders looked dubious as well. She felt a twinge of fear, then a rush of inspiration. She walked to the window seat, opened it, and took out a family tree her mother had embroidered. "My family," she explained. "See here? My grandmother China—that wasn't her real name, but that's what she was known by—was a widow when she met my grandfather Alexander. Her first husband was a man named George Low."

They were losing interest, politely nodding as she forced them to pass around the sampler of her mother's early and rather inept needlework.

"George Low came over to work on the railroad, you know," Callie said.

"Excuse me, this is so interesting, but won't dinner be cold soon?" The young mother was always worried, as was everyone else, that the next moment would bring another howling colicky spell for her child.

Callie slowly dished fricasee while she continued her geneology. Nico completely lost interest and buttered his corn bread. Good, she thought. It was he who had taught her the art of losing her audience.

"Now George Low had a much younger brother, the baby of the family, really, and that's this gentleman. Hiram Low. An artist. Lovely family, although all his brothers are gone now. Interesting, isn't it, what happens to a family? There are so many stories about the Low brothers. You'll find them fascinating. At any rate, technically, perhaps, he isn't actually my great-uncle, but, more precisely, the brother-in-law of my grandmother's first marriage, but still, we were the only family he knew of in America." Gideon raised his brows and rolled his eyes, then coughed to hide, she was sure, a laugh. The rest of the faces around the table were well and truly glazed. "So of course we welcome him," Callie said.

There was a moment's silence, and then the Misses Stevens picked up their forks. "Welcome to America, Mr. Low," they said in chorus. "Please join us tonight when we read *Ivanhoe* together," Emily added.

Callie looked around. All faces smiling. The mysterious Mr. Low, who looked like all the other Orientals, didn't he, had been of only momentary interest. Now, chicken fricasee, corn bread, and news of the baby's colic, memories of the Stevens girls' father, and of the war in Europe were more important.

"You've changed," Nico said a winter evening almost a year after Mr. Nakata-Low, had arrived.

She patted her hair, which was edged at the temples with early silver. "So have you." A year's growth had further elongated her angular son, but it had also pushed the little boy back somewhere and now there was a hint, a look, of the man waiting to emerge. "We're getting older, I guess." She picked up the chopping knife and began slicing carrots.

"Not that. Don't get angry if I say it but . . . you're nicer."

"How?" She put the carrot slices in the pot and turned to face him. He shrugged. "You don't get as angry."

"Maybe there isn't as much to upset me."

"Come on, Ma. There's plenty stuff."

"I know," she said softly. "Like Hitler, and the war, and Dad far away in the middle of it."

"And even," Nico said, "like that." He pointed to the middle of the floor, where his shoes and bookbag lay. Then, as his mother squawked, he scooped them up. "But you saw them before," he said. "When I came in here, you were staring at them."

She sighed, and then she smiled. "You won't believe this," she said, "but I was looking at them as a composition. A painting I'd call *The Boy*. What do you think?"

"I think you've really changed, is what I think."

She tried to grab him for a hug, but he was a wiry escape artist who peeked into the stockpot. "Now," he said, "if only your cooking would change. Stew again?"

She didn't even remind him how lucky he was to have food. She simply stirred her stew and admired its beautiful texture and colors.

24

"Of course I'm happy they're coming!" Callie smacked the rag down and recently caught dust motes escaped back into the air. "Why wouldn't I be? Why would you ask? Haven't seen them— haven't seen him—in seven years. Never saw my own granddaughter. Why wouldn't I be happy?"

Her husband and father sat in easy chairs near the parlor fireplace. She could feel the look they exchanged without needing to see it.

"Maybe you're nervous," Gideon suggested. "Overexcited."

Sometimes he acted as if she were still a baby, not a grandmother. She was fifty-one years old, for heaven's sake, not fifty, as Nico's card had said. Imagine, he almost never wrote, never called, never visited—and then a birthday card out of the blue with the message "How could we not celebrate your half-century?" Was she supposed to tell him that he was a year late? Or simply be grateful that he remembered her at all?

The only picture she had of Nicolette was of a baby. She wouldn't know her own flesh and blood if she bumped into her.

It made Callie's heart shrivel.

Maybe it was her own fault. When he'd brought Alison Marshall up here, Callie hadn't liked her at all, and it probably showed.

But how could she possibly like the girl? Oh, she was pretty

enough, if you liked cotton-candy women. All pink and gold. White-gold hair and pink fuzzy clingy sweater. Little gold chains, gold charms, pink-polished nails, and delicate touches so you'd be sure and know she had money. Maybe not big money, not astounding money, but enough so that she wasn't likely to develop wrinkles worrying over her next meal. Rich, certainly, compared to the Prinz family.

It wasn't the money that bothered Callie. Let Nico have it easier than the rest of them. He'd always seemed uncomfortable with his family's style of living, and he wasn't strong enough to handle it, anyway. A little money could help buy his dreams, let him pursue the stage and acting.

But what had set Callie's teeth on edge so that she could barely manage even a false smile was that this confection of a girl acted like all of them were toys. "Cute" and its cousins were her favorite words. The house was "cute," Rafael—and Nico's—Portuguese-Spanish background was "sweet," Callie's name was subject for exultation. ("California!" Alison squealed. "Like the state," Gideon needlessly explained. "She was a child of a new world and none of our old-world names fit her." "Adorable!" Alison yelped.) Callie—and Nico's— Chinese-Yankee heritage, next explained, was "precious" and after that Callie tried not to listen as the girl chuckled and exclaimed at the house's "unbelievably darling" artifacts—the adorable ancient carved plate that held small treats for a house spirit nobody completely understood anymore. The precious animal carvings on the bedroom doorway, the stairwell, the luscious history on the kitchen fireplace. The something-or-other old quilts. The cunning samovar. God knew what else.

Cute! Callie felt all of them, their history, their triumphs, their art, and their worth shrink into a little bundle, trinket size. As if, because they were different from the Kewpie doll's people and friends, they weren't fully human.

Alison chattered in her overanimated manner. "My family's so *dull* in comparison. So ordinary. Just like everybody else I know and they know. They've been here *forever*, and all my ancestors, far as anyone knows, are English or German." She shrugged her angora shoulders and Callie knew that she was supposed to be impressed by the old, unmixed lineage. Alison squeezed Nico's arm. "But Mendocino, and this house, and all of you, well, it's so different, so *exciting!*"

As if she'd picked Nico out of a toy store, as if he were some kind of daring experiment on her part, a walking, talking jigsaw puzzle of a

man who would shock and amuse those exactly alike friends and family. Had she ever noticed that he was alive and human and more than material for chitchat with less "cute" friends?

Callie had held her tongue and listened politely. She heard how they had met in San Francisco when Nico was studying at Berkeley and Alison was vacationing with her great-aunt, and she felt personally responsible for their misalliance. It was the sack in the samovar, her insistence that her son go to college that had placed them in proximity. He would never have met an Alison here at home. They weren't a local breed.

Several months later, Nico wrote her. He'd quit school, not seeing its purpose in his life, and moved to New York to try his luck at acting, and happy day, amazing coincidence, Alison lived in Connecticut.

Callie had heard no more until one November day when she received a brief letter informing her that Nico and Alison had impulsively run away to Maryland to marry. "Finally gone and done it," as he so unromantically put it. He was sorry he couldn't tell them in advance, or invite them to witness the ceremony, but they were a long, long way from Mendocino, and besides, they hadn't exactly planned out the whole thing. And there hadn't been any formal celebration. Just a little party after the fact given by Alison's parents.

Callie tried very hard not to care. The party must have been small, casual, and Alison's parents were under no obligation to invite her. Besides, it was a hard trip to Connecticut, and an expensive one, too. Maybe it had been a kindness, a conscious decision not to put Nico's parents—not to mention his aging grandfather—to any trouble. She sent them a letter of congratulations and love and, suddenly very timid, asked if they would like the old quilt—the intricate one the family called the "Sarah" quilt—as a wedding gift. Alison had seemed to really love it. Or, perhaps, another object that the bride had admired at length, Anna's basket with the hummingbird feathers woven through it?

Both items were heirlooms, family treasures, but that would not have been enough to offer a girl like Alison. However, Callie had heard that similar items were being sought by antique dealers and sold for enormous sums in big-city galleries, so she felt confident that they were offering something that Alison would understand to be of value.

Nico answered promptly and politely. The quilt and basket were parts of the old house and they'd feel dreadful moving either one to

their apartment—all Danish modern blond wood, anyway—but many, many thanks for the offer. They were quite well. Nico had a chance at a small part off-Broadway and Alison was having the time of her life fixing up their place.

Callie read and reread the polite, friendly, distant note. She was sure it had been prompted by Alison, refusing to sully her Danish modern life and quarters with her mother-in-law's ancient trash.

"Send them one of your paintings," Rafael suggested.

"Oh, for heaven's sake! She'd never want my dribbles and scratches!"

"Nonsense. You're good. Everybody says so. People buy them."

"At sidewalk sales. That doesn't count. For all I know, there's some kind of right and proper Danish modern blond art, anyway."

"She loved your paintings," her husband insisted. "Remember how she carried on about them while she was here?"

Callie sighed. "You don't know much about courting, do you?"

"Been a long time," Rafael murmured.

"Nobody insults the boy's mother then," Callie snapped. "But later, when you're his wife and you live a whole country away, all rules are off. She *hated* everything in this house."

Rafael shook his head and returned to his newspaper. Domestic politics didn't interest him.

Callie was left with the problem of the wedding gift and it hovered above her like a vulture, day and night. Finally, she settled on her original idea. A piece of art, or craft. Something special that nobody else could give them. Something that would last. She visited every artist friend in the area, and there were many. The Depression's empty houses had been offered for a few hundred dollars, a sum that artists, already attracted to the remote north coast's natural grandeur, could afford. Mendocino had become a mecca for artists and craftsmen and now there was a burgeoning community.

Callie even visited Hiro Nakata—no longer needing to hide inside the silent, anonymous Hiram Low—who had a tiny two-room house at the edge of Mendocino City. He was still painting, although he looked so glassy and fragile that she feared the next large storm would lift and carry him out to sea.

She finally had a friend carve a large salad bowl and serving pieces out of the blondest, palest, most exotic woods he could find.

It was beautiful. A historic salad bowl with a raised rippling wave motif on the side. A signed work of art. She was intensely proud of it. It did justice to the groom's side of the family, showed that they

had taste, imagination, high esthetic standards—and an awareness of blond wood.

They received a polite thank-you from Alison, who did not seem to understand, or at least to make any mention, that the bowl had been handmade for her, or that she would never see another quite like it. She didn't even comment on the serving spoon and fork—one a redwood tree, the other a bear. But then, as she explained, she was rather rushed for time, and so perhaps she had meant to say more, but couldn't.

What puzzled Callie most was the engraved name at the tip of the notepaper. Mrs. Nicholas Prince.

Prince.

When Rafael saw it, two furious dots of red stained his cheeks.

Gideon adjusted his glasses, wiped them off, then studied the card again. "What the devil has he done? Who's he become? What did he do with the person he used to be?" He tossed the heavy cream-colored note onto the side table and half closed his eyes. His hand curled around the smooth handle of his walking cane and banged it once on the floor. Then he crossed his arms over his chest and looked as if he might sleep.

Callie wrote regularly, discussing Gideon's still-futile efforts to create a redwood park, a preserve, Rafael's adventures in the world of haberdashery, and her own fledgling career as an artist.

They received a greeting card at Easter, another on Mother's Day.

Callie wrote less often.

In June, they received a third card, but this was a heavy little square with a pink border and an engraved message.

"Alison and Nicholas Prince announce the arrival of their daughter, Nicolette Marshall, May 29, 1954."

"I had no idea," Callie said, but that wasn't completely true. It didn't take a mathematical genius to figure out that November to May wasn't quite a baby-making season, so some of her questions about the elopement were answered.

Neither Rafael nor Gideon counted, computed, or commented, so she did it for them, and then they said she was small-minded, which was ridiculous. She had nothing against the baby, its speedy arrival, or its parents. She just didn't like surprises when the friendly thing would be to have been given a clue as to how things were.

Nicolette, judging from the enclosed snapshot, was beautiful, although the men in the house squinted and made stupid remarks,

acting as if the little girl looked like every other baby.

Callie would have liked to knit for the child, but instead she bought her granddaughter the most expensive, outlandish, hand-knit leggings, jacket, and cap she could find, all pink like the inside of a shell. Let that baby know she had faraway grandparents who could do right by her.

Rafael squawked when he saw the bill, but he had a good enough job in the haberdashery in Fort Bragg, so Callie ignored him.

For the next six years, Callie wrote the Prince family, asking when or if they might visit and bring Nicolette. For six years, she waited for a specific response—or for an invitation to come to New York and see for herself. But Alison wrote jolly letters full of exclamation marks, statistics ("She's walking now!!!" "She's wearing a size four!!"), and no substance or invitations. Christmas cards, Christmas gifts—each year plaid robes for Gideon and Rafael, chenille for Callie, thank-you's for the baby's birthday gift, for their Christmas gifts, for the anniversary gift . . . and nothing else.

Not even a new snapshot in three years.

Well, today she'd meet the girl and she'd be sure to take her own pictures.

Callie went to check the rooms upstairs. Mr. Nakata's old room was as flooded with sunlight as was his painting above the bed. Callie plumped the pillows and straightened the quilt her mother had made. The room was in perfect order, with clean linens and a bowl of roses on the nightstand. Still she smoothed the quilt again, checked for dust on the picture frame, and made sure there were fresh towels in the brand-new upstairs bathroom. Then she checked the bedroom with the old brass bed. She had propped Nico's beloved childhood teddy bear on the pillow and wondered if Nicolette would enjoy it and whether Nico himself would remember it at all.

Would he recognize anything? Anyone? Acknowledge it? He seemed to have developed amnesia about his past.

And then she sat down on the brass bed and took deep breaths, one after the other, again and again, to still the fearful racing in her heart and bloodstream. She wanted so much, hoped for so much, hoped that somehow, in the short time allotted her, she'd be able not only to convey what she felt, but to make Nico—and Alison—feel it as well.

This is you, she wanted to say. This is all we ever had to give you—a house full of memories, a history uniquely yours. But it's

331

something, so don't forsake it so completely. Life and ties and meaning can't be this cool and formal. What you've done isn't called bettering yourself.

Perhaps they would stay for a week or more. They'd be in California for quite a while, she knew. So maybe they'd stay and let the trees and the ocean and cliffs work their magic, help Nico remember his childhood, his past, help Alison and Nicolette bond and become rooted here. They would leave again, of course, but not as thoroughly as they'd left years earlier.

Perhaps they'd even send Nicolette for summers with her grandparents. They could fish the river and hunt for shells and explore tidepools. They could walk the old streets and tell stories of days remembered. They could sit in the house on foggy mornings and bake gingerbread men and create new history.

She would send that child home fat with a sense of the generations of miracles wrought to create a little girl from New York.

She heard the gravel crunch outside and stood up quickly, smoothed the child's quilt, and rushed to the tower window.

There they were, Nico's dark head close to his wife's navy blue hat as they helped the child out of the backseat of their car. Callie watched Alison carefully adjust the child's navy coat and white gloves and straighten the rim of her hat. It took a moment to realize and become depressed by the fact that the two of them wore mother and daughter outfits.

"They're here!" she announced, rushing down the stairs. The men she lived with might as well have been in comas for all the attention they paid anything. She opened the door before Nico could ring or knock, excitement pounding at her temples.

And then she felt as shy as a girl at her first party.

They stood, a few feet apart on either side of the threshold, smiling awkwardly. Callie didn't know whether to rush and hug, to say something clever that would end the tension, or to burst into tears.

She felt so plain, so unadorned. They sparkled and shone. Especially Nicolette, an elfin creature with large green eyes and—the hat did not completely hide it—curly red-gold hair. Callie smiled smugly. They could keep her any distance they liked from this child, but the two of them were kin, related through hair pigment if nothing more, and they would have to notice it every single day.

"Are you the one who's my grandmother?"

Her voice was large and brassy, a complete surprise out of the budlike mouth. Callie burst out laughing. "I am," she finally said. "I

am indeed. And if you're the one who's my granddaughter, why don't you come right on in?"

Alison and she kissed the air next to each other's cheeks and Nico, tall and handsome but as uncomfortable-looking as ever he was at twelve, hugged her awkwardly.

The afternoon moved along too quickly, skidding by on polite amenities and superficial discussion of much that Callie had hoped they could talk about at length. All she could deduce was that Nico was not getting work—he spoke vaguely of possibilities, some commercial work for television, an experimental Off-Broadway play. He worried her. He was taking on some of the scaled-down grayness that had become Rafael's mask after the crash.

Alison, however, was fine, perky and busy with good works, hoping they'd be able to move to something larger soon, possibly a house in the suburbs. All the same, Alison was too young to have those deep, disappointed tracings at the side of her mouth.

Everything was wonderful, they both said, but it was obvious that things were not going well and that they were never going to talk honestly. Abruptly, prematurely, they'd exhausted all obvious topics. The silence stretched. What on earth would they talk about the next few days?

"The house is exactly as I remember it," Alison said, ending one painful lull. Her manner and style were a lot calmer than they had been, and even if her rare letters still contained an excess of exclamations, she no longer spoke with so many of them. "How unusual of you to keep it unchanged."

She didn't use any form of address and Callie understood why. She wouldn't call her mother-in-law by her first name, surely didn't feel ready for plain and simple "Mother," and if she tried for the "Mother Prinz or Mrs. Prinz" business, then she'd run smack into their different last names.

"Actually, there are some changes," Callie said while she poured coffee and milk and brought out the cookies she'd baked. Fancy swirly numbers for the adults and, for Nicolette, gingerbread men with raisin eyes. "We went and got a television, as you can see. Sold the cow. Turned the barn into a garage and storage shed." She could see in Alison's cool eyes how insignificant the changes really were. The furniture was out of date, preserved and recovered for comfort and utility, not looks or value. She could also see that the house was old-fashioned, odd to begin with and now weathered into an eccentric museum piece.

333

She felt as shocked and suddenly protective of the place as if it had been her baby, declared homely by a passerby. "Oh," she said, "and I nearly forgot—there's two full baths upstairs now. Remember those god-awful bathroom lines, Nico? During the war, when we had those boarders, it could be something. Now, of course, there'll be nobody up there but you. I've fixed up the corner room and the one next to it, the new room—"

"New!" Gideon shook his head. "Good Lord, Callie, I rebuilt that room in ought-six! We should stop calling it new!" He chuckled and Callie could hear the nervousness propelling him. She also felt a need to race, talk nonstop, ease the bubbling in her veins. Only Rafael seemed cool, watching his son from a distance.

"You know how those names stick," she said. "That's what Mama called it. Anyway, my painting things are all over the landing, the tower, and I hope you don't mind. I'm entrenched up there—it has the best light of anyplace I've ever found. You must like to paint, Nicolette. We'll paint together one of these days. Did you bring any messy old clothes? If not, I'm sure I'll find an old shirt of Grandpa's. In fact, where are all your suitcases? How silly of us not to have brought them in."

She knew she sounded like a fool, but she couldn't stop herself. Alison was aiming pointed glances at Nico, soundless airpuffs leaving her lips, and if Callie stopped making noise, if she even let those puffs become words, something very wrong would be let loose into the room.

"I can loan you one of my smocks for painting. Does that sound like fun? We could—"

"Nicholas," Alison whispered harshly.

"Mother," Nico said. "Mother, I—"

"I know, I'm ignoring you. But I have plans for you, too. For all of us. We'll have to go see the town. It's changed, Nico. Lots of new people, more tourists all the time. We could—"

"Mother! I'm afraid you—"

Rafael leaned forward in his chair. "Why did you change your name?" he demanded. "Didn't even warn me. Not one word. Why?"

Alison's fair skin developed rusty blotches. "Nicholas didn't change his name," she said. "He Anglicized it."

"Anglicized?"

"Made it less . . . foreign. Made it . . . American."

"American!" Rafael looked at her with complete disbelief, then he

turned his gaze onto his son. "What the devil am I, then? Didn't I fight in the war? Don't I vote?"

Alison's lips were so tightly clamped there was a white pressure line around them.

We aren't cute anymore, Callie thought. Maybe even her Nicholas had lost his adorable, precious exotic flavor. Alison didn't smile, not even at him.

"Well, you know, Dad, people would hear it and spell it this way anyway," Nico said mildly. "And in the theater, you don't want to be typecast as some kind of . . . as a . . . I mean they don't know the difference between Spanish or Portuguese or Mexican or anything, and as soon as you have a name like that, you know the kind of parts you get."

"No, what kind?" Rafael asked.

Nico looked acutely uncomfortable. "Bandits," he said softly. He shrugged—the first familiar, heartwarming thing he'd done—and stopped himself.

"Anglicized!" Rafael said again. Then he slumped back into his chair and fiddled with his pipe and said no more.

"Nicolette," Callie said, "I want to know all about you. Do you have a nickname? Something easier than that mouthful?"

The little girl's enormous green eyes went from her mother's face to her father's and back to her grandmother's. She shook her head.

No nickname. Such a tiny creature with such an ornate and lengthy tag. Ah, well. New topic. "What's school like? What do you do there? What's its name?"

"Nicholas!" Alison hissed.

"Preston," the child answered. She bit off the ear of her ginger-bread man. "It's the same school my mother went to. Mostly we sing songs and our teacher reads us stories, and sometimes we go on trips to the firehouse, maybe, or the zoo, and—"

"Maybe we can take little trips while you're here," Callie said. Nicolette smiled and nodded. "We have a dwarf forest nearby, did you know that? The ground's so poor that full-grown trees are smaller than you are! You'll be like a giant. And there's—"

"Nicholas!" Alison was no longer subtle.

"Mother." Nico sounded very tired. "There's some misunderstanding. We can't take little trips or do those things. We aren't staying long."

Callie looked from one to the other. "Then we'll have to cram a lot into tomorrow—"

"No." Nico's voice was very gentle.

"We have Great-aunt Alice's car, you understand," Alison said briskly. "We must get it back to her."

"Is she driving? I thought your letter said she was ill. I thought you were out here for two weeks." She was ashamed of herself for saying what they all knew, for begging for them, but there it was, and what else was she to do? In a few hours they planned to disappear again, before she'd even found a place to take hold of them, to touch.

"Well," Alison said, "there's so much to see in this amazing state that two weeks is barely any time at all!" She flashed a bright white smile at her mother-in-law and then a barely concealed look of fury at her husband.

"You'll stay for dinner, won't you?" Callie asked. Her voice was little more than a whisper.

"It's a long ride back to—" Alison began.

"I'll make it early," Callie said.

Rafael and Gideon behaved as if nothing odd were going on, but that was their way.

Maybe it was a male family trait. Nico—Nicholas Prince—sat like a dummy, letting his nasty little wife stomp out all traces of his family and past.

No. That wasn't fair. Nobody was coercing him. He was a grown man and, whatever the reasons, this is how he wanted it, or agreed to it. He had always wanted to be different from them, and Alison and distance, obviously, were the price he was willing to pay.

Rafael and Gideon also knew what they wanted and what mattered. They bowed to the inevitable and simply didn't bother with the rest. "Don't scattershoot," Gideon was fond of saying. "Take careful aim and save what you can."

The old clock hiss-ticked. Alison ran one perfect nail back and forth in a groove of the sofa's wood trim. Nico looked as if he might say something, but then he swallowed, three times, and took to studying the clock's pendulum. Gideon watched his great-granddaughter neatly dismember the last of the gingerbread men. Rafael's eyes were half closed, but directed at his son. He, too, appeared to have things to say, but chose not to.

Save what you can. Callie cleared her throat and spoke in the most natural voice she could manage. "Nico, while I get dinner to-

gether, why don't you and Alison drive into the village? I don't believe she's ever seen the area." She paused, then couldn't resist adding one more incentive. "It's terribly cute."

Alison didn't need prodding. She wanted out. "Nicolette," she said, "go find your—"

"Please let her stay with me," Callie said.

"She'll get in your way."

"She'll help me get dinner and bake some gingerbread men for the road and for Great-aunt Alice."

"Can I, Mommy? Please?"

"It'll give you time alone together," Callie said. Oh, how polite they were while a struggle to the death raged. Let them try and touch that little girl! They understood. She was releasing the two of them, permanently, and with great pain, but the child belonged to her and this house, at least for one afternoon.

Their faces showed that they understood and that they'd give her one small victory.

Waste, Gideon thought. Waste and more waste. He sat in the old rocker, close to the kitchen fireplace, and knew that the happy sounds at the table belied the chilly despair he and Callie felt. Callie had just shown Nicolette how to punch down bread dough, and the little girl giggled and pummeled away. Gingerbread men were in the oven, and in a minute Callie was taking her granddaughter to see her favorite tree. The secret tree, she called it, because she'd spent lots of her childhood at its base, reading and dreaming and planning, and the tree was so wide that her mother could never find her behind it. They had already explored the house and pulled everything out of the window seat. Callie had let the child choose a souvenir, and Nicolette now clutched the old nested dolls carved by the Russian.

The only thing missing from this peaceful domestic scene was the future. This was it, the complete history, beginning, middle, and end of the Ross-James-Prinz-Prince generations.

They would never be back. Didn't take a genius to recognize that. They'd scatter and be lost and forgotten and as good as extinct, whether or not some unsuspecting descendant wandered the face of the earth. Not knowing was a kind of death, and so many people didn't know, floated loose and rootless as if the human race started from scratch with their birth.

What a waste. He looked, as he often did, at the Russian's fire-

place freize with the village, the fort, the tipis, the populous ocean, the trees, this house. He didn't know who all the people were in and around the carved house.

And of what he did know, all was gone or about to be. The otters dead, the trees heading for extinction, the Indians lost and debilitated, and now the house, the family, about to disappear.

Would any of this last in that little red head of hers? And was a six-year-old's memory of a single afternoon and a set of wooden dolls enough of a keepsake if everything else was lost?

Poor Callie. She was such a good, feisty woman. Life hadn't been easy on her, but she managed, she survived. She was something like a tree that way. But she was also very human, and she'd wanted so much more from these people and this day. Maybe she'd find comfort in her paintings.

Rafael was pale, easy. He'd hide inside his newspapers and in front of the television, his new passion.

And Gideon? Well, he always had a place to turn, letters to write, meetings to attend. He'd keep as busy as his bad back and weak knees would let him.

He knew they thought he was cracked. But he loved the trees, and they'd come to represent the hope of this world, of misty time stretching in both directions, of peace and endurance and strength. He knew the tree Callie was taking Nicolette to see, and it had probably been around during the Crusades, or even earlier. How could you let something like that be hacked into picnic tables? The waste had to end somewhere. You had to save what you could. Save that tree. Save as many as you could.

But people? People were just too damned hard.

PART VII
1 9 7 3

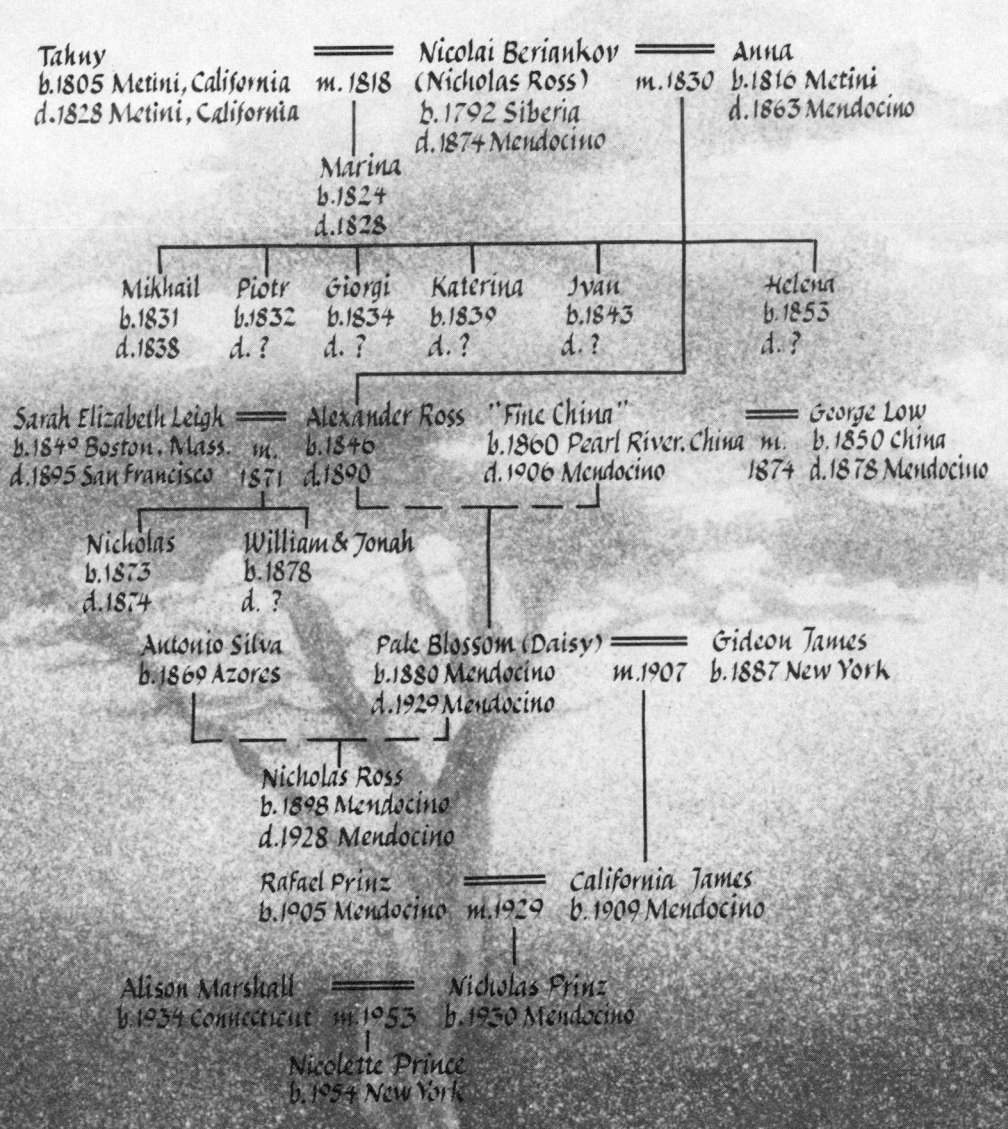

Tahny
b.1805 Metini, California
d.1828 Metini, California
m.1818

Nicolai Beriankov
(Nicholas Ross)
b.1792 Siberia
d.1874 Mendocino
m.1830

Anna
b.1816 Metini
d.1863 Mendocino

Marina
b.1824
d.1828

Mikhail
b.1831
d.1838

Piotr
b.1832
d. ?

Giorgi
b.1834
d. ?

Katerina
b.1839
d. ?

Ivan
b.1843
d. ?

Helena
b.1853
d. ?

Sarah Elizabeth Leigh
b.1849 Boston, Mass.
d.1895 San Francisco
m. 1871

Alexander Ross
b.1846
d.1890

"Fine China"
b.1860 Pearl River, China
d.1906 Mendocino
m. 1874

George Low
b.1850 China
d.1878 Mendocino

Nicholas
b.1873
d.1874

William & Jonah
b.1878
d. ?

Antonio Silva
b.1869 Azores

Pale Blossom (Daisy)
b.1880 Mendocino
d.1929 Mendocino
m.1907

Gideon James
b.1887 New York

Nicholas Ross
b.1898 Mendocino
d.1928 Mendocino

Rafael Prinz
b.1905 Mendocino
m.1929

California James
b.1909 Mendocino

Alison Marshall
b.1934 Connecticut
m.1953

Nicholas Prinz
b.1930 Mendocino

Nicolette Prince
b.1954 New York

25

It was beautiful on the bluff. Sunny but crisp, the fragrant air suggesting cider and woodfires. Despite the strong breeze off the ocean, Callie was warmed by a deep reservoir of contentment. "Proud of me, Papa? We did it, didn't we?" she murmured, then she caught herself. Watch it. Doddering old ladies talked to themselves. Bad enough to do it home alone, but if she did it in public, she'd get herself locked up. She straightened her gloves, pulled her jacket tight, and stood straight.

We did it, she said again, but this time deep inside. The town wouldn't be lost. Saving it had been a battle hard fought and well won, and once again Callie congratulated herself and Mendocino on survival. A young woman standing nearby intercepted her smile and returned it.

"See any?" The girl nodded toward the ocean.

"Not yet," Callie answered. "Not today."

"Ever have?" She had a scrubbed face and straight brown hair that was nearly to her waist. You heard all kinds of things, mostly worrisome, about the young people, the flower children, who'd been arriving for a while now, starting experimental communities in the woods, living off the land, but most of them, like this one, were beautiful and fresh-looking. Or was that a function of their youth, no matter

how they squandered it? In any case, they didn't seem any stranger or more troublesome than the flappers of Callie's youth.

This one looked nice enough. Probably nineteen, about Nicolette's age. Callie immediately tried to erase the thought. Did no good to think about any of them. They were as gone as the dead, but in a sadder, unnatural way. Thinking or wondering about them brought on a dull ache that throbbed for days. Bad enough carrying a dead father and husband around every minute of every day, talking to them out loud so that people in the market gave pointed, worried looks. She was sufficiently weighed down and didn't need any more ghosts in her pockets.

"Excuse me, but have you?" the girl said. Her voice was louder, her enunciation clearer.

It was a talk-to-the-deaf-old-lady voice. Callie almost protested, then she realized the girl was justified—the old lady's mind had been wandering. The girl was waiting for an answer, again. But for the life of her, Callie couldn't remember what the question was. "Have I what?" she asked.

"Seen a whale. Ever."

"Oh, yes. Oh, my, yes. Lived here all my life and seen them every migration, more or less."

"Is it worth waiting for?" The girl shivered. "They're getting impatient," she explained, pointing at two fringed and bearded men stretched out on the bluff. Their expressions were glazed and unchanging. It was hard to believe they felt impatience, pain, or a pulse. It was probably true what people said about the drugs kids were growing in the woods and smoking and eating.

"I can't say what's worthwhile for anybody else," Callie said gently. "But I find the whales exhilarating. Every sighting's a discovery, as if they're brand-new and just invented and fantastic. I mean that size, that spout, that whole watery world. I know they aren't signaling me, but all the same . . . I guess it's how the astronauts will feel someday finding a completely different, but friendly, civilization." She stopped, embarrassed.

The girl nodded. "I understand."

"They don't show up every day, you know."

The girl nodded again.

"Some people who come here, well, I think they believe those are performing whales, that this is a scheduled show, like Disneyland."

"Or Marineworld."

Callie looked at her.

"Jumping dolphins, juggling seals, that kind of thing."

Callie raised her eyebrows. She hadn't heard about that one. All these make-believe countries and worlds for earthbound explorers. Was the town she'd just helped save another one? Mendocinoland! Big whales! Big trees! Little village! See-touch-smell quaintness!

Well, it was a different kind of place. Or a familiar one. There'd never been enough money to tear anything down, so, unlike more affluent cities, the old town with its solid redwood heart endured. She'd been told that it gave people the same glad feeling that the invented Main Street in Disneyland did, made up for something lost.

On the other side of the whales, on the other edge of the deceptively peaceful ocean, American boys had killed and died again, and the war and turmoil at home had been almost as violent. Nothing was unquestioned, untouched, unchanged; not families, not women, not students, not prejudice or practice, not laws, not love or marriage or values. But Mendocino stayed the same, a solid object to hold on to for balance. Mendocino could be trusted. Callie looked lovingly at the village.

Her memories raced up and down its sidewalks, back and forth in time, from a wild-haired ten-year-old selling Victory Bread in a town with more horses than automobiles to an unflaming flapper cheering for the Fourth of July fireworks to a young mother counting pennies for a pair of shoes to a—a what?—a sixty-four-year-old widow-artist-activist?

Two things had stayed the same, her unruly hair and her town, although the former, while still unmanageable, had gone from fire to ash, from long curls to the shortest, easiest cropped style she could manage.

But the town, the backdrop of her life, was almost precisely what she remembered from her earliest childhood. Except that there was no more lumber stacked on the bluff, no chute sliding freshly milled wood down to waiting ships, no whistle shrieking workers back from lunch, no clatter of hobnailed boots on wooden sidewalks. And unlike her hair, it had brightened up. When she was very young the houses had been white or ochre, then they'd faded to gray neglect. Now they were bright pastel confections.

Artists, artisans, hippies, and tourists instead of lumberjacks and millworkers, but nasturtiums still curled around picket fences and the same gingerbread house trim glinted in the clear autumn sunlight.

"Look!" someone shouted. "There's one!"

Callie turned, and there it was, the arc of back, the spouted greet-

343

ing, and the rush of joy that nearly knocked her off her feet.

There were whistles and shouts. The young girl clapped her hands and chuckled.

"Aren't they something?" Callie said.

A second spout was sighted and cheered.

"We're killing them, aren't we?" It wasn't a question. The girl looked wistful.

"Some of us are. And some of us are trying not to let the others do it. Haven't you heard about the whale war?"

The girl grimaced. "What's the point? There's this guy in our house—he's into Kafka, you know? He has this quote on the wall. 'In your battle with the world always bet on the world.' And there you have it."

"I don't know who your Kafka is," Callie said, her voice sharper than it had been, "but I prefer the words of Gideon James, who said, 'Save what you can.' He spent his life trying to save the remaining redwoods. Didn't get them all, of course, or even most, but there's a park now, a safe place for some of them. Men like him got Congress to make that national park. Maybe saving what matters to you isn't as fancy an idea as Mr. Kafka's, but it surely gets more done." She looked back to sea. "Lord knows," she said, "there's always something needs saving."

The girl looked confused. She was very young.

"They were going to build a hotel," Callie said quietly. "A big one. And apartments. And maybe even a landing strip."

"Where?" The girl had found an apple and was systematically biting out a line around its middle.

"Right here. On the headlands, where we're standing." It was still unimaginable to Callie. Abhorrent. Like imprisoning the town, building a concrete barrier between it and the ocean so that a few rich and happy vacationers could hoard this view. "Now they can't," she said. "The headlands will be a state park. And this is the best part—the whole town's becoming a special historic zone, so no developers can make it some high-rise nightmare. Can't ever be anything except what it is."

"You stopped them?"

"Yes," Callie said, "we stopped them." The wind was stronger, penetrating through to the center of her bones. The girl shivered and picked up a large woven bag. Her zombie friends stirred. Callie bid the girl farewell and tried to remember where she'd parked her car.

Two whales and a victory lunch had knocked its location out of her mind. She walked a few steps, remembered where the car was, and then turned back.

"Listen," she called to the girl. Her voice was strong and sure. "When you get home, make sure and give your Mr. Kafka the message, won't you?"

The girl looked at her companions and then at Callie. "What message?"

How could she have forgotten already? Maybe that stuff they smoked made them more absentminded than an old lady. "Tell your Mr. Kafka we stopped them! Tell him that sometimes you can battle the world and win!" Then she waved and headed home.

She thought she had imagined it, stitched it together from fairy tales and half-remembered chitchat.

All those dreams of it, and here it was, half-hidden by trees, its silvery sheen and the wavy glass in its strange tower catching the afternoon sunshine.

"I'll be a minute," she told the driver of the faded blue pickup.

Jesse snuffled and began to fret.

"No, no," she whispered. "Shhhh. Let Mommy catch her breath, get her bearing." She stood at a distance, rocking him in her arms, cooing soothing nonsense while she watched the house.

Then she swallowed hard, walked up to the porch, and lifted the heavy door knocker.

Jesse made a kittenish sound. It wasn't a cry, it was a wistful, hopeful baby noise. Maybe they still shared part of their nervous system and he, too, felt a rise of expectation and excitement.

She peeked through the window. Weird. It looked the same, she thought, although her memories were more emotional than descriptive—crannies and secrets, chests full of strange objects, stories everywhere, good smells, laughter—not specific sofas and end tables, so she didn't know, couldn't tell.

She knocked again. Gave it lots of time. Knocked one last time. There was no response.

She shrugged, trying to feel nonchalant about the missed connection. It didn't work. She felt bitterly, irrationally disappointed, like a baby, like Jesse would feel once he had enough words and memories for a tantrum.

Maybe it wasn't meant to be. They said you can't go home again,

and she knew that was true. But maybe you couldn't go home again to somebody else's house, either. Well, she'd tried. It wasn't in the cards.

She backed off, watched the house from a distance, then climbed into the pickup truck and left.

Callie sat in the window seat, watching the sunset. Window seat sunsets through the trees had become a ritual, alternating with sunsets over the ocean, seen from the tower.

The shadows intensified, low ferns glowing yellow and lime in the late-slanting sun. It was never twice the same.

But she was delaying the inevitable. "All right, now," she said. She stopped, pondered whether talking out loud to oneself was as dangerous as talking out loud to the departed, decided they were both acceptable if one were hard of hearing and alone, and relaxed. "No more excuses, then. You promised that once the town business was settled, you'd get on with it."

Tomorrow she'd call a realtor. It hurt to even think about it. Often, lately, she found herself apologizing to the house. Out loud, too.

Well, but she was lonely and the house expensive to keep up and she was too old and stiff to take in boarders, run the stairs a thousand times a day and cook enormous meals every night. No. She wanted to paint, wanted to spend her time at the art center, needed to be with people. The place was ridiculously large for one old woman. After Gideon had died, even Rafael had talked about moving into town, although he'd gotten to be nothing if not downright cheap and spending money on anything bothered him. Still, he announced that the house they'd lost forty years earlier was available again. Some of those hippies were in it, but it was for sale. Pretty cheap, too, because it didn't have an ocean view.

They could have gone, played bride and groom again, started over, but this house had held them and they'd delayed and postponed until one day Rafael's heart gave out.

Now it was time to move before more developers and tourists came up and made everything too expensive.

Pity this place was out of the historic district so that anybody could buy and demolish it. Put up a plastic, anonymous motel. She shuddered. Maybe she'd get an agreement to save some of it. She'd take the fireplace mantel, the newel post, the otter door frame. And no matter who bought it or what became of it, of course she'd take the

old Russian's plate. It was such a pretty thing with its carvings, although the crackers on it looked almost as old as it was. And, dear God, she'd have to find a place for all the things in the window seat. She wasn't sure what all of them were, but they would surely have to move with her. She couldn't save the house, but she could hold on to its soul and memory, its keepsakes.

She stood up and lifted the pillow-covered lid. One by one, she transferred the contents of the deep chest to the kitchen table.

And, oh, the table itself, with its generations of scars and burns. Initials carved by little boys' pen knives. The "NJ" her brother had left on the table's lip. A tiny "Nico" carved by her son on one of his less obedient days. The burned curve of a cakepan, dropped when her mother felt faint. The silent, sinister gash Callie always wondered about.

But if she was going to carry on about a table, what was she to do with the doorway that had notches marking her growth—or the one marking Nico's? Or the family messages scribbled under the wallpaper in the living room? Or the photographs on the walls, on tables, loosely thrown into boxes in closets? Or the balalaika nobody knew how to play? Or the rosebush planted for her father's seventieth birthday? Or the old graves at the back? Their flat markers were overgrown with huckleberries, but they were still intact. Rafael and Gideon were buried in town, in the cemetery, but what of all the rest of them? Even the infamous corpse by the river was beginning to feel like an heirloom.

She looked at the clumsy but endearing sampler that had saved Mr. Nakata. Her mother had embroidered it as a young girl. What a family, she thought, looking at the names. We are a tree—roots in every direction, each tapping a different part of the forest. But in the end, they all fed the same sturdy trunk, produced the same leaves, kept growing as one thing even if . . . even if . . .

Who knew what belonged on those top leaves now?

She made herself strong coffee and sat down at the kitchen table. Maybe nobody would want the house. In any case, it wouldn't be easy selling it. Who needed eight bedrooms except the hippies, and they couldn't afford anything. The one time she'd talked to a realtor, shown her the place, the woman had been appalled.

"My clients want modern appliances," she'd said, regarding the kitchen with horror. The Wedgwood stove still worked perfectly after fifty years. Why change it? Besides, it had warming drawers and turkey ovens and it was beautiful and lush, not antiseptic and skimpy in

the way of new ranges. But the realtor couldn't see it. She wanted long, laminated counters, tile floors, wall ovens, things that buzzed and chimed and cleaned themselves.

"What is *this!*" she said.

"A sink. Made of a redwood log. We don't use it anymore, of course, but it's too interesting to throw away, don't you think? See, here's the drain, and this lid goes on top of it."

The realtor sighed.

"Dark wood is not in style now," Callie was told as they walked through the house. "Perhaps if you painted it, the place would look a bit more . . ."

"It's varnished virgin redwood!"

"People don't varnish redwood anymore. Makes the whole house old-fashioned."

"But it is old-fashioned. It's a hundred and thirty years old. Doesn't that make it all right? Everybody loves the old houses in town."

"Those are historic," the realtor said with next to no interest. She was inspecting the downstairs bathroom, sighing and making notations on a checklist. "Who lived here?"

"My family."

"Well, with all due apologies, did they do anything important? Would anybody recognize their names or something that happened to them?"

Callie shook her head. "They were ordinary, like most people."

"Then it's not historic, you see?"

"Things happened to them," Callie said with some force. The woman was a blockhead. "They have a history."

"For clients, it has to be zingy. Sexy. You know what I mean? What did your people do?"

"They were carpenters and lumberjacks and my father was a merchant marine and . . ." Even she knew that Rafael's job in the haberdashery didn't qualify them for stardom.

What had they done? She pondered the question. They had survived against enormous odds. They didn't make the world any worse for their having been here. They struggled and made do with their times and their lot. Sometimes they made a good difference. But that obviously wasn't enough. "I guess people like us need modern plumbing to be sexy," she said.

"You got it," the realtor said. "You do have a nice view upstairs, though," she allowed. "They'll probably want to tear this place down anyway. It would cost too much to remodel."

After that interview, Callie did nothing further about the house. No need to rush in the wrecking crew.

Look at these things, she now thought. Look what survives, sometimes without any meaning except what you assign it. She didn't know which baby's head the little knit cap had warmed or how you made tea in the samovar or what child had drawn a rough but charming, excited picture of a snowy day, or why a little girl named Sarah Elizabeth Leigh had written, "I am afraid of Indians. I am afraid of dying," in her journal, or whether she had truly killed her sister, or what to make of a small carving of an angel with a spear in his side or an old wooden flute. But she knew these things were markers, that they mattered. They were what her family had done.

And there they'd stay until she was buried and they were scattered or sold in somebody's country store. Or thrown away by whoever cleaned out her new place. Who'd want a yellow menu just because it featured some unknown Daisy's Victory Bread? Or a daguerreotype of a family standing in front of a long-gone hotel?

There were letters tied in packets, held together with rubber bands and ribbons, and among them a half dozen envelopes spanning several years and marked Return to Sender or Addressee Unknown.

But the addressee, one painfully remembered Nicolette Prince *was* known. Only her whereabouts were a mystery. Nicolette Prince had disappeared as had Nicholas Prince, although not together.

Nico had gone first, when the marriage ended. She and Rafael found out about the divorce through a few lines scribbled at the bottom of his Christmas card that year. Nico was looking for a permanent place, he wrote, and so there was no return address on the envelope. His message was for his grandfather as well. She had written to tell them of Gideon's death, but obviously Nico had already been gone. For the next few years, he sent cards to all three of them on most birthdays and holidays. Callie always wondered if he knew how similar his messages were, how unchanging and unsatisfying his life seemed from year to year. He was always up for what could be an important role, he was always about to move, he was always well, and he never said anything about his ex-wife or his child.

Once, a friend claimed to have seen him on her favorite soap opera, and Callie forsook canvas and paints for two weeks straight, glued at midday to the otherwise ignored television set. But if, indeed, her son had been on the show, he no longer was.

For a while, she hoped he'd come to town on movie or television business. Hollywood used Mendocino in place of New England, al-

though why they didn't use it as itself, she couldn't say. This way, they were always fussing about sunsets because they happened on the "wrong" side. In any case, Nico never appeared.

Eventually, there was only one card, at Christmas, and the same year Callie's letter to Nicolette came back with its mysterious "Addressee Unknown." Nico's cards stopped altogether two years later and never again could Callie locate her granddaughter.

She wasn't sure why she'd kept the returned letters, except as mute tokens of something she couldn't save, something precious and lost. And now she was going to lose the house, too, and she didn't know what would become of all the memories resting in the corners after the wrecker's ball knocked them away. She sipped her coffee as the room grew darker. Outside, treetops burned in a yellow-orange sunset flare, but Callie was no longer watching.

She heard the scrunch of gravel and stopped dusting. She didn't expect anyone. Had not, after all, called a realtor. First, she'd decided to give the house a thorough cleaning so it would look its best. First, she'd wait until she didn't feel as if she were committing a crime, murdering something.

She looked outside and saw a blue pickup truck. A young woman got out, then leaned in and pulled out an infant and put him in a sling she wore on her chest. She was very lovely, her hair pulled severely back into a long braid. Medieval-looking with her pale oval face and fine features, and with that baby, a Madonna, like ones Callie had seen nearly half a century ago in Italy.

But her clothing reminded Callie of her own childhood, of her mother's long, calico everyday dress. Those hippie children dressed oddly, sometimes like Indians, sometimes like cowboys, sometimes like panhandlers, sometimes, obviously, like Daisy James.

The girl approached the porch, then the driver of the pickup stuck her head out her window. "Lavender!" she called. "You forgot this!" She held out a backpack.

Lavender went back to claim it, then again, looking worried and determined, approached the door and knocked.

"Yes?" Callie opened the door halfway. Sometimes they sold things —clumsily made pottery or weavings—as a way of asking for money, and Callie was so annoyed by the slipshod craftsmanship, she turned them away. But this one had only a baby and the backpack.

"I'm..." Her voice was strangled and small. She cleared her throat. "I'm Laven—my name is Letty Hendricks and I know this

will sound weird, but I wondered if I could see your house, if it isn't an imposition. I was here the other day, but nobody was home, so . . ."

Callie shook her head slightly. "Are you a realtor, then?"

The girl shook her head.

"It isn't for sale yet."

"I wanted to see it, not buy it."

"I'm a little confused." That was a definite understatement.

"Listen, this must be a bother. I'm sorry. It was just an impulse." The girl backed off. "Thanks anyway."

"No, wait. Why don't you tell me what you wanted to see?" Callie asked. "And why."

The girl shrugged. There was something so familiar about the angle, the expression. Ah, but Callie kept doing that, looking for signs and portents, connections where there were none. So what if a million years ago a little Nico, who never had many words until he discovered scripts, had shrugged in just that way? That had nothing to do with the here or now. Even if the pulled-back hair was a shade of red-gold well remembered. "Try, won't you?" Callie prodded.

Lavender, or Letty, cleared her throat and breathed deeply. "When I was little, I visited this house. Or one like it. I'm not sure. It was just once, but I never forgot, and I thought if I was ever anywhere near it, I'd visit, and I was up in Humboldt with friends, on my way back to San Francisco, so here I am." She shrugged again, to wash away the emotion. "But I could be wrong. I probably am. I was only six. Kids mix things up."

Six. She said she had been six. The shrug, the expression, the hair. Callie put her hand to her head. There was pressure building between her eyes, a dizziness she had to stop. It was like delerium, seeing half of something imagined, knowing it wasn't real but still fearing and believing and wanting it. She had to stop her mind from running to the edge of a cliff and leaping off. Too much didn't make sense, anyway. "Your name is Letty? Or Lavender?"

"That's what my friends call me, what I call myself," she said. "Lavender Sunshine. Letty Hendricks is my real name, but it's so stiff. And this is my son, Jesse Sunshine. Well, actually, you can't really see him because he's all scrunched and sleeping." She picked up the backpack. "Thanks, anyway," she said. "I'm sorry to have bothered you."

"Wait—please feel free to look around. But tell me why you visited here? Do you remember?"

"My grandparents used to live here—if this is the right house, of course. Maybe you knew them, even though it was a long time ago. They're dead now. Their name was Prince."

"No," Callie said softly.

"You didn't know them?"

"Prinz. With a *z*." Callie's head spun, whirled, opened, and unfolded. She braced herself against the wall. "Letty is short for Nicolette," she whispered.

The girl nodded, wide-eyed. She opened her mouth to question Callie, but she was stopped by a loud howl in the sling.

"Come in. Both of you. I'll explain, and you'll explain, and it'll all make sense soon." Callie took off her glasses, rubbed her eyes, wiped their corners, and continued. "Right away, though, there's two important things to know. One, your grandmother isn't dead, and second, my great-grandson is hungry. First things first."

They waved off the pickup and said no more until Letty was settled on the old sofa and Jesse was nursing with a lip-smacking gusto that had made Callie laugh years ago when her own son did it. He was fine-featured, with enormous dark eyes and skin the color of tea with milk.

Letty sighed. "She told me you were dead."

"Your mother?"

She nodded. "I know why she must have done it, but all the same, it's cruel."

"Why? Why would she do such a thing? I wrote and wrote—I can show them to you—but you'd disappeared."

"It wasn't exactly a friendly divorce. My father barely ever saw me again. She made it really hard, I think. He didn't support us. She always mentioned that. She didn't even like my name anymore—sounded too much like his, so she started calling me Letty. Then, when she remarried, we moved to Virginia, and my name was changed to Hendricks, so nothing of my dad was left, and I guess you were part of him." She shrugged. "Besides, she was—odd—about his family. Your family." She paused a moment. "My family."

"Like how?"

Another shrug. "She called you nobodies. They used to fight about it, and even now, if I mention Dad's family, she acts embarrassed and makes fun of them. 'The Model U.N.,' she calls you."

"Yes," Callie murmured. "Seems I recall how the name had to be changed so it'd be American."

"She said nobody in this family ever was or did anything."

352

"They did the work of the world," Callie said. "But that's not enough for some people."

"She'd act like I was saying something dirty if I mentioned them in front of other people. She called you refugees." Letty looked angry.

"I know a real estate lady she'd love," Callie murmured.

"She belongs to the D.A.R., believe it or not. Very into ancestors. Hers. See, Dad hasn't done very well. Mostly, he's a bit player or an extra. You know, one of those people who fill out a scene, but you never notice them or know who they are. Mom says it figures, that he comes from a whole family of extras."

Callie pursed her lips. "Extras are like the Greek chorus, perhaps?"

Letty shrugged. "Something like that."

"If I recall my twelfth grade teacher, then, they're there to bear witness. That's an important job." She sighed. "Oh, who cares? Tell me more about my son. Do you ever see him?"

Letty shook her head. "He's in L.A. I used to get Christmas and birthday cards, but I never saw him. Mom says he drinks a lot and has for years, but I don't know. When I was in L.A., I tried to find him, called about a hundred Princes before I gave up." And again, her father's shrug. How was it that Alison hadn't managed to remove that, too?

The baby, satisfied, stopped nursing. Letty lifted him to her shoulder and patted his back. Callie became engrossed in this most ordinary, most marvelous process and was shocked, when she looked back at her granddaughter, to see that her nose was bright red and she was blinking back tears.

"He's called Jesse because he's an outlaw baby." She tried for a smile. "Like Jesse James." Then her face crumpled. "I don't know what to do," she said. "I have to find a job, something to do, a place for us. I was living with people, but things are different now. I have a baby. It's not a good scene, not with Jesse, not for him. And she won't even talk to me anymore."

"Who?"

"My mother. Because I'll corrupt her other children. Because I left home. Because I had Jesse. Because I kept him. Because I'm not married." She sniffed and managed a smile. "All of the above. She thinks I did this to spite her."

"Where's his father?" Callie asked softly.

"Vietnam. Or maybe he's home, since the truce. It won't matter, either way." She stood up. "Mind if I look around, then?" Jesse was asleep on her shoulder.

"Could I hold him?" Callie whispered. She settled into the carved rocker and sighed with pleasure. "Take all the time you like."

She should have had dozens of babies, if for nothing else than moments such as this. She closed her eyes and slowly rocked, loving each tiny pulse of the baby's breath on her neck.

Of course, babies grew up. She had a momentary picture of hers as a drunk, aging, out-of-work actor, then banished it, replacing it with his sketched likeness as a child dancing in the river's shallows.

"I thought it would be smaller or less interesting than I remembered, but it really does have all those wonderful nooks and crannies. It's not like anyplace else I've ever been. That's why I never forgot it."

Callie was so far away, inside her own dream, that her granddaughter's voice startled and confused her for a second.

"It's enormous," Letty said.

"Enormous is right," Callie said. "Too much to handle. That's why I have to sell it."

"What a shame!"

Callie nodded. "I agree. Makes me sad. This is outside the protected area and has a view, so they'll probably tear it down and build some kind of hotel. It's too big and old-fashioned and not sexy enough."

Letty said nothing, but stood by the staircase, her fingers idly tracing the floral carvings on the newel post. "But safe," she said softly. "Isn't that how you described it when I was here? Or in your letters?"

"Probably. This has always been a place where anybody could come and be safe. Your mother was right in a way. We were all refugees of one kind or another."

"I remembered," Letty said softly. "It stuck in my mind like the good promise made in a fairy tale, and when Jesse was born, I kept hearing it over and over."

Callie cleared her throat, softly, so that the baby wouldn't wake. "Letty," she said, "I could find a new place with room for the two of you."

"Oh, I couldn't . . ."

"For as long as you need. Until you know what to do, where you want to be. Things like that."

"I didn't mean for you to feel you had to—"

"I know, but I'd love it all the same."

"You don't even know me."

"We're family. I'm willing to try."

Letty moved around the room, touching, inspecting, visibly remembering. "Wasn't this a boardinghouse once?" she asked.

"More than once," Callie said. "My grandmother took in boarders last century. And I took them in during the Depression and the war. Maybe more times than that, I'd have to think. Why?"

"Why couldn't it be one again?"

"Oh, child, I'm too old for that now."

"I'm not."

"I want to paint."

"I want to work, earn my keep and my baby's."

"There's all those meals, endless stews and giant casseroles. You'd hate it."

Letty shrugged.

"Besides, nobody stays in boardinghouses nowadays. The very sound of it goes with varnished redwood and unfashionable stoves."

"How's that?" Letty asked, then she waved away any explanation. "Listen, we don't want boarders. We want people passing through, we want tourists."

"I don't see the difference. We had salesmen who only stayed a night or two, people like that."

"Maybe, but tourists want to eat out, try different restaurants. When I was thirteen, we went to England to visit my stepfather's relatives, and we stayed in places that didn't serve dinner. They were houses, like this one, and all they served was breakfast. For tourists. Couldn't we manage that? I make great French toast. I can squeeze oranges." She was almost skipping around. "And after breakfast, I'd clean up and care for Jesse and manage things so you could go off and paint." She stopped and looked at Callie intently. "Well? How does it sound?"

It sounded marvelous, miraculous. Too good to be possible. "It's hard work," she said. "Very hard."

"I'm tough. I know what they say about kids my age, but I'm a worker."

"No vacations."

"We'll close for two weeks."

She controlled the urge to burst into tears. "We'd need more bathrooms. People want that."

Letty considered. "Fine. We'll rent a few rooms first, then, when we've made money, we'll add bathrooms."

"But isn't the house too old-fashioned?"

"Are you kidding? People will love it! Look at this great old furni-

ture, the quilts, the beams, the carved beds, the brass one—are you kidding? And then there's your stories—remember how you told me about the people who had been here and you showed me all those things from the window seat, and then for a while you wrote me letters with more stories, and lots of pictures, remember?"

Callie nodded.

"Those letters made my mother crazy," Letty said. She put a hand on her hip and made her voice shrill. "'Another message from the United Nations, she'd say." Letty shook her head with disgust. "Forget her. Look at this!" The girl dipped into her backpack and rummaged until she pulled out a scratched and paint-chipped Matryoshka doll. "You gave this to me," she said. "I saved it for Jesse, but we'd be glad to donate it back to the house. One more thing you could tell stories about. Or maybe we'd have a brochure. You could design it—"

"There must be something seriously wrong with the idea," Callie said.

"Why?"

"Because it's too wonderful. The whole place is suddenly humming, can't you feel it? It's all too right. It must actually be impossible, or illogical."

"At least immature," Letty said. "That's always a favorite."

"Impractical."

"Unworkable."

"Unreasonable."

Callie stood up, carefully cradling her great-grandson. "Perfect," she said. "In the family tradition."

"When do we begin?"

Callie smiled down at the newest leaf on the old sampler. "In all honesty," she said, "I think we began a long, long time ago."

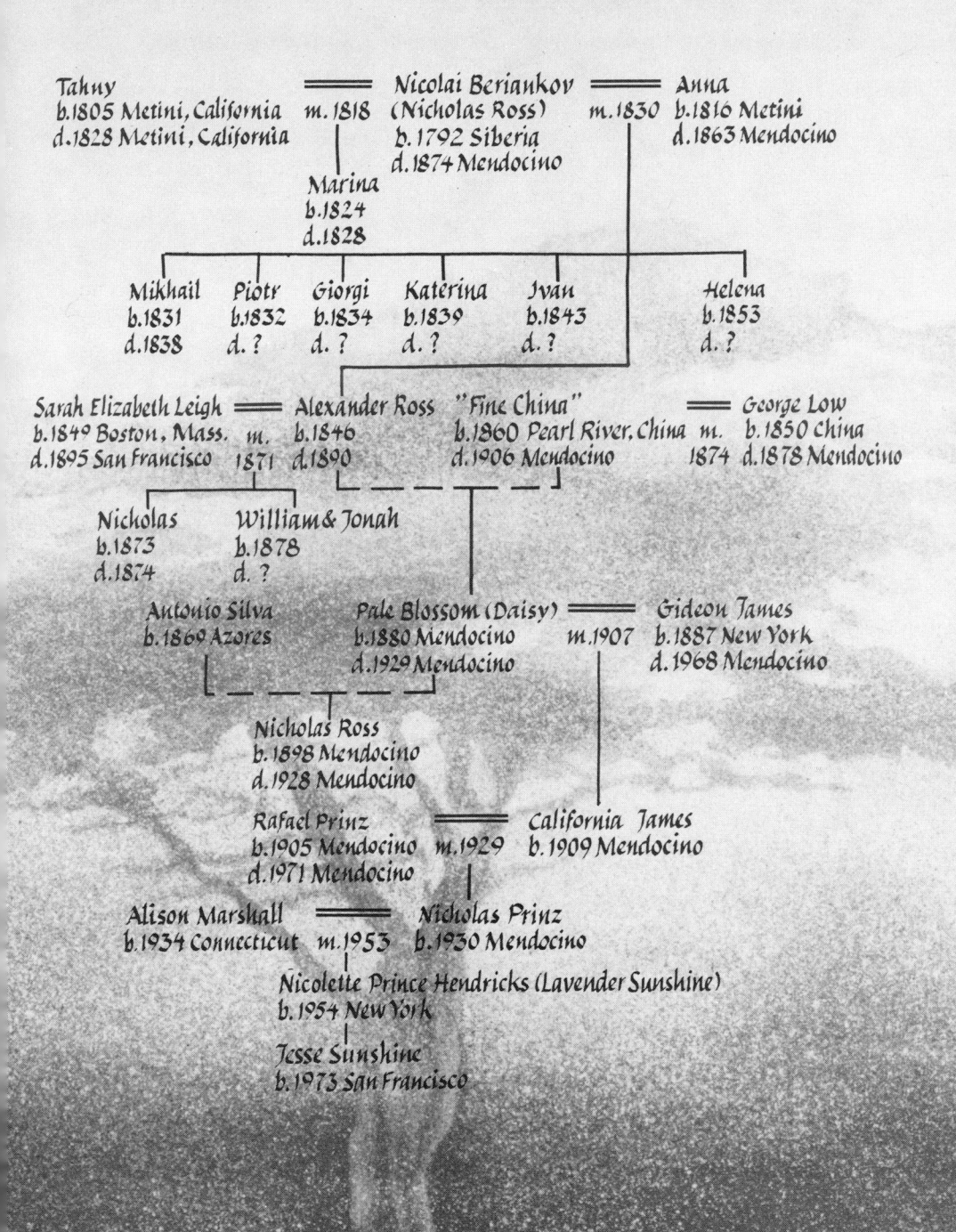

Tahny
b.1805 Metini, California
d.1828 Metini, California

m. 1818

Nicolai Beriankov
(Nicholas Ross)
b. 1792 Siberia
d. 1874 Mendocino

m. 1830

Anna
b.1816 Metini
d.1863 Mendocino

Marina
b.1824
d.1828

Mikhail
b.1831
d.1838

Piotr
b.1832
d. ?

Giorgi
b.1834
d. ?

Katerina
b.1839
d. ?

Ivan
b.1843
d. ?

Helena
b.1853
d. ?

Sarah Elizabeth Leigh
b.1849 Boston, Mass.
d.1895 San Francisco

m.
1871

Alexander Ross
b.1846
d.1890

"Fine China"
b.1860 Pearl River, China
d.1906 Mendocino

m.
1874

George Low
b.1850 China
d.1878 Mendocino

Nicholas
b.1873
d.1874

William & Jonah
b.1878
d. ?

Antonio Silva
b.1869 Azores

Pale Blossom (Daisy)
b.1880 Mendocino
d.1929 Mendocino

m.1907

Gideon James
b.1887 New York
d.1968 Mendocino

Nicholas Ross
b.1898 Mendocino
d.1928 Mendocino

Rafael Prinz
b.1905 Mendocino
d.1971 Mendocino

m.1929

California James
b.1909 Mendocino

Alison Marshall
b.1934 Connecticut

m.1953

Nicholas Prinz
b.1930 Mendocino

Nicolette Prince Hendricks (Lavender Sunshine)
b.1954 New York

Jesse Sunshine
b.1973 San Francisco